HERE I AM

The Life of John the Baptist

A Novel

Moira Quinn, O.Ss.R.

- For you
my Carmelite Sisters
mercy, peace and joy
Moira

F
Ov H

HERE I AM, The Life of John the Baptist
Copyright © Moira Quinn, 2006

Revised edition 2014

REDEMPTORISTINE NUNS OF NEW YORK, INC
89 Hiddenbrooke Drive, NY 12508-2230
HERE.I.AM.book@gmail.com

Quinn, Moira, 1955 –
    Here I Am, the Life of John the Baptist/Moira Quinn
    p. cm.

ISBN 0-9763715-3-7

1. John, the Baptist, Saint – Fiction.   2. Bible, N.T. – History
of Biblical events – Fiction.
3. Christian men saints – Fiction. 4. Palestine – Fiction.
I. Title.

BS2456.Q56 2006
813'.54-dc21   2006909976
[FIC]

INTRODUCTION

I was sitting in a bar in Wantagh, Long Island with a friend one December evening in 1980, when we got to talking about how prominent John the Baptist was in the Gospels. I was a hairdresser at the time going to daily Mass during Advent. For some inexplicable reason I was intrigued by John and wondered what happened before he came out of the wilderness to baptize. I don't remember exactly how it came about, but I said something like, "Wouldn't it make an interesting story?" And my friend said, "Why don't you write it yourself?"

So I did.

But first, I went to the source, the Jerusalem Bible, and took notes on all the passages and footnotes pertaining to the Baptist. Next, I went to the public library and picked up an old book, "Jesus and His Times" by Henry Daniel-Rops.* Then I simply began to write. I just began on page 1 and let the story unfold itself: characters appeared and scenes took shape. Even I was astonished by the story. I'll never know where I got the chutzpah to begin such a project because I never dreamed of doing anything like this before. I truly believe it was written under the inspiration of the Spirit.

While musing on the life of John the Baptist, I began to muse on my own life and felt my youthful dream of becoming a nun reawaken when I followed the outstretched arm of John the Baptist pointing to the Lamb of God. I discovered the desire within me to give my life to Jesus, just as John had done. I entered the Order of the Most Holy Redeemer, the Redemptoristine Nuns of Esopus, New York on March 25, 1988.

In the monastery I was introduced to the computer which made polishing my novel so much easier. I also met knowledgeable people who continually sparked my imagination. My novel took on new life.

Like a mother nurturing her growing child I wrote my novel, and when it was ready to go out on its own, I sent it to publishing houses only to have it turned away. Disappointed that no one wanted my child, I shelved it for nine years until inspiration beckoned again last year. My child was still growing, new insights came to light, characters needed to have their voices heard, so I began to write again.

This time I surfed the Internet, gleaning historical and religious details to add depth to the story. In the interim I even painted an original piece for the cover. And now, after countless polishings, the novel has crystallized into a vibrant account of one man's life.

I humbly offer my novel for you to enjoy. **HERE I AM** is dedicated to Ruah, the Creative Breath of God, who inspired and changed my life. May she inspire yours.

Moira Quinn, O.Ss.R.
June 24, 2006
The Nativity of John the Baptist

As Advent began in 2013, I was drawn to revisit this work that holds such deep meaning in my life. In this revised edition I have added more details and polish, yet the story of love and devotion remains the same.

September 14, 2014
Exaltation of the Cross

*Henry Daniel—Rops. Jesus and His Times. Dulton Publication. January 1, 1956

ACKNOWLEDGEMENTS

'Here I Am' has been in the making for more than half my lifetime! Along the way I have been encouraged and supported by my family, community and friends. I wish to thank Marianne Santalone Certa for her words on that cold wintry night - they sparked a flame that has lasted all this time. My sister, Paula Q. Smaldone, was the first to copyedit the manuscript and pointed out where clarification of certain scenes was necessary.

In the spring of 2014, I engaged Sr. Angelique Dryden, a Sparkill Dominican, to copyedit the work. She was a fount of information. Despite her remark that some pages may look like the "Slaughter of the Holy Innocence," I am grateful for her input and gentle corrections.

In writing the novel I picked up inspiration from every imaginable resource. When I used quotes from the Bible, I compared various translations, and then pulled phrases from an assortment of texts and Liturgy of the Hours looking for just the right words to express the intention of the scene; consequently, I am unable to credit any one Bible as the source. But mostly I want to thank John the Baptist who continues to point the way, and the Spirit whose inspiration is ever present.

I

The lots were drawn. The bull was slaughtered and its blood collected. The sweet white smoke of frankincense coiled through the air. On this most solemn day, one man alone would offer sacrifice in the Holy of Holies to the Almighty Creator on behalf of all the people of Israel.

Zechariah was the chosen one.

Slowly the old priest climbed the fifteen steps to enter the sanctuary where no Gentile would dare pass. On the arch above was an inscription written in four languages: Hebrew, Greek, Arabic and Latin, 'Anyone who is taken shall be killed; he alone shall be answerable for his death.'

The venerable man had passed through the thirteen gates, one more beautiful than the last, to reach this point. As he climbed he considered the past. Twice a year his division had come to serve the Temple. While serving, it had always been his personal petition that he and his wife would be blessed with a child. Over the years they longed for a son, but now they were an old and lonely couple with no one to continue their bloodline. He had been a priest for a score and twelve years, and his wife was well beyond childbearing.

Zechariah stood inside the final gate high above the Temple courtyard. The noise of the crowd below had faded. The cedar door plated in gold with its grape vine design stood open. A magnificent wine colored drape embroidered with every known flower of the world covered the sanctum. He adjusted his tallith; the linen prayer shawl with its indigo stripes woven along the edge and cornered by tassels covered his shoulders. The other sacred garments he wore were made of the finest white linen and had been put on over his ritually bathed body. The priest lifted the drape and stepped into the sacred place.

Sunlight filtered through the latticed windows dimly patterning the sanctum floor. Before him were the golden altar and the seven branched candelabra. With eyes lowered, he added more frankincense to the censer. Gently swinging the burner, the priest walked into the dark opening of the Holy of Holies, obscuring the Divine Presence with the fragrant smoke.

This day, the Day of Atonement, was the only day of the year when a priest would actually enter and come before the Omnipresent Lord and stand in the midst of the Navel of the Universe.

Taking the blood of the animal with a hyssop branch, he sprinkled the altar consecrating it to the Lord. For a second time, he lifted the incense and let the smoke waft in the Holy Place. Then once more he sprinkled the blood of the bull, expiating all his sins and those of the people.

When the ritual was done in accordance with the Law, he paused with eyes closed for a moment and silently begged, 'Mercy,' as his prayer rose with the incense to heaven.

"Zechariah."

His eyes flashed open. The Sacred Place was filled with a light that had no source.

"Do not be afraid. Your petition has been heard."

In the depths of his heart, Zechariah had indeed cried out his old, now absurd, plea.

"Your wife, Elizabeth," continued the commanding voice , "shall bear a son and you shall name him John. Know that he will be great before the Lord of all. The child will be filled with God's Spirit and will prepare a perfect people, holy and just, for the coming of Lord. Rejoice!"

"This cannot be," protested Zechariah, terrified by this unseen yet present being. The old man squinted; his eyes could just barely distinguish in the brilliance of the light a form from which the voice emanated. In his bewilderment, the priest argued, "I am an old man and my wife is beyond her fertile years."

"I am Gabriel. I stand in the presence of Yahweh," the light grew bolder, "and have been sent to you to bring you this good news. But because you have not believed my words, your speech shall fail you, and you will be unable to communicate until the day these things come to pass."

In an instant, the apparition vanished. Zechariah, dazed by what he had heard and seen, stumbled out of the Holy of Holies. He made his way down the long steps. At different levels, fellow priests and Levites stopped him, asking what had kept him so long in the Sacred Place. He opened his mouth but not a sound came out. His speech was gone! Zechariah no longer doubted all would come to pass as the angel Gabriel - for he believed it was an angel - had said and fell on his knees in fear and homage praising the Lord.

When he awoke, Zechariah was giddy with joy and would have sprung from his bed had not his friends held him down. He had fainted from emotion, and the doctor who had been summoned could find no cause for the priest's strange ailment and behavior. Zechariah tried to restore himself to some degree of dignity long enough to assure the people around him that he was fine. The old priest tried to explain through gestures what had transpired in the Holy of Holies, but they did not understand.

Zechariah's mind whirled. The Creator was going to bless him and Elizabeth with a child. Elizabeth! How he longed to see her, to tell her, to hold her. She was going to be a mother, have the baby her arms longed to hold. A son! A son who would be herald of the Lord! The MESSIAH was coming!

His eyes brimmed with tears of joy and gladness for himself, his wife, and all the people of Israel. "For unto us a son is given!" his heart cried out. Zechariah's friends saw his tears and tried to comfort him, knowing how this mysterious ailment must distress him. Again the old man tried to explain his behavior. A son. My son - the herald of the Messiah! The Messiah!

He motioned for a writing tablet, but when it arrived and he tried to put down his thoughts, it came to him that perhaps the angel had made him mute for more than one purpose: in addition to demonstrating the power of the Creator, perhaps he was to be silent about his son and the Messiah. Zechariah trembled under the magnitude of the knowledge he possessed. He wrote nothing. He wished to go home. Only Elizabeth would he tell. How he longed to see his dear wife Elizabeth!

Elizabeth, a handsome woman with silver strands of hair coming from beneath her veil, anxiously paced the courtyard having received the news from a messenger just hours before that her husband was ill. She prepared his room and had a soothing broth ready for his arrival home. Zechariah was in good health and spirits before he left for Jerusalem to serve his week in the Temple. She had not gone with him to the Holy City since as a priest he would abstain from having relations with her, and at her age she was content to stay home. She wondered what could have happened.

Hearing the clatter of a wagon outside, she rushed to open the door and saw her husband smiling and waving his arm in greeting. His grey eyes sparkled, his face bright, his silky white hair and beard neatly groomed. Zechariah jumped down from the cart like a young man and gave her such a warm and tight embrace.

"Husband, what is this?" asked Elizabeth, relieved but startled by his enthusiastic public display. "Someone has played a cruel hoax on me today and sent a message that you were ill. But, thank the Lord, you are well."

Zechariah merely smiled with his arms still encircling his wife.

"Why would someone send such a message?" she continued. For a moment she thought he was going to whisper the answer in her ear when he gently nuzzled her neck. His soft whiskers tickled, and Elizabeth blushed at her husband's demonstrative behavior. Remembering they were still outside their home in the street for all passer-by to see, she quickly broke from his embrace and said with mock scorn, "Come inside the house!" Once inside she asked, "So, how was Jerusalem? As busy and bustling as ever, I suppose."

She led him to the table in the courtyard where the broth, bread and wine were waiting for his arrival. Zechariah's arms slipped around her waist again. Amused, her mind flew back to when they were young married lovers, and her husband was always amorous and eager. She turned in his arms to face him. Zechariah's eyes twinkled with hidden knowledge. It looked to Elizabeth as if he had something wonderful, extraordinary to tell her. "Well, tell me!" And when he did not answer she continued with a laugh, "Must I drag it out of you? How was your week? How did you place?"

A shadow crossed the countenance of her husband's face. She felt his breathing deepen. "Something has happened!" Elizabeth gazed into the depths of his eyes and was suddenly filled with concern, "Please, tell me. What has happened?"

Zechariah opened his mouth to speak, but no sound came from his lips. Then, lightly at first, he touched his lips to hers. Elizabeth's entire being melted under his tender kisses, forgetting the concerns of a moment ago. Together they climbed the stairs and entered their bedchamber.

Six months had gone by since Zechariah's return home, and he was still unable to speak. Yet, Elizabeth and her husband were content. To her utter amazement, Elizabeth had conceived and was bearing a child! At first, she did not comprehend what was taking place in her body. And when she felt life move in her womb, Zechariah's silent reassurances calmed her, and they rejoiced in the gracious gift of life from their Creator.

It was early spring now, and Elizabeth sat on the terrace overlooking the courtyard, relaxing from her chores of spinning and sewing new clothes for the child to come. She was watching a sparrow's nest in the almond tree that her husband had planted in the courtyard. Two chicks had just hatched and she delighted in seeing the new life. So fixed was her gaze watching the tiny nestlings that she did not hear the knock on the door or notice the girl with long braided hair down her back when she entered the courtyard. Only when she heard her name being called, "Elizabeth, Aunt?" did she rise, as quickly as she could, holding her belly to see who had come.   Below was a simply dressed lone traveler carrying a bundle.

"Mary!" she cried out, rushing down the stairs, as fast as she could, to embrace her sister Anna's only child.   At that moment, light dawned in her being with the appearance of her young niece at her home, and everything was made clear regarding her mysterious pregnancy.   Elizabeth exclaimed, "Holy are you and holy is the One in your womb! How is it that you have come here to me? From the moment I heard your voice, the babe in my womb has been dancing for joy!"

"Then you know it, too!" Mary exclaimed. "I had to come to share this great thing with you. I have so much to tell you. May I stay awhile in your home? And if I can be of any service…"

"I would be honored." said Elizabeth.   "Zechariah! Come. See who has come to be with us to share our joy - my niece Mary."

Zechariah came down from his library upstairs.   On seeing the radiant young woman in the courtyard, his eyes grew moist; he, too, by the grace of the Creator's Spirit, recognized Mary as the mother of the Messiah and bowed before the maiden.

After the couple made Mary welcome, she told her story:

"Some days ago, while I was alone and quiet in my room, a being of light appeared to me. The light spoke to me, not in words that my ears could hear, rather the voice sounded in my heart. It said, 'Hail gracious one, beloved of the Lord.' I trembled at the appearance and the greeting. I believe it was an angel of the Lord. It said its name was Gabriel."

At this point, she paused and smiled because Zechariah was nodding his head in affirmation.

"The messenger continued saying not to be afraid for I am favored by the Lord: that I shall conceive and bear in my womb a Son and shall name him Jesus! That he shall be great among the people, and the Lord will give him the throne of David.

"I asked the angel how shall this happen, for I am just betrothed and have not yet had relations with my husband.

"Gabriel answered the Spirit of the Most High would envelop me and said the child to be born will be the Holy One, the Son of the Most High! As proof of this promise, the angel said that you, Aunt Elizabeth, one who had been called barren, had conceived a son in your old age and were in your sixth month, for nothing is impossible with Yahweh!

"Though quivering at hearing the name of the Ineffable, I opened my arms to the light and said, 'I am the Lord's. Be it done unto me as you have said.' Then the angel disappeared."

When Mary finished her remarkable story, Elizabeth rose up and rejoiced, "Blessed are you who believed! Praise the Lord for the promise of old is fulfilled in you, Mary."

Mary joined her Aunt in praising the Most High, "My whole being sings the greatness of the Lord! My spirit rejoices! For the Most High has imbued me with lovingkindness, doing this great thing in me. Blessed be the Name. The Most High has shown us mercy and has indeed remembered the promise made to Abraham and Sarah and all our ancestors!"

Elizabeth's labor began late in the night, yet she waited for the dawn before she whispered to her husband, "Arise. Tell Mary to bid the midwife come. Today you will have a son."

Such a flurry of activity erupted after Zechariah clapped his hands, signaling the time had arrived. From then on the women took over. Their servant, Abigail, was in and out of the room fetching and carrying out orders given by the mid-wife. Mary sat by her aunt's side, holding her hand and heartening her with encouraging words.

At midday, Zechariah tapped on the bedroom door and beckoned Mary to come out. With a twinkle in his eye, he pointed to the crowd below in the courtyard. There, before her eyes, were her parents, Anna and Joachim, and her betrothed, Joseph. There, too, were his parents, Jacob and Deborah, and his brothers and their families. Her heart was filled with wonder and happiness. She had not seen her parents for three months. And as for her betrothed - she had left on uncertain terms and awaited word from him there in Ain Karim.

When their eyes met Joseph spoke in a loud and clear voice, "I have come for my wife."

Mary blushed with excitement. They had not faced each other since the day Mary had told him she was with child. He had come! She felt so honored that Joseph would make the long trip to claim her as his own. At this point Mary's parents rushed to embrace their child, and the others gathered around and exchanged eager greetings. Finally, Joseph pulled her away from the crowd.

He was almost twenty; tall with square shoulders and the strong arms of a carpenter, and honest brown eyes. Despite his outward calm, he too was excited to meet her. She was fourteen with rosy cheeks, sparkling hazel eyes, and warm almond colored hair. She had changed, though; there was a certain softness about her figure, and she had a glow about her that came from the bearing of life within.

"You look beautiful, Mary. You've gained weight," Joseph blurted out when they were alone. He blushed beneath his youthful beard. Men do not comment on women's appearance. "I mean, how are you?" Mary blushed also.

They had been engaged a short while when Mary came into the carpenter shop to tell Joseph all that the angel of the Lord had said. Though he knew her to be a guileless girl, he could not comprehend what she was telling him. Confused and afraid to break their engagement outright for fear of exposing her to scandal, Joseph agreed that Mary should visit her kinfolk in Ain Karim so he could have time to think and decide what would be the best way to handle their troubling dilemma.

Joseph told her of the days since she went away; of how he thought day and night weighing all the possibilities regarding her unexplainable pregnancy: his right to shun her knowing the child she carried was not his, but fearful that would leave her open to being accused of adultery. Under the Law, the penalty for such a crime was stoning. He cared too much for Mary to allow any harm to come to her. He could marry her quickly, and they could move to another place where no one knew them, but that would mean leaving behind everyone and everything they had ever known and loved. Or he could marry her, and stay and bear the scandal, shame and gossip that would afflict them for the rest of their lives.

Finally, he came to the conclusion that Mary should live with her relatives in Ain Karim and he would quietly release her from their betrothal. Being a righteous man, his conscience would not permit him to marry her even though he knew her to be innocent of any wrong doing.

Sleep had been difficult with all this weighing on his mind, but after the decision was made he fell into a deep, dream-filled sleep. He dreamt an angel of the Lord appeared to him and said, "Do not be afraid, Joseph. Take Mary as your wife. It is by the touch of the Creator Spirit that this child has been conceived in her. She will bear a Son and you, of the lineage of David, shall name him Jesus, for he will save his people by winning them back to the Lord."

And as he awoke, a passage from scripture came to him, "Behold a virgin shall conceive and bear a son, whose name shall be God-with-us!"

His heart beat with exhilaration. Joseph now understood all that Mary had told him. The time of which the prophets had spoken had come to pass and his betrothed was the woman of whom they had foretold. His heart was opened to the truth, and he believed. Praising the Lord, he quickly went to his family, as well as to Joachim and Anna, and persuaded them all to come with him to claim his betrothed, marry her, and bring her back to their home.

"Mary," Joseph began, taking her hands in his big, rough carpenter hands, "on the day we were betrothed, I declared before our families and friends that you are my wife and I am your husband. Yet, now you are 'the virgin with child' our Holy Scriptures foretold. You are to be the mother of our Messiah. And the Messiah is to come from the House of David." He took a deep breath to compose himself and continued, "I, Joseph, son of Jacob, of the House of David, a humble carpenter, though a virgin myself, ask that I may be the father of your Son in this world. I love you, Mary. I want to be your protector, provider, the father of your child, your husband."

Mary looked deep into his handsome face, his hopeful eyes and responded, "Joseph, I love you, too. There is no man I know of who is more caring, gentle or wise. And there is no better man that our Son could call father here on earth than you. I will be proud and honored to be your wife and for you to be father to our Son."

Suddenly, cries of a newborn were heard from above. Mary jumped up clasping her hands in front of her. Joseph watched from his seated position as the brightness of Mary's face gradually became solemn. Her hands slowly moved down to feel her own small yet growing belly. He knew she wondered at the miracle of an elderly woman conceiving and giving birth, and herself, a virgin with child, and pondered what all their futures would hold.

"And what will be your son's name?" inquired the curious family and friends who had gathered in the courtyard when they heard the astonishing news that the Lord had blessed the old couple with a child.

His mother answered evenly, "He is to be called John, for the Lord has been gracious to us."

Since the newborn's birth, the people had disputed over the name of the boy with some saying, "There is none of your family called by that name. The custom, as you well know, is to name the child after one of your beloved dead."

Despite their nay-saying, on the eighth day the proud father took his son to the synagogue to be named and circumcised. Zechariah sacrificed a lamb and gave five silver pieces to the priest, dedicating his firstborn son to the Almighty.

Zechariah's neighbors were still babbling over the choice of 'John' as the child's name when he returned the babe to his mother. They had gathered to celebrate the dedication of the boy, but their constant, well-meaning advice annoyed him. No amount of gesturing could stop their harping at the mute man until the power of the Lord opened his mouth, "His name is John!"

Zechariah, having found his voice, blessed the Creator, and filled with Spirit, prophesied saying, "Blessed be the Name of the Holy One of Israel! You have visited your people with your mighty hand of mercy. You have raised up a voice for our salvation..." His eyes fell on Mary, and Joseph who stood by her side. "...Salvation has come from the House of David as promised of old remembering the holy covenant. Therefore, let us all worship the Almighty without fear in holiness and righteousness all the days of our lives."

Taking his son in his hands, Zechariah held him aloft and said, "And you, my son, will be called prophet of the Most High. You will walk before the Promised One to prepare the way. With knowledge of salvation, you will instruct the people. And through the forgiveness of their sins, those who dwell in darkness and the shadow of death will be guided into the path of peace and justice!"

Then he walked over to Mary, placed the babe in her arms and said, "Because of the tender mercy of our Creator, the dawn from on high has broken upon us."

When the celebration of John's dedication was over and the excitement of Zechariah's regained voice subsided, Joseph took the priest aside and said, "Mary and I wish to be married immediately. Would you do us the honor of witnessing and blessing the ceremony?"

"Mary and you want to marry immediately? Well, not today! So much has happened today. Elizabeth is tired. And preparations have to be made. Elizabeth will be so pleased to hear this news!" Zechariah, having found his voice, had taken to speaking out loud. "Why all the rush? Oh, of course, I see. Mary is in her third month. Joseph has his carpenter's shop to get back to. He is a good man...owns his own carpenter shop....every man needs a trade. Oh, this is why he brought his own family and the in-laws-to-be with him here. And all the supplies needed for a feast. How considerate. How fine. This is what he planned all along. He said so when he first arrived and claimed Mary as his wife. Now he has been away from Nazareth and neglecting his business for too long, and they need to get settled in their own home." Then to Joseph, "Tomorrow. Tomorrow evening I will raise the wedding canopy."

Joseph patiently listened to the old priest, realizing he was making up for nine months of silence. "Thank you."

"The pleasure is all mine. I have a son. My wife is well. Mary and you will be married tomorrow. And I shall see my Salvation! Bless you both! Bless us all!"

Joseph had indeed made the journey with Mary's parents and his family knowing he would not leave Ain Karim without taking the maiden as his wife. He wished both sides of the family to be there for this joyous and solemn occasion. It was not the autumn wedding they had hoped it would be after the harvest when music and dancing, food and wine would last for days and days. But he had convinced them all to come to the hill country in Judea with as much as their small caravan could handle to make this festive day as beautiful as possible.

Mary's mother, Anna, also came prepared; she brought from Nazareth her daughter's wedding dress. Girls at the age of ten begin to make and embroider their dress in anticipation of their wedding.

In the amber light of the setting sun Anna helped her girl dress. She brushed and scented her daughter's hair, and waited for the groom to arrive. When Joseph entered, as was the custom, he was wearing the garland crown his mother had just woven for him. His groomsmen, his brothers, were also in attendance to testify that the young woman was indeed the groom's bride. Dressed as any other virgin bride with her crown of coins about her forehead, Mary looked radiant.

Joseph, on beholding her youthful innocent beauty, was filled with longing for her, yet the curves of her body bespoke the presence of the Holy Child within. Suddenly, he was overcome with awe for her being. Mary was like the Temple in Jerusalem; her womb was the Holy of Holies which held the Divine, the Son of the Creator of the Universe!

Picking up the veil on the bench beside the door, Joseph approached her somberly and lifted it over her head and said, "You are my wife." Then he reverently whispered, "My virgin wife now and for ever."

Mary's eyes filled with tears. She nodded; she understood. Theirs was to be a special, holy love. Their longing for, and the fulfilled promise of the coming of the Messiah was to unite them in a way more than any physical consummation ever could.

The sun had set. The time had come to begin the wedding. Observing the law regarding new mothers, Elizabeth, being ritually impure, would watch the wedding from the terrace above with baby John snuggled in her arms. Zechariah stood under the chuppah, the marriage canopy with the groom dressed in his finest tunic. Joseph's parents stood alongside him with his brothers. Joachim and Anna, holding candles, awaited Mary. Everyone was in place.

Mary came slowly from the upper room. Her veil covered her face, and in her hands she carried her wedding gift to her new husband. Her parents took her by the arms and guided her down the stairs and across the courtyard amidst a joyful chorus of praise. The chuppah, set up under the starlit night, itself invoked the blessing of the Almighty on the couple. Seven times the bride and her parents circled the canopy, acknowledging her husband beneath it to be the center of her universe. When they came to a halt before the groom, Zechariah lifted the bride's veil and folded it back. At that time Anna kissed her cheeks and presented their only child to Joseph, then stepped back.

Mary unfolded her gift to her husband and draped the new tallith with its tassels across his shoulders. For the first time now he was a man enveloped with the aura of light which marriage imparts; a complete man under the Law. In his turn, Joseph produced a simple gold ring and placed it on his bride's forefinger, saying, "Behold, you are consecrated to me with this ring, according to the Law of Moses and Israel. As this ring encircles your finger so, too, shall I encircle you, protect you, provide for you." With that Mary held up her ringed hand for all to witness, and everyone raised an Alleluia!

On a little table placed beside Zechariah stood the betrothal cup from which Joseph and Mary had first promised themselves to each other. The priest filled the cup to overflowing with wine and blessed it, then handed it to the groom. Joseph drank and held it out to his bride. With both their hands holding the cup Mary drank the wine.

Zechariah then asked all the people to bow their heads for the final blessing. Spreading the fingers of his raised hands, dividing the four in two, he prayed the seven-fold blessing, "Blessed are you, Lord, Creator of everything for your glory. Blessed are you, Lord, Creator of man and woman in your own likeness. Blessed are you, Lord, let this couple be very happy as Adam and Eve were once happy in the Garden of Eden. Blessed are you, Lord, Creator of joy and celebration, rejoicing and jubilation, pleasure and delight, love, peace and friendship. Blessed are you, Lord, who make groom and bride rejoice together in each other when they become one soul in two bodies. Blessed are you, Lord, may this couple rejoice in the Child you will bless them with. Blessed are you, Lord, may the blessings of this joyful day fill all the cities of Judea."

Thus the wedding ritual was complete and Joseph and Mary were united in marriage, and all present cried out, "Amen! Alleluia!"

II

The two boys stole back into the city while the others still slept. They reached the Temple steps at dawn as the Levites were assembling at the Nicanor Gate. At the moment the sun rose, the trumpets sounded the new day. Twenty Levites, custodians of the Temple, pushed against the massive bronze doors. The boys watched in awe as the enormous double doors rumbled open. At the exact same time, voices within the Temple and without the city took up the morning prayer, "Hear, O Israel, the Lord is our God, the Lord alone. You shall love the Lord your God with all your heart, and with all your soul, and with all your strength..."

Jesus stood at the threshold of the Temple and chanted with all the other faithful. John, by his side, softly prayed the holy words also. When that was done John anxiously made motions to leave but Jesus remained mesmerized looking down into the Temple courtyard over to the sanctuary. Passover had ended and it was time to be going. Their parents would need their help to prepare for the journey out of Jerusalem.

At the same moment, the boys turned to one another and said, "Let's go back." "Let's go inside."

"What?"

"I want to speak to the priests and elders," answered Jesus.

"You c-can't interrupt those important men. What would you say to them? You are only t-twelve!"

John, thirteen, a whole six months older than his cousin, was not ready to discuss anything with the elders, though his father had taught him well. His father said one day he would proclaim some great message to the people, but John knew himself to be too shy and awkward to speak in front of anyone... especially the elders of the Temple.

"I must be about my Father's business," replied Jesus.

16

"Then let's g-go," said John and added, "Your father is a carpenter, and our families are on their way back to my home. We've stayed too long already."

They stood eye to eye for a moment, and then Jesus merely smiled and considered the Temple again.

"Jesus," John pleaded. "My parents are old and need my help. We must g-go!"

"You are right," agreed his cousin. "Go help your parents. I will be all right in my Father's house."

"Why do you speak in r-riddles?" protested John. "Your house is in Nazareth. You will lose your way home if you do not c-come with me now. Besides, you are too young to be alone in Jerusalem."

Jesus purposefully descended the fifteen curved steps into the Temple courtyard. He made his way past the merchants selling doves and lambs and the money changers in the Court of the Gentiles. John's heart beat wildly. There was no time to run after Jesus to persuade him to come away. He could stay no longer. "Well, d-do as you must," John shouted in frustration. "But hurry. Do not be overly long." By then, Jesus was ascending the fifteen steps leading to the sanctuary where inside many priests and scribes were gathering to discuss the Torah, pray, and perform Temple sacrifices.

John ran from the Temple, threading his way through the narrow streets crowded with fellow pilgrims trying to leave the Holy City after Passover. He felt guilty leaving his cousin behind and could not help but wonder what Jesus would say to those learned men. Compared to himself, Jesus, for all his youth, had wisdom beyond his years and would be at ease speaking to them. And by thinking that, John feared he would never be the orator his father wanted him to be.

When he reached the campsite, John saw that most of the work had already been done by Abigail. She was their servant, the nursemaid of his childhood and his friend. But now she scolded him severely. His father scolded him also, and said, "Where have you been? Did you not know there was work to be done? And you worried your mother, disappearing that way."

"I am s-sorry," answered the boy. "I was with Jesus at the T-temple." Then to make amends, "I will do all the rest of the packing. G-go, sit in the shade, Abigail. All of you sit, and I will bring you water to d-drink when we are ready to go so you will be fresh for the journey. The cart will be packed in no time!"

"He is such a good boy," said Elizabeth quietly to her husband. "And if he was with Jesus, what harm could come to him?"

Every few years, Joseph made some time and took the family in the opposite direction from home to go to Ain Karim after Passover so the two families could have some quiet time together. After their leisurely half day's journey, the carpenter and the old priest entered the familiar courtyard. Joseph had brought his ass which carried all the supplies they had needed for being on the road. "Jesus, come and help me," called Joseph as he began to unload the animal. There was no answer. "Mary, where is Jesus?"

Mary, Elizabeth and Abigail had arrived with a group of women ahead of the men returning to Ain Karim. Mary stopped what she was doing and looked about. She answered, "He is not with you? I heard he was with John earlier this morning, so I supposed he accompanied you here with the men. He must be here. I will find him." She crossed the yard and called out, "Jesus? Jesus?"

"John was with us," said Joseph, beginning to feel uneasy.

Elizabeth appeared on the terrace landing when she heard their exchange and began to call, "He is not up here. John? John? Where is Jesus?"

John, a thin youth with straight brown hair and dark round eyes came sheepishly from the direction of the kitchen. "I – D-didn't he catch up? I – I last s-s-saw him in Jerusalem."

"What?" cried Mary, suddenly alarmed. "Where in Jerusalem?"

"We went to the T-t-temple before the sun rose to see them open the gate. Then Jesus wanted to stay and talk to the elders. I c-c-could not stop him. He went into the T-t-temple and I left to help my father. Honestly, I thought he was g-g-going to catch up to leave with us at the last minute."

"When he did not come with us I assumed he was traveling with the women," said Joseph.

"I have not seen him since he went to sleep last night and now it will soon be dusk," fretted the young mother to Elizabeth at her side. "My son is alone in Jerusalem. We must go back now."

Mary would have rushed out into the night had it not been for her husband who said, "It is a long walk back to Jerusalem. It is not safe to travel at night. We will leave at first light."

She turned to him with tears brimming in her eyes, "But he is all alone."

"He will be all right, Mary. Nothing will harm him," said Joseph taking her into his arms. Joseph, himself, was trying hard to be strong and logical. "If I know our son, some kind person has already taken a liking to him and brought him home and they are feasting him with food right now. You know how easily he makes friends."

Then he saw John's guilt ridden face and said, "Do not reproach yourself, John. You are not to blame. Will you come with us back to the Holy City and show us where you last saw Jesus? With your help we will find him in the morning, so do not worry."

"O-of course I will help," cried John, anxious to make amends. "I would g-give my life to be of help."

By midday all three were standing on the threshold of the Temple. Naively they expected to see Jesus where John had last seen him.   They thought he would be waiting for them, but he was nowhere in sight.

Joseph entered the Court of the Gentiles and asked among the money changers about his son.   Then he went over to the sellers of doves and lambs, and then to the groups of pious men in the courtyard.   Meanwhile, Mary and John remained at the Nicanor Gate and asked all the people coming and going about Jesus.   No one had seen a lost boy.

When they came together again they searched the streets around the perimeter of the Temple.   They went to the Golden Gate, the Sheep Gate - Jesus was fond of animals and perhaps he was drawn to where the men bought and sold livestock. They also went to the Gate of Benjamin and finally to the Garden Gate from where they had first entered Jerusalem in the morning.   Everywhere they went they inquired about a missing boy but to no avail.

The light of day began to fade as the sun sank below the walls of the city.   Mary began to weep from worry and exhaustion at the thought of being separated from her only son another day.   Reluctantly, she set up a makeshift camp for the night while Joseph went to buy some food.   John wandered about looking for sticks to make a fire.

When the carpenter returned with bread and fruit he tried to get his wife to eat, even though his own stomach was in knots. John sat silently. He could not eat either.

At night a hush fell over the city.   The three gathered themselves together against the darkness and prayed.   They trusted in the Almighty and that Jesus would be well for another night and they would find him in the morning.

The distant trumpet signaled the new day. With dawn's first light they began the morning prayer, their voices mingling with those of the faithful throughout the city. Jerusalem came to life. Farmers entered the city with their grain, fruit and vegetables for market, while day laborers left to go work in the fields. Joseph and Mary and John began their search all over again.

They wandered the narrow maze of streets and kept the Temple in view and questioned all who would listen to them about the lost boy. At midmorning they found themselves once more at the Nicanor Gate. They peered down into the courtyard.

"Th-th-there he is," shouted John. "Jesus!" called Mary and Joseph as they followed John into the Temple. They could see Jesus walking towards the inner courts with a Pharisee. All three ran and shouted. Jesus and his companion stopped half way up the steps at the sound behind them.

Mary took Jesus into her arms and said, "Son, we have been looking for you everywhere! We were so frightened when we discovered you were not among our company when we returned to Ain Karim! How is it you did not come when we left Jerusalem?"

Jesus remained silent in his mother's embrace.

"Allow me," said the young Pharisee. "I am Nicodemus. I have been watching after your son. My wife was more than pleased to feed him. He came into the inner court two days ago. He said you would be back for him. In the meanwhile, I was astounded, and so were the other doctors of the Law, with his keen questions and insights, and his love for the word of our Holy Scripture."

"I am the Word." Jesus whispered in his mother's ear and gently broke her hold, then spoke louder, "Why did you look for me everywhere when you knew I would be in my Father's House?"

Mary sat down on the Temple steps and gazed up at her son and wondered what his words meant. Joseph, on the other hand, comprehended what he meant by 'Father's House' and laid a hand on Jesus' shoulder to restrain him. Husband and wife looked at each other; was their son aware of his self being?

"Of course, if you want to be a carpenter like your father," continued Nicodemus, misunderstanding, "Then go back to Nazareth and callus up your hands. Would that you were the son of a rabbi! You have the wit and intelligence to be great among men!"

"Thank you, Rabbi Nicodemus," said Joseph as he helped Mary up. "And may the Lord, blessed be the Name, reward you for the care you gave our son." To the others he said, "Come. We must start back if we are to reach John's home by dark."

"Yes, thank you, Rabbi Nicodemus," said Jesus. "I look forward to our meeting again." Then Jesus turned to John who stood off to the side. He looked lost. "Hey John," he smiled, "race you to the Garden Gate!"

"Do not go any further than the gate. I do not want to lose you both!" Mary called after the two as they swiftly walked through the courtyard, then broke into a run as soon as they passed the Temple Gate.

"Boys!" exclaimed Nicodemus. "You can be proud of your son. He is special. For one so young, he is very wise…and compelling. People will be drawn to him."

Jesus reached the gate first with John close behind. Both boys, laughing and exhausted, collapsed on the ground. When they caught their breath, they realized they were sitting among the beggars.

"I feel sorry for these people," said John thoughtfully. "What s–s-sin have they committed that the Lord Almighty would make them blind, lame or poor, and then forget them?"

"Our Father in heaven is all lovingkindness. These people are no more or less guilty than anyone else you see. God is not punishing the lame, blind and poor. Nor has God forgotten them," Jesus answered. "Rather, they are in our midst as an invitation to us to mirror and manifest to one another the compassion of the Merciful and Just One."

"I-I wish there was something we c-could do to ease their s-suffering."

22

Jesus nodded and turned to the man with a twisted leg next to him and said, "Do you have a place to stay?"

The man blinked with surprise at the question and shook his head back and forth.

"Jesus?" whispered John, alarmed.

"I overheard a man yesterday in the Temple telling a friend that ever since his wife died it has been difficult for him to do all the chores around the place like milking the goat and feeding the chickens. He said nothing of pay, but would be happy to share his home. You know, offer someone a place to sleep and some food in exchange... I suspect he is lonely, too." Then Jesus asked, "Would you be interested?"

"I used to milk goats when I was a lad before I came to Jerusalem and busted my leg to pieces," exclaimed the man with the crutch and begging bowl. "No one wants to hire me as a day laborer when they see my crutch, but I am able. I would be glad to do chores in exchange for a bed and food. Where is this man?"

"Not far," said Jesus as he helped the man up. "My cousin and I will show you the way,"

In a few minutes they were knocking on a door.

"Who is it?"

Jesus spoke up, "I heard you were looking for someone to help you with your chores?"

The door opened. An old man peered out. "Do I know you?" asked the man looking from boy to boy to man.

"No, but I understand you are willing to share your home with someone who could help you, and my friend here," Jesus pointed to the man with the crutch, "could use some work and a place to stay."

"I am Josias. I am good with animals and I even know how to cook!" said the cripple earnestly. "Don't mind the crutch; I can get around fine."

"Come in, come in. I am Micheas, son of Rubin. Welcome," said the old man who saw past the twisted leg and saw another man like himself: alone and in need. He took an instant liking to his new friends and said, "Come in, boys. You are welcome, too."

"Jesus, we must be at the g-gate when your p-parents arrive," John whispered urgently.

"You are right. We must take our leave. Shalom to you both, Micheas and Josias. May you be blessed with peace, health and happiness. Deal honorably with each other and prosper."

"Wait," said the old man. "Here is a copper coin for each of you for your trouble."

"It was no tr-trouble," said John shaking his head.

"Thank you, sir," said Jesus as he took the coins and gave one to John.

At the head of the alley, they saw Joseph and Mary pass by. They ran to catch up and surprised them when they popped out from behind. They all continued along with the boys in the rear.

John held the coin in his hand. It was hot in his hand. He had not wanted to take the money and he did not understand why Jesus did. You should not get paid for doing a good deed. Ahead was the Garden Gate where all the poor begged for alms. Jesus helped one but there were still so many more. As they passed the crowd John thoughtfully dropped his coin into the bowl of an old woman.

Jesus saw all this from the corner of his eye and smiled. He bent down and gave his coin to a little blind boy.

When the two families were reunited again, Elizabeth and Zechariah had a grand homecoming feast prepared for the weary travelers. After the meal, they all sat around the fire pit relaxing and watching the flickering flames.

"Mother, tell us a story," said Jesus.

"Oh son, aren't you too tired for stories?"

"Please," Jesus implored. "Tell the story about my birth."

Mary saw her son's eyes shift to John. He was not looking to be backed up in his request as much as alerting his cousin that this was something special for him to hear.

After Jesus' revelation earlier that day, Mary understood her son's desire to be about his Father's business. Nevertheless, she and Joseph had discussed and prayed about the matter and decided that Jesus needed to be obedient to them; their son needed to mature in age before he could truly begin his destiny. However, the birth of her son was a blessed event, and she would willingly share the story with John if it would help Jesus and her young cousin know each other better.

"It was the time of the great census ordered by Caesar Augustus. The whole country was on the move; everyone had to return to their family town to be registered. My delivery time was near, but we were obliged by Roman law to be counted among the House of David in Bethlehem.

"We made the journey slowly. I rode most of the way on our ass; it took us five days before we reached the tiny town. We arrived on the last day of the census and had to wait in a long line with all the other people who had converged on Bethlehem from all over the country. It was then my labor began. As soon as we were counted and our names signed in their great book, Joseph rushed to the inn to find us a room, or a space in the courtyard at least. But Bethlehem was overcrowded and there was no room anywhere, and we knew no one in town on whom we could impose.

"Joseph explained to the innkeeper our dilemma and pleaded for any place where we could find shelter. Finally, he took pity on us and suggested we use his brother's shepherd's cave where animals and tools were kept on the outskirts of town near the grazing fields.

"We found the cave - it was a dark and damp place, but Joseph made me a bed of fresh straw and built a fire to keep us warm. My labor pangs were strong by then, and I was frightened to give birth by myself. As I lay on the straw, the glow of the fire threw its light across the arch of the low ceiling and it lightened my heart somewhat. You see, light is a symbol of hope and my son to be born was my Hope.

"A midwife came. We were so grateful; she was sent by the kindness of the innkeeper. Now with her there and Joseph by my side and knowing I was in the care of the Source of all Life, my fears left me. When I delivered you, my beautiful first-born, I praised the Most High whose lovingkindness is boundless and placed you, my son, on my husband's knee, declaring to the entire world that Joseph was your father.

"All the next day I rested. Your father bought food, water and more straw for there were still no lodgings to be found.

"But that night, just as we were falling asleep, there was a tapping at the wooden door that covered the cave's entrance. Five shepherds stood there asking to see the newborn. They claimed a mysterious shining being appeared to them saying, 'Rejoice, shepherds! Behold, I bring you news of great joy. Today in the City of David, your Savior has been born, the Promised One of God. You will find the infant this night rolled in linen and lying in a manger.' Then the messenger was joined by other heavenly voices singing, 'Glory to God in the highest and peace to all people on earth!'

"Very quietly they peeked at you in the manger and uttered hushed exclamations of joy. But when they left we could hear them loudly praising the Most High and spreading the good news, 'The Savior is born! The Promised One! The Messiah!' "

John half dozed on his mother's lap, struggling to stay awake through the last part of his cousin Mary's story; he could not keep his eyes open any longer after such an eventful day. He dreamt he saw Mary showing off her baby to scruffy looking shepherds and heard voices saying, 'The Savior is born…. The Messiah….' And his own voice was the loudest of all.

"Alleluia," cried Zechariah, Elizabeth and Joseph.

John's eyes snapped open, hearing the shout of praise. His eyes locked onto Jesus' across the glowing embers; John's young cousin's eyes glistened - Jesus smiled and nodded his head in encouragement. John wondered what the dream meant.

After breakfast the next day, Jesus was helping his father pack their ass for the trip back to Nazareth. John pulled him aside. "M-may I ask you something?" John started timidly.

"Sure, anything," answered Jesus.

"At the T-temple yesterday – your f-f-father's house, your father's b-b-business," stammered John. "I had a d-dream last night." Words did not come easily to John: his face turned red, he closed his eyes and after a moment's silence continued, "I don't understand it, but I have a f-feeling that it is something special concerning you – and m-me. So, all I want to s-say is that if you ever need my help, you can c-count on me. D-d-do you need my help?"

"Yes!" Jesus smiled broadly. "Someday. When we are older."

"Jesus," called Joseph. "It is time to go. Say good-bye to John and his parents."

"Shalom, cousin, peace. Listen to your father. And grow strong before our God." Jesus waved as he ran to his mother and father, "See you next Passover."

III

Mary came down from the women's gallery of the synagogue with her friends. Her pleasant expression faded when she saw the solemn faces of her husband and son.

"One of the elders has a traveling merchant staying with him," began Joseph quietly. "He brought a message from Ain Karim. Your Aunt Elizabeth has died, and Zechariah is weak and failing."

Sudden sadness enveloped Mary. Her own beloved parents had died within the last few years: first her father and then her mother. Now her aunt with whom she shared so much was gone too, and soon her venerable uncle would join them in eternal rest - all her loved ones.

"But John," she whispered. Her heart went out to him. Though he was living in the community of the Essenes, he would now be an orphan living far from his sole relatives, especially the One he would someday herald.

Jesus put his arm around his mother.

Mary wiped a tear from her eye as she thought of her nineteen-year-old son who would someday bring peace to Israel. She rested her head on his shoulder, absorbing the promised hope his presence exuded. Then, looking to Joseph, asked, "Husband, would it be possible for us to go to the hill country to bring solace to John and offer our final farewell to Zechariah before he joins our ancestors?"

Joseph nodded in agreement and took his wife's hand. There was nothing in the carpenter shop that demanded his immediate attention, and he, also, felt it was important for Jesus and John to be together at this time in their lives.

Late on the fourth day of the week, Joseph, Mary and Jesus arrived at the home of Zechariah, the ancient priest of Abijah in Ain Karim. The carpenter had closed his shop, informing the neighbors that they would be away for at least two weeks to be with his wife's family in their time of sorrow.

From the doorway they could see and hear many people inside the courtyard loudly lamenting. They arrived too late. Zechariah was dead. Sorrowfully, they moved through the courtyard seeking John. Instead they found Abigail, the good-hearted servant who, when widowed, young and alone without children, was taken in by John's parents to help the elderly couple care for their newborn. To the family, she was more kin than servant.

"You! Here!" exclaimed Abigail. "How?" She was at a loss for words between her surprise, grief and gratitude for their arrival.

"The traveling merchant brought your sad news about my aunt," said Mary. "We came as soon as we could. I am so sorry we are too late to say our farewell blessing to Zechariah. Where is John?"

"John is still at the cemetery," answered Abigail. "He would not come away. Both his dearly loved parents lie side by side in the tomb. The dear old man died in his sleep last night... John was with him...he is taking it very hard...he told us to leave him alone with his parents...."

Abigail could not control her cries any longer and broke down completely. Mary encircled the woman in her arms and they wept together while Joseph stood respectfully to the side. Jesus also shed tears for his great uncle; his heart was moved with grief. Moreover, he felt sympathy at the sight of all the mourners who thought of death as the end of life. He was the first to see John standing at the doorway and spoke softly, "There he is."

John looked dazed. Mary and Abigail, Joseph and others all moved forward as one to bring the young man inside, but just as Mary was about to reach him, he backed out the doorway and fled back down the street.

"He is not ready to face us all..." said Abigail apologetically, knowing her John. He had always been a quiet boy, content with his studies, happier to be the listener than the speaker - he showed signs of being awkward before people. He stuttered. Yet, now, these last years with the solitary Essenes, who lived out in the desert by the Salt Sea, he seemed at ease hidden away among them sharing in their ascetic life of righteousness, but she missed him terribly. "He knows we care. And he truly loves us too, but he needs time to grieve by himself."

The morning sun peeked over the courtyard wall as Jesus sat on the steps leading up to the terrace. He had waited up very late for John's return and rose before there was light in the sky. He longed to see his cousin. John's dog nudged Jesus' arm for attention, aware of the grief in the household and her master's absence. Jesus petted the dog, and it brought comfort to them both.

"Who is your friend?"

"You remember Spicy," Jesus answered the light footsteps coming down the stairs. "She is the stray pup John found in Jerusalem last Passover."

"Oh, yes," said Mary sitting down beside her son and petting the dog. "I thought John called her that because she smelled so bad!" They both laughed at her joke and then were silent for a while. "John is not home."

Jesus looked into his mother's tired hazel eyes; she had not slept well. He kissed her cheek and said, "I'll find him." Jesus slapped his thigh as he walked across the courtyard. "Come on, Spicy; let's go find your master." Spicy beat him to the door and, as soon as it was opened, darted around it and was gone down the street.

The town's marketplace was already busy with activity with vendors setting up for the day when Jesus arrived. He had passed many an alley and doorway, keeping an eye open for John. He made inquiries at the stand selling fruit and bought some grapes. The man knew John's family, of course, and

30

offered his sympathies but could not help. None of the other vendors could either.

Just outside town was a lush vineyard that had a fresh spring-well that flowed endlessly. Jesus came upon Abigail there by the fountain, surrounded by her friends. Usually the townswomen would be exchanging good-natured gossip amidst the beauty as they fetched water for the day's use from the spring, but Abigail's eyes were red and watering as her friends tried to console her over the lose of her loved ones. He joined the circle of women and said, "Abigail, do not weep for those who have died. I promise you - you shall see them alive in the house of our heavenly Father."

Abigail was astounded by these words spoken so gently by young Jesus, and yet with such conviction that she felt immediately upraised.

"I am going to find John and bring him home."

When Jesus left, Abigail found it easy to blink back her tears, sensing all would be well. She said good-bye to her friends, picked up her filled water jar, and headed back home with a peaceful heart.

On the outskirts of town Jesus took the road climbing up the hills to Jerusalem. Ahead of him, the sun rose above the terraced hills laden with vines, while behind him to the west were the rolling grasslands leading to the Great Sea. Going some distance up the road, he stopped and shielded his eyes with his arm from the glare of the bright sun, surveying the route ahead. To the left he thought he could see someone sitting alongside the road. He increased his walking speed to get a closer look, then slowed down when he saw it was indeed his cousin. John's back was to him and Jesus could see John's shoulders heaving up and down and heard him sobbing. Quietly, Jesus stopped within a hand-breadth behind his cousin.

"Oh God!" cried out John in despair.

"Here I am. Why do you weep?"

John stiffened and covered his face; he did not want the stranger to see him crying. Taking in gulps of air he tried to regain his composure.

"Tell me why you weep?"

Lowering his hands he saw the shadow of the man behind him patiently waiting for him to speak. He did not turn to the compassionate voice, yet felt its outpouring of sympathy and in it found the courage to begin.

"M-my dear mother died...after a brief illness...then, within the week, my wise father died...just the night before last...they were old, married over fifty years...they had a beautiful, long life together. I am their only son born to them in their later years. It was my f-father who was ill, but my mother died so suddenly...then he failed quickly and followed her. I reached Jerusalem before I knew where I was. I had turned away from those who love me...gathered at my home...I thought I wanted to be alone. B-but I want to be home. I was on my way...but...but I found my d-dog d-dead in the road." John's eyes filled with tears again as he stroked her golden coat. "I s-suppose she came searching for me...I passed a band of Roman s-soldiers on horseback...she liked to chase horses...nip at their legs...I guess there was an accident."

Jesus leaned over his cousin's shoulder. John cradled Spicy in his arms. The dog was quite still. Jesus felt overwhelming mercy toward his cousin in his suffering; Spicy's death was more than John's already broken heart could bear - it was all too wrenching. He leaned over and placed one hand on John's shoulder and the other on Spicy's still warm side and said, "She is not dead, just asleep."

At that the dog's eyes fluttered open, she squirmed in John's arms and licked his face. His surprised cries of joy filled the air. For a while he was lost in the delight of having Spicy alive. And then he wondered: How could this be? Spicy was surely dead. What miracle has happened? Spicy leaped from his arms and scampered around to the stranger behind him.

John turned to look and saw Jesus smiling down at Spicy vigorously rubbing her head.

In that instant the miracle was forgotten. John was so glad to see his cousin he jumped up to embrace him and cried out, "You are here! How? When?"

Jesus told him they had received the news in Nazareth of his mother's death and had arrived yesterday in Ain Karim. The pain of his loss filled John again. He apologized for leaving; he had blindly entered the doorway of his home and only saw the courtyard filled with lamenting people. If he had truly looked and seen Jesus and his parents, he would not have left. Jesus enfolded him in his arms once more and John grew calm.

Spicy tugged at her master's cloak. John looked down at his playful dog. He was sure she was dead. How did she come alive again? Jesus touched her! John pulled away slowly and gazed at Jesus in wonder. There was serenity, sureness in Jesus' expression that no one else possessed.

I wonder," said John.

"What?"

"How…I – I," stammered John not knowing how to put into words the strange, vague awareness inside him. "Could it?…I wonder?" He shook his head, then said, "My f-father called for you the last day of his life."

"We must be on our way. Mother and Abigail are concerned for you," said Jesus. As they began to walk Spicy raced ahead of them and then back to John's side. Jesus asked gently, "What did your father speak of during his last few days?"

"Well, he was mostly pr-praying with the psalms and quoting the prophets. He knew all the Holy Writings and could recite them by heart," replied John.

"For instance?"

" 'A shoot will come out of the stump of Jesse, and from his roots a branch, and the spirit of the Lord shall rest upon him.' " said John and went on, " 'but you, O Bethlehem, though you are small among the clans of Judah, out of you will come one who will rule over Israel, whose origins are from old, from ancient times. And his greatness will reach the ends of the earth, and he will be their peace.' "

"What do you think he meant by those words," asked Jesus.

"I believe he was referring to the guaranteed future of the Davidic line and the prophecies concerning the Messiah. The first quote was from Isaiah, the other is Micah. Both suggest the Messiah will be of the Davidic line. But why he spoke them on his deathbed, I do not know; only that he longed for the Messiah to come, as do we all."

Jesus smiled for two reasons: He, the Messiah, was before John and second, it fascinated Jesus that his cousin did not stutter when quoting the scriptures or when expounding their meaning. "Did he say anything else?"

John nodded and continued, "Now, after he said that a number of times, it was as if they gave him confidence and peace, my father seemed to search his mind for a particular text. Finally he began to pray the psalm about waiting for redemption, 'Out of the depths I cry to you, O Lord. Lord hear my voice! ... I wait for the Lord, my soul waits. I hope in his word... O Israel, hope in the Lord! The Lord will bring mercy and grant full pardon for steadfast is his love.' Because of his weakness, his voice rose and fell but it was very strong on the last line, 'It is HE WHO WILL SAVE Israel from all their sins.' "

Jesus sighed his own name.

John stopped in his tracks. He suddenly realized - yes that was the literal translation of his cousin's name. That strange vague feeling came over him again. How often during his last hours did his father pray that psalm! And John remembered at the time he wondered if his father was trying to communicate something to him. "That is r-remarkable!" exclaimed John.

"What is?" Jesus stopped also.

"I remember my f-father praying that psalm many times. After he was silent for a while, he said softly, 'God will give you a sign: Look, a virgin is with child and will give birth to a son and will call him Emmanuel, God-with-us.' It was then he said your name, 'Jesus.' I thought it was curious at the time, but now it is utterly m-mystifying to think that he was also actually c-calling your name over and over again while he prayed that psalm."

"Do you know why?" Jesus asked gently. When John stared at him blankly, Jesus said, "Were there any other prophecies your father spoke of?"

"Yes," he answered slowly because he sensed he was supposed to know why but did not. "From Jeremiah, 'A voice is heard, weeping and mourning: Rachel, crying for her children, and she will not be consoled because they are no more.' This is such a sad quote referring to the Assyrian invasion, yet my father's voice was full of hope and joy as if its message was one of a better future."

John continued, "Then he quoted from Hosea, 'Out of Egypt I call my son.' Now these last two," John spoke knowledgeably from his life-long study of the sacred texts, "are really obscure if they refer to the Messiah. They are also in contrast: the quote from Jeremiah is about exile, while the other is about Joshua's delivery of the Israelites to the Promised Land by crossing the Jordan as the Lord bade him after the death of Moses.' "

Again John stopped short. The name Joshua is a form of Jesus.

"John," said Jesus as he too stopped. They were already outside the door of John's home. Their time had gone too quickly. Jesus wanted to continue their conversation. John did not know Him yet. "Your father would be proud of your understanding of the scriptures. I understand you have been overwhelmed with sorrow these last few days; nonetheless, try to take these quotes and prophecies out of your head and place them in your heart."

John wondered what his cousin was talking about.

"Did your father utter any prophecies concerning you?"

"M-me?' exclaimed John. What did Jesus know that he did not? "Me?" John was aware that his whole life was under his father's guidance: his studying under his father's tutelage and then in the synagogue, and then his training living the life of righteousness with the Essenes were only building blocks for some mission his father said he was born to perform.

Even though his father had tried to prepare him over the years by telling him he would someday proclaim a great message to the people, he still felt himself to be the most unlikely, and unworthy, person to stand before the people of Israel.

Now Jesus, John always thought, would be better suited for the task, being much wiser than himself and a natural speaker: persuasive, yet gentle in his...

"You are the prophet of whom it is written in the book of Malachi, 'See, I am sending my messenger to prepare the way before me. Who can endure the day of his coming? For he is like a refiner's fire: he will purify the descendants of Levi and refine them like silver and gold, until they present offerings to God in righteousness.' And, 'Lo, I will send to you the prophet...' "

"What are you saying?" blurted out John. "I am no prophet!"

" '...before you.' " Jesus went on steadily, "And the prophet Isaiah, 'A voice of one crying out in the wilderness: Prepare the way of the Lord, make straight his paths. Then the glory of the Lord shall be revealed and all people will see it together.' "

"See what?" cried John, fearful and bewildered by his cousin's words and still blind as to what his mission was to be, "W-who am I that I should be called a pr-prophet? What am I to c-cry out?"

"Here is your God," Jesus answered simply. "See, the Lord Yahweh has come with might to gather the sheep in his arms."

Their eyes locked. John could not believe his ears and the authority with which Jesus spoke the Blessed Name of the Unutterable. His mind was filled with clouds, and yet a golden ray of light was beginning to prick through the darkness. His heart was pounding.

"Peace, John," said Jesus, touching his cousin's elbow. "Try to take all these prophecies out of your head and hold them in your heart. We will speak again later."

Because they were in front of John's house, Mary heard them speaking outside the door and opened it to greet them both home. Spicy ran past them into the yard. "The shepherd has found his lost sheep," announced Jesus as he kissed his mother and saluted his father.

John still stood in the street, his mind a muddle, trying to see through the clouds. Mary and Joseph embraced him and ushered him into his own courtyard. Outwardly he accepted their condolences with composure, but in truth, his head was reeling.

That week, they mourned the loss of Elizabeth and Zechariah as a family. John spent much of his time in the solitude of his room agonizing over the prophecies and wondering what were the expectations of him. His father had always said that John would someday fulfill a mission that he had been born to perform. And then on his deathbed his father quoted many prophecies relating to the Messiah. Was that the message he was to proclaim to the people? Was he a prophet? Jesus said so in so many words. If this be true, how was it he did not feel it within himself? Who was the Messiah? John did not know his own self. How was he to know the Messiah?

The week of mourning was over. Worn out by speculation, John came out of his room and looked below into the courtyard. Joseph and Jesus were fixing something, while

Mary and Abigail sat pleasantly under the almond tree talking. His relatives would be leaving in the morning; it was time they got back to Nazareth. John decided that for the remainder of their time together he would put aside trying to understand the prophecies and just be with the family.

He paused there on the terrace as he watched them all below, and mused on how much Jesus favored his mother in looks. Jesus was definitely Mary's son. No mistaking it. Jesus was as tall as Joseph, but that was it. He suddenly became aware of how much he loved them all and would miss them terribly after they left, especially Jesus. Unexpectedly, a great shaft of light shattered the darkness of his mind; the clouds parted and the light grew brighter and brighter.

"Jesus, come up here!"

Jesus excused himself from his father's side and climbed the stairs. When he stood by John, he followed the direction of his cousin's fixed stare. It was upon his mother. Jesus could feel the tension radiating off John. Jesus knew his cousin needed to hear the answers to all his questions from his own lips. "Let us go to your room."

Once inside the room, Jesus waited quietly for the questions to come. John had followed slowly; he was blinded by the light of revelation; his mind was dazzled, and terrified. He had to know. He had to ask. "Is your m-mother..." John could scarcely say the words his throat was so constricted by the unbelievable inspiration flashing in his mind, "a virgin?"

"Yes. All things are possible with the Author of Life. I was created in my mother's womb through the Holy Spirit."

John's mind fumbled about trying to grasp Jesus' words. His heart was pounding; he tried to think logically. "You were born in Bethlehem. That I know. You are of the House of David!"

"Yes, John," said Jesus. "Joseph traces his lineage back to King David. My mother placed me on his knee designating him my earthly father."

" 'A shoot, a branch will grow from the stump of Jesse.' " John said. Then he asked. "Do I remember correctly that your family once spent time in Egypt?"

"Yes, at the time when Herod the Great slew all the infant boys in Bethlehem."

" 'Rachel weeps for her children…' " murmured John closing his eyes. Everyone knew of the infamy wrought by Herod nineteen years ago and how the women of Bethlehem were bereft of their newborn sons while Jesus…startled, John opened his eyes and whispered, "He was looking for you!"

" 'You will return to your own land so there is hope for your future.' " Jesus quoted Jeremiah.

" 'Out of Egypt I call my son.' " John continued. " 'Hope in the Lord.' "

The prophecies were like pieces of a puzzle handed down to the people of Israel by the prophets of old. These all concerned the Messiah. John always thought Jesus to be an exceptional person and trembled now in the blazing knowledge of this bright and terrible light as the pieces came together to reveal Jesus…'He-who-will-save!' Jesus…the Promised One… the Messiah!

John was dazed by this new-found knowledge. He felt as if he was going to black out and staggered over to his bed. Jesus put an arm around John and helped him sit and then knelt on the floor in front of John and watched, and waited. When his eyes could focus again, John looked in turn for the first time into the eyes of the Messiah. He felt overwhelmed by the person in front of him even though it was his own cousin whom he had always known and loved. John's mind jumped from cloud to ray to cloud. It frightened him.

"I am here," said Jesus. He appreciated his cousin's bewilderment and fright. "Do not be afraid."

Still, with his mind in a whirl jumping from cloud to ray, John could not put into words all that was going on inside him. All he could say was, "How?"

"Yahweh," Jesus began to make clear his being, yet when he saw John wince when he said the Holy Name, said, "Abba God planned that the salvation of the Children of Israel would come through the Son."

"'God-with-us,'" groaned John. Not only did Jesus speak the personal name of the Lord again, which is so holy no one may utter it, but he reeled at the momentous thought that his cousin was also the Son of God. He turned away.

Jesus laid his hand on John's shoulder until John could look upon him again and continued gently to explain, "Abba God is my Father in heaven. I was begotten in my mother through power of the Holy Spirit. Joseph is my virgin father. I love and respect him above all other men on earth."

John breathed deeply trying to calm himself. With all his might he tried to make sense of it all and humbly ventured, "But how do you know all this?"

"I learned it through my mother's love of telling stories. She was wont to share all the cherished memories she held in her heart, all the great things the Most High had done for her. Like gentle rain upon tender grass, she showered stories on me from my very beginning. I have pondered them, prayed over them, believe them. I believe my mother. I believe Abba."

Though his cousin's words were mystifying John believed Jesus. Yet, John was sad and said, "Why didn't my father tell me stories?"

"Your father taught you in a different way. Like an eagle rousing its young, hovering over its little one, he spread his wings over you to protect you, guide you until you were ready to hear it. Now."

Fresh tears sprang to John's eyes. His father was trying to tell him all along, particularly on his deathbed, the only way he knew how; through the Scriptures. John sighed at his own density. Inhaling deeply, he was determined to learn it all and said, "May I-I ask?" And when Jesus nodded in encouragement, "How are you, a p-p-poor carpenter's son...what are you to do?"

"Thus says Isaiah, 'I will bring salvation to the ends of the earth. I will lay down my life for my sheep.' " Jesus tried to use words John would be familiar with. "I am the Lamb of God."

"Salvation," whispered John full of hope. He did not grasp though the meaning of the phrase 'Lamb of God.' He wondered at the time a week ago when Jesus found him and brought him home that he mentioned sheep and even called himself shepherd. It was odd that Jesus talked about being a shepherd when he was a carpenter. Now he said he was a lamb. John's poor mind strove to sort out all the words and prophecies and revelations that sparked in his head. It was strange, but the only thing John could think of was the unblemished lambs that were sacrificed at the Temple at Passover. Jesus was like an unblemished lamb. Lightning flashed through his mind: Sacrificed!

"No!" John's voice thundered as he broke away from Jesus and paced his small room, suddenly heartsick.

"Peace, John," said Jesus sitting back on his heels. Though unable to foretell the future, Jesus came to the same conclusion as John now did of the inevitable end of any prophet who is wholly faithful to Yahweh. " 'I will bring mercy and grant full pardon,' that all who believe in me may have eternal life." Then Jesus said with great passion, "For love of you and all the people of God; for love of Abba."

"No!" John agonized. He fell to his knees pleading, "I do not want to proclaim your death!"

"You will be proclaiming my life! My life!" Jesus assured him. "And eternal life for all those who believe in the Son of God."

All his life had been in preparation to be the herald of the Promised One, the Messiah. Clouds were beginning to form in his mind as he strove to gain understanding: he was to be the Messiah's herald. He felt unworthy of the mission, so unprepared. Unexpectedly he recalled something from their past. Astounded, John inquired, "At the T-temple…when you were twelve… you wanted to begin, didn't you?"

"Yes"

"But I was not ready."

"Neither of us was ready, John. And I was too young." Jesus laughed remembering the occasion. "My parents said it was not the time." Then he spoke more soberly, "I am still too young. We are both too young, John. It is written, 'There is a season for every purpose under heaven.' And the season has not yet arrived."

John accepted this with relief but now that he knew the truth of his mission he wanted to prepare himself in earnest except he did not know how or where to begin. When they were thirteen and twelve, he had offered Jesus his help, and now he willingly reaffirmed his pledge of self and said, "What is there that I can do for you now?"

Jesus discerned from his cousin's intent look, the way he held his shoulders taut, how his straight brown hair, wet from perspiration clung to his forehead, that John needed a new direction in life. His book learning and love of the Holy Writings, well taught to him by Zechariah and the rabbis, along with the solitary way of the Essenes, had shaped him into a man full of righteousness, but John lacked the give and take of life experienced among the people. Jesus spoke, "Let me ask you this. Which is the greatest commandment?"

"There are two," replied John. "The first is, 'You shall love your God,' " he whispered these words to the Son, "and I do…'with all my heart, with all my mind, with all my soul, and with all my strength.' "

Jesus smiled tenderly, "And the second?"

"You shall love your neighbor as yourself."

Pleased with his cousin's response, Jesus stood up and laid his hand on John's shoulder saying, "John, love your neighbor."

IV

It was time for John to get on with his life.

Thirty days had passed since the bodies of Zechariah and Elizabeth had been laid in the tomb. On the first day, the day of burial, neighbors came to share in the bread of mourning and drink the ritual cup of wine with the family after the procession home from the cemetery, while hired flute players and keeners made a doleful din in the corner. The first week of mourning had been spent inside the home with the family. No work was done.

In the weeks following Joseph, Mary and Jesus' departure to Nazareth, John did not go out more than a couple of times - only to the synagogue and home again on the Sabbath. He silently came and went and the townsfolk respected the young man's grief. He remained in his room, recounting what he had learned about the Messiah and his own role. Reading and studying the Torah had been his chief pleasure in life. Now, every passage, every word was on fire with new meaning. Jesus was the Messiah. He, himself, was to be his herald. He spent many long hours in prayer seeking guidance as to how to proclaim the Messiah's coming but could find no answer. Jesus had assured him, though, that words would come when the season was ripe and for now all he was to do was to love his neighbor.

Didn't he love his neighbors? Of course he did. However, the question gradually dawned on John: Who were his neighbors? John suddenly realized he had led a very sheltered life up until now as the only child of elderly parents and then living outside the world with the Essenes. Now, like a caged animal, John paced his room anxious to escape but afraid to leave his cage for the unknown. How was he to love his neighbor?

On the morning after the period of mourning was complete, John appeared from his room freshly bathed and dressed in clean clothes. It was common for the extremely pious not to wash and to wear old clothes during the thirty days of mourning. Rather, John, unlike the Pharisees, followed the customs of the Essenes and ritually bathed entirely every day and wore white to signify his profound sorrow. He now put away his sorrow and, though unsure of the direction, was ready to walk his destined path.

Abigail watched John eat his morning meal as she kneaded dough. She was glad to see him eating because for the last month he did nothing but fast. The only food he had allowed himself were vegetables and flat bread, and those sparingly. He had brought down two small scrolls with him and had placed them beside him on the table. She wondered what they were.

"I'm glad you have come downstairs," began Abigail. By his silence she knew something was on his mind. She knew he contemplated his future for she had heard him pacing the floors at all hours of the day and night. Abigail was curious and wanted to help her boy so she asked, "So John, what are you going to do today?"

"I have written two letters," John spoke deliberately. "I am going to the market to find two messengers. The first letter is to the Superior of the Essenes informing him I will not be returning to the community to take my vows at the Qumran monastery. They are pious men. Their discipline and love for truth, justice and charity draws me but I will not come to know the world, as I must, if I am that far separated from the world.

Not daring to look in her direction he continued, "The second letter is going to the Temple in Jerusalem. As you know I was offered, as my right as a member of the priestly class of Abijah, the opportunity to sit at the feet and learn from the wise and gentle Rabbi Hillel. I am going to decline that offer, also."

"O John," Abigail exclaimed. She was relieved he was not taking vows with the Essenes because that would mean she would never see him again. But not going on with his studies to become a respected priest? "What would your father say after all he had hoped and dreamed for you?"

"I believe my father knew the path I am destined to follow," said John in answer. "I assure you I am not abandoning the life my father envisioned but fulfilling it. I can no longer secrete myself away by the shores of the Salt Sea nor can I bury my head in books or sit at a master's feet when my single desire is to serve the Lord, my one true Master."

Abigail had never heard John speak like this. His sincerity was obvious. She wondered out loud, "How are you going to accomplish this?"

"I-I do not know," John answered truthfully. "I will find the answer among God's people."

It was not hard for John to find two couriers to take his letters to Jerusalem and Qumran, especially after he ignorantly paid them twice the usual amount for such an errand. He breathed deeply to calm the nervousness he felt after implementing his resolve to separate himself from his former way of life and follow the direction Jesus had indicated. His life among the people was now to begin.

Standing in the market place, he looked around it as if it were for the first time. On the eastern side stood the synagogue; how he longed to go inside that holy place where all was familiar. He turned away and began watching the people buying and selling and bartering everything from fruits and vegetables to dried fish to baked bread to sandals and blankets. He had never really considered other people's lives before. He realized how isolated a life he had led. Many of the vendors must have risen before dawn to bring in the produce of the fields from the outlying areas. Other trades people traveled from town to town to sell their specialty wares. Women carried large vessels for water across the square to the spring outside town and then hauled them back home after they were filled. Some did this many times in one day. Fascinated, John stood engrossed by the variety and activity of the people around him. He wondered how he was going to love his neighbor.

John felt a little tug. Someone was reaching into the coin purse tied to his belt. A pick-pocket? Swiftly he grabbed the wrist firmly. "You shall not steal!" he cried, whirling around to face the thief. It was a boy! A boy of about nine or ten years of age! Though the lad was scared, he had a defiant look in his eyes as he tried to wriggle free. John continued sternly, "Where are your parents?"

"Ain't got none," said the boy, jerking to free his arm. As he did three coins dropped from his hand to the ground.

John stared at the boy's dark sunken eyes, dirty matted hair and rag covered body. He could feel the bones of the lad through the skin of his wrist. The child was starving! John picked up the three coins with is free hand and said, "Our God has said, 'You shall not steal.' "

Fear engulfed the boy, frightened that the man was going to hand him over to the authorities for punishment, or beat him himself.

"Rather," continued John, "Ask, and it will be given you."

The boy stared blankly at him.

"Open your hand." John nodded his head solemnly.

The boy did so, not knowing what to expect. The man place the three coins into his palm plus two more! He gaped at the handful of coins in amazement. What kind of man would show such mercy!

"Do you have a place to stay?" John asked kindly. When the lad gave no answer he said, "Come home with me."

The boy's eyes filled with tears and he flung his arms around the man's waist; no one, no one had ever done anything like this before, and he cried for the first time in many years of his short life.

John felt a rush of embarrassment as the boy clung to him sobbing; John did not know what to do with his own arms. He looked around and saw that the people continued about their own business and no one paid them any attention. Tentatively, John began to pat the boy's back.

While he waited for the boy to regain control, John continued to look around the square and saw people he had never noticed before in Ain Karim: beggars, a blind man not far from the gate leading to the spring, sick old people, and other starving children much like this boy in his arms: people living on the fringe of society. His mind went back to when he and Jesus helped the beggars at the Garden Gate in Jerusalem. Slowly, awkwardly he began to stroke the boy's dusty hair. John now knew how he was going to love his neighbor.

"My name is John. What is yours?"

"Jacob." hiccoughed the boy.

"Well, Jacob, let us go to my home and eat, and then you can tell me about yourself."

"Sir," said the boy. "Here," and he thrust the five coins back at John. "Sorry."

"They are yours." John said kindly.

"Can't take 'em," said Jacob with tears smarting his eyes again. "Not if'm goin' to your place."

"All right, but keep one."

The boy could not get over the man's generosity and allowed himself to be led as he rubbed more tears away.

Spicy jumped up to greet her master when John opened the door, then turned to the boy and sniffed. The dog jumped up putting her paws on the boy's shoulders and began licking his face.

"Don't be afraid," said John when he saw the boy start but then laugh. "That is Spicy. She likes you. Abigail, I'm back. I brought home a friend."

Abigail came from the kitchen and saw the boy frolicking with the dog. "And who do we have here?"

"His name is Jacob and he needs a place to stay."

"Little one," she called. "I am Abigail and it just so happens that I just made some soup and bread. Are you hungry?"

"Yes'm!" Jacob's dark eyes widened as he inhaled deeply smelling the aroma of fresh baked bread surrounding the plump woman.

John and Abigail watched the boy eat tentatively at first then devour everything in sight, not even leaving a scrap for Spicy. When the boy had his fill John asked, "Jacob, how is it that you have no one to care for you?"

"My amma's dead," he answered wiping the crumbs from his face with the back of his hand.

"Poor boy," exclaimed Abigail sympathetically. "And your father?"

"The dirty Romans crucified him," he said bitterly. "My abba was a gamblin' man. Lost everythin' we had; our farm, and even our goats! The Romans caught him stealin' and kilt him. So now I ain't got no one. I can take care of myself," he bragged. The prideful defiance was back in his voice. He had to be tough to survive. The young boy glared at the two adults sitting before him but then remembered their kindness. His heart melted, "I sorry," Jacob cried, instantly realizing how much he missed his family and how he really didn't want to be on his own. He wished to start his life over again. "From now on I'll never steal again. I swear, God can strike me dead if I ever steal sumthin' again!"

"Goodness Gracious!" gasped Abigail.

"Do not swear by the Almighty." John hushed the boy and said a quick prayer on his behalf. "God knows you have had a hard life. A lad like you would always be good given the proper love and understanding." John glanced at Abigail and she nodded reading his thoughts, "With the Almighty's help, Abigail and I will help you."

Jacob was thrilled to hear this and jumped up and threw himself into Abigail's arms giving her a big hug. Holding him snug in her arms she began to laugh, "Boy, you need a bath!"

Jacob was asleep as soon as he was snuggled beneath the blankets. Spicy lay on the bed beside the lad with her head on his chest. "Instant friends," said John closing the door. When he and Abigail were alone downstairs at the table he said, "What would you say if I began to bring home other people, strangers who need help, like Jacob?"

She cocked her head and said, "And do what with them?"

"I have noticed that there are so many needy, lonely people who can't do for themselves. Only today I truly saw the need," John began. "I have been blessed with so much. So I have a plan. I could feed them, clothe them, shelter them…"

"This house isn't big enough to care for all the needy people of world," laughed Abigail.

"…I could find them housing, employment…"

"That is a big task," remarked the woman realizing how serious he was.

"It will be hard work, but my father left me a great deal. He was a wealthy man from the trade business and from being a priest. I want to share all he left me with the less fortunate." Then he said in a businesslike way, "In fact, you can cook and wash and nurse…" Finally John looked at Abigail and saw her usual cheerful face had gone straight. "…You can…"

"Am I just a servant in your household?' she asked coolly.

In truth and by rights, a man never had to explain or consult about anything with a woman. However, Abigail had cared for him since the day of his birth and now he had treated her indifferently and by his careless way of proposing his idea, had hurt her feelings.

John stood up and went to her side and then knelt before her. "I'm sorry," he said. "I-I said it all wrong. Forgive me.

You are my second mother. I love you. I don't know what I would do without you."

He was her boy. Abigail smiled and opened her arms to him. When John had confidently rested his head on her bosom she stroked his hair. She knew he was under a great deal of strain these past months, and he didn't mean to be unfeeling. In truth, the last months had been hard on them both, ending with mourning the loss of beloved Elizabeth and Zechariah.

John looked up and said, "Abigail, would you please help me care for our people, the poor of Ain Karim?"

"I would do anything for you, John," she responded. "I love you." She smiled, "Besides, you know me, the more people around, the more things for me to do, the happier I am." Abigail laughed and pulled his ear, "Anyway, it is pretty dull just cooking and doing for you!"

The first week passed quickly. Jacob played with Spicy, laughed and ate; he never knew he could be so happy. Abigail was also in her glory cooking hearty foods to fatten up the skinny child and was just plain delighted to have a youngster in the house again.

On market days, John went there to meet people in hopes of finding a real home for Jacob. Feeling awkward about approaching the various people, he always bought something from the vendors before engaging them in conversation. The merchants looked at him as if he were crazy after John stuttered the situation and what he wanted to accomplish: finding a home for a needy child. In the end, all John had to show when he got home from his excursions to market were tunics, pots, jugs, sandals, rope, a lot of dried fish... Abigail accepted all the merchandize, knowing the motive for its purchase, and was saddened that no one wanted to help. Neither of them said anything to Jacob about their intent.

Finally, late the following week, John came home and called out, "Abigail, Jacob, I brought home a friend. This is Core. He is a shepherd from Bethlehem."

With a trained eye Core sized up the lad and saw that he was strong and healthy and happy - on the spot he took an instant liking to the boy. He nodded to John and said in a most friendly manner, "Glad to meet you folks."

"Come in and have some refreshments with us," offered Abigail.

"Don't mind if I do," said Core.

John spoke, "I met Core today when he brought in his fleece to market and we got to talking. He and his wife have been blessed with four daughters but no sons and he was looking for help to manage his large flocks."

Core was a middle-aged man with broad shoulders and an even boarder smile. His big square hands moved with the grace that comes from caring for animals.

"And I was asking John, here," the shepherd broke in, he had been munching on grapes, "if he knew of a lad and a sheep dog that'd be willing to live with me and my family and learn the sheep business. He'd become a part of my family. Me and Judith, that's my wife, would adopt him and he'd inherit everything I own, such as it is, when I am gone."

Jacob was sitting opposite Core with Spicy between himself and John. The boy sat on the edge of his seat caught up with the shepherd's story. He hankered to work with animals again, as he had done before the bad times. "Please, sir," said Jacob eagerly, "Could I be that boy? I useta have goats! I don't have a sheep dog, but I'd work real hard ta make ya proud."

"Spicy would make a good sheep dog, wouldn't you girl?" said John scratching her head.

"But she's yours!"

"As a going away present."

"Going away?"

Jacob hadn't reckoned that if he went with Core it meant he would be leaving John and Abigail. How could he leave them after they had been so good to him? But to live with a real family and work with animals and have his own dog... Jacob threw his arms around John's neck, "I'll never forget ya!"

"Praise God!" cried Core who came around the table and scooped up the boy and placed him on his knees. "Today I have a son. From now on you are Jacob, son of Core."

The man turned to John with glistening eyes and said, "Thank you for finding me a son."

The next day John and Abigail bade farewell to Jacob and Spicy. John did not know whom he would miss more: his frisky dog or the energetic boy. Sadly, John watched as Core and Jacob, hand in hand, went down the street, turned the corner and went out of sight. John whispered to himself as the three walked away, "So this is my path."

Abigail nodded and sighed, "I wonder what friend you will bring home tomorrow."

V

Side by side, John and Abigail worked. They fed, clothed and sheltered the homeless. To the poor they offered their support. Together they nursed the sick and buried the dead.

In the beginning, John became an object of speculation among the merchants in Ain Karim. He attended every market day, the second and fifth day of the week, and bought so many blankets, straw mattresses, jugs, wash basins, and the like that the shop owners inquired whether the son of Zechariah was going to open an inn in his parents' home.

This speculation arose because during the first few months of his new life, John did not know how else to meet and talk to people. His response to their inquiries would be to smile and vaguely nod his head and continue to buy clothing, belts and sandals for the friends who stayed awhile in his home. As a consequence, it was not long before the vendors appreciated John's intent and became a network of people who willingly put out the word when one of John's friends needed a permanent home or work.

One of their first friends was an acquaintance of Abigail's. She brought him home with her one morning after hauling water for their daily needs. She announced, "John, I brought home my friend, Mosallam."

"You are the blind man I have seen near the spring," said John recognizing the man. "May the peace of our Lord be with you. Welcome to our home."

"And with you," replied Mosallam and said, "Abigail thinks you may be able to help me." He was a bearded man in his late twenties with long dark hair pulled back in a plait. His face was bright and lively regardless of the fact that his eyes were covered with a milky haze.

"Do you need a place to stay?" inquired John. "Where do you live?"

"Wherever my mat is," said the blind man unrolling the sleeping mat he had tucked under his arm and sitting down. "You would be surprised where people like me sleep."

"No; saddened," commented John. "How do you pass the day?"

"I beg," he shrugged.

"He makes straw dolls for the children," said Abigail and added, "he made that sleeping mat himself out of whatever he could get his hands on. He is quite good."

John noted that the mat did indeed look well made despite having been woven together out of scraps of palm and wild grasses. "Do you have a business?"

"Me?" laughed Mosallam. "No, who would buy from a blind man?"

"I would," proclaimed Abigail nudging John with her elbow. "Given the proper materials to work with I have a feeling his work would rival that of that traveling weaver."

"Really?" John was surprised. "Can you make anything else other than mats or dolls?"

"I can. My father was a master weaver. I wasn't always blind," stated Mosallam. "He was the one who taught me how to weave. I was a lad when my eyes began to cloud up. My parents encouraged me to explore the world around me. They taught me to be unafraid of my darkening world and to carry on as long as I could. May the Lord bless their souls. I am so grateful to them. But who would put any stock in a blind man? Who would buy from me?"

"I would," said John.

"Really?" It was the blind man's turn to be surprised. "You know as well as I do our society casts off people like me. They figure I have sinned, or my parents, blessed be their holy memory, and God's vengeance is upon me, so they have as little to do with me as possible. Oh sure, they give alms to the poor blind beggar, but I have my pride and know in my heart our gracious and merciful God has something better planned for me than sitting around with my hand out waiting for charity. I don't want to get, I want to give!"

John was impressed with Mosallam's eloquence and passion; his faith. "You are a man of true vision," said John. "If you are as good as Abigail thinks you are, we can go into business together and get you a stall in the square. What would you need to make some display items that we could put out for exhibit to see if there is a market for your work?" John realized all along that Abigail had brought home this man so he might get the chance he needed to use his Creator-given talents for the benefit of their town. "Tell me what you need, and I will buy the raw materials for you."

Dumbfounded, Mosallam just sat there amazed at the opportunity being offered. He tried to imagine what it would be like not to have to beg for food and for scraps of materials anymore. To make a living out of making baskets, mats…

"Say something," prompted Abigail.

"Yes! Thank you. Yes," beamed the blind man now that his secret dream had a chance of becoming a reality. "To think I'll have proper materials to weave at last! May the Lord bless you!"

Mosallam's work was undeniably extraordinary. His baskets were beautiful yet sturdy, his mats light and flexible, his fans delicate and well balanced in the hand, and his dolls charming. The people of Ain Karim readily bought from the blind man once they saw his wares, and he was soon taking orders. And within a year, Mosallam had rented his own quarters nearer the market.

One night after sharing a meal with his friend, Mosallam got down to business and said, "John, would you mind if I bought out your share of our partnership?"

"Why?" asked John at the sudden proposition.

"I don't need a middleman anymore. Of late the suppliers have been coming directly to me to push their materials."

"Didn't I do a good job?"

"It's not that. You're very conscientious," said Mosallam. "But the suppliers are making too much money off you, John. You don't haggle!"

"I know. They are good and honest men, so when they quote a price I pay it. I don't see the sense in all the arguing and name calling just to save some money."

The blind man chuckled at John's description of these men; basically, it was true. "It's a game, John. They enjoy haggling. They call each other names to see who can say the most outlandish things. The next time you go to buy something, haggle. Call the man a son-of-an-ass and see what he says."

"I can't," laughed John. "It's just as well then if I'm not your middleman. You will do better without me."

"It is because of you I am the man you see before you today. May the Lord bless you!" said Mosallam and impulsively gave John a great big hug.

Abigail, who had been listening from the kitchen while the men had their business talk, was so proud of both of them. When it was time to say good night she handed Mosallam his walking staff and called as he left, "Now don't be a stranger now that you have become a rich, independent merchant."

John and Abigail fell into a routine over the years. They rose early with morning prayers and worked tirelessly throughout the day. At home, Abigail fed and cared for their guests while John went about quietly meeting people, extending his field of friends to local farmers, vineyard owners, oil pressers and the like. He believed friends were everywhere: some to be helped, others who could help. At night they enjoyed a companionable meal with their friends and prayed before retiring, thanking the Almighty for the blessings of the day.

John's reputation for being a good, honest man, caring only for the welfare of the unfortunate, grew to the extent that people even sought him out.

Once, as John prayed long into the night, he heard someone knocking at the front door. He lit a lamp and went down to open it. Before him was a young woman with an infant in her arms. Beside her she held the hand of a small child. She looked exhausted, distressed. Hurriedly she handed over her children to John and backed away with tears in her eyes. "Take my children. I cannot care for them anymore," she cried. "I will be back for them someday, God willing." Then she fled into the night.

The child, a girl of about three years of age, began to cry as her mother ran. John put the lamp down and wrapped his free arm around the crying child to soothe her. Her cries woke the baby and Abigail. Together they settled the children into Abigail's room for they were too small to sleep alone.

"What happened?"

"Their mother will be back. She doesn't know when, but she will be back."

"Did you notice the girl's club foot?"

John nodded and kissed her on the cheek good night.

Another day, early in the morning, John found a terse note under the door. It read, "My old man is crazy. I've had enough. You take him. He is in the market."

Immediately, John left the house. How anyone could abandon one's own parent was beyond his imagining. Usually, he felt pity for those who could not care for their own, but this note was so cold. As he ran to the market he prayed to understand human nature. Shortly, he scanned the empty market place and saw a lone figure on the far side. He could hear the frail voice calling, "Mother? Where are you? I want to go home."

"Here I am," said John gently. "Are you ready to come home with me?"

The slight, thinly dressed elderly man peered up and smiled. The grey head nodded.

"Can you walk?"

The old man lifted his arms as children often do when they want to be carried. John walked home with the man cradled in his arms. As they went along, the aged man began to sing a child's song. John sang, too.

John shouted his exuberant good-byes as he left Mosallam's house. The blind man had invited him over with his haggling friends for the evening meal. They had feasted richly, and John departed, feeling relaxed. The bright moon in the dark sky cast sharp shadows in the streets as he made his way home.

"Hey, where are you going?"

"What?" said John as he peered around the darkness until he saw a woman a step or two behind him. He had passed her in the dim light of the alley. She stepped forward into the moonlight and pulled up her gown exposing her legs.

"It doesn't cost much for a little fun."

The voice was young. John stepped closer. Her cheeks were round and smooth. She was young. He said, "Come home with me."

John saw her hesitate a moment before she linked her arm through his. It was late, and the girl came away willingly with him, a stranger.

Silently, they walked through the streets, entered his house and went upstairs to his room which was the only empty one in the house that night. He would sleep on the roof that night, it was pleasant enough, and he had done it before. He lit a small ceramic lamp, collected a few things, and taking the blanket off the bed, said he would return with a fresh one.

When John returned with blanket in hand and opened the door, he was astonished to see that the girl had removed all her clothes and stood in the golden lamplight. His heart began to beat hard against his chest. She was a beautiful woman. Then his heart stopped when he noticed the bruises and scratches on her body. She had been abused. In a strained whisper he said, "Lie down." After carefully covering her body with the blanket he said, "May the peace of the Lord be with you. Sleep well."

Something wet fell on her face. He was gone, so she wiped away the wetness with her fingertips and touched them to her lips. Salty. Tears? Why, he was he crying!

He was not the first that night. And it looked like it was going to be a good night when this one came along and invited her to his place. That had never happened before. Because he was neatly dressed, smelled clean and had not been drinking, she took his arm. They had walked at an even pace without talking. That was not new; men didn't bother to talk to her when they were doing their business, and if they did, it was usually lewd and ugly. And another thing was different: this man was not in a hurry unlike the others who, sometimes brutally, used her, laughed at her with contempt, and flung a few coins at her on the ground.

This was going to be different! Such a large house and a bed! Once alone in the upper room, she quickly undressed and waited for the man's return. When he opened the door she saw he was startled to see her naked, but he didn't leer; rather, his gaze was something more like awe. When he told her to lie down, she seductively stretched out on his bed and waited for him to come to her. Only instead of coming on her, he slowly covered her body with the blanket, being careful not to touch her body. It was then the tear fell on her face.

His actions and those words of his, "May the peace of the Lord be with you," filled her now with such a sudden shame that she rolled over and wept long and bitterly into the night.

She awoke with a start, remembering where she was and the night before. She could tell by the light in the room it was late in the morning. She jumped out of bed and looked for her clothes; they were not where she had left them on the floor. Instead, a wash basin with a towel was set up in the corner. A new gown and a new belt and a new pair of sandals were laid out beside them.

Washing and dressing quickly, she stepped out of the room onto the terrace. Below, two children played in the yard chasing each other, one had a club foot but that didn't slow her down. There were other people sitting at a long table in the courtyard talking.

"Come down and have some breakfast," a fat woman said cheerily.

She was hoping to get away without being noticed but, now seen and not knowing what else to do, she obediently came down the stairs and sat at the table. The couple nodded to her excusing themselves, and she was left by herself.

The fat woman called from the kitchen, "Help yourself to some fruit while I get the bread out of the oven."

It was peculiar that the woman, or the couple, did not question the appearance of a stranger in the house. It was almost as if she were expected. She wondered where the man from the night before was. At that moment, he emerged from another upper room carrying an old man in his arms. He put him down in a chair in a sunny spot by the tree in the courtyard. He stroked the old man's hand and touched his face. Then he turned and saw her. He smiled.

She wanted to hide after last night. How could he smile at her knowing who and what she was? She hunched her shoulders forward and bowed her head, letting her hair fall over her face. Presently she felt fingers combing back her hair and twisting it to keep it out of her face.

"Good morning, dear child. Did you sleep well?"

It was his voice, so kind...and combing her hair with his fingers.... She lurched forward onto the table and sobbed into her arms...she felt so undeserving of his kind attention.

"John? What have you done?" said the woman responding to the young woman's cries. She felt him move away as the big woman gathered her into her arms. She said, "There, there now, tell Abigail what the matter is."

When she could catch her breath she croaked, "It's not him. It's me. I'm the horrible one."

"Now what could you have done that's so horrible?" crooned Abigail.

The girl merely cried all the more, burying her face in the woman's soft chest.

John, knowing the answer, took the seat opposite her and asked without reproach, "How did you, one so young, come to that sort of life?"

How could she tell them her miserable story! Obviously, these people were fine, righteous people and if they knew she was a prostitute...then it dawned on her; he already knew. She lifted her head to look at him and saw only compassion, not condemnation, in his face. And on the woman's face too! Somehow she found the courage to trust them with her story.

"My father is a violent man. He beat my mother and was rough with my brothers and me. When I turned twelve my body began to change and he..." her voice was barely a whisper and she squeezed her eyes closed trying to block out the depravity, "...he started to touch me all over. I was so frightened and ashamed. I didn't know what he was doing. And when I told my mother I saw the fear in her eyes. She was frightened of him, too. I knew she couldn't stop him. So I had to get away, I had to run away."

The girl trembled as she spoke. She opened her eyes and saw that the two people before her were not revolted; their faces showed concern for her plight. She went on, "I left our small farm. I had no one to turn to, nowhere to go but the streets. I had to beg for food to survive. Then one night, a man said he'd pay me for a little fun. I did not know what he meant, but when I found out it was no worse than what my father did to me. I let him do it and he gave me money. I soon found out there are other men who want the same, so…"

Her voice trailed off, and she covered her face in shame when she heard how ugly her words sounded to her own ears. "O dear Lord, what am I to do now?" she cried. She had learned in one brief night that there are truly good people in this world. She had propositioned this man, and he had paid her in kindness. This woman, also, had welcomed her as if she were her own daughter. She could not help but cry, "I am so ashamed. I don't want to go back to the streets, but what is there for me? I have no family, and I am not a virgin; no good family will have me as a servant. I'll never be a wife." The real horror of her situation was all too frightening. "I am doomed to be outcast. I'll be like the lepers!"

"Stay with us," John said reassuringly to allay her fears. "You will have a place here." He thought of how sin begot sin, yet the innocence within her reached out to the light of the Almighty's saving grace. He said, "Your father gravely sinned against you, and it is sad that your mother was so wounded herself that she did not have the strength to rescue you from your father. But you, in your confusion and need for survival, you too have gone astray."

"Yes," she cried full of remorse, her face red with shame. "But, dear God, what am I to do?"

"You must become innocent again." said John. "We will take you to Jerusalem where we will buy a lamb and you can offer an expiatory sacrifice at the Temple to blot out all your sins."

"Yes," she now cried with some hope in her voice, and with determination said, "From this day on I will never, ever lie with a man again!"

"Don't say never, dear child," said John. It was his turn to blush. "I have seen your beautiful body, and someday someone will see the beautiful person you are inside, as well as out, and ask for your hand in marriage. And he will be a sweet and tender lover to you, and you will have beautiful children together."

The girl blushed also, recalling his look of appreciation the night before, and sighed wondering if his prediction could ever possibly come true. She had been through so much; she doubted.

"Please stay with us," said Abigail, filling the silence. "We can help you forget your past and find a better life. What is your name?"

"Nizanna," replied the girl, lifelessly.

"What a beautiful name!" exclaimed John. "It means blossom, doesn't it? And that is what you are."

Nizanna looked at him skeptically.

"You know, Ain Karim is surrounded by vineyards. I've seen the vine-dressers mercilessly pruning the vines after the fruit is gathered, and you think nothing will ever grow on that vine again. But come spring it buds forth with the tiniest of blossoms. They may appear small and modest; nevertheless they are the promise of future abundance." He smiled at her unsure face and continued, "You have been mercilessly pruned by life. Yet, it is in God's mercy, the ugly and dead parts of you have been cut away, and you will blossom, imperceptibly, like the grape flower, to become the beautiful woman you were always meant to be."

She was incredulous at the outpouring of his kind words, his generous offer to welcome her into his home, his offer to buy a lamb at the Temple in Jerusalem that she might blot out her sins with its blood, his prediction of a happy future… "May I really stay with you?"

"Please, Nizanna, please, dear child. Stay with us." said John.

She felt embarrassed, for though he was not much older than herself, she wished she was his dear child. Finally, shyly, full of hope she answered, "Yes."

Every year, John and Abigail, and whoever was in the house at the time, went up to Jerusalem for Passover. John always made it a point to see Jesus and tell him all the things he was doing to love his neighbor. His cousin was impressed with all that he heard. Yet, when John asked, "When do we begin?"

"When the season arrives," Jesus would simply answer. However, when he noted his cousin's restless manner this Passover, Jesus added, "There will come a time when you can longer contain yourself and the words will flow from your mouth like the Jordan River."

Passover had ended, and for the first time in six years John and Abigail were alone in their home in Ain Karim. There was no one - no friends they were ministering to at the moment. They sat at their long table and reminisced about the times past with all their joys and tears.

The rejected old man had died peacefully in his sleep surrounded by caring people. They laid him to rest in a plot that John had bought to bury others who had no one to care for them in death.

The woman with the two children returned after a two-and-a-half-year absence. She had been recently widowed when she left her small children in John's care and went to work in an inn in Jerusalem. There she met her new husband and together they came to reclaim her children. She wept to see how much they had grown and how healthy and happy they were. And when they ran to her arms she swore she would never let them go again. She thanked John and Abigail for their kindness and for never letting her children forget they had a mother who loved them and was coming back for them.

Recently, Nizanna had married one of Mosallam's haggling friend's sons. Abigail had instructed her on all the duties of a woman: cooking, baking, cleaning and leading the Sabbath prayer. Not long afterwards Nizanna got a position as a servant in the haggler's household. His youngest son, Elam, was attracted to her sweet nature and set out to woo the young woman. At first she was leery of his attention but was soon won over by his thoughtfulness and respectful persistence. Nizanna truly blossomed into the beautiful woman she was meant to be on the day of her wedding.

As they reminisced about the many people who had passed through their lives, Abigail suddenly gripped John's hand as she clutched her chest. The color drained from her cheeks and her eyes rolled. She had had minor spells before but had always dismissed them. This time, however, the painful episode did not abate and Abigail passed out. John had to carry the poor woman to her room where he spent the whole night by her side in prayer.

In the morning Abigail awoke and felt incredibly weak.

"Are you feeling better?" John asked hopefully.

Abigail was horrified to hear from her own mouth mumbling and gurgling sounds when she tried to speak. She tried to move but she could not lift even her little finger. The spasm in her chest and the pounding in her head from the night before had robbed her of all her strength. A tear rolled down the side of her face.

When John squeezed her hand he felt only limpness. She was paralyzed. He dried the tears from his dear friend's face and said, "I love you, Abigail. I am here."

The next three days John never left her side. He bathed and dressed her to make her as comfortable as possible. He brewed teas and broths as she had taught him, hoping that she would recover. She showed no signs of improvement. John then began to recount all the happy times they had together: his childhood, their work together…. He spoke of his everlasting gratitude to his second mother…. He prayed.

On the fourth day Abigail closed her eyes and died in peace. John took it upon himself to ritually wash and anoint his dearest friend with perfumed oils as a final act of mercy, as he had seen her do so many times before for others, and dressed her in finest linen for her burial.

When the news of the good woman's death became known, people from far and wide gathered at John's house to mourn with him the passing of his second mother. And when the time came, many willing hands bore the woman's body in procession to the cemetery. It was not necessary to hire professional mourners to lament and wail, for kindhearted Abigail was genuinely loved by one and all.

John laid Abigail to rest beside his beloved parents in the family's sepulcher. At his insistence, the mourners left John at the burial site to return to his house for the customary bread and wine of mourning. All alone, John watched the cemetery caretakers roll the great stone across the entrance of the tomb. Unrestrained tears streamed down his face while he rocked in prayer commending all his loved ones into the hands of the Almighty.

VI

John stayed closeted in his home the first week of mourning. On the eighth day, he went for a walk, aimlessly wandering the surrounding area of Ain Karim. The winter rains had soaked the ground, and the spring sun had warmed the land causing a profusion of plant life. The vines on the slopes were still bare, but the roadside danced with flowers: leggy bright red anemone, tall blue lupins and brilliant yellow groundsel. The fields, too, waved with colorful flora: bold yellow wild mustard, frilly white wild carrot and soft yellow fennel. The sturdy magenta thistles stood their ground in the breeze. Their sweet fragrances mingled with the earthy smell of the green fields. Birds sang in the blossoming almond orchard. Men and women worked. Children played. All this life was going on around John, yet he saw none of it, so joyless was his mood.

He found himself at the cemetery and once again poured out his heart to the Lord. Though he prayed, his heart was still raw with grief. He turned away.

In town again, he naturally took the street which led to his home. He opened the door and there was no cheery welcome from Abigail. The courtyard was empty; there were no friends who needed his help to occupy his mind. Loneliness suddenly engulfed him. His home had become a vacant house.

Up the street he fled. He did not greet anyone as he made his way through the streets, and the townsfolk did not intrude upon his grief. He ended his flight in front of Mosallam's house. It was only midday, and the blind man was not at home; he would be working at the market until dusk.

John was exhausted from lack of sleep. He had dared not rest while he was caring for Abigail, and this past week found no rest while mourning the loss of his second mother. Overcome with weariness, he wandered down the cool alley beside the weaver's house and climbed the outside steps which led to the sunny dry roof. It was there Mosallam stored his supplies: sun dried sweet grass, the wider, coarser bulrush and other grasses John didn't recognize. There he sat surrounded by the smell of the fields and waited for his friend's return.

It was pitch black when John awoke. Uncomfortable and unsure of where he was until he felt the bulrushes pressing into his back, John got up and made his way down and out of the alley and found the door. He knocked.

"Who's there?" called Mosallam through the bolted door.

"Me. John. May I come in? I cannot go home."

Four days had passed since John had come to his house in the middle of the night. Mosallam's life had changed dramatically ever since good, kind, ever-cheerful Abigail had introduced him to John. The blind man grieved the passing of his dear friend but was now more concerned with how John was taking her death. John slept while Mosallam worked, ate little and spoke less. The Sabbath was about to begin and Mosallam prepared the evening meal as John sat listlessly at the table. The blind Mosallam was at ease cutting and cooking vegetables, building cooking fires… Fires! It suddenly occurred to him that all the while John had been with him not once did he ask for a lamp to be lit; a sighted man in the dark.

"Well, John," began Mosallam, concerned for his friend. "What are you plans?"

"I'm not sure," John answered, unable to think of the future while bound in the grip of grief.

"Will you be returning to your house soon?"

"I don't know."

"John, have you thought about your future?" the blind man asked. When John did not respond, he tried again. "Thanks to you there are very few people left in our town who need real help. Friends are taking care of friends. What are you going to do for the rest of your life?"

"I'm not sure," said John sullenly. "I may leave."

68

"My house?" When there was no answer, "Ain Karim?" Mosallam was getting frustrated with the lack of response but persisted, "Are you going to return to the Essenes?" The blind man knew his friend had once belonged to that community of ascetics.

"No."

Mosallam continued to probe, "If you leave, what will you do with your house?"

"I don't care," he said, and he did not; it was a just an empty house now and he did not want to think about it.

"It is a beautiful house. Will you rent it, or sell it?" prodded Mosallam.

"What does it matter?" said John through gritted teeth. He did not like being needled by the man's relentless questions.

"What does it matter?" shouted the blind man. "You could rent it and receive a good monthly income. I suspect you have very little to live on. Am I right in saying that you have spent most of your father's wealth on your friends? You never were a good business man, John. Your house is a splendid place. You could sell it and become a rich man."

"I don't want to be rich," retorted John, rubbing his forehead, feeling more and more agitated by Mosallam's voice.

"So, where will you go?" said Mosallam, not letting up, "Up to Jerusalem?"

John did not answer because he did not know. Turmoil imprisoned his mind, and there were no words to express how he felt.

"Talk to me, John," barked Mosallam. "Sometimes you are as slow as a mule and dumb as an ox! What are you going to do with your life?"

John bolted to his feet, his shoulders tense, his fists clenched. He could not take any more harassing. Could not Mosallam understand that he was in pain! Why was he tormenting him? John was furious, but not a word passed his lips.

The blind man felt the wave of silent anger. What kept his friend from confiding in him: control, pride, egotism? "Why do you hold back? If you don't want to confide in me, tell me to mind my own business." Nothing. The tension in the air was tangible. "John, just say, 'Mind your own business you son-of-an-ass!' and I will."

John laughed fiercely at his friend's challenge. John knew Mosallam was only trying to help. And with that laugh caught in his throat, it quickly turned into sobs.

Mosallam rocked his friend in his arms. After John became quiet, the blind man gave him a little shake and said, "Talk to me, John."

"I-I am afraid." John began. "You are right: I know my work is f-f-finished here. Ain Karim is now a community where people reach out and c-care for one another. I am unsure where my path leads me. There is something I must do...b-but I lack the c-c-courage to begin. I cannot explain it any more to you now, I'm sorry...I feel forgotten...a-a-alone."

Forgotten? thought Mosallam, by whom? And alone? The people who raised him and loved him the most were gone, true, but there were many others who loved and respected John. Because of John, it was as if their town of Ain Karim had become the kingdom of God on earth. John said he was afraid. What else is there for him to do? Mosallam comprehended that his friend was at a crossroad in his life, and, from his own experience, knew how the lack of direction could weigh heavily on a man's mind. Having no solution to offer his friend Mosallam said, "Tomorrow morning we will go to the Sabbath services at the synagogue and ask our Creator for guidance."

John and Mosallam covered their heads as they entered the synagogue and took seats in the rear. John closed his eyes in prayer. It was his habit always to pray for those for whom no one cared: the lost and lonely who needed help. Except now, he prayed for himself: the lost and lonely in need of help - to be shown the way.

After the initial prayers were said, someone got up to do the reading. With eyes still closed, John listened to the somewhat familiar sounding voice as the words of Isaiah drifted in his mind, "...though I thought I have labored in vain, my reward is with my God.... I will give you as a light to the nations, that my salvation may reach the ends of the earth.... The Holy One of Israel has chosen you.... How could I forget you, when behold: I have etched you on the palms of my hands. Fear not."

"Jesus!" whispered John, rising to his feet to see who it was that read, but it was just a man from Ain Karim closing the scroll and returning to his seat.

On leaving the synagogue John felt reborn. The words of the prophet Isaiah, and the voice that spoke to him, still sang in his heart. He was conscious that the holy words were spoken for his benefit, to comfort him, strengthen him, encourage him that he was not alone; God was with him.

Mosallam sensed John's mood had changed and asked, "Did I hear you say your cousin's name? Is he here?"

"No," answered John with a yes in his heart.

"Did you pray for guidance?"

"Yes. And I am ready and unafraid to follow my path."

"What do you plan to do?"

"Well, I'll tell you, you son-of-an-ass!" laughed John. "I'm going to continue my work ministering to the people, but not here in Ain Karim where I am comfortable and sheltered in my own home. I will leave tomorrow."

"What? Tomorrow!" exclaimed Mosallam at the suddenness. "What about your house?"

"My friend, will you do me a favor?"

"Anything."

"Live in my home."

Mosallam gasped at John's request.

"Give up your rented rooms and live in my home. Keep it for me until I return. You could store your supplies upstairs, make a workroom..."

"John, I couldn't ," said the blind man. "I'll pay you rent."

"No," he said, throwing his arm over his friend's shoulders. "I don't want your money. All I want is someone I love to take care of my home."

The next day John welcomed Mosallam into his new home. John looked around the courtyard with its flowering almond tree in the corner, the table and benches set up for meals, the terrace with the three bedrooms opening on to it with the kitchen and storage rooms beneath.... so many memories.

"I'll get my things," said John as he bounded up the stairs. The walls in his room were bare except for the small tapestry his mother had woven long ago. He sighed to think how just seeing that on the wall comforted him with so many fond memories of family and love. Still, he was anxious to be going and to begin his new path. He rolled up the blanket on the bed and tucked it under his arm. From the corner he took his father's walking staff and an old soft leather pouch off the desk. From off the shelf of the storage room he collected a small wineskin that he could sling over his shoulder to be used to carry water.

Mosallam felt what John had brought down. "Is this all you are taking?"

"No," replied John, going to the front door and removing from the peg on the door frame the mezuzah which contained the great commandments. "And this," he said, handing it to the blind man. "This mezuzah was my father's and his father's before him. I want this piece of home with me."

When it came time to leave, the two men stood in the doorway hugging. Then Mosallam, being practical, produced a pouch and pressed it into John's hand saying, "I know you care nothing for money, but you will need something to live on. Take it as a traveler's blessing."

"Bless you my friend!" said John humbly accepting the gift, and after giving Mosallam a final embrace was gone.

John headed east out of Ain Karim. This time, he delighted in seeing the variety of beautiful spring flowers as they swayed by the roadside and hearing the songs of the birds as he walked along. They were welcome companions as he left his home and traveled toward Jerusalem. He skirted the Holy City in the late afternoon and pitched camp at dusk between Jerusalem and Bethany. In the morning, the second day of the week, market day, John went into Bethany and bought bread and cheese and filled his wineskin at the well.

John stood at the crossroads and decided he did not want to go back into Jerusalem – it was too large a place to begin with. Bethany was still too close to home and too much like his own home town. Qumran to the east, where the Essenes lived by the Salt Sea, was not the place his path led him either, though he had felt at home there with their life of prayer, austerity and righteousness. Jericho, the City of Palms, just about equidistant from Jerusalem as Qumran to the east, but north of Qumran, was a good day's journey. He decided that is where he would begin.

He struck out down the road and could see Jericho far below off in the distant plain, but soon his descent became rather steep as he entered the deep crevice that led ever downward though the wilderness. He had to be careful where he stepped; loose stones and gravel were constantly shifting under his feet. At one point the high sheer rock walls closed in on him and he had to practically squeeze through the pass. An ominous blood-colored vein of ore slanted through the rock wall: he had come to the place known as the Red Ascent. It was not an easy walk and he was glad when he came to a bend in the narrow path and saw the way grew wider. The land was desolate and did not get nearly as much rain as in the higher elevations.

Not far onward, he saw three men coming up the Red Ascent. John had heard that the road to Jericho was sometimes dangerous with robbers by day and jackals by night, but these seemed like ordinary men coming toward him, so when they stopped in front of him he greeted them.   The men looked thirsty from their hard climb, and he was about to offer them some of his water when he noticed one fellow held a club. The man in the middle was big, with wild hair and cold grey eyes. The third disappeared around him.   He was surrounded.   His stomach instantly tightened into a knot.

"Give us whatcha got," growled the big man.

John quietly laid down his staff, removed the blanket roll he had strapped to his back and handed over to the second man his money, water and food.

"What's that around your neck?"

"Something of worth only to me," replied John evenly to the big man.   He had put his father's mezuzah in the old leather pouch and wore it around his neck. It was not his intention to anger the robbers but, still, this was his only treasure and something holy.

At that, the man with the cold grey eyes turned as if to leave, but instead, swiftly pulled a knife and lunged forward, slashing at the pouch around John's neck, tearing through his tunic and deeply slitting his upper chest and left shoulder.   As the man pivoted to reverse and strike again, John caught his arm and struggled for a moment but the other man clubbed him hard in the ribs.   John fell to the ground and soon lost consciousness as the men continued to club and kick him.

The midday sun burned down on John as he lay on the side of the road.   The robbers had stripped him of his clothes, taken all his belongings, even his mezuzah, and pushed him off to the side.   He could not move for the throbbing of the knife wound and loss of blood, and each ragged breath was a struggle against the pain of his broken ribs.   With no strength all he could do was turn his head from the blinding sun.

Time passed slowly.   At one point John heard footsteps. He squinted and saw a well-to-do man about to pass by.   John tried to call out, except only a moan escaped his lips as he stretched his right arm out to the man. The man paused for a second but hurried along. John closed his eyes again and wondered why, in heaven's name, the man had not stopped.

By mid-afternoon, his skin felt as if it were on fire as he lay on the rocky ground. John prayed someone else would come soon. He was full of trust; he knew this was not his end and that the Almighty was with him. A shadow covered his face. John saw another man, a Levite by his dress, standing over him, inspecting him. But when the man saw that he was still alive, he backed away and ran. From that little exertion, and dismay at being left alone again, John blacked out once more.

Water! Cool water was passing his dry, cracked lips. Small amounts of cool, refreshing water were being carefully given to him. John peered up gratefully at the stranger who cradled him gently in his arms. The man laid him down once more and cleansed his wounds with wine. Then the stranger soothed his burnt skin with a fragrant balm to aid in the healing. After he had finished dabbing on the ointment, the stranger covered his naked body with a length of material.

When his mind cleared some, he was astonishment to realize the stranger was a Samaritan. He became conscious of this when he took in that the man who was nursing him was calmly speaking in an accent he hardly understood. To John the sound was beautiful. The Samaritan next got his arms around John's back and knees and lifted him on to his donkey. John fell peacefully asleep with his head resting on the animal's neck and the Samaritan's steadying hand on his back.

When John awoke, he found himself in a room barely large enough to walk around in. Bright sunlight came through the small window above the narrow bed. He tried to sit up, but the sharp pain in his ribs caused him to fall back down. His skin felt tight and hot to the touch from all the exposure to the sun. Fingering the bandage covering his knife wound John shivered, recalling his ordeal.

The door opened. A woman plainly dressed with disheveled hair said dully, "You're awake."

"Where am I?"

"Red Inn. Three days now. That Samaritan brought you here and gave the innkeeper two denarii to take care of you."

John blessed the man remembering his mercy and kindness.

"Stay in bed as long as you like." She continued without emotion, "That Samaritan said he'd make up the difference on his return if it cost us more." She was turning to leave as she mumbled, "I'll bring you something to eat."

"Thank you. My name is John, son of Zechariah," he said to her back, hoping to learn her name.

By the end of the week, John was strong enough to move about the room and look out the window. Zara, he found out her name from the innkeeper, Uriah, bought clothes for him and charged it to the Samaritan's bill. Early the second week he felt strong enough to go downstairs to the main room where meals were served. There were a few travelers there eating and resting while escaping the heat of the midday sun. Zara appeared with a tray and headed for the stairs but, when she saw John already standing in the hall, left the tray on the nearest table and left without a word.

John took a seat at the empty table in the corner and was about to eat when loud voices erupted, "We don't eat with infidels." "Pagan, get out of here. This is Judea – go back where you belong."

John saw two men had gotten up from their table and were shouting at a man in the doorway. He was a Samaritan. His Samaritan. John got up as quickly as he could and positioned himself between the men and said, "Peace, brothers, we are all travelers here and guests of the innkeeper." Then turning to the Judeans, "Do you really believe you will be corrupted if this man has one meal here, or is your faith that weak?"

"Who do you think you are? Solomon?" said one of the men mockingly. But after a period of silence under John's weighty stare, they backed off and moved to the other side of the room.

"Thank you," said the Samaritan in heavily accented Hebrew.

"Join me," invited John, motioning to his table in the corner.

"You would not be offended eating with an infidel?"

"How could I be offended by the man who saved my life!"

John went on to profusely thank the Samaritan for rescuing his life and paying for his lodging. He explained that the man need not pay anything more for John had decided to stay at the inn, with the innkeeper's permission, and work to pay off all the debts he accrued. He explained that when he was in his room regaining strength all that past week he thought on the Samaritan's example of mercy and generosity. It inspired him, and after a while, it became obvious that he need not go to Jericho to look for people in need; there was much he could do to love his neighbor right here at the Red Inn.

John helped wherever he could: served meals and drinks, cleaned rooms, tethered and fed the animals for the travelers…. Uriah the innkeeper was grateful for another pair of hands; he was an older man and Zara couldn't do all the work. The inn itself consisted of a large hall set up for eating and sleeping. A kitchen was on one side and the stable area on the other. There were a few small rooms upstairs for the innkeeper, Zara, and John and other guests who could afford it. Red Inn was situated halfway between Jerusalem and Jericho, one of the few level plots of land on the steep Red Ascent. By mid afternoon, the towering cliff cast long dark shadows over the inn, but at dawn the ground and rock walls were ablaze with hues of red: a glorious fusion of sun and earth.

The nickname 'Solomon' stuck with John. The inn attracted a strange mixture of people from all over Judea, Samaria and Galilee crossing paths with traders from Damascus and Antioch and even far off Basra and Riyadh. Rogues and merchants, priests and beggars all stopped there. Uriah and John declared the inn to be neutral territory and even went so far as to rename it 'Shalom Caravan Inn.' All those who entered were equals. If there was a dispute among the guests, all would gather to hear both sides of the story and John/Solomon would decide what was fair. If the parties would not abide by his ruling, they had to take their argument elsewhere.

The months went by, and John had long ago recovered his strength and paid his debt, but he made no attempt to leave. He liked the work and met many friends. And people were astonished to find help, support, and an understanding ear in such an out-of-the-way-place. All were open and grateful to him except Zara, who remained distant and silent; she rejected any effort on John's part to be her friend.

John always slept soundly after a long day's work, but one night he was jarred awake by a thud against the wall. He listened in the dark and could hear a man's muffled angry voice, another thud, and then a woman's cry. Zara was in trouble. He bounded from his straw mattress and flung open her door. A man had Zara by the hair and was beating her with his fist. John lunged at the man, pried him off her, and cast him out the door. The man, already off balance, fell down the stairs that happened to be opposite Zara's room and lay in a heap at the bottom.

Zara had crumpled to the floor moaning. Her gown had been torn off her shoulders but she made no move to cover herself. She felt a blanket being draped across her, and then heard the door close. She raised her head, but as soon as she saw that John was still in the room watching her she said hoarsely, "Get out!"

This time he would not accept her rejection - not this time; he knew her misery. Silently he stood guard, not only for her protection, in case the man had a mind to return, but for her whole being. She needed help.

She screamed when he did not go, "Leave me alone!"

"Why?"

"Why? What's it to you?" she yelled. "What's it to you whether I live or die?"

"I care for you." He said quietly.

"So, you want to be my lover, too," she growled like a trapped lion backed into the corner. Slowly she staggered to her feet.

John's heart ached for Zara seeing her wretchedness and he knew, in her loneliness, she took traveling men to bed. He spoke without reproach, "Love is a gift that ought to be given to a husband."

"Don't play Solomon with me." She accented her words with a hard slap across his face.

"You've been so hurt. If it makes you feel better, strike again." He took a step closer.

Absolute rage rose up in Zara at his intrusion into her life. She couldn't stand to see the look of pity and patience in his eyes. She raised her fists but could not bring herself to strike him; instead, she turned and pounded the wall. As much as she hated him, she knew he was not her problem, and that made her angrier. Soon she began to tire and slumped against the wall. The next thing she knew, she felt him take hold of her wrists; he was too close behind her. Zara automatically froze, pressed herself closer to the wall and growled deep and slow, "Let go."

"I am your friend," said John. He understood Zara was trying to beat away all the men who had ever hurt her, all her pent up fury over all the unhappiness in her life. She needed basic, real love. Zara needed to be held like a baby in its mother's arms.

At his words, though, she shuddered. She was not ready, so John stepped away. He planned to leave but at the door he paused; something deep inside him made him turn to her once more and say, "You will never find true love in the arms of strangers."

Back in his room John could hear Zara sobbing. He prayed that she might know God's mercy and be guided out of her darkness into the way of light and peace.

The cock crowed in another day. From where he lay, he could see the beginning of a beautiful dawn. He heard the clucking of the hens in the yard and something else – breathing. Zara knelt on the floor beside his bed, her hands gripping the edge of his blanket, her head down in her arm. She was sleeping. She must have come in sometime during the night and was too shy to wake him. John slowly raised himself up on one elbow.

She felt him move and said, "Forgive me."

"I am not angry with you."

"Then help me get out of here. I want to be free of all this."

"Running away does not solve problems. You will never be free until you face your darkness. Walk through your darkness and into the light."

"How, Solomon," Zara cried. She still had not moved from her position on the floor with her head down on her arm as she gripped and released, gripped and released his blanket. Her hair covered her face. "Tell me how!"

John stroked her soft hair as a mother would her child's. How could he say what he must without inflicting more pain or guilt on her? He had to speak the truth no matter what, so he spoke without a hint of scolding, "Turn away from this meaningless life you have taken on. Face in yourself what is wounded; only then will you heal and find true love. Would you not rather have one good and faithful husband than many bed partners who are only bound to hurt you in the long run?"

80

"Face," Zara pulled her head away from his touch, "...wounded...face," she muttered. Abruptly she sat up straight and threw back her hair, caught it up with one hand; anger flashed in her eyes, bitterness in her voice, "Now, who would marry a face like this?"

John's mouth opened. He had never noticed. Zara had a long, red, ghastly scar that ran from her temple down to her jaw! Anytime in the past few months when he looked at her, he saw only her defeated posture, her sad eyes. He wondered what tragedy had befallen her, but did not ask. Overcoming his shock he said, "Good men don't marry for outer beauty. It is what is in the heart..."

"Truly? Do men want to see into a woman's heart?" she challenged him. "Men. That is not what they are looking for."

John challenged her, "You use them as much as they use you."

Tears stung her eyes, her lips quivered but she did not speak.

John got up and brought over the wash basin and cloth. Zara's face was bruised and still had dried blood on it from where the man had punched her in the nose. Kindly, he helped her up and seated her on a stool and gently washed her face, careful not to hurt her any more than she had been.

Docile to his administrations she choked back tears and whispered as he rinsed out the cloth, "They make me feel as if someone cares for me...for me...even if it is just for one night."

"But what of the day?" asked John, as he set aside the bowl. "True friendships are the light of life! They are so much more fulfilling than those fleeting pleasures of the night."

"I have no friends," said Zara with fresh tears brimming in her eyes. "No one will ever love me!"

"God is constant love," exclaimed John. "Do you not know that the Creator of heaven and earth loves you beyond all telling?"

Zara shook her head, "Not me."

"You most of all," replied John, then quoted the psalms, "Scripture says, 'The troubled call out, God hears and frees them. God stays near the brokenhearted, heals their wounded spirit.' " John looked her in the eye. "Call on God's mercy and the Almighty will free you."

"Truly?" sighed Zara. "I so want to believe you, Solomon."

"Believe me," said John. "I am your friend."

"Can a man be a woman's friend?" Zara knew unless you were his wife, his daughter, or his mother, a woman was nothing to a man and that they did not associate with one another.

"I can," John smiled. He watched her ponder this, absently fingering the ugly scar on her face. He took her hand away and held it and said, "I can. I am."

Zara laughed; he was so simple, so naïve, but she needed a friend, needed something, someone to believe in. She had observed John long enough to know he had a good heart. Once she started laughing, she couldn't stop thinking of the incongruity of it all: after all those years of loneliness to have a friend who is a man, no less. And if Solomon said God loved her, who was she to argue? Her laughter brought new tears. Tears of sadness, tears of joy, tears of relief. "I haven't laughed like this in years," Zara confessed, "Or cried so much since I was a child."

John nodded and smiled himself. "It's good for you to cry and even better to see you smile."

Zara had gone back to her room and had fallen asleep. John knew she was exhausted so he covered for her, doing all her chores. She finally came down when it was almost dark. John got her something to eat, and they sat at a table talking quietly. The few people who would be staying at the inn that night were already making themselves comfortable with their blankets on the floor alongside the stable area.

A man appeared out of nowhere next to Zara - the same one from the night before. "You weren't in your room," he said, ignoring John. "We have some unfinished business."

Zara had not slept the whole day; she had pondered all that John had said and prayed for God's mercy, the courage to accept God's love, and the ability to respect herself as a person worthy of true love, and for the strength to face her darkness and walk in the light.

Zara did not cower from the man's hard eyes but she did turn away to look at John; his eyes were encouraging, which gave her the confidence to tell the man, "I will not be receiving you in my room any longer. Good night."

"What do you mean?" scoffed the man, grabbing her wrist to pull her up. "Come on." Then the man took in John sitting there and recognized him as the man from the night before. He sneered, "So, is this your new lover?"

John started to his feet. "Solomon," Zara said. The man already had taken a step backwards, though he still held her wrist, remembering his fall down the stairs. Thereupon, she said with that low growl John had heard the night before, "Let go. I won't be receiving ANY man in my room."

The man threw down her arm when he saw something new in her eyes: strength instead of submissiveness, self determination instead of that hungry, needy look she usually wore. She would no longer be the easy diversion she had been the other times he stopped in the inn. And besides, she found herself another.

Zara smiled at John. She was filled with a curious feeling of power and joy at her new- found freedom. And John was proud of her; she was strong, and with that confident, relaxed smile she was beautiful!

VII

In the months following that night of tears and laughter, Zara became another person. No longer surly and silent, she was giddy with enthusiasm for life. She hummed while she worked, joshed good-naturedly with the patrons, and became as playful as a kitten. Although almost thirty, she became youthful again, recapturing her lost years. But more important than her newly acquired light-hearted nature, she became the best friend a person could desire as she continually thanked God for all the goodness and mercy shown to her.

One time, Zara called over to the stable area that Solomon was needed. John was working with the animals and could hear something was going on. When he stood up and looked over the half wall that separated the patrons from the animals, he saw two men shoving each other. Their faces were crimson red as they stood nose to nose. John separated the men and explained the rules of the inn: "Shalom Caravan Inn is neutral territory and all quarrels are settled by me, Solomon."

Solomon took his seat in the middle of a table with the innkeeper Uriah and Zara flanking him in the rear. The two men took up opposite positions at the sides of the table. The spectators, the few guests in the hall at the time, turned their benches toward the tribunal and paid close attention to the proceedings. John nodded toward the older man, out of deference to age, to begin.

"I sold this man two goats about five months ago." He was a farmer, plainly dressed with graying hair and beard. "A buck and a doe: the buck was three years old and the doe about six years old, if I remember rightly, when I sold him the pair. They were fine, healthy specimens."

"Fine? Ha!" cried the other man. He was much younger than the farmer, not quite twenty by the looks of him and richly dressed. He had soft hands. "The billy died and the nanny gives no milk."

The shouting erupted again. "Goats? Is this one of your larks, Zara?" said John over his shoulder beneath the hubbub.

"I wish!" she answered with glee.

Solomon raised his hands for order then addressed the young man, "Why did you buy the goats?"

"I am one son of many in my father's household. I have it in mind to prove myself to him by becoming a cheese maker, so I bought the goats to start a flock but now…"

The farmer shook his head from side to side at the naiveté of the young man. Obviously he knew nothing of goats or of cheese making.

"Where are the goats now?"

"The billy is dead," exclaimed the younger man. "I had to put it out of its misery. He broke his leg when we were looking for pasture in the Red Ascent. And I can't get the nanny to give milk. She is fat and lazy. Last night when we arrived she was sick: bleating and shaking. This morning I heard no sound from the stable, so I am afraid she is dead, too!" The rich fellow leaned forward across John and yelled, "I paid a great deal of money for those animals. I want my money back."

"No!" countered the farmer. "I sold them to you in good faith. When I owned her, she gave milk. It was because you didn't want to buy her kid that she naturally dried up."

John questioned the young man, "Am I to understand you did not check on your animal this morning?"

"What use is it to look at a dead goat when I know she is dead?"

John bowed his head in thought for a moment as the spectators took up the chant, "Solomon, Solomon…" His face was straight when he raised his head and hands to call them to silence. He addressed the two men in grave tones, "You will both abide by my rule?" Each nodded. "Farmer: Repay the man half the price of the two goats. Young sir: That is for the nanny. You may not collect on the billy for I wager you and friends had a fine feast the day he died."

The spectators, the young man's friends among them, roared with laughter at the truth of it. The young fellow blushed with anger at the laughter, but was appeased to get at least something for his loss.

"Shake hands," John instructed them after the money was handed over. "And I will buy you both a drink." To Zara he whispered, "Bring two mugs over to the stable."

In the back stall Zara found John stroking a goat. Coming closer she saw two tiny goats; twin kids. "Oh, John," she exclaimed, "This isn't THE goat?"

"It certainly is! The joke is on that ignorant fellow," laughed John as he shook his head. "No wonder she gave no milk and was fat and lazy; she was pregnant!"

"What about the mugs? Our drinks are at the other end of the hall."

"Well, there's plenty of milk here and I promised my friends a drink."

Zara preceded John back into the hall with two mugs of warm foaming milk and set them before the two opponents. John followed with the twin kids cradled in his arms and the nanny trotting behind him and placed the newborn goats in the lap of the farmer. "These and the doe now belong to you."

The farmer accepted them with great delight and thanked Solomon for his wise judgment.

Then John said to the young man, "If you really cared for your goat you would have checked on her this morning and found a lovely surprise, but, as it is, you have forfeited this fine flock."

The spectators roared again with laughter at the goings-on and at John's witty remark. The young man blushed furiously.

Quickly Solomon, to be kind, gave him some advice, "The human mind may devise many plans, yet it is the intent of the Almighty that will be done. You want to prove yourself to

86

your father? Then be a wise son; that is a father's pleasure. So whatever you endeavor, remember, hard work always bears a profit. Now go in the peace of our God."

The night was dark as only the old crescent moon hung low in the western sky. Even though the spring day had been warm, there was still quite a chill in the evening air. It was late by the time John finished tending the animals in the stable area and was about to lock the courtyard gate for the night.

"Hey! Wait! Can I get food and lodging?"

In the blackness John could make out a figure coming toward him from the road. "Certainly. Come into the hall and warm yourself by the fire while I make you a plate."

John led the way and motioned the man to be seated at the bench and table by the fireside. There was always something hot on the fire: onions and lentils, sometimes even meat. John scooped up some stew and put it in a bowl and grabbed a hunk of bread and turned to the man and stopped short. The man was big with curly black hair and cold grey eyes. It was the man who had slashed and robbed him on the road to Jericho.

"Well?" said the robber impatiently as John just stood there.

His stomach twisted in a knot as he set the food in front of the man and asked, in a barely audible voice, if he wanted something to drink. When the man nodded, John backed away into the kitchen area. Once out of sight behind the wall that separated the kitchen from the hall, John steadied himself by leaning on the food preparation table.

Zara was sweeping the floor when John came in. She saw him trembling and asked, "What's wrong? Are you ill?"

"I just left a man in the hall," John answered. "It is the man w-who r-r-robbed me a-and left me for d-d-dead on the road..." He had closed his eyes as he tried to blot out the mental pictures of that harrowing experience.

"Oh, John! Did he threaten you? Has he come to rob us? What does he want?"

"F-food and lodging," said John as he pressed his hand against the ridge of the scar that ran across his upper chest. "He did not recognize me."

"Then what is the problem?" Zara half laughed because she was so relieved. When he did not answer she looked at him closer and saw on his ashen face fear and loathing. "So, you are human."

John winced. Her remark cut him to the quick. If only she knew how hard it was not to falter: how he consciously put the needs and cares of others before his own and was always on guard against his own apathy and disregard for the less fortunate, as well as disgust for those who did not live the Law, how he tried with every waking moment to be found worthy of his destiny. With Zara's words he suddenly realized how he had denied his true feeling about being assaulted those many months ago. Tears came to his eyes.

Zara was sorry for her jest when she witnessed his anguish and pain. She watched as he desperately tried to regain control of his feelings of dread as he filled a mug with beer. As he was about to go back out she was inspired to say, "May I play Solomon?"

He looked at her blankly; this was no time for foolery. Yet, once he noted that she was in earnest, he nodded that he would listen because he despised the anger and hate he felt in his heart toward the robber.

"If I were you I would bless the man...." Zara continued despite John's dumbfounded look. "I bless him. I do! For if misfortune had not befallen you - you would never have come here to stay in the inn. You have made a difference, John, ever since you began to work here. It has become a place where travelers can find shalom: peace, a warm fire, someone to listen to their stories, counsel, friends... You have changed my life. I might be dead, or worse, if it had not been for you. Bless him, John, bless him."

88

John understood the wisdom of her words and was grateful. His heart had begun to beat more slowly and he took a deep breath as he went out to serve the man his drink.

"What took you so long?" growled the robber.

Involuntarily, John shuddered when he heard the tone of voice. In spite of which, he again took a deep breath and set down the beer and said, "May the peace of our God be with you and bless you."

"Wha?" said the robber, really looking John up and down for the first time. "What did you say to me?"

"May the peace of our God be with you and bless you."

"Do you know me?"

"I do." John's voice was shaking but he went on, "You robbed me, beat me and left me for dead not a year ago."

"And you bless me!" laughed the man loudly. He stopped as soon as he observed the other's sincerity. After he gulped down the rest of the beer he said, "Where do I sleep?"

"John." Knock, knock, knock. "John, wake up." He rose sleepily in the dim moonless light of dawn. Zara stood in the hall with her shawl wrapped tightly around her against the morning chill. "The robber just left," she exclaimed. "He told me to give you this." And she handed him a pouch.

Curious as to what the robber would give him, John felt the old leather pouch; his heart quickened. He loosened the drawstring and slipped out the content into his hand. It was a mezuzah. The mezuzah the robber had stolen from him. His mezuzah! Tears sprang to his eyes as he said a prayer of thanksgiving and pressed the mezuzah to his lips. He turned back into his room and sat on the bed rocking back and forth, holding the treasure to his breast.

"What is it?' asked Zara from the door.

"My mezuzah," said John holding it out for her to see. "Of all the things stolen from me that day, this was the most precious."

She looked at the daintily carved tube. It was just large enough to fit in the palm of John's hand.

"This was my father's before me and his father's before him," he explained while undoing the top and removing the miniature scroll from inside. "The scroll contains the words from Deuteronomy in the Torah, 'Hear, Oh Israel: the Lord is God, the Lord alone. Therefore, you shall love the Lord your God with all your heart, and with all your soul, and with all your strength.' It also says that in return for our fidelity, the Almighty God will bless us with seasonal rain that we might have grain, wine and oil, and grass for our animals. The mezuzah is affixed to our doorposts so as we enter our home, we are reminded of the covenant we have with the Almighty."

"It is beautiful," Zara said in a hushed tone, moved by John's devotion.

He was quiet in thought for a while, then spoke out loud to himself, "Last night the setting moon was a crescent. In fourteen days Passover begins with the full spring moon. I shall be going."

"And you will come back here after Passover?" asked Zara, hoping she did not hear finality in his voice.

"No," he answered gently. "This mezuzah has reminded me I must be along my path. If what you said last night was true, then my work here is completed. And I have a desire to see my family and friends at Passover." John took in her forlorn expression and said, "Why don't you come to Jerusalem, too? Have you ever seen the glory that lies beyond this desolate place?"

"No, but I would like to," she said truthfully. "I lived in Geras in Perea beyond the Jordan when my parents were alive. Uriah is a distant relative and took me in as a servant when I had nowhere else to go. My family was not religious, so we never went up to Jerusalem for Passover. It is strange that I came here many years ago and never went any further, what with Jerusalem being so close. Yes, I want to go and see the great Temple. And when I'm there I want to offer a personal sacrifice for all that God has done for me."

That night John and Zara and Uriah sat talking after the day's work was done. John informed the innkeeper of his plans to leave Shalom Caravan Inn and suggested that they all go up to Jerusalem for the celebration of Passover. Uriah, ever the business man, heard John out but argued it would be too busy at the inn with all the pilgrims on their way to Jerusalem. John conceded this yet countered that they need not leave until the last patron was on his way to the Holy City, and they could easily be back at the inn long before the floods of travelers began their journey back home.

"And there's another thing," lamented Uriah after agreeing that John's plan could work. "Who will I get to take your place?" He was sorry John would not be coming back with them; he was a good worker and a good friend. Shalom Caravan Inn had become such a pleasant place to live and work ever since John had joined them. Just being around John, Uriah had become a more peaceable man himself.

"How about Yehudi?" suggested John.

"That imbecile?" cried the innkeeper. "That vagrant?"

Yehudi had wandered into the inn not a month ago begging for food. Now John was considered tall, but this man was a head taller with massive shoulders. He was poorly dressed and hungry, so John gave him shelter in the stable with the animals, food, and a tunic of his own that came too short on the fellow, and too tight across the chest but it covered him. Since then Yehudi would go and come whenever he needed food. It was true Yehudi was simple and had the mind of a child in a giant's body, yet he was kind and gentle and was more than willing to do anything in exchange for a few meals.

"Yehudi needs a home," John countered. "His needs are few. He is eager to work. Of course, he does need to be given detailed directions but once given, he works tirelessly and meticulously."

91

The innkeeper considered John's proposed replacement.

"Please, Uriah," pleaded Zara with a wink to John. "If we are to lose Solomon, isn't it just as well to have a Sampson around if a dispute occurs? One look at Yehudi and they will all be quiet as lambs!"

All three laughed heartily, and the innkeeper agreed.

They arrived late in Jerusalem but still in time before the markets closed to buy some unleavened bread, wine, eggs and parsley and salt for their Passover meal. They had met another small group of people coming up the Red Ascent and had agreed to purchase an unblemished lamb to share between them. By the time they arrived, the Holy City was crammed with pious Jews. Every possible space was taken up by the influx of pilgrims: houses were filled with families, and inns were serving three times as many patrons as usual. John and his group decided to camp outside the city.

It was decided between the men that John would recount the Passover story. Customarily, the eldest of the group held that honor, but Uriah and the head of the household of their fellow pilgrims did not feel they could tell the Passover story with enough due reverence or detail. And so it fell to John to answer the traditional questions posed by the youngest male, "Why is this night different from all the rest?"

Reciting from memory the Book of Exodus and leading the Hallel, the psalms of praise, John spoke from his heart:

"Give thanks to the Lord; make known God's deeds…. By means of Moses and Aaron our God performed mighty signs and miracles in the land of Egypt when Pharaoh oppressed Israel with bitter slavery and would not let them go. So the God of Israel turned Egypt's waters into blood." John began to recount the ten plagues. "God swarmed their land with frogs. God filled the air with gnats and flies. God struck down the livestock with a deadly disease. God caused festering boils to torment both humans and animals alike. God threw down lightning and hail and roared with thunder ruining the barley and flax. God spoke and a numberless black cloud of locusts came and devoured all the green in their land. God sent darkness over all the land of Egypt.

"Because Pharaoh's heart was hard, he would not relent and let Israel leave, so the Destroyer descended upon the land. The God of Israel told the Chosen People through Moses to sacrifice an unblemished male lamb and with its blood paint the doorposts and lintels of their homes. On seeing the blood, the Angel of Death passed over the Chosen People's homes sparing their children and struck down all the first born of Egypt, both man and beast alike. Dread fell upon Pharaoh and he ordered Israel to depart."

"Why do we eat unleavened bread?" asked the boy.

"Because the people of Israel left in such a hurry!" laughed John. "Israel left that land singing, full of joy at the wonders God had wrought."

"So why do we eat parsley dipped in this salt water?" the youngster also wanted to know.

"The salt water reminds us of the tears we shed while we were slaves, but the parsley symbolizes our freedom and new life in the Promised Land." Then John concluded the telling of the Passover story by saying, "And that is why, my children, to this day, we keep this festival of seven days as a remembrance of how the Holy One of Israel freed us from the hands of the Egyptians."

The next day, the three from Shalom Caravan Inn and the other family went into the city. The men passed into the Temple to join the other pious men in the Passover services, while the women escorted Zara to the women's court where she could offer her expiatory sacrifice of a pair of doves for her past sins and sing her prayers of thanksgiving to God.

During the days that followed, John eyes scanned the vast crowds, looking for Jesus and his family. This was the first time he had failed to meet with them in Jerusalem.

Early on the sixth day of Passover, John began to say farewell to his friends as Uriah was anxious to get back to

Shalom Caravan Inn ahead of the pilgrims. The innkeeper pressed John to return with them, but John was ready to take up his path again, though he did not know where he was headed.

"I want to give you something," said Zara. "I made it out of the pouch your mezuzah came in. It was in the hall when I left your room. I bought some yarn from a merchant at the inn and worked on it in my spare time. I hope you like it and will always remember me."

The old leather pouch was transformed. Before it was a simple brown drawstring bag, but now it was covered with blue weaving with a Star of David on the front. It was beautiful, and he said so. "I thank you from the bottom of my heart. You are an artist! I did not know you possessed such a talent, Zara. It is wondrous!" John exclaimed. "I have an idea: come with me to Ain Karim."

Zara blushed at his effusive praise for her handiwork and was taken aback by his sudden proposition.

"Once you wanted to leave the inn, but I said you could not run away to solve your problems." Zara nodded recalling that day she had asked him for help. John continued, "You have faced your darkness and now walk in the light. You are free to leave."

"What would I do?"

"You have a great artistic talent, and I want my friend Mosallam to see this, and if he thinks it is as good as I think it is he will help you start your own business. Are you ready to begin a whole new life?"

"I never dreamed of such an opportunity," she said, overwhelmed by his proposal, but the more she let it play in her mind, the more she liked the idea. "Oh, Solomon, do I dare? I know I have talents that I have not yet used, but what if…"

"Let your eyes be fixed ahead; walk in the light of the Lord and your way will be firm," said Solomon to encourage her, knowing this was a big step. "I am confident in your potential, and my friend will be impressed with your handiwork."

Uriah was quite upset at Zara's decision to leave the inn. Now he was losing two good workers. And anyhow, a woman in business was a preposterous idea.

John knew what the innkeeper's reaction would be, so he had already lined up a woman to take Zara's place. He was never idle when it came to seeing to people's needs and blending them with other people's wants so that their lives would be mutually beneficial.

John led the way through the shadowy streets. They arrived on the outskirts of Ain Karim just after the sun had set on the western horizon. But the tips of the trees on the eastern hills still caught the afterglow of the sun's rays. He stopped at a house that was dark and knocked.

"John," whispered Zara, noting that all the other places they passed along the way had their lamps lit. "Are you sure this is the house?"

"Mosallam! Open up. It's John."

"John!" came the joyous shout from the other side of the door. "Welcome my friend! I can't believe it!" cried Mosallam as he flung wide the door and grasped John twirling him around. Abruptly he stopped when he bumped into another person and put out his hand to steady that person. "Pardon me...uhmmm madam."

"No offense taken...uhmmm sir," she laughed.

"Mosallam. My friend Zara."

They were exchanging pleasantries when John interrupted, "Did Jesus and his family come by here during Passover?"

"No, John," answered Mosallam and added, "I sent word to them after you left that Abigail had died and you had gone to follow your path."

John was grateful for the kind service and felt a pang of guilt and sorrow for not having thought of it himself. He also felt a bit lonesome; this was the first time in his life he had not spent Passover with his family. With a sigh he put these thoughts aside and said, "Do you suppose we could light the lamps?"

"I was wondering about that," whispered Zara.

"Excuse this inconsiderate man," chuckled Mosallam as he rushed about to light the wall sconces and clay table lamps. "You must be hungry, too. I was preparing something for my own meal when you knocked. There is plenty. Come and sit while I get it."

"Mosallam!" called John as he crossed the courtyard, "What do I feel beneath my feet? Persian rugs? You must be prospering."

"I hope you don't mind since this is your house," said the man a little apologetically.

"This is your home; be comfortable."

Questions raced through Zara's mind: This is John's house? Then why did he work at the inn? John's path. She had heard him refer to it before but had no idea what it meant. Who was Abigail? His sister? His wife? Who was Jesus? She realized how little she knew of him other than he was her best friend and was generous to anyone who needed help. And how was this man who lit the lamps going to judge her work? In the light, she could see now the man's eyes were clouded, opaque, blind. How could he judge her work?

Mosallam put together a fine meal and the two men spoke easily, catching up on each other's lives: John's adventures at Shalom Caravan Inn and the blind man's thriving business. At one point Mosallam said, "We are neglecting the lady."

"Sorry, Zara," said John. "Zara is a weaver, also."

"What?" shouted Mosallam in mock offense. "You would bring competition into this house?"

"Not a weaver, John," corrected Zara. "I embroider."

"She made this," said John as he handed the pouch to his friend. "What do you think?"

The blind man took the pouch and, lightly at first, ran his fingers over the item for design. Then he slipped two fingers inside and found a field of continuous stitch with half crossed stitches where the pattern was raised on the outside. With his nail he scratched at the stitches to see if any came loose. None did. "Now, tell me the colors. I recognize the Star of David."

Zara was amazed that he identified the design and how meticulously he went over her work and was even concerned about color. John answered, "The field is fair blue like the sky and the star is golden like the sun."

"It's a fine piece of work. Where did you learn?"

"All girls begin to embroider when they are about ten in preparation for the day they marry. But I just observed others and copied what I saw."

"Ah, a natural artist. Do you have any more samples of your work?"

"No," responded John, "but, with your permission, we would like to stay here and Zara could make some things for you to judge. Ultimately, if you deem her work deserving, would you be willing to sponsor her in a small business?"

"Certainly," said Mosallam without a moment's hesitation, remembering how John had made him the same offer years ago. "By all means, go to the market tomorrow and purchase whatever you need: yarns, silks, linen. Make a variety of things. Be creative. See if you can get a loom."

"I have a small one here," interjected John.

"I have never found one. Where is it?"

"In my old room," John answered. "Joseph, Jesus' father, made one for my mother a long, long time ago. You know the tapestry in my room? Anyway, after my parents died, Joseph built a suspended rack hanging from the ceiling in my room where I could keep my treasures: my father's scroll and writing tablets, my mother's jewelry..."

"No fair hiding things on a poor blind man!" exclaimed Mosallam as he laughed and shrugged his shoulders, "After all, this is your house."

"This is our home," corrected John. Then trying to suppress a yawn he said, "It has been a long day and it is getting late. Which room do you use?"

"I stay on the first floor in Abigail's old room. The place is much as you left it. I keep your room always ready for you."

"Thank you. Zara can have my room, and I will sleep in my parents'."

John said he would give Zara a proper tour of his home in the morning so, for now, he led her upstairs to the terrace: the first room was his parents'. It had four beds tucked together from when he and Abigail had friends residing with them.

"Who was Abigail?" asked Zara, wondering who this woman was that used to sleep on the first floor.

"Abigail was my second mother. She was the first to help me find my path," replied John simply.

Mosallam followed them upstairs and told John that friends still come to stay in the rooms when they need a place. The blind man did not mind, in fact, he enjoyed the company and was more than glad to give to others a little of what he had received. The second room had more beds like the first but the third room had only a single bed. It was John's room: freshly made, with a basin and towels laid out as if he were expected.

Mosallam pushed past Zara and John into the room. Armed with his walking stick he tapped the ceiling and, sure enough, located the suspended rack right over the bed and let out an, "Ah-Ha!" Zara, trying not to laugh at the blind man's antics, caught sight of the tapestry on the wall and commented on how lovely it was. Zara continued to smile as she listened to the two men talk about their friends. No wonder John felt at home at the inn – he was practically running one from his own home. Only here, they were truly his guests. John was forever doing what he could to help the less fortunate. She came to the conclusion that this must be John's path: to help others. And Mosallam was like John in that they both had good hearts. She felt a deep sense of gratitude for their willingness to help her start a new life.

Zara was reluctant to take John's room but he said, "Please make yourself at home. I have slept in every room in this house, including the roof and in the courtyard. You are not putting me out. I'll see you in the morning."

A month went by before Zara knew it. She worked on her embroidery from sunrise to sunset. At first her fingers were terribly stiff from the intricate work, but soon they became nimble, gaining skill from constant repetition. She enjoyed every moment of the day, because she was exercising her gift to create beautiful things.

The first thing she did was to embroider a simple design on a tunic. Next she decorated a cushion, and then created a floral pattern on a shawl. She even tried her hand at John's mother's loom. Since she had no formal training, her design was unique and ingenious.

On days when Mosallam was not at his stall in the market, he joined Zara in the courtyard and wove. Zara sometimes would just sit and marvel as his masterful, agile fingers composed the most wondrous works of craftsmanship she had ever seen. Mostly they worked in easy silence, yet when they spoke, each listened to the other with utmost interest. They enjoyed each other's company.

One evening as the light was fading, Zara snipped the last thread of her needlework. She smiled as Mosallam continued to work, oblivious of the gathering darkness. As a cue it was time to stop, she handed him her latest effort. After he went over her piece, a sash, he smiled apprehensively at her.

"Don't you like it?"

"Yes. It is very good."

She could tell something was on his mind. All afternoon he had been silent. It was not her place to pry into his affairs but his whole demeanor made her feel as if he was pondering whether he should do something or not. Well, curiosity got the better of her, so she asked, "What is on your mind, sir?"

Mosallam remained quiet for a moment, then smiled; he too was recalling their first meeting. Her cheerful spirit gave him the courage to ask, "Madam, may I ask a favor of you?"

"Of course."

"May I see your face?"

Zara was taken aback by his request and began to tremble because 'to see' meant 'to feel.' She had not thought much about her scarred face since John had helped turn her life around and made her feel normal. When she first began going to market, she felt the townspeople's stares and heard their whispering. But slowly, as they got to know her, she became a familiar face, a friendly face. It was always so difficult to meet new people. What would Mosallam think of her ugly face? Stop these thoughts, she told herself; Mosallam had accepted her sight unseen when they first met. If there was anything she had learned in the last year, it was to trust. Mosallam had accepted her, and she liked Mosallam; she trusted him. "Yes, Mosallam."

Mosallam's hands trembled as he gently touched her face: her forehead, the arch of her brows, the delicate eyelids and feathery lashes. His index finger traced the high bridge of her nose and his thumb followed the bow of her soft full lips. He fanned his fingers across her smooth cheeks until one hand paused at a point near her eye and traced the arc down to her chin. Both hands slid down her strong neck. Lifting his hands he pushed back her head covering and ran his fingers through her billowy hair. "A woman of texture," he murmured, "thank you."

John had come in quietly and witnessed this scene. In the dim light he saw Zara's and Mosallam's bashful awkwardness that followed that moment, so he announced himself, "I'm back. You working in the dark again?"

"Speaking of work," Zara jumped up, feeling very self-conscious and grateful to step away from Mosallam. "Where were you all day?"

"I did some day labor. I met with friends." he answered casually.

"John has a knack for making friends and helping the less fortunate," explained Mosallam.

Neither had to explain any further; Zara knew all about John's friends. She had seen him in action at the inn.

While they sat down to have their evening meal it was Zara's turn to observe the features of the blind weaver. He was in his mid-thirties. His face was animated with expressive eyebrows, a strong nose, long beard, a kind face. His brown hair was silver-streaked and plaited in the back, unusual for a man - but very sensible. He was neither tall nor short, fat nor thin. She liked him immensely. She blushed at her thoughts and excused herself from the table.

The next morning Zara and John sat at the courtyard table eating their breakfast in silence, lost in their own thoughts. Yet, when Mosallam came out from his room, John saw Zara's face light up.

"Are you alone?"

Zara signaled John by putting her finger to her lips. He recognized the familiar mischievous twinkle in her eyes. John, open to an early morning lark, winked and answered, "Yes."

"I have something important to ask you. Are you in love with Zara?"

John gazed at his friend's earnest face in quiet surprise. Then he looked at Zara; her eyes were wide and her cheeks were pink. They both knew what was coming. "No, we are just good friends."

"Good. Do you think she likes me?"

John watched the color in Zara's cheeks deepen. "I'm sure she does."

"She is a fine woman. I know we have only known each other for a short while, but I sense a fine woman there. She is talented, giving; we think and feel the same way about many things. Her rich laughing voice fills me with delight. Have you noticed how she hums while she works? I could go on and on…" exclaimed Mosallam. Then after a moment to catch his breath he asked timidly, "Do you think she could care for a blind man?"

Zara sat motionless, tears welling up in her eyes. When she still did not make her presence known, John said, "I remember Zara once asked me who would marry a face like hers."

Jolted, Mosallam pounded his fist into his hand, "There is nothing wrong with her face. It is textured, beautifully textured. I love her, John. Do you think she would marry me?"

The scarred woman bit her lip as tears rolled down her cheeks recalling her sordid past, her desperate search for love. How could her heart feel as if it were brimming over with joy while at the same time shriveling up with sorrow? For she knew she had to be honest with Mosallam about her past. "Mosallam," her voice was deep with emotion, her eyes downcast, "I am not a virgin. In truth, I have had many lovers - loving none of them and none of them loving me."

Mosallam was shocked for a moment, realizing how she had heard his every word. In spite of which, he regained his composure rapidly; he had professed his love and was at peace. And now she had given him another reason to love her; she had risked everything, knowing it might drive him away; his respect for her expanded. She was a fine woman.

Finally he said, "Madam, from the moment I met you I knew you were not a maiden – traveling alone with the likes of John." He laughed softly to himself, knowing the kind of people his friend associated with. "Being blind not only sharpens a man's senses, but also his perception. Hence, I knew you were … an experienced woman." Mosallam reached out to her, stroked her bowed head and wiped away the tears from her eyes and said, "You are a woman of texture. To me you are perfect. I love you. Will you marry me?"

102

"Yes!" cried Zara, throwing her arms around the kindest, most loving man in the world.

After that happy and tender moment had passed, Zara rested her head on Mosallam's shoulder. She saw John standing there with his arms crossed over his chest grinning at them broadly. She said, "Well, Solomon, what do you think?"

"See where your larks lead you?" he laughed, shaking his finger at her. "I'm glad for both of you. I had hoped my two dearest friends would discover each other."

VIII

The bride and groom exchanged vows of fidelity and love under the chuppah. It seemed like the whole town came out to see Mosallam in his tasseled tallith and Zara with her gold ring drink from the blessed wedding cup. Zara was radiant in her gown which she had embroidered herself, incorporating a set of pearls Mosallam had given her as a betrothal gift.

The celebration lasted for days and days and when the last guests, the blind man's haggling friends, left, John made moves to leave also. "Dear friends," he said, "I leave you to get better acquainted." He good-naturedly thumped the groom on the back and winked at the bride. Then, seriously, he blessed them, "May your love reflect God's love for both of you and be like the rings you wear: a love that is without beginning or end."

With those words of blessing, he turned toward the door.

"You are leaving now?" exclaimed Zara, seeing he was leaving as if he were going out for an afternoon stroll. "You can't just leave! Aren't you going to take anything with you? A blanket, water skin, money…?"

"What, and get robbed again?" laughed John. "No, thank you."

"But where are you going? What are you going to do?" asked Mosallam, also full of concern.

"To Jerusalem. I will travel with no possessions like my friends, and find work and food along the way. Don't worry. I plan to come back to Ain Karim often. But let me assure you, I will not impose on you too much."

"Nonsense," protested Mosallam. "Remember, this is your home."

"OUR home," said John at the same time as the blind man.

"Yes, John," said Zara, giving him a long hug, "Come back to our home soon. God bless you."

104

John spent the next few months dividing his time between Jerusalem and Bethany. First, he merely observed the homeless, the poor, the hungry. He spent much of his time sitting side by side with these people, as Jesus and he had done when they were young, seeing how they truly lived and learning of their needs.

He found day labor in Bethany and the surrounding areas to supply his own needs. Men who desired work assembled in the early morning hours at a central location where merchants or land owners picked from among them those to labor in the fields or tend vines, pick fruit, tote loads, or haul water. After receiving his daily wage, John bought as much as he could and shared what he had with those less fortunate who could not sustain themselves or their families.

Once he went to Ain Karim for the Sabbath, and Zara refused to let him leave until she could fatten him up again before he returned to Jerusalem. The couple suspected he gave away all his food more often than not.

When John was not selected for day labor, he would use that opportunity to go out to deserted areas outside Jerusalem to pray and to think and to be one with the Almighty. He had continued to practice what he had learned as a teenager regarding the contemplative life with the Essenes. He would exit the Holy City through the Garden Gate and take the road toward Emmaus.

On one such day, as he wandered the hills, he came across a footpath, hardly visible but there, and wondered where it went. He decided to follow it for a while to see. He pondered his own path in life as he walked along this nearly invisible trail: both were unknown with obstacles strewn before him.

On coming around a turn, he caught sight of something up ahead. As he approached, he saw two figures, one bending over the other. It looked as though they needed help. John rushed forward.

The one standing heard the approach and turned, picked up his bell from the ground and sounded it, loudly crying, "Unclean, unclean!"

John came to an abrupt halt. Lepers. The man was covered from head to toe with strips of filthy material. Only his shadowed eyes and one gnarled, almost fingerless hand that rang the bell were visible. The other figure lay unmoving in a heap at his feet. A breeze floated by, carrying on it the stench of decaying flesh. John's stomach churned and he ran, stopping only to retch by the side of the road.

Back again by the Garden Gate John stared in vain at the glorious gardens that graced the hillside along the eastern wall of Jerusalem. Neither their beauty nor their sweet fragrance could erase the sight and smell of those two people.

John had bathed entirely, ritually, even though he had not touched them for fear of contamination, as soon as he came to a stream. Nor could he bring himself to go inside the city until nightfall when the new day began and the period of impurity was ended. So there he sat.

As night fell, the area became deserted. Herod's palace was situated near the gate, and the Roman soldiers assigned to Herod when he was in residence paid little attention to the bedraggled man who sat practically at their doorstep. When a sudden evening storm lit up the sky and the winds and rain lashed at John, he made no move to go into the city and find shelter. He hunched over his knees and thought of how he had abandoned those two poorest of the poor. With each thunder clap, Zara's words echoed in his ears, "So, you are human."

It was ingrained in the Chosen People's mind to equate the horrendous disease of leprosy as a punishment from the Almighty for some extremely grave sin. With this mentality, it was fitting, therefore, that the afflicted be banished from family and village, lest they contaminate the rest of society by their obvious guilt.

John's natural instinct was revulsion, but he knew better. His mind cast back to when he and Jesus had sat among the

106

beggars at this very gate and Jesus had said, "Our Father in heaven is all lovingkindness. These people are no more or less guilty than anyone else you see. God is not punishing these people, nor has God forgotten them. Rather, they are in our midst as an invitation to us to mirror and manifest to one another the compassion of the Merciful and Just One."

Morning found him still huddled by the gate quaking with inborn dread, yet he was resolved to do what he must. Cold, wet and stiff he got up and took the road back toward Emmaus and found again the little path that led further into the hills to the lepers.

It was not long before he came upon signs of habitation and saw a narrow passage that snaked its way between two high, undulating walls. He was sure he had found the entrance to the lepers' settlement. Praying for strength and wisdom, he approached, calling out softly at first, then louder in a hoarse voice, "Man? Man?"

"Unclean," warned a voice.

"I know. May the peace of our God be with you," responded John, making his way through the winding passage. "I apologize for leaving you and your friend in your time of need yesterday."

"Come no nearer. What do you want from us?"

John heard the suspicion in the man's voice. He smiled painfully at the irony of the situation; both of them uneasy about coming together. John continued forward and answered, "I want to be of service to you, if I can. How is your friend?"

"Dead."

The word echoed off the walls vaulting over John's head as he came out of the shadowy passageway into the light. Yesterday was gone, as was that man, but today and tomorrow he would do what he could.

At the first sight of the clearing, John's mind took in and formulated all that could be done for the lepers. Broken bits of pottery, frayed, empty baskets, and garbage lay strewn all about. His heart leapt for joy and he praised the Lord for there was a well long forgotten by civilization. Natural forces had carved out caves along the ground level, and he could see in the shadows other lepers huddled together in their thin rags. He could do nothing for the deceased but he could, would do something for these others who were as much children of the Father as he was.

John called to them to come out, not to be afraid; he had come only to help them, not condemn them. And slowly, haltingly because of their infirmities, they came. There were seven in all: three men, two women, an adolescent boy and a beautiful baby girl. The women hid their deformed faces and held on to each other. One man dragged himself on his rear for he had only stumps where feet had once been and those oozed with sores. He was blind. Another man had grotesque growths all over his body that were so deforming that John took a step or two backward when he came into view.

"Afraid?" said the leper whom he had seen on the road the day before. "How can you help us if you can't even stand the sight or the smell of us? You should be afraid. You risk contamination just by being here. You do not belong here. Go. Leave us. We are lepers!"

John was astonished to hear a note of pride in the man's voice. He was pleased that they had a sense of self-worth. "I belong where I am needed," he responded as he reach out and laid his hand on the shoulder of the man with the hideous growths.

The lepers all gasped that this stranger would dare touch one of them. "You are unclean now!" cried the leader of the community. "You cannot leave us now!"

"Peace. Do not be afraid for me. I have studied the Torah all my life. The Lord gave Moses and Aaron the laws regarding leprosy and cleanliness to protect the individual, as well as the community. Since that time, in our desire to fulfill the letter of the Law, we have forgotten mercy. There is no law that says I may not touch you." John said these things to gain the lepers' trust, knowing full well he would have to

108

scrupulously, ritually, purify himself before the day was out, before he would become clean again and be able to enter a city or town.

John went on to say, "It was written by Solomon in the Book of Proverbs, 'Refuse no one the good on which they have a claim when it is in your power to do it for them.' You do have a claim: as children of Abraham and Sarah, you, despite your dwelling apart, befittingly have the right to your integrity. And it is within my power to ease your situation. What can I do for you?"

The lepers for the first time in a very long while felt hope; hope that was almost dead was suddenly alive again in the form of this man. No one had ever spoken with such authority on their behalf or even dared come among them. Now, with such a proposal, they pressed in on him with all their hopes and dreams, needs and wants. They were so desperate and appreciative and overcome with awe and joy that they kissed his hands and feet, leaving them wet with their grateful tears.

Humbled at being reverenced this way, John brushed away his own tears, knowing it was the Hand of the Almighty that had brought him here to do this work.

As the day went on, they all sat and talked about what was needed most. John noticed the lad and the little girl were not like the others. The boy had scaly skin, red from constant scratching, but not true leprosy with its facial deformity and blindness, and fingerless hands and feet, and oozing sores. And the baby girl had not a blemish on her. He asked, "To whom does she belong?"

"Me," they answered in unison.

The leper whom he had deserted on the road the day before gave a coughing laugh at John's puzzled look and spoke for the rest, "All that we have is held in common, thus each person may by right claim a thing as his or her own. Now, it just so happened not too long ago we were all out on one of our scavenges under the starry night when we heard a baby's cry. For some unknown reason, but probably just because she is a girl, she was rejected, as we were rejected. Rather than leaving her to die of hunger or exposure or to be eaten by jackals, she became mine, hers, his. She is ours.

John was deeply moved by the simplicity and eloquence of the leader's words, and the compassion of them all. He further learned that they all had been abandoned or driven out by family or town and somehow had found each other. They truly loved their neighbor.

When it was time to leave, John blessed them and dubbed them his hidden friends - for their sake, and his own, he thought it best, for now, not to speak openly to other people about the lepers – and pledged that he would return with aid. Once John left the lepers, he was careful to stay clear of Jerusalem, and it was long after nightfall by the time he arrived at Ain Karim.

"Merciful God!" exclaimed Zara as she tripped over the naked body lying across the threshold. She was on her way out in the early light of a new day to fetch water. Bending over the man she screamed when she saw it was John. "Mosallam! Quick! Help!"

All day and all night John shivered with chills from fever and in his delirium mumbled, "...hidden frrr..." and "...don't be afraid." On the morning of the second day, the fever broke and the following day, he was strong enough to join them at table.

"In your delirium you were worried about something: hidden friends?" asked Mosallam. He and his wife had questioned each other in private as to who they might be. It was obvious that John had come home to seek their help, which they were ready to give. Nevertheless, they were curious as to who these people were.

Zara noticed the guarded look in John's eyes and knew he was concealing something. Prompted by her poking, the blind man continued his questions, "Who are these people,

John? Why did you say in your fever, 'Don't be afraid.' Are you afraid?"

"Not any more," answered John, knowing deep down there would always be a certain amount of fear and yes, revulsion, concerning the lepers. That day when he left his new friends, he made his way up the barren hills toward Ain Karim. As dusk gathered he tore off his clothes and buried them deep in the sand and covered them with rocks because he had no fire with which to burn them. He found a lonely stream and washed and washed and washed before he came close to town. Then he waited, naked and cold, until it was completely dark when no one would be about to see him sneak into Ain Karim. Fever and exhaustion overcame him as he crawled the last few feet before he reached his home and fell unconscious.

"It was curious," he continued. "But when I looked into their eyes, all my fears disappeared." John stood and walked behind Mosallam, laying his hands on the blind man's shoulders, and gazed down at Zara and said, "My hidden friends' needs are urgent, so I'll put my fear aside that I might serve them. Only, I cannot do it alone. Therefore, I've come on their behalf to ask if you would help me help them."

"Just say the word, John, we are ready to help in any way we can," said the blind man, patting John's hand.

"They need clothes for three men, two women, a lad and a little girl. Blankets, baskets, vessels for water and oil, food, a broom, perhaps seeds to plant…"

"Sounds like they need everything! Is this a family in trouble?'

"Yes," hedged John.

Zara saw he was evading the question and could keep silent no longer. "John, why don't you tell us something about these people?" When she saw how he hesitated, she said, "Solomon, don't judge us incapable of understanding or lacking in compassion."

"I'm sorry. It is just that I don't want you to worry."

"Do you have cause to worry?" exclaimed Zara. "This secrecy about your hidden friends and talk about being worried and not too afraid of whoever these people are frightens me more than not knowing, John!"

"They are lepers!" he blurted out.

Mosallam and Zara gasped. Those who associated with lepers were in danger of contamination and becoming outcasts themselves.

John knew they were shocked and said, "My hidden friends live in caves, wear rags, scavenge for food in the dark like animals. The beggars in Jerusalem are living like kings in comparison. At least they receive alms and assemble in the Temple to worship and hear the Torah read. My hidden friends are ostracized from society, shunned by family and friends, barred from synagogue, forced to live and die..." John's heart was enkindled as he spoke of all he had seen and felt in the last few days. Inflamed, he pleaded that mercy be shown toward the lepers who, through no fault of their own, were rejected and abandoned by the Chosen People.

The couple had never heard John speak so poignantly, passionately before and assured him that they would not abandon his hidden friends. That very day they all went to the market and bought provisions. The next day John left.

With a borrowed donkey laden with supplies, John made his way back to the leper colony. They were amazed that he was actually true to his word and were filled with gratitude. John had staked the donkey inside the passageway keeping the animal outside the open area and carried the supplies into their camp. The lepers clustered around the bundles and rejoiced at all the new things he had brought: clothes, utensils, fresh food, various sized vessels, oil, grain... Those who were able helped set out all the items, but before the clothes were distributed John hauled water from their well and helped them bathe.

One by one John helped them undress, bathe, cleanse and dress their raw flesh, and left them to bask in the warm sun.

Though his stomach turned at the sight of this one's deformity or that one's smell, he realized, just as he had told Mosallam and Zara, that he forgot to be afraid of these lepers when he heard their stories and looked into their grateful eyes. When everyone was clean, they all got new clothes, and he burned their putrid rags. That night, after being clothed, fed and warmed in their new blankets, the lepers slept comfortably for the first time in many, many years.

During the following weeks, John continued to visit his hidden friends and, after the autumn rains fell, he helped them plant a small garden of wheat. He had learned a little about gardening from his mother and Abigail, who both tended their own kitchen garden, and from working day labor. When the little sprouts began to appear in the lepers' garden, they were thrilled and watered it by hand when it looked dry.

Although he no longer had any personal fear of the lepers, he always kept new garments for himself hidden along the way near a stream so when he left their presence he could ritually bathe and redress in clean clothes.

John continued to work day labor in the city and helped other friends in Jerusalem as well as the lepers. When he could afford it, he brought them fresh supplies, for he knew they still scavenged for other things. For the lad with the bad itchy skin, he inquired of an old healing woman about remedies and purchased from her the purest of flax seed oil. He applied it to the youth's scaly skin and bandaged his hands with strips of cloth so he could not scratch. Ultimately, it was John's hope that someday they would all be cured, or at least become as self-sufficient as they could be. And with their wheat growing, they were well on their way.

It was spring. Passover was at hand and John met Mosallam and Zara for the feast in Jerusalem. John, again, searched the crowds hoping to meet Jesus and was disappointed when he did not see his family for a second year in a row.

On the seventh day, the last day of Passover, Mosallam said, "Zara and I would like to meet our hidden friends." When the blind man sensed John's unease, he continued, "We have heard you speak so often of them that we feel we already know them. We would like to meet these good people face to face. And since we are so close…"

"They are lepers," John reminded the couple in whispered tones, careful that no others would hear him.

"And I'm a blind man," retorted Mosallam. "They won't bother me."

"And I'm not afraid," Zara chimed in. "You speak so warmly of them. And I, of all people, know not to judge by people's looks. They sound like a lovely family, and we'd be pleased to meet them."

John could think of no reason to dissuade them, so he agreed, but cautioned them not to announce their intentions to anyone lest they cause unwarranted alarm.

As a result of their decision they found themselves on the road to Emmaus, walking three abreast with Mosallam in the middle. They each carried parcels of supplies for their hidden friends. Along the rocky footpath off the main road, they walked in single file with the blind man's hand on John's shoulder to guide him to the leper colony. When they came to the passageway to the concealed community, they paused as they heard singing. Upon entering the colony, though, the singing abruptly stopped at the sight of two strangers with John.

John put them at ease immediately by moving among the lepers, reassuring them: smiling, taking the fingerless hand of a woman, rubbing this one's back, tousling the lad's hair, lifting the baby girl. He greeted them all individually, then said, "I have brought with me today some friends to share in your Passover celebration. They are Mosallam and his wife, Zara. They are your benefactors. Without their help, I would never have been able to assist you."

The blind man could feel the change in tension. At first when they arrived, the lepers were silent and guarded, but after

John had introduced them one by one, they came forward and thanked the couple for their generosity. Mosallam felt the outpouring of their love. Zara held tightly onto her husband's arm and smiled shyly at the lepers; for once in her life she was at a loss for words.

The eldest male called for attention as they had not finished their own worship and invited the guests to join them. John and Mosallam sat on the ground in the front while Zara sat in back with the two women and the baby. The lepers took up their singing: snatches of this psalm or that - everything from a solemn Yom Kippur hymn to a joyous psalm of thanksgiving usually sung at the Feast of First Fruits. Someone started a Passover song only to trail off and have it picked up again by someone else.

John realized what they were doing. The last time he had seen them he told them it was Passover and he would not be seeing them for over a week. Obviously, none of them had any real training in religious worship, and most of them had been outcasts for such a long time that they sang from the heart whatever fragment of praise they could think of to the Almighty.

The elder among them addressed the assembly with a remembered passage from the Torah:

"Moses led the Chosen People through the Reed Sea out of Egypt and into the desert. There they wandered for forty years yet they were not alone. The Deliverer cared for them by sending manna from heaven and quail to eat in the wilderness and, after many trials, led them to the Promised Land."

He continued with a reflection on how they, too, were a chosen people, chosen to wander in the wilderness yet never alone. They had no Moses, but the Deliverer had sent them John. This man could not lead them to the Promised Land; however, he did renew their faith in the mercy of the Lord and eased their suffering, so that the place where they did dwell had in truth become a promised land.

A loud AMEN was said in chorus.

John was moved by their devotion and humbled by their words of praise on his behalf. They who lived in exile accepted the will of the Almighty and strove to live by the Law as best they could. At that moment his heart was so filled with love for the Almighty, so filled with love for his friends, so filled...

"The Lord has sent me to comfort you; he will make your wilderness like Eden; joy and gladness will be found in you, thanksgiving and the voice of song! For the Promised One comes! The Redeemer of Israel has chosen you. Take comfort; your Messiah comes!"

...with the Spirit. John had risen to his feet and stood with arms outstretched. An inner fire glowed within his being and he had spoken out. Still half in a daze, John knew the words he spoke were first proclaimed by Isaiah long ago, yet they had not come from him, but rather through him. He had no forethought of what he was going to say. He was just as startled as those who were staring up at him; never had he spoken thus. All the lepers whispered. Mosallam took hold of his hand which now hung by his side.

"Peace be with you all," said John, returning a gentle squeeze to Mosallam's hand. His heart was pounding but he knew he had to speak, so he swallowed hard and continued, "The Spirit of the Lord is upon me. I, the herald of the Lord, announce to you this good news: your Savior comes! Like a shepherd he will feed his flock and gather the lambs in his arms. Your Savior will comfort you and will have mercy on all who suffer. He will renew your strength and establish justice throughout the land. Your Messiah comes."

"Hosanna!" "Praise the Lord!" "Alleluia!" cried the lepers. Generally, such words would be deemed as almost blasphemous, for who could speak for the Lord? Yet these people loved John, trusted John, believed John, so their shouts of joy and praise echoed all around.

When John's mind cleared, he saw the lepers dancing, in their own clumsy way, reveling in the good news. The blind man still held on to his friend's hand, and Zara came to their side. They questioned him, but he stood mute having no more words for them. With eyes on the brink of tears, John wondered if he had done the right thing. He longed to see Jesus.

By midafternoon he made motions to leave. The lepers did not want John to go; they had feasted and now wanted to hear more of this wondrous news. John said, "The One who has been foretold by the prophets down through the ages is soon to be among you. We must be found worthy of the Messiah's coming. My friends, love one another."

After he said goodbye to each one of the lepers in the colony and promising to return to them again he silently walked ahead of Mosallam and Zara, pondering what to do. When he came to the road leading back to Jerusalem, John waited for the couple to catch up, weighing which way to go.

"Is this the path you have so often alluded to?" asked Mosallam. And when no answer came he repeated his question, "John, is this your path?"

What could he say to his friends? He had referred to his path often enough in their presence, but now, by his own admission, it was more than just helping those in need. He could not evade the question any longer and acknowledged solemnly, "This is my path: to prepare the way for the Lord. I am his herald."

"Then why are you not proclaiming it to the world?" cried Zara.

"He told me I am first to observe all things around me and love my neighbor…"

"You know him!" she broke in, filled with excitement. "You know who the Messiah is? Who is he? Where is he?"

John silenced her questions with his sober stare. Considering he had questions of his own to ask the Messiah, he would say no more except, "Say nothing of what you have witnessed today. For now just hold this in your heart." Then he turned and looked down the road and said, "I must leave you for a while."

"Why, John?" asked Mosallam. For a reply the blind man was gathered into his friend's arms. From experience, Mosallam understood John's inability sometimes to put into words all that was in his heart. Motivated by concern, Mosallam whispered the same questions he had years ago after Abigail's death, "What will you do? Where will you go?"

"I feel I need to distance myself from all that is familiar to me for the time being to gain perspective about all that has happened along my path thus far," said John. "I am going to the north country. I want to visit my cousin Jesus and his family in Nazareth. I have not seen nor heard from them for two years now, and I wonder what has become of them."

"Then go, John," said Zara, embracing him also. Never did she or her husband dream of the magnitude of his path. And now that they had glimpsed his greater mission, they realized he had to be free to do and be whatever the Messiah required. "Go, and do what you must, knowing you are loved by us and blessed by the Lord."

IX

Nazareth was a good five day walk from the Holy City, yet John arrived late on the fourth day, having rested little along the way.   When he arrived, John asked for directions to the carpenter's house, since he had never been to the Galilean village before.

John spotted the place by the workbench in the yard in front of the home.   The carpenter shop was an attached extension as large as the small house.   John paused outside the yard, imagining all the years Joseph tended his craft with Jesus by his side as apprentice.   Long shadows were cast everywhere as the sun slid down below the hills.   The smell of cooking drifted in the air and lamps were being lit inside the house.   He had not seen his family for two years, and now that he was here, John felt awkward about approaching the door unannounced.

"John," said a voice from the far end of the shop.   John turned and saw Jesus with arms out in welcome.   As they embraced, his cousin exclaimed, "You came quickly - four days!"

"You knew I was coming?"

"I felt the Spirit move.   Whom have you told?"

John felt decidedly uneasy, realizing Jesus knew something had happened and that he was coming.   With eyes cast to the ground thinking his cousin would chide him for proclaiming the good news before the proper time, confessed, "I –I told Mosallam, you know him, the blind man from Ain Karim, and his wife Zara.   We were visiting our hidden f-fr-friends…"   He paused.   Out of the corner of his eye, John saw Jesus cross his arms over his chest waiting for the rest of it.   "…at the l-leper colony."   John heard a 'humph' from his cousin and looked up to see Jesus wide-eyed.   "I couldn't help it!" he added rapidly.   "They all are good people.   Generous and loving and such faith; such innocent devotion!   They likened themselves to the Chosen People in Exodus wandering in the wilderness. They needed to know the Almighty loves them and is with them!"

Jesus tried to hide his smile behind his hand and said, "Lepers you say! My, my! How did it feel?"

Realizing Jesus was rather amused, John relaxed a little and said, "It was as if I was watching myself in a dream. Suddenly, I was standing with my arms out and words were pouring from my mouth. When I realized what was happening and that everyone was staring at me, I became nervous and confused and tried to continue what I had begun."

"Good."

"Does this mean we will begin soon?"

Jesus' gaze penetrated deeply into John's being, and then eased away. John flushed under his cousin's stare. But the other took his arm and said, "Come inside. Mother will be pleased you have arrived."

Mary was indeed glad and kissed her cousin on both cheeks in greeting. "It has been far too long since we have been together." As she set another place at the table, she said, "Jesus thought you might be coming," then motioning to her husband sitting at the head of the table, "Joseph is joining us tonight."

Mary never changed: small and sprite, hazel eyes sparkling, her hair was still a warm brown peeking from underneath her head-covering. But Joseph, John had almost missed him in the low lamplight, appeared shrunken and fragile.

"It is wonderful to see you once more," said Joseph. "I wanted to greet you properly - please excuse me for not rising."

John took the carpenter's callused hand and felt the years of wear as he bent over and kissed Joseph's brow and said, "I have come for a long visit, my kinsman. I have missed you, also, very much."

At supper, they all wanted to hear of John's adventures so he told them of his work at Shalom Caravan Inn and his dealings with the leper colony. They sat in amazement, for it was unheard of for anyone to associate with lepers. Then John

120

told Joseph and his wife of how he felt moved to speak of their son, the Promised One, to his hidden friends.

After the meal, Jesus saw his father had grown tired and helped Joseph from the table and went to another room through a narrow door.

"How long has he been like that?"

"My husband stopped working in the shop about three years ago. His back, legs, arms and hands have progressively deteriorated until he is as you see him today. Jesus has taken over the carpenter shop, though he always consults with his father for advice and guidance."

"I missed seeing you at Passover."

"We could not make the long journey to Jerusalem. It would have been too much of a strain on Joseph."

Jesus returned and brought out a jug of wine and two cups. This was the time when men relaxed, sharing a drink and conversation. Jesus was about to pour some in John's cup, but his cousin shook his head. Jesus poured some wine in his own and sat down as his mother got up and began to busy herself with the cleaning up.

As John watched Jesus drink, his mind became jumbled with thoughts wending back to when his own parents instructed him that he must never drink wine or strong drink, as he was dedicated to the Lord from his birth to proclaim a great message to the people. When they died, he was so grief stricken that he longed to share in the cup of mourning, but remained steadfast to his promise to them. And then he thought of Spicy, his dog, and how she was dead on the side of the road; but Jesus had brought Spicy back to life - he was sure of it now. John wondered out loud, "Surely, you could do something for him."

"Time and nature will take their course," said Jesus solemnly, taking another sip of his wine.

"How can you let this go on when Joseph is so afflicted?"

In that moment, the silence was deafening as Jesus' eyes bore into John's. From behind they heard a sniff, and Jesus looked over his shoulder to his mother whose head was bowed. Jesus bade her sit by his side and put his arm around her and calmly explained to John, "Time and nature will take their course. We are all born. We all live our lives. And we all die. Even I will die, John. I love my father, but some things cannot be changed." Then he added ever so gently, "Joseph knows that I love him and that I Am with him."

John's face burned with shame for having doubted Jesus' compassion towards Joseph and for hurting Mary. With throat constricted he addressed her, "I am sorry, Mary."

"I know you spoke out of concern for my husband."

"No," cried John. He stared hard at his own clenched hands not daring to look Jesus' way. "I presume too much. Forgive me for causing you pain. Both of you."

"I love you, John."

John gazed into Mary's face and beheld nothing but tenderness and ready forgiveness. Jesus' countenance exhibited the same. Tears came to John's eyes with feelings of unworthiness. He was harder on himself than those who loved him.

"You are tired, John," said Mary, seeing his emotion. "Would you like to retire? You can share the corner with Jesus. We have plenty of blankets and pillows."

John looked around the room. Like many humble homes, the main room was also the sleeping room. He noticed it used to be bigger; Jesus must have added a wall to make Joseph a little room so he could have his peace and quiet. There was a nook with a blanket hung over it. Mary probably slept there while Jesus slept on the opposite side of the room on a mat. John had never realized how humbly they lived.

John looked at them both; Mary was so understanding and Jesus' steady gaze made him feel as if his mind was being read. Jesus lowered his eyes and John was filled with a renewed sense of awe of his cousin. He humbly asked, "May I sleep with Joseph? I could help him if he wakes in the night."

"That is not necessary – Jesus and I take turns caring for him."

"Please. I would be more comfortable doing what I know how to do. I have cared for many sick people. Let me do this for you."

"As you wish," smiled Mary seeing her son nod in approval. "If you need anything, call."

Jesus went to the nook and got out the sleeping mats, blankets and pillows and handed some to John. Ever since Jesus had revealed himself to his cousin, John had been over-awed by him, and now that they had not spoken for over two years, he felt John's trepidation. He was glad John would be staying for a long visit – it would give them time to renew their relationship. Jesus showed his cousin his father's little room.

The next morning, John helped Joseph bathe and dress and carried him into the main room. Mary greeted them cheerily and set out a light meal for her husband and gave John whatever he wanted. Jesus had already eaten and was at work in the carpenter shop.

When Jesus came in at midday, he asked John if he would care to see the shop. John followed him, wondering what his cousin would say to him once they were alone, but Jesus merely showed him all the tools that lined the wall and explained their uses. On the work table in the middle of the shop were pieces of cedar that Jesus was carving and sanding into legs for chairs. In spite of Nazareth's being a simple village, some rich merchant had heard of Joseph's and Jesus' craftsmanship and ordered a set of chairs.

As days went by John became more at ease with the family, experiencing them in their daily life, and fell into a routine. After breakfast, if Joseph was feeling well enough, he would carry him out to the shop and they would watch Jesus work. Often Jesus would ask for assistance and John would hesitantly come forward, claiming to be all thumbs. Be that as it may, John picked up skills easily and was soon working comfortably by Jesus' side.

John always enjoyed learning new things, so Joseph instructed him on the various woods they used in the shop. The sycamore, when properly treated, was worm proof and became hard as iron and was therefore desirable for making tools. Oak, pine and ilex were for common use, while cedar from Lebanon and oak from Bashan were expensive, highly valued, and thus used only for special orders. Even old vine trunks were used for small items like racks. Jesus taught John how to check a beam for straightness and how to measure off a plank. He showed John how to file and sand, and how to chisel the wood with an adze to notch the pieces together.

On one hot day John was stripped to the waist so he could freely move his arms as he sanded a long beam. He was preparing to rub in the oil from the flax seed to varnish the piece, when he felt Jesus' eyes upon him. Jesus often paused in his work to see how John was progressing, so he looked up expectantly.

"How did you get that scar?"

Jesus' eyes were on the long red line that tracked across John's chest over to his arm. Involuntarily, John shivered despite the heat of the day as his hand fingered the lumpy line. "Thanks be to God, I am still alive. It is a wonder..." responded John, as he went on to relate the story of the good Samaritan who had rescued him. "...I shall never forget the kindness of that man."

"Nor will I," said Jesus.

As the weeks went by Joseph became noticeably weaker. Finally it came to the point where he remained in his little room while Mary sat by his side. She spoke quietly with her husband of their life together and of her gratitude for his protection when she was found to be with child, his generous support of their family, and their loving companionship. At night John would come in and make Joseph comfortable in the little bed and then roll out his own sleeping mat on the floor beside the failing man and take some rest.

Joseph died.

John was a light sleeper. The sudden silence woke him. Joseph had stopped breathing; he had peacefully slipped away. John went to the door to tell the family but he saw that Jesus was already standing by the nook where his mother slept. He could hear them crying as they came towards the little room. Mary went in first and caressed her husband's face and smoothed his brow. Then she stepped back so Jesus, as was his duty as son, could place two small coins on the eyes of her husband to close them and ensure that in death Joseph would behold nothing save the Glorious Visage. Together the cousins lifted the body of Joseph off the bed and laid him on John's mat so as not to taint the bed further with a corpse. Jesus stood and rent the left side of his garment while John, as kin rent the right, as a symbol of the fabric of their lives being torn away with the death of their beloved. Mary loosed her hair.

Jesus said softly, "I shall go and tip over the water jar outside the front door to announce the death of my father. The neighbor women will come in the morning when they see the sign and prepare my father's body for burial."

"Please," said John humbly. "It would be an honor if you would allow me to perform the rites for burial."

"That is a woman's undertaking."

"I have done this many times for my friends," replied John. And when Jesus did not argue, John continued, "I will fetch the basin and water. Do you have any perfumed oil and linen for the shroud?"

Mary had prepared for this day and brought out lengths of linen she had woven from flax; the spring plant from which the fine threads were made that represented the Tree of Life. She also had oil and a new lamp that would stay lit for the seven days of mourning. She passed these all to her son.

Jesus, though, went to the cabinet in the main room and withdrew a carved wooden box.

"That was given for you, my son," protested Mary.

"Let us honor my father with these gifts."

As John undressed the body he could hear their exchange in the main room and wondered what was in the box. Jesus came to the door and placed it alongside John. It was a box carved out of a single block of cedar, highly polished with a design of the Star of David in the center, surrounded with a laurel wreath etched into the lid. Inside was a sealed jar and two lamb's suede pouches.

"My father made this box. It is his finest work," said Jesus quietly. "It contains the treasure the three foreigners presented to my mother on the occasion of my birth. The jar contains myrrh with which to anoint the dead. One pouch contains frankincense and the other gold. With the gold I will buy a tomb in the morning. Use the myrrh oil. I will bring a burner that we may light the incense."

When Jesus returned with the live coal, John dropped the precious frankincense onto the glowing ember and the soothing scent quickly filled the room.

After washing the body, John broke open the sealed jar and poured the myrrh into his palms and, praying all the while, massaged the dark, richly aromatic oil over the face and body of his kinsman, staining away the pallor of death.

John then unfolded the linen Mary had given him to wrap the body. He was having difficulty in such a small room so he beckoned Jesus who had remained at the doorway throughout the ritual to come to his assistance. Jesus knelt beside the body of his father and held his shoulders while John arranged the cloth beneath. When they laid the body down again Jesus crossed the arms of his father over his chest. His hands lingered over them while John put his arm across his cousin's shoulder. Together they wept. And Mary, hearing their lamentation, rushed in, forgetting the sack of dried flowers and spices she had saved to perfume and adorn her beloved and cast herself over the body of her husband.

126

Jesus gathered his mother into his arms and offered a prayer, "Father of all Mercy, hear my plea for my father, Joseph. Lord Sabaoth, send Michael, Prince of the Heavenly Host, and all your angels to march with the soul of my father until they bring him into your glorious light and peace."

The seven days of mourning that followed the burial of Joseph were filled with such an outpouring of sympathy and love for the family. The carpenter was not a rich man; he held no prominent position in the village, yet his wisdom and counsel were often sought by his neighbors. His charity could be witnessed in every home in the district. He always lent a helping hand when someone was in need. When a man needed a trestle erected in his yard, Joseph was there. When a poor widow was without a mortar and pestle, an anonymous gift of one was discovered outside her door. Or when a damaged water trough needed repair, Joseph was there to fix it, without ever asking for recompense. His neighbors appreciated his skill as a carpenter, but even more than that, they respected Joseph as a righteous man among men.

Twenty-one days after the first week of sorrow John again put the same question to Jesus as he had when he first arrived in Nazareth: "Are we to begin soon?"

John felt his face turn crimson under his cousin's gaze. Perhaps it was too soon after the death of Jesus' father, but the Spirit did move him to speak, so was it not time for the Messiah to come forward?

"Before I answer you, let me ask you a question," said Jesus. "Why should the Messiah come?"

John was confused by the question. He, Jesus, the Messiah, was already here. Words tumbled out of his mouth, "The Chosen People have waited so long for the Promised One and for the glory of Israel to be restored by the Son of David. Is it not time to set up your kingdom? Time for Israel to triumph over our oppressors the Romans? You are the Messiah of

Israel! And, as you have instructed me, I have loved my neighbor. My friends would rejoice in your coming!"

When John answered like any other man, Jesus looked around the workshop where they were standing and said in reply, "Does this look like a kingdom? Do I look like a king? A warrior?" There was a touch of heavy-heartedness as he spoke. "You have yet to understand why I have come."

"Then tell me what I do not know!"

Jesus shook his head, sighing to himself: Years ago I told John I was the Lamb of God. He did not recall or understand. Did his cousin not know the words of Isaiah? "...he had no appearance, no majesty that we should look at him, desire him. Yet he was wounded for our transgressions, crushed for our iniquities; upon him was the punishment that made us whole. Like sheep we had gone astray, turning to our own ways. So God laid upon him the punishment for our crimes. For the love of the Lord he was led like a lamb to be slaughtered to make of his life an offering for the sin of all..." "Where are my sheep?" murmured Jesus, and then louder said, "Go back among the people, John. Scrutinize everything you see and think of who I Am."

"You give no answer!" exclaimed John; he longed to know, to understand. He felt frustrated that all his life his parents and Mary and Joseph knew of the Messiah's embodiment in Jesus. Did his father, Zechariah, and Jesus know the exact direction his path was to take, or could they only speculate so they spoke in obscure terms, like just now when Jesus murmured, "Where are my sheep?" It was evident he was to discover the full direction of his path on his own, alone. And what was he to scrutinize? How would that clarify anything? John's thoughts were so confused and painful he abruptly shouted, "Then I will leave. Now. Alone."

"You are not alone, John. You are etched on the palms of my hands," reassured Jesus. "You are on your path. You have done all things well. Nevertheless, there is something only you can do for me, but how it is done is up to you to discover and implement."

John's heart ached hearing the love and encouragement from the lips of the One whom he loved; he remembered when he heard those words of Isaiah spoken to him when he was beginning his path. He was not alone. Those words were a balm for his wounded soul, and John, sorry for his outburst, said, "I will pray."

John struggled against sleep as he kept vigil throughout the night in prayer. Slowly he paced the yard outside the carpenter's small house. With each step he felt every part of his foot from heel to ball to toe, heel, ball, toe…. As he walked he prayed to comprehend the mystery of his life, his path and his role as herald of the Messiah.

As night wore on to its darkest, a dream came to him, yet it was not a dream for his eyes were open and his mind was clear:

He walked on a path, crooked and thorny. Wild bushes grew along the way. Two hands, his own (or another's - he could not tell), pruned the wild bushes.

He walked in the sun. The path, once crooked, was straighter, but the wild bushes still needed pruning. Two hands, his own (or another's – he could not tell), pruned the wild bushes. Bleeding fingers pricked off the thorns.

He walked in the Sun and all along the way the path was dressed in splendor as the bushes burst into glorious bloom.

John wondered.

Dawn came and John thanked Mary for making him welcome in her home for the summer and again expressed his sorrow at the loss of her husband, Joseph.

He then went to the carpenter shop to bid farewell to Jesus. As they stood face to face, John said, "Our lives are a mystery: there may be pain but the unfolding is not to be rushed for the outcome will be more beautiful, more wondrous than imagined. I will be patient. I will trust."

"Good, John," said his cousin and put out his arms to embrace John.

John took a half step backward. He said, "You are the Messiah, the Son of God." He lifted his arms behind his head and gathered up his hair and giving it a twist, took a small saw from the rack on the wall and sawed off his hair. He handed his hair to Jesus and said, "My life is yours."

Jesus, aware of the effect his being had on John, solemnly accepted the hunk of hair in one hand and placed the other on the back of his cousin's neck. He could feel John trembling beneath his touch. Jesus said, "John, be not afraid of me. I am a man as much as you and need your love as much as your help."

"You will always have my love," said John, wrapping his arms around his cousin. They hugged long and hard. Then John stepped away and walked before the Son.

X

From the first moment John saw the sea he felt drawn to it. Yet ever since Jesus told him to scrutinize everything a certain restlessness overcame him and he wandered from town to town. Though not staying in any one place for very long, John always stayed along the golden shore of the harp-shaped Sea of Gennesareth. Try as he might to be aware of every person and thing around him, John still felt as if he were groping blindfolded on his path not knowing what was 'the one thing more' he was supposed to do.

Initially, he came to the Greek/Roman city named after the latest Caesar, Tiberius. They also renamed the sea after him, though the people of the district still called it by its most common name, the Sea of Galilee. John discovered that few Jews actually lived in Tiberius because it was a defiled city, having been built on the site of a burial ground. When he found work, his attempts at caring for the less fortunate were rebuffed. The Roman settlers were suspicious of a Jew offering citizens of the Empire aid.

Further up the coast, in Magdala, he fared a little better and found work drying fish which was sold throughout Israel. After a couple months he moved on to Capharnaum. Still, no matter where he went, he felt restless and left this fishing village for another, Bethsaida.

A boy's piercing scream sliced across the waters, jarring John out of his morning prayers. Newly arrived in Bethsaida, he had slept under the stars and awoke at dawn to see the fishermen already about their business. The boat had just reached its most distant point and was beginning to circle back again to shore. The two in the boat had been dropping the nets with their floats and sinkers, which, when hauled in by the other fishermen on shore, would entrap the fish. From John's location he could see now only one person in the boat. The other was gone. The boy, alone in the boat, screamed and gestured frantically. The men on shore waded forward shouting. One man from the group dived into the sea and swam hard to the spot. When there, he drew his knife and disappeared beneath the water.

Moments seemed like forever, but finally the man resurfaced, dragging the limp body of the other to the side of the boat. The boy helped pull both men in. As they began to row, the men on shore took up the slack of the nets and pulled with all their might. John joined them at the end of the line.

They dragged the boat to shore. Now grouped around the boat the one man stumbled out while the lad sat there crying as the other man lay motionless in the bottom. "Do something, Simon," cried one of the fishermen, "help him."

"Damn it," swore the eldest of the group. "I wish to God there was something I could do. Look at him. He was under too long."

Grief showed on all their faces as they stood around confused and dazed by what had happened. John, too, stared at the lifeless man in the bottom of the boat; he appeared to be in his early twenties. John whispered a prayer, "My God, help him."

Immediately, he himself jumped into the boat and rolled the man onto his stomach, sat on the man's back and began to slide his hands from the lower back up along the spine to the top, pressing hard all the way. Some water came out of his mouth. John rolled him over again but the man's chest was still not moving. John took a deep breath and put his mouth over the other's and breathed hard. Again. And again. When the man still did not respond, John fisted his hand and gave the man a solid thump on the center of his chest and then began to alternate between breathing into the man's mouth and pushing down on his ribs. John did this nearly a dozen times. Soon more water came out of the man's mouth and he finally began to breathe on his own.

The fishermen gaped at the stranger in alarm and wonder, but when they saw their companion's eyes flicker and then breathe on his own, they knew he was going to live and they raised a shout of joy.

"Quiet," commanded John. "The morning air is cold on his wet body. Where does he live?"

Swiftly, the fishermen lifted their friend who had drowned and carried him down the beach. The youth who had been in the boat raced ahead of them and darted into one of the white-washed houses that lined the shore. A high pitched scream arose from inside and out came a girl running to meet them. When she saw the limp body, she covered her face and bawled. The youth had followed her out and shouted at her trying to explain, but she could not hear him.

John, who had followed the men down the beach, grabbed the girl by the shoulders and shook her and said, "He is alive. He is alive!"

She heard the voice and understood, yet could not control her sobs as they became cries of relief. Strong arms encircled her, soothed her, and gradually she calmed down and rested securely there.

"He needs you. Are you all right now?"

The voice was unknown to her; his accent was not Galilean, but Judean. She opened her eyes slowly to see the arms, the shoulder, the face of a man she did not know. The girl broke from his clasp and scurried into the house.

The fishermen came out and stood a little way from the door. "What happened out there?" John was close enough to hear the eldest, Simon, inquire.

"He was badly tangled in the nets," answered the man who had dived in. He looked to be the younger brother of Simon.

"In heaven's name, if there is anything wrong with the nets or trouble of any kind, come to me," said Simon, placing his hand on the shoulder of the youth who had been left alone in the boat after his partner fell in, "or James. Do not be afraid to ask questions. Always check the nets. This must never happen again. We are all fishermen. We are family. A man gains strength when, like a strong and trustworthy net, he is bound and connected to the people he depends on."

The girl appeared from the house and rushed at the lad shouting, "Don't you ever frighten me like that again, saying my brother is dead!"

"I didn't," protested the boy. "I said he drowned."

The men groaned.

"Why do you keep saying that?" she exclaimed, still distressed by what had happened.

"Because he opens his mouth and words spill out," said one of the men, wrapping his arms around the lad's neck and clamping his hand over the fellow's mouth.

"Look who is talking," said the boy, shoving him away. It was plain to see they were brothers. "Stop it, James."

"Never mind," said Simon, putting an end to that. He turned to the girl and spoke sincerely, "As God is my witness, I thought we had lost him. I take full responsibility. If there is anything I can do for you, let me know. Is he better?"

"He is asleep," she replied. "But what happened?"

"Philip became entangled in the nets somehow and lost his balance and fell overboard. Andrew dived in to rescue him."

"Thank you, Andrew."

"Do not thank me alone. There is the man who brought your brother back to life," said Andrew, pointing to John.

"Good fellow, join us," said Simon, calling him over.

"I thank you from the bottom of my heart," said the girl.

"Thank our God's loving mercy. The Creator gave life back to the man, not I." John was not just speaking humbly. His efforts to revive the man weren't his own. The last thing he remembered before the men carried the man to the house was saying a prayer. He felt a bit disconcerted because, again, his action and words were guided by the Spirit and he moved as in a dream.

134

"Amen," said the girl and boy.

"Amen," said the three fishermen.

"There is nothing more we can do here. Let's go and inspect the damage Andrew has done to the nets," kidded James.

"Don't start," said Simon, obviously the leader. "This is no time for teasing. I am sure we will be able to handle whatever needs to be done." To the girl he said, "I'll send my wife over to give you a hand tonight."

"My mother, too, would be glad to assist," added James sincerely.

"Excuse me," interrupted John. "If the young lady will allow, I would like to offer my services rather than disturb your households."

"Yes, thank you," she answered quickly, recalling how, after all, he had brought her brother back to life and how safe and secure she felt in his arms.

"Wait," said Simon, eyeing the stranger. "Are you a physician?"

"I? No," he answered. "I am John, son of Zechariah, of Ain Karim, a wanderer practiced in caring for the ill."

"She has no money to pay…"

"But I would welcome his assistance!"

"I ask for nothing."

Simon studied the stranger and the girl; would it be responsible, respectable to permit this stranger entrance into the household of a girl of marriageable age without the consent of her brother? Yet, he had to laugh at himself; after the wondrous thing this man had just done, how could he doubt his character? And he knew the girl to be a good girl and was merely grateful, indebted to him. Simon sensed the rightness of the situation and said, "You may stay, outside, and help."

"The young lady's name is Adah," introduced James with a romantic tone in his voice and a twinkle in his eye.

John smiled at the girl whose face turned red at the introduction. The fishermen laughed as Simon pushed James to the rear. John did not catch what was so amusing, but he could tell there was real affection underneath all the banter and jostling that went on among them.

Adah did blush. She knew the men, her brother's partners and friends, would think her, a maiden, too forward in accepting a stranger's help over the assistance of the neighborhood women. But she was not being forward; she saw in this man not only someone who had saved her brother's life but someone in whom she could place all her trust, a pillar of strength to hold on to. Adah lowered her eyes from John, and especially the fishermen, and said as demurely as she could, "If I may, I will call you when I need your help. Thank you." And with a little curtsey, she hurried back into the house.

The men laughed again as the girl scurried away and breathed a sigh of relief that all would be well as they moved down the beach back to their nets. They thought Adah guileless. And the outsider, John, was worthy of their trust, given the heroic actions he had performed that day.

The lad lingered near the outsider. He, too, saw in the man a person to be looked up to. He was the only one who had yet to be introduced, so he announced, "My name is John, too!"

John walked the beach but kept the house of Philip and his sister, Adah, in sight. He saw the girl do her chores outside so as not to disturb her sleeping brother. The fishermen sat around the widely spread net and meticulously mended the torn areas. Villagers moaned when they saw the men were not in their boats and complained that they would starve with no fish today.

As the light of the setting sun skimmed the water of the lake, John sat in prayer in the small kitchen garden beside the house, gathering the last warm rays of the late winter sun. Adah, shyly and without a word, placed a plate of food by his side. Before she could slip away, John asked, "How is your brother?"

136

"Still asleep. Should I wake him to give him food, also?"

"No. Right now he needs to sleep. Let him wake on his own accord and by then he will be ravenous," John said reassuringly.

"Where will you sleep?" asked Adah. She understood why Simon said the stranger had to stay outside, but she still wanted to be hospitable. "My brother and I both sleep in the main room. If I tip over the table and give you some straw you could have a private corner..."

"Please do not go to any trouble," responded John. He realized Adah was a maiden of perhaps thirteen, marriageable age, and it would not be prudent for him to sleep inside her home. He had learned earlier that she had no other relatives in the world save this brother, so until Philip was well, it would be unseemly for him to accept her offer to sleep inside. "The air is lovely. I enjoy sleeping under the stars. Still, if you need me, do not hesitate to call."

Long before dawn, Adah did tap on John's shoulder to wake him. He was wrapped up in his cloak, huddled beside the kitchen wall. "My brother is tossing and turning with fever," whispered Adah. "His breathing is odd. What should we do?"

John entered the house. It was just as the girl had said: a main room where they lived and slept and, in the winter and rain, cooked and ate. He told her to build up the fire and light the lamps. The ill man lay on a mat in the corner of the room. He was restless and trying to free himself from his blanket; he was probably dreaming of being entangled in the nets. John knelt beside Philip and felt his forehead and listened to his chest. "He must still have some sea water in his lungs. That is what is causing the fever. It must come out if he is to get better. Do you have mustard, salt and oil? I will need some hot water, too."

Adah removed from the shelf a small sack of mustard seed and a chunk of salt and jar of oil and put them on the table.

John found a mortar and pestle and began to crush the seeds into powder. He scraped off some salt and added that to the mustard and poured some oil over it to make a paste. He then added some hot water to liquefy the mixture. While waiting for it to cool a little, he asked for an empty basin and if they had any anise or fennel with which to brew some tea.

John helped Philip sit up and had the man drink the mustard concoction as quickly as possible and asked Adah to hold the basin in front of her brother. Abigail had taught him that the pungent mustard drink would purge the body of infectious fluids. Philip, groggy with fever, drank the stuff in two gulps and almost immediately began heaving and vomiting the acrid fluid. John held the man's forehead and rubbed his back when the man's stomach was empty but continued to dry heave. Eventually he began to cough and hack and spew out the remaining tainted water from his lungs. The heaving went on even after there was nothing left to come out.

"Sweeten the tea with some honey and let him sip it; it will soothe his stomach and throat," said John as he laid the man down again and took the foul basin from Adah. He went down the beach, dug a hole and buried the putrid mess. On his return the sweet smell of fennel filled the room.

"Who's there?" asked Philip, seeing a stranger enter the house.

"His name is John," said Adah holding the tea to his lips, "he has saved your life."

"The nets!" he croaked, remembering his ordeal. Then, realizing he was safe in his own home, lay back and let his eyelids close.

Adah was relieved; Philip's fever was almost gone and he slept peacefully. John watched from the door as she tended her brother and went outside again knowing the crisis was past. He gazed up at the morning stars and thanked the Almighty.

Not a moment had gone by, or so it seemed, after he had wrapped himself up again in his cloak to resume his own sleep, when the youth John was standing over him, talking faster than a flying fish, "You slept outside? How is Philip? Can I see him? Why didn't you come to my house to sleep? Two houses down. We have plenty of room…"

John raised his hand to stop the boy's chatter. The sun was just peaking over the horizon and it seemed the fishermen were already busy with their work. "Philip is well. The crisis is past. Don't go in now; he is still sleeping. You can see him later. It was a fine night to sleep under the stars. Hear, O Israel, the Lord is God, the Lord alone…"

Young John smiled and joined in the morning prayer and as soon as they were finished said, "Come fishing with us."

"Let me check on Philip first and get something to eat. I'll see you by the shore in a little while."

"Right. See you in a little while," agreed the boy and raced down the beach.

John knocked at the door and was welcomed in. Adah already had a cake of flat bread cooking on the oven-stone. She offered it to him along with a handful of figs. As he sat down at the table she excused herself saying she wanted a word with Simon.

In the light of day John looked around the room more closely; Philip lay on his side softly snoring. He noticed that the shelf on which folks normally kept their food was almost bare. He had eaten fish and onions the night before but now there was just this handful of figs and bread. This was a poor household.

Philip stirred on his mat, suddenly aware of someone in the room. "Who's there?"

"I am John," he answered. "You had an accident with the nets yesterday. I offered my services to your sister to help care for you and she accepted with Simon's approval."

He tried to sit up but he was too weak. "Where is my sister?"

"I believe she has gone to the market," responded John. He thought she probably asked Simon for an advance on her brother's pay so she could feed Philip and himself. "She will return shortly. Are you hungry? She left you this bread and some figs."

"Yes," said Philip, suddenly aware he was very hungry.

John had not touched the food so he gave it to the weak man. He also found some tea and honey left from the night before and offered that too. At that moment Adah came back with an armful of food from the market. John made for the door for it was not his intention to be a burden on the family.

"Are you leaving?" exclaimed the girl. "We have yet to thank you properly!"

Simon had given her money. She had bought enough food for the day but wished to show John, and Andrew, their appreciation by preparing a small feast in their honor. She knew her brother was too weak today and it would have to wait until he was fully recovered, but if the outsider left... She rushed to her brother and whispered in his ear, "This man brought you back to life after you drowned. And then I was so frightened last night that you were going to die! But this man knew exactly what to do to help. Twice he has saved your life! He is a wanderer with no place to go. You must invite him to stay with us so we can show our gratitude."

"Please, sir," said Philip, feeling the same as his sister, "I owe you my life. I offer you the hospitality of my home. It would be an honor if you would accept."

"Thank you. I accept your generous offer." John accepted their hospitality because he realized he could still be of help to the family until Philip got back on his feet; he could find day labor and supplement their household income until the brother could provide for his sister again.

John went to the shore where the fishermen were working and as he approached heard James say, "We are done. All the torn sections are mended."

"Well," threw out Simon, "while we have the nets spread out like this, why don't we reinforce the whole thing? We'd have to do it sooner or later."

"Right," agreed James. "We may as well check the sinkers and floats while we are at it. We don't want anything like what happened yesterday to happen again."

" 'Morning, John," said young John, seeing him standing there.

"Ah, our co-rescuer!" cried out James, grandly wrapping his arm around Andrew and saluting John. "How is our friend, Philip?"

"He is better, thanks be to God, but will need a few more days of rest to fully regain his strength," answered John, then asked, "Do you have any work for me today?"

"Andrew and I usually team with Philip, James and John here," said Simon. "Do you know how to mend nets?"

"No. But I dried fish in Magdala before I came here."

"Well, we don't have any fish so you might as well go take a walk," said Simon.

John was about to go when James said, "Maybe we could use you in the afternoon."

"Wait," called young John. "I'm an apprentice and I earn half a day's pay to watch and learn and try my hand at things."

Simon took the bait. After all, this man saved his friend's life. "That is true. You are welcome to stay and earn a few small coins for yourself and learn some things in the bargain."

So he did. That day and the days that followed and even after Philip resumed his work, John stayed on with the fishermen. He drew a great deal of satisfaction working on the boats and found true friends in the good-hearted fishermen. He continued to live with Philip and his sister, Adah, bringing home his share of the fish. However, unbeknownst to his friends, John would often go off and spend his pay aiding the poor in the village.

Spring soon arrived and John inquired among the fishermen who would be going to Jerusalem for the Passover. None were. Simon had said it was impossible to go when the people of Bethsaida grumbled that their bellies were empty when they did not fish the two days out of the Passover week as well as the Sabbath. And just to go to Jerusalem was a six day walk. They had a responsibility to the village.

So the night before John left, Philip organized a feast in his honor to show his gratitude and bid farewell to the man who saved his life. All the fishermen and their families came to the celebration. They had all come to love and respect John who was no longer the stranger, the outsider, among them. They looked on him as one of their own. And in the morning, when he was ready to be one his way, John hugged the fishermen as they climbed into their boats and he began his journey south to Jerusalem.

With less than a half day's journey left to the Holy City, John heard his name being called by a woman. He turned around and saw Jesus' head among the crowd. Quickly, he pushed his way back through the pilgrims and embraced his family. At John's suggestion they headed towards Bethany in hopes of meeting Mosallam and Zara who always stayed in that village during the Holy Days.

"I have become a fisherman on the Sea of Galilee," declared John, telling his family of what he has been doing since last they saw him. "I met fine, good-hearted men in Bethsaida, but they would not leave their village or people to come for the Passover. They said they were fortunate to have a synagogue with a rabbi to instruct them and lead them in services. But how could that compare with the beauty and the glory of the Temple and the sacrifices!?"

"Are you going to return to the sea after the Holy Days?" asked Mary.

"I enjoyed living and working by the sea," admitted John.

"Why don't you go back?" asked Jesus. "And if you find yourself there when Passover time comes again, stay and experience how a small village synagogue observes the Feast."

John gave his cousin a sideways glance. Jesus had spoken casually enough, but he detected a subtle suggestion, a direction, perhaps a marker on his path. He wondered what the next Passover held in store for him.

It was not long before they did find Mosallam and Zara near Bethany. John was delighted to see that Zara was with child. He congratulated them both and introduced her, and remembered Mosallam, to his family. They raised a tent between Bethany and Jerusalem and in the shadow of the Temple celebrated Passover. They attended the services during the days and feasted on lamb, unleavened bread and bitter herbs during the nights, all the while singing psalms of praise at their campsite under the full moon.

On the final day of Passover they sat around the campfire having an amiable conversation when Zara asked, "John, remember last year at this time you spoke to us of the Messiah? Does your family know? Tell us more about him."

John could not believe his ears - here was Zara asking about the Messiah while she was sitting right next to Jesus. He shot a glance at his cousin and saw Jesus faintly smiling as he gazed into the fire. John's throat became dry and constricted as he looked from Jesus to Zara to Mosallam. Their faces showed interest in the new topic. Only Mary's sharp intake of breath belied to John that she, too, wondered what he would say. He was bewildered by his predicament.

"Why do you ask John about the Messiah?" asked Jesus, breaking the silence.

"Because John said he was here!" exclaimed Zara.

"Wife!" said Mosallam suddenly remembering, "John asked us not to mention this."

"Oh, John," gasped Zara, covering her mouth.

"Never mind," said Jesus. "If the Messiah were here what would you want of him?"

They all looked at him, questioningly.

"Let us say it was within his power to grant whatever you ask. Mosallam, would you ask him to cure your blindness?"

A look of wonder and excitement crossed the blind man's face, but he turned thoughtful and answered slowly, "No." Feeling the amazement of the people around him he explained, "Though there was a time I thought my blindness was a curse from the Almighty, I now thank and praise God for my sightlessness. I have often wondered what kind of man I would have been sighted. Would I have developed my skills to the same degree? Would I have met John? My beautiful wife?" As he spoke he reached for her hand. "No, I am content. Because of my blindness I have been richly blest."

"And Zara," said Jesus, "what would you want of the Messiah?"

"Like Mosallam, I am content." Then she added with a laugh, rubbing her belly, "But I do wonder, though, what I am having?"

Jesus searched her face; she had laughed but her eyes bespoke worry. She was having her first child and she was over thirty years of age and in her eight month. Gently, he placed his hand on her belly and said, "A healthy child."

"Oh! Did you feel that?" cried Zara. "Mosallam, quick! Feel here!" She placed his hand over the spot where the baby kicked and confessed, "The baby has not moved in days. Secretly, I thought something was wrong with the baby because I was tired from the pilgrimage. But the baby has never kicked like this before. It's dancing inside me!" she laughed. "I, too, have been blest with all I could desire. Praised be our God!"

Jesus gazed fondly at the happy couple, and then turned to Mary, "Mother?"

Tears glistened in her eyes as she rejoiced in the couple's bliss and remembered her own pregnancy, and how her

Aunt Elizabeth had made the same remark about unborn John dancing in her womb. "Isn't the Most High wonderful!?" She gladly continued speaking to her son and the others, "For me, each day is such a gift! Each day is a revelation of the Most High's love for us all! And in the Messiah we will see it. He will free us from fear and loneliness, and open our hearts to accept God's copious love and let true peace enter into our lives."

Jesus kissed his mother's brow and looked at John, "Well, what do you have to say about the Messiah?"

Throughout the conversation John tried to be open to the Spirit but was not moved to speak. Just a year ago he was filled with the Spirit, yet now, when asked directly, he failed to utter a single word. Questions taunted his mind: 'What can I say? Why can't I just say the Messiah sits at the Feast with us now? Would they believe me? Would they believe in him? God Almighty...!' John could not look at any of them in the face. His eyes had been fixed on the sole of Jesus' sandal. "What am I to say?" he finally said softly, sadly, "I am not worthy to kneel and undo the strap of his sandal."

Mosallam and Zara sensed John's distress and excused themselves, saying they had a busy day ahead of them tomorrow with their return journey to Ain Karim. Mary, too, excused herself, but not without first putting her arms around John.

John's eyes stung feeling Mary's compassion, tenderness, love. His heart felt as if it was breaking, for surely it was evident to Jesus that he was inadequate to be the Messiah's herald. He was afraid Jesus would leave him also - and afraid he would stay. Jesus did stay and John's eyes rose to meet his cousin's and he cried out in anguish, "Why me? Why did you choose me when I l-lack the c-courage and the talent to be your herald?"

"You are mine, John. Remember to be patient with yourself."

"And when you touched Zara's b-belly, the baby came alive again, didn't it? You preformed a miracle in my sight and I said nothing. Not a word of praise or thanks! What more proof do you need that I am un-unworthy...?" John stood up abruptly and half turned from the dying fire and Jesus. "...Forgive me."

"The fullness of time is almost at hand," said Jesus, rising quickly to John's side. "John, John. You are my herald. Put your trust in me. When the time comes your voice will surely sound loud and strong." While Jesus spoke John turned slowly to face his cousin and when their eyes met, Jesus said, "My trust is in you."

XI

"May I come home with you?"

John put aside all his anxieties of the night before and was able to give a warm farewell to his family when they broke camp in the morning. It was Mosallam he turned to with the request and said, "I would like to be present when Zara's child is born. I could help you arrange for a woman to see to her personal needs."

"We've already found a woman. She starts next week. Besides, you don't have to ask to come to your own home, John. Zara and I miss you all the time."

Because of Zara's condition, they took their time reaching Ain Karim. Her spirits were high ever since she felt renewed life in her womb. She assured the men she was not the least bit tired from their journey, yet she slept the whole next day.

One morning the following week, Susannah arrived. She was a local widow who had no sons. Her daughters were married and had gone to live with their husbands' families. Wiry and full of life, she said she had many a good year left in her so she offered herself when she heard the blind weaver was looking for someone to attend his pregnant wife and help care for the child. They were all taken by her independent attitude and were sure she would make an interesting match for Zara.

When Zara's labor began two weeks later, Susannah notified John, who went to the market place to inform Mosallam. They did not need a mid-wife as Susannah had had five of her own and had practiced midwifery for others, so she knew all the techniques of birthing babies. Mosallam, on hearing the news, left his stand without a single word, leaving the customers to John. The patrons and Mosallam's fellow merchants laughed and shouted their good wishes to the back of the blind man as he hurried home.

A baby boy was born as the sun set. For her age, Zara had an easy time of it and the baby was perfect. Mosallam held the squirming creature on his knees and marveled at the tiny hands and feet and chortled when he heard the baby's hearty cries. He wanted to hold his son forever, but Susannah gave him back to his mother to nurse and shooed the men away so Zara and the baby could rest.

On the eighth day after the birth, Zara handed the baby to her husband to be taken to the synagogue to be named and circumcised. John and practically all the men in the town escorted them. When the priest asked the father the name of the baby, Mosallam answered, "Zechariah." John was surprised and flattered. On their way home the blind man explained that neither he nor his wife had family and considered John their closest kin and so to honor him, they chose the name of his deceased father and named their boy Zechariah.

On the thirty-third day following the naming and circumcision, Zara went to the synagogue to be ritually purified in a bath and to be prayed over while Mosallam offered an unblemished male lamb to redeem his son as Moses had prescribed in the Law. All firstborn males are sacred to the Lord and it is required of every father to ransom his firstborn in remembrance of the strength of the hand of God on the night of Passover when the Almighty spared the firstborn sons of the Children of Israel in the land of Egypt.

Not long after Zara's purification, John took his leave of the family, leaving them in the capable hands of Susannah. She indeed had made a fine addition to the family. John had enjoyed this time of relaxation and sharing in the experience of a new baby, along with the opportunity for more prayer and study, but he knew in his heart it was time for him to resume his path.

John decided to visit his hidden friends outside Jerusalem. He was amazed to see how well they were doing; their garden was abundant with herbs and vegetables and the young grape vine promised to bear fruit. He learned from the lepers that, occasionally when they still scavenged, they found baskets of grain and fruit obviously left for them on their footpath. No one knew of their location, so John concluded that Mosallam must have arranged it. Bless him. Though the improved diet did not cure their illness, it did ease their suffering.

Astonishingly enough though, the lad who had scaly skin had grown tall and his skin was almost totally clear. And the little girl was still without blemish; she had not become infected living among the lepers.

Bartholomew, now sixteen, was well enough for John to propose that he be taken to Jerusalem so the priest at the Temple could declare him clean. He petitioned for the little girl, Dinah, to be returned to society also because she was never leprous and he could easily find her a loving home.

The invitation to free these two dear ones from the leper community broke their hearts. However, their children deserved to live a normal life: a life full of hope, one with a happy future. So it was with great lamentation and optimistic joy the lepers blessed their beloved children and granted them a new beginning in life.

It was an emotional parting a few days later. Bartholomew and Dinah wept greatly when they left with John for they knew they might never see their leper family again.

The journey to Jerusalem began late in the afternoon. It was not a long walk, but three- year-old Dinah, already worn out from crying, needed to be carried. Bartholomew carried her until they were within sight of the Holy City. John and the children bathed themselves ritually, put on new clothes and slept outside the city to abide with the laws of purity. In the morning John picked up Dinah and walk ahead of the lad. Bartholomew, with bell in hand, rang it loudly and called out, "Unclean," keenly feeling the shame of being an outcast. John walked backwards most of the time and spoke words of encouragement to the young fellow. He also tried to prepare them for the vast crowds of people they would encounter in the city.

They came in not through the Garden Gate, the closest to the footpath, but rather went around Jerusalem and entered the Golden Gate where they could pass directly into the Temple without walking all the way through the city with Bartholomew ringing his bell and calling "unclean."

Inside the Temple John ushered the lad to the leper room. It was a closet specifically constructed in the women's court where the priest could inspect the stricken. When the priest drew back the curtain and examined the lad he asked, "Has he been living apart from society?"

"Yes," John answered. "But his skin has so greatly improved I brought him here for you to judge."

Pale blotches from where his skin had healed covered his body. The priest pointed with a stick to a patch of crust between the lad's shoulder blades and said, "Shave his head and bring him back in seven days."

Quickly they left the city and set up camp in a deserted place. Bartholomew looked forlorn as John shaved his head in accordance with the priest's instructions. "The priest did not reject you," reassured John. "He just needs to be sure before he declares you clean. Take this period of waiting to give thanks to the Almighty for the great mercy God has bestowed on you and as a way to prepare yourself for the future. All will be well!"

During the week of waiting Bartholomew told John his family lived in Bethany not far from where they were camped. Under the cover of night they stole into the village and the lad pointed out his house. He recounted how, eight years earlier, he had been driven out by the villagers because of his skin ailment which they thought was leprous. His family was powerless to save him, especially after their Rabbi would not intervene and told him to go find his own kind. Bartholomew told of how he wandered in the wilderness nearly dying of hunger and thirst before the lepers found him and took him into their family. He spoke of how they loved and cared for him during the second half of his life.

On the sixth day John told the children that he was going off to do some day labor, which he normally did, but rather this day he went to Bethany instead and knocked on the door of the house where Bartholomew had once lived. The woman who answered was not terribly old but her face was care worn. Delicately, he asked if she had a son named Bartholomew.

"I once had a son by that name, but he was taken from me." Sadness filled her voice.

John sensed the woman believed her son had died by the way she responded. "If he were to return to you," John asked, "would you welcome him?"

"Welcome him? I prayed night and day for his return." She said almost bitterly, "I walked the desert to try to catch a glimpse of him. Can a mother ever turn from her child? No matter how..." Tears brimmed in her eyes. "I had always hoped but..."

"Hope still!" exclaimed John. "If all goes well, your son shall be returned to you, whole and unblemished, tomorrow. Woman, pray and prepare."

"Who are you? How do you know this? Are you a prophet?"

"A prophet?" whispered John and then out loud with a slight smile creasing his face, "No, a messenger. One who proclaims good tidings, a time of favor, a time of mercy." Tears filled his own eyes, knowing he was also speaking of the Promised One. "A son shall be given you."

The woman covered John's hands with joyful tears and kisses, intuitively trusting wholeheartedly in the messenger and said, "May my son's return be the gracious pleasure of our God who has sent you to me."

The next day John and Dinah stood aside as the priest examined Bartholomew again. John had rubbed the youth's back with fine sand and oiled his skin to polish away any remaining crust. The crust had flaked away leaving a smooth white area where it had once clung. "He is healed. He is clean," declared the priest. "Go and buy two turtle doves, some cedar wood, hyssop and a length of scarlet yarn."

John ran and purchased what the priest required for the purification rite. The priest took one of the birds and slew it over an earthen bowl, mingling the bird's blood with fresh spring water. The priest then tied the scarlet yarn around the cedar wood, hyssop and the living bird and dipped them into the bloody water and then sprinkled the lad seven times. In addition, the priest dabbed blood on Bartholomew's right ear lobe, right thumb and right big toe. Finally, the priest pronounced him ritually clean and gave the youth the live turtle dove to set free.

Bartholomew held the dove firmly yet gently as he left the leper room and walked to the center of the Temple's court. There he threw the bird up into the air. Thrice it circled, gaining its bearing before it flew off over the Temple. At that Bartholomew let out an exuberant whoop of joy. Like the dove, he was free!

A leper proclaimed clean was still required to bathe, shave his head again, even his eyebrows, and put on new clothes. John had anticipated this event and had bought new clothes for both the lad and the girl and delighted in watching them splash around in the pool of Bethesda.

When they were dressed, they bought an unblemished male lamb as an atonement offering. Bartholomew wiped tears from his eyes as the lamb was led away. They were not for the lamb that would soon be slaughtered, nor for himself did he cry, rather, he cried for those he had left behind - his family of lepers.

A short while later they found themselves on the streets of Bethany and walking down the alley where Bartholomew used to live. Suddenly, a woman rushed upon them and cried out, "I've been watching and waiting for you all day! Did not all go well? Where is my son? What news do you bring?"

Wordlessly, John stepped aside so the woman could get a better view of the lad.

"Amma!" Bartholomew instantly recognized her.

The mother blinked in astonishment at the tall youth with a shaved head. In her mind time had stood still and she expected to see a small boy. Trembling she reached up to caress his cheek and felt fuzz. Her boy was a young man. Tears of sorrow over the lost years welled up and overflowed with tears of joy as the mother and son hung on to each other so tightly that it seemed they would never be separated again.

Their cries and laughter brought people out of their houses. The mother had not told anyone of the possible return of her son, wanting to surprise them all. Brothers and sisters, grandparents, friends and neighbors, young and old all joined in the excitement. The father finally appeared after being mysteriously summoned from working in the field. He stood dumbfounded gaping at his son. When he came to his senses he pressed Bartholomew to himself long and hard. After that he proclaimed a feast in honor of his son who was once dead and now had come back to life.

For days they feasted and made merry, celebrating the merciful goodness of their God who had restored their son to family and friends and village. Even the Rabbi came with a blessing. John stayed on the outskirts of the celebration with shy Dinah playing in an adjacent garden and eating treats brought to them by Bartholomew, his mother and his sisters.

The morning after the feasting was over and when all the guests had gone, John said, "Today, Dinah, we will go to Jerusalem and find a good family for you to live with." John thought there would be no problem placing such an adorable child. "After breakfast we will say good-bye to Bartholomew…"

Dinah's young mind did not comprehend all that John had said but she understood 'good-bye to Bartholomew' and began to bawl, "Bar-ta-mew! Bar-ta-mew!"

While John was trying to comfort and reassure her, Bartholomew came in running and swept her up in his arms. As she calmed he asked, "What made her cry?"

Before John could finish his explanation the youth raised his voice, "No you won't. She is mine!"

John was not prepared for the lad's reaction. He grasped Dinah's fear of leaving the only person she knew, but it failed to dawn on him that Bartholomew's attachment to the girl would be even stronger and that he would be unwilling to let her go.

Bartholomew's mother came in at the same time and heard the exchange. She asked, "Do you care so much for this girl?"

He turned to face his mother, then looked down at Dinah nestled securely in his arms. He said, "She is my child. She is as much a part of me as I am a father and a mother, a brother to her. She has known me all her life. I am all she has. And she is mine. I love her. I cannot let her go. Oh, amma!" He was about to beg. However, he drew himself up tall and looked his mother directly in the eye and said, "Mother, I cannot let her go. You know I love you and am happy to be home at last with the family, but I will not be parted from Dinah. If there is no room for her here, with me, we will go."

Bartholomew's mother was filled with pride for her responsible, caring, independent son. He was not a boy. He was a man. "Did I say anything about her leaving? I know what it is like to be separated from the child you love." As she spoke she cupped his face in her hands, "Of course, she is staying! I wouldn't have it any other way."

John was pleased with the way it worked out. It had not occurred to him that Bartholomew's family would want another child. So, he bade them farewell as Dinah snuggled in her new amma's arms.

John sat wearily on the grassy beach by the Sea of Galilee. He had taken a walk north of the town of Gamala to pray in solitude and think. He had spent the last six months moving from town to village to town aiding the poor, the sick, the orphaned, the widow, the oppressed... He did what he could for the people of Jericho and Ephraim, Gadara and now Gamala. Something always left him with a sense of dissatisfaction every place he went; thus, after a month or so, he would move on to another town.

He was feeling despondent because everywhere he went it seemed to John the people he met not only lacked material wealth but spiritual health. Was he the only one who cared for the welfare of the poor? Certainly there were enough prosperous people around who could show charity to these less fortunate ones.

And had the Israelites ceased to look for, long for the Messiah? On the Sabbath the synagogues were full. The assembly, however, seemed spiritless as they half listened to the Holy Writ and recited without thought lengthy prayers. If being in a holy meeting place did not inspire them to reach out to the Almighty, what hope was there for the man sitting next to them? Evidence of this lackadaisicalness bore as its fruit failure to keep the Sabbath holy. He saw hard-heartedness, lack of respect, avarice, envy, licentious behavior, wrath, theft.... The people struggled, sometimes violently, against the oppression of the Roman occupation. And collaborators overtaxed the populace.

John, as a member of the Pharisee sect, began to realize how hypocritical the religious leaders of his day had become in their over-zealous strict observance of every minute detail of the Law while their own hearts grew cold to the real needs of the Israelites and showed them little mercy.

There were those who would dress in their finest linen to be honored by the crowds one day, and then on the next, put on sackcloth and moan about how unworthy they were of their many blessings, though all the while, ignoring the poor among them. The bleeding Pharisee would rather smash his nose against the wall than see a woman passing on the street. John recalled once during the Feast of Booths, a time of thanksgiving for the harvest, pilgrims processing, singing psalms and waving palm branches in their right hands while holding a citron in their left. Among them were Pharisees who loaded themselves down with bundles of palms and citrons for the sole purpose of demonstrating their great devotion. Additionally, there were always quarrels among the Pharisees and Sadducees.

He shook his head. John had met kind, honest people who sought and held God in reverential awe. Last Passover in Jerusalem a young Pharisee named Gamaliel, grandson of Hillel, preached to the faithful in the Temple. He was righteous, yet gentle and wise. Holy. He thought of all his friends and how they were blessed and shared their blessing, and how they looked forward to the coming of the Promised One. Jesus.

Jesus, the Messiah, the Son of God was among the Chosen People. Had they ceased looking for the One who is to come? Did they not long for the salvation promised? He prayed fervently. How could he, the herald of the Messiah, prepare the people for his coming?

"John. John."

At hearing his name being called he looked up and saw two boats rowing close to shore. A young man shouted his name again and waved. It was his friends from Bethsaida: Philip, James and young John in one boat and Simon and Andrew in the other. He waded out into the water and was pulled aboard amidst much laughter and back slapping. It was good to see them again. Instantly, he forgot his concerns and was easily persuaded to return with them to Bethsaida.

XII

John jumped out of the boat, helped shore her, and immediately began sorting the catch and inspecting and folding the nets just as if he had never been away. The fishermen had been far south of their village when they spotted John sitting on the shore. They were thrilled when he joined them in the boats and had not refused their invitation to come with them to Bethsaida

Philip insisted John come home with him and be his guest, as his door was always open to the man who saved his life. The other men shouted 'unfair' for they all wanted time with John and had a lot of catching up to do. Finally, it was decided they and their families would get together in a little while for an impromptu meal on the beach as a welcoming celebration. The families often got together to share a meal, especially at sundown after the Sabbath if they had had a good week at sea.

On their arrival at the house Philip and John found all was in order, except Adah was where to be seen. Bread, hot from the oven, was cooling on the table, lentils with garlic and onions were slow cooking over the fire and the floor was swept clean. While they waited for Adah to return to organize the food and things needed for the celebration, Philip and John washed.

"I'm sorry I wasn't here when you got back. Zebedee wasn't feeling well and I was helping his wife....John!" Adah had rushed into the house explaining loudly why she wasn't home to welcome her brother and to see the surprise James said was waiting for her at home. John filled her eyes. There he stood, tall, broad-shouldered with sun-streaked hair and those same steady, honest brown eyes. It was almost a year since she had seen him and he was more handsome than she remembered. She blushed at her thoughts and for her boisterous entrance.

"Good evening, Adah," said John with a friendly smile on his face. "I hope it does not inconvenience you, but your brother has offered me the hospitality of your home again."

"You are always welcome to our home," replied Adah, pink-cheeked and eyes lowered.

"We are eating with our friends on the beach tonight," said Philip. "Get things ready."

Adah nodded and quickly gathered what they would need. In her basket she packed the bread and cheese, wooden plates and cups and knives for the three of them. On the beach they would cook the fish caught that day. From a peg by the door she slung the wine skin over her shoulder and got the basket on her arm. With her free hand she lifted the pot of lentils and headed for the door. As she began to walk John took the hot and heavy pot from her and walked on ahead.

They arrived at the shore to find the fire already burning high and all the men sitting around it talking while the fish cooked. Adah offered wine to all present. All accepted except John who merely said, "This company of good friends is intoxicating enough for me."

Adah joined the wives of Zebedee and Simon as they organized all the food they would serve. Everyone chatted happily as they got re-acquainted, eating and drinking what was laid out before them. By the end of the meal Simon's three children were wild and noisy and over tired by the day's excitement. John caught the littlest one by the hand and brought her over to her mother. Instead of just leaving her there, John sat down with the little girl in his lap along-side the women who had formed their own circle so they could talk as they pleased. The two other boys came over to see what was going on and sat down on either side of the man. John started them off with a song and they all joined in to sing. When the little one began to doze, he talked a while with the women and then when all was calm, he returned to the men's circle after receiving a grateful nod from Simon's wife, Gali.

When he was gone Adah listened as the older women praised John. She watched John from the corner of her eye and thought, in agreement with her friends, how he was not like the other men. Her brother and his friends were good men, yet John was different. He was considerate of people, even of women and children; he did not think it was beneath him to help a woman with her chores or take time to give attention to other people's children. And the way he spoke – it was not just that he had a Judean accent; he was something more than a fisherman or a day laborer. Even with her limited experience beyond her village and their Rabbi she knew by his bearing and words he was educated, wise, pious.

Over the next few days Adah noticed that John fell into the same routine that he had followed when he was with them the year before. John washed scrupulously before doing anything. He prayed before retiring and rose early to pray before going out with the men to fish. After they returned from fishing and seeing to the nets and sorting the catch, each man received a share of the fish. The rest went to market to be sold and Simon would give them their share of the monetary profits the next day. As soon as John got home he would thoroughly wash. Sometimes he would ask for bread before he would leave with his share of the catch and disappear for the rest of the day. She wondered where he went and why he ate alone. Curiosity got the better of her; one day she followed him.

John went to the market in Bethsaida. He walked among the stalls and spoke with the trade folk. He bought some figs and cheese and a jar of oil. He went over to a group of poorly dressed youths loitering about the market and offered the fruit to them as they talked. After awhile John went off with some of the fellows and headed for the poorest section of the village.

Not knowing the lads or what exchange went on between them, Adah followed them at a distance and saw them go down an alley. She trailed them into the smelly, gloomy passageway. She covered her nose with her shawl. Quietly she approached where they had gone in and peeked through the cracks of the door.

John was conversing with the people inside but she could not make out all that was being said. From what she could see, they, like her own small house, had only a large main room, except they were a large family. John gave them his food, fish and all, and she could tell by his gestures he was offering them assistance to supplement their meager way of life. The people were grateful for his concern and blessed him over and over again for his generosity.

When she saw John preparing to leave, she rushed from the alley and crossed the closing marketplace. At one point she had to push her way through because two men had begun an argument and people were crowding around to add in their own two bits. As she reached the street leading to the shore the shouting abruptly stopped. Adah glanced over her shoulder and saw John standing between the men with a hand on each one's back. One spoke. John nodded. The other spoke. John nodded. He lowered his head; it appeared he was thinking, and when he raised it again, he spoke at length. She could not hear his words but she saw the tension between the two men ease away and in the end they all shook hands.

That night Adah lay on her mat and thought of John. She was right - he was something more than just a fisherman. He was selfless; he displayed a willingness to come to the aid of others. He was thoughtful, wise, a peacemaker. A man of prayer and discipline. Yes, he was different than anyone she had ever met before in all her fourteen years.

Recently, when she became a woman, Philip spoke to her about her marrying. Usually, women by the time they were her age were already betrothed. But he said he would not marry her away to another family without her consent. He wanted her to be happy in life. Following their parents' death Philip had been a good brother and guardian. And ever since John had saved his life, Philip had had a great appreciation for everything and everyone around him, so much so that Philip told her he had resolved not to rush her into an unhappy union and was content to have her live with him awhile longer.

At fourteen many girls were already married and having children. Adah wanted a home of her own and children, but no one among their friends or in their village caught her eye. Until now. John was the man she wanted to share her life with and have a share in his life.

Another Sabbath would soon be over and Adah stood in her doorway thinking as she watched the sun set. A month had gone by and still John was unaware of her feelings for him. Quietly Adah had set about doing what she could to be a part of John's life. During the week she baked extra bread to offer him as he left the house, knowing that he would go into the village to help the poor.

Every Sabbath day, after the service and eating something, the men gathered on the beach to discuss the Talmud, complain about the Roman occupation and plan for the coming week. The women meanwhile kept close to home keeping the small children quiet. John always spent the Sabbath afternoon alone in prayer.

As today's Sabbath sun got closer to the horizon, Philip came back to the house for the evening meal. In fact, he was already eating. Adah was about to call John in, when she stopped herself. Silently she went to the little kitchen garden on the side of the house where he sat bathed in the golden rays of the sun. He prayed with is eyes closed, his face serene, his breathing so shallow his chest barely rose and fell; it was so unlike the men in her village who mumbled aloud their prayers while they rocked back and forth, or swayed side to side. It looked so peaceful. She wanted to share in that peace.

Just then she heard the trumpet from the synagogue signaling the end of the Sabbath and saw John inhale deeply. She spoke in a soft voice, "May I speak with you, John?"

"Of course, Adah."

161

"Do we keep the Sabbath well?" she asked. She and her brother always went to synagogue in the morning. She knew John, being a Judean and a frequent pilgrim to Jerusalem for the feasts, was learned in such things and would be a fair judge of how they kept the Lord's Day.

John was pleased she was concerned and had showed interest. He had noticed the farther north one was from Jerusalem the more lax in their observance the people tended to be. He thought the probable reason was that five hundred years ago when the Jews returned to the Promised Land after being exiled in Babylonia, they came home to find their land overrun by Arameans, Canaanites, Phoenicians and Mesopotamians who had battled over and settled in the verdant region of Galilee. Then there was the influence of the Greeks and the Romans - not to mention the Samaritans who claimed the land in between Judea and Galilee. Yet to their credit, the Jews in the north had a simple trust in the Almighty that never wavered. He said, "Why do you want to know?"

"My mother died when I was born and my father when I was nine. Philip has raised me properly, but I have no woman relative to really instruct me." She blushed for she wanted to add that if she were to be his wife, it would be important for them and their children to know how to honor the Lord's Day fittingly. Instead she simply said, "I want to reverence the Sabbath rightly. I know you are a learned man and I believe you would not be unkind if I asked."

"You keep it well," he said, rising to his feet and washing his hands up to his elbows in the basin kept for such a purpose by the side of the house. He smiled at her intent expression and said, "Would you like to learn more about the reasons, ritual, and traditions of the day?"

"Yes, please!" she said earnestly.

"Very well. On the fifth day of the week, the day before preparation day, I will instruct you when I get home from fishing."

162

On the morning of the day Adah received no inkling from John that he remembered his offer, but went about her business trusting in his word. She went to the market and bought what she thought they would need: enough food and lamp oil to last them through the Sabbath. She did her daily chores: she hauled water from the village well, gathered fuel, baked bread and cooked, and swept the floor.

Philip came in first, broke off a hunk of warm bread and ate.

"Where is John?" asked Adah as casually as she could, hoping her brother would not sense her feelings of anticipation.

"Washing, as usual. And, as usual, he says he has something to do this afternoon." With that Philip got up having finished gulping down his food, and went out again.

Adah smiled when John did come in and gave her a slight nod as he passed her brother going out the door saying he would be back later. Suddenly, she felt anxious to be alone with John, but he, full of composure, took a seat at the table and began as if he were posing a question to another man when they discuss the Talmud. "Why do we keep the Sabbath holy?"

"It is the Lord's day," she answered simply.

"Yes," said John and expounded, "Long ago the Almighty spoke unto Moses and he, in turn, delivered this message to the Chosen People: God made the heavens and the earth, the land and the seas and all their array in six days and on the seventh day God rested. The word Sabbath itself means 'day of rest.' God blessed the seventh day and made it holy, separate from all the other days of the week. That is why we labor six days and rest on the seventh, that we might worship, thank and contemplate all the marvelous deeds the Almighty has done for us."

His tone was formal as he adeptly explained the purpose of the day. However, when he began to reminisce about the day of preparation and Sabbath with his own family, he became more relaxed. He spoke of seeing his mother and their friend Abigail grinding grain for bread for the Sabbath and then

163

watching it magically rise in the bowl. How herbs were collected from the garden, vegetables and fruits were washed and prepared, and enough food was cooked for that night and to be eaten cold the following day and night. Also their fine clothes were made ready and laid out. His own jobs were to sweep the courtyard and gather plenty of fuel for the fire and fill all the lamps with oil, for if the fire went out or the lamps ran dry, you could not relight or refill them until after the sunset of the Sabbath day.

All this had to be done before nightfall. At twilight the hazzan, the man in the synagogue who leads the congregation in prayer, would take the Sabbath trumpet up to the roof of the synagogue. Two blasts are sounded at the sighting of the first star – laborers came in from the fields. Another two blasts are sounded at the sighting of the second star – people washed and put on their Sabbath clothes. And again two more blasts were sounded at the sighting of the third star – and 'the Sabbath begins to shine' as women everywhere lit the lamps to banish the darkness.

The meal, set out before the first trumpet sounded, begins with a threefold blessing which he recited for her to learn. On Sabbath morning they rose singing a psalm, 'It is good to give thanks to our God, to sing praise to your name, Most High. To proclaim your kindness throughout the night, for you make me glad, O God, by your deeds; at the work of your hands I rejoice...'

Adah sat enraptured, listening to John speak. And when he spontaneously broke into song she joined her voice with his in singing the well-known psalm. John nodded his approval, then continued.

Everyone went to synagogue to hear the word of the Lord. After singing psalms, listening to the scriptures and instruction, and worshipping together as a people, everyone went home to eat for the first time that day. The rest of the day was spent relaxing with the family and mulling over in one's heart the greatness of the Almighty and giving praise for all the blessings received during the week.

At sundown the trumpet sounded again ending the Sabbath. They washed, offered the blessings unto their God for the gifts of light, wine and food, and then sat down to a delicious cold meal. Thus, according to age old traditions, the Sabbath was conducted.

The next morning was the day of preparation. Adah was busy as soon as the men left the house for work. Using the provisions she had bought the day before, she set about cooking for the Sabbath. First, she set to simmer on the fire a pot of lentils, onions and seasoning that would be delicious either hot or cold. The sun was at mid-point when she took the bread out of the oven and put in a fancy spice cake. In a skillet she fried more onions and garlic and aromatic herbs in oil to make a sauce to dip their dried fish into. By mid-afternoon she had swept out the house, gathered fuel for the fire, and was filling the lamps. She laid the table, filled the water basins, and placed towels and a change of clothing out for her brother. The sun was sinking to the horizon as she combed her long hair and dressed. Adah poured the wine as the sun touched the hills.

The trumpet's first blasts came just as Philip and John entered the house. Philip noticed the care with which the table was set, the food laid out, and the wine poured. The trumpet sounded again and Philip saw a change of clothes, his only other, and a towel by the basin; he began to wash as he eyed his sister scurrying around the room getting a taper from the fire and shielding it from any draft. When the trumpet sounded for the third time Adah lit the two little lamps on the table and he heard her say softly, "Let the Sabbath begin to shine," then louder, "Blessed be God, Creator of the Universe, who has made us holy through the commandments and commanded us to kindle the Sabbath light."

Philip had sat down and was about to eat when he noticed John and Adah still standing and his sister looking beseechingly at him. She whispered another prayer John had taught her, "Brother, may you shine in the Torah." It had been such a long time since they had observed the Sabbath properly that it took Philip a moment to understand they were waiting for him to invoke the blessings for the Sabbath meal. Solemnly, he stood up again and prayed, breaking the bread and handing pieces to John and his sister, "Blessed be God, Creator of the Universe, who brings forth bread from the earth."

"Amen," responded John and Adah.

Lifting the wine cup he prayed, "Blessed be God, Creator of the Universe, who creates the fruit of the vine to gladden our hearts." Philip sipped the wine and passed the cup to John, who only reverenced the wine then passed it Adah.

"Amen."

Then placing his fingertips in the salt dish he prayed, "Blessed be God, Creator of the Universe, by this salt may we who partake of this Sabbath meal be purified. May it be a sign of our unbreakable covenant with you and be joined in peace and friendship with those seated around this table."

"Amen."

On Sabbath morn as they prepared to leave for the synagogue, Adah softly sang the Sabbath psalm, "It is good to give thanks to the Lord, to sing praise to your name, Most High…" Philip marveled at the change in his sister and happily joined in her song of praise. From inside the house they could hear outside John singing also.

Together they walked the short distance to the synagogue. Philip and John sat inside on benches with the men, while Adah and the other women of the village stood behind the lattice wall. The congregation prayed, sang, and listened to the Holy Writ and the commentary.

By midday the service was over and they went home to break their fast. Philip left after he had eaten to join his friends down at the beach. John retired to the side garden to pray while Adah, not being able to do any chores, even the simplest task, found a quiet place down by the shore and sat there gazing out

166

over the sparkling waters of the sea. Though her mind often wandered here and there, she always returned to thoughts of how good God was to her and was filled with peace.

Philip came back late in the afternoon, hungry again. He sat at the table picking at the dried fish and dunking the bread in the aromatic sauce. Adah washed, as did John, when they heard the trumpet signal the close of the Sabbath. Adah saw Philip at the table and brought the basin of water over to him. He looked up from his food quizzically; he was almost finished eating. His sister whispered, "Let us end the Sabbath as we have begun."

Philip did as he was told for he remembered the night before, and that morning, and how right it all felt. He washed and prayed, "We give thanks to you, God of our ancestors, who has kept us safe in life. Preserve us in this life that we may serve you with all our heart, with all our soul, and with all our strength."

"Amen."

"Blessed be God," prayed Philip, lifting a bowl of aromatic spices from the table and inhaling the fragrance before passing it around for the others to smell, "May these spices remind us of the Sabbath joy which filled our hearts this day."

"Amen."

Taking the wine vessel, Philip filled his cup to overflowing as customary to symbolize the blessings of the Sabbath spilling over into the work week, "Blessed be God, who renews our strength. Grant us a good week, a week of peace; may gladness reign and joy increase."

"Amen."

Philip and Adah drank while John reverenced the wine as he had done the night before.

It was now dark in the house and Philip lit a new lamp saying, "Blessed be God, Creator of Light! Give us light for all our days, hope for the future, and we bid you, Merciful God, make haste in giving us the Messiah. Come, Lord, come!"

"Amen."

When all was done in accordance with the Law, Philip was filled with so much pride that he gave his little sister a warm embrace and said, "You have renewed in me a love for the beauty of the Sabbath. This past year I have appreciated everything around me thanks to my rebirth," he gave a nod to John. "Yet, out of habit, I have neglected to observe the Sabbath with due reverence. It was my fault that we grew lax in showing our gratitude to God. But thanks to you, Adah, my eyes are open to this beautiful, meaningful day."

"Thank John. It was – He taught me how to conduct the Sabbath," she explained. She was about to say it was because of John that she wanted to learn to do it properly, only that was not altogether true. Something else touched off a longing inside her that wanted to honor God in a special way on the Sabbath.

"Thank you, John," said Philip to his friend. "And now it seems that because I have neglected Adah's religious upbringing, I am again in your debt."

"I did nothing. In your hearts you know what is good and holy and pleasing to our God. You just needed to be reminded that we owe our complete love and devotion to the Almighty." John smiled at the brother and sister. Adah had indeed prepared a beautiful Sabbath and Philip rose to the occasion by graciously leading them in the ritual prayers.

Without further ado they all ate and finished their meal. As Adah began to clear away the dishes Philip remarked, "Someday you will make someone an excellent wife."

Adah blushed as she caught John's eye and he smiled at her. She felt warm all over. Did he know how much she had grown to love him and hoped to share his life? She prayed he felt the same.

John held her gaze. Her deep blue eyes glistened in the lamp light. There was a tenderness there that he found very appealing. Truly she was a sweet girl: respectful, earnest, thoughtful, generous, good...lovely. She lowered her eyes modestly and moved away from the table. John sighed. This was the first time he thought of Adah as a woman and there was no room in his life for the feelings that suddenly welled up in his heart.

There were not many fish in the net. Simon looked at the meager catch, then at the five men. "John and John. Why don't you both go for a walk. We'll sort this out."

The sun was at its zenith as the two Johns strolled down the beach. John liked his young friend and enjoyed their many walks together. For a lad of fourteen he was very keen. At thirteen, like other boys, he had finished his study at the synagogue school and become an apprentice following his brother, James, and their father, Zebedee, in the fishing business. Young John had loved to study the Torah and could express himself quite well on matters of the Law and held many insights into human nature.

"What is your view of the Messiah?" inquired John, wondering what the thoughts of the lad might be.

"I wish he were here now!" exclaimed the youth. "We need him now. It seems to me we have drifted away from our covenant with God and hardly ever, really and truly, long for the coming of the Messiah. As evidence of this I see how badly we tend to treat one another, being concerned only for our own welfare. Do you think the tax collectors are honest? Why do some charge more than others? Have you seen that Sadducee in our village?" At this the lad began to mimic him. "He wears his phylactery so large and tight on his arm and forehead that he lists to one side like one of our boats when we have piled too many fish on one side. The phylactery, like the mezuzah on our door posts, is an outward sign of our covenant with the Eternal, not a burden. And have you noticed those sanctimonious Pharisees who lecture the people on being generous to the poor while dressed in their purple and finery? It does not help that the Romans have got a hold on us, but something insipid has come over us and drained away the purity that befits us as the

Chosen People. If only the Messiah were here to lead his people. He would bring us back to Yahweh again…"

John was astounded to hear the youth speak so. His voice grew louder and louder with every word, and in his excitement pronounced the Ineffable Name of the Almighty, something not even the Rabbis would dare to do. How did this young man come to know all this when he himself had only just begun to observe the failings of the people? And he, who knew Jesus, still could not bring himself to openly speak of the Messiah. Why was his own tongue silent?

"There is no need to shout," said John, humbled, as he put his arm around the younger's shoulder. "I am in full agreement with you."

Young John looked up at his friend. He idolized the man beside him. He felt proud that the man took an interest in him, treated him as an equal and respected his opinions. He asked, "Do you think the Messiah will come in our lifetime?"

"Yes."

"Do you really think so? What makes you say that?"

"Your faith," said John with a lump in his throat and a pang in his heart. What stopped him from saying the Promised One is among us in the man Jesus?

Young John, always sensitive to others, heard the tightness in the man's voice and was reluctant to ask any more questions as they headed back up the beach.

XIII

"What is wrong with your sister?"

"Why?" Philip stopped folding the nets and crossed his arms over his chest and asked James, "What has she done?"

"Nothing," said James affably. "Only I greeted her yesterday and she just floated by."

Philip began to think. She was different lately - the last Sabbath and all. In fact, ever since John returned to stay with them, a change had come over her. It was subtle but, now that he thought on it, her eyes were always on John. Her concerns had become what he did, what he needed. Her eyes – Adah had the eyes of a woman in love. It was clear to him now. How was it he had not noticed it before? Philip smiled. His little sister was in love, and with a man he admired above all the rest. Philip said, "Adah has not said a word to me, but I think she is in love."

"With whom?" exclaimed James.

"Why are you so interested? I thought you were engaged."

"I am. I am. I'm asking for Andrew," laughed James.

By now all the fishermen had gathered around to listen and laughed. Andrew laughed too, glad to be included. He was soft spoken, yet he quietly took in everything and was the first to act if anything needed to be done. It was Simon who eventually said, "So, who is she in love with?"

"Why John, of course," replied Philip.

"My brother!?" James blurted out.

"Don't be a fool," said Philip. "John. My house guest."

"Ahhhh," all the men said approvingly.

"Quiet friends. He is coming," said Andrew, seeing John and the younger approaching.

"Yes. Not a word to John," said Philip looking over his shoulder. "I don't think he knows how she feels and you are not to tell him." Then to James in particular, "And you are not to tease Adah either."

"Me? I wouldn't do that," said James, drawing himself up tall. "She is like one of my own sisters."

"That's what I am afraid of."

"All finished?" asked young John.

"Just about," said Simon.

John did not stop by the nets but continued by lost in his own thoughts.

"Maybe he is in love too," whispered James.

Simon gave him the cold eye, then shouted after John, "Hey! Don't you want your pay?"

It was the fourth day of the week. Simon always gave the men their pay early: the day before the big market day before the Sabbath. Whether it was a good week or a poor one, the men always got their share. Simon became captain at thirty-three when his father, Jonah, handed down the business to him, the eldest son. Though he was firm, and many times gruff, he was always fair and all the men looked to Simon as a born leader.

John accepted his pay and headed toward the house. As he got closer he looked around for Adah; she was not in the garden and the house was empty. On the shelf where the family kept their supplies there was a jar that held the household money. John took it down and heard only a couple of coins rattling inside. Simon had given him six coins and he did not need all that to get what he needed in the market for his friends because Adah always seemed to have plenty on hand to give when he went off by himself. He dropped four coins into the jar.

"What are you doing?" exclaimed Adah behind him.

John returned the jar to the shelf.

Adah thought Philip had somehow been able to put more money into the household funds but now she realized John was adding to it also. "Philip would not approve. Nor do I. You are our guest," she said as she reached for the jar.

172

"Please," said John, intercepting her hand and holding on to it. "I cannot go on accepting your hospitality week after week if you do not let me contribute to the household. And Passover is coming next week. You will need the extra money for the Feast."

Adah let her hand rest in his though she dared not look up into his eyes lest he see how much she cared for him. She longed for John to ask her brother for her hand in marriage, but Adah did not want to openly sway him. Their marriage had to be his own desire.

She bowed to his words for she did wonder how they were going to manage Passover. At that moment she remembered the year before and that John went to Jerusalem for the Feast. She did not want him to leave, but she had no hold over him. Adah withdrew her hand from his and asked, "When will you be leaving us to go to the Holy City?"

"I decided not to go this year," said John recalling Jesus' suggestion that he stay wherever he was for the Holy Days.

Adah was suddenly filled with joyful hope and wanted to do everything possible to make his stay in Bethsaida a memorable one. So she asked with merry anticipation, "Is there anything special we should do for Passover?"

"Our God is good, give thanks! God's love is forever! Our Lord of lords, give thanks! God's love is forever! God alone does wondrous deeds! God's love is forever! God remembers our distress! God's love is forever! Holds out a mighty arm! God's love is forever! God in heaven be thanked! God's love is forever!" The words sprang involuntarily from John's lips. Earlier he had felt humbled when he heard young John's zeal for the Lord. It filled him with doubt, yet these words that just spontaneously came to him filled him with comfort and encouragement. They reminded him that no matter how he felt, or how long it took for him to begin heralding the Messiah, the Almighty's love was with him and deserved to be thanked and praised.

Adah was puzzled by John's strange response and asked, "Isn't that a psalm?"

John, lost in his own thoughts, did not answer.

"Yes," said Philip answering for him. He had just come in. "It is from the Hallel, a group of psalms we sing during the Passover season."

"John is not going to Jerusalem for Passover!" Adah informed her brother with a twinkle in her eye. "He is staying with us!"

Philip plainly saw his sister's happiness contemplating John's remaining as their guest. Yet, taking in John's reserve, Philip wondered how it was that his friend did not see how Adah loved him? He decided to give John a little more time before he would have to speak to him about Adah's heart. "Well then," he said, "We must plan a special feast. I have already asked Zebedee and his wife, and James and John to join us. Their sisters will be with their husbands and families." Philip walked over to fetch the money jar and was surprised when he upended it how many coins spilled out onto the table. "Adah, where did all this money come from?"

Stricken, she did not know what to say.

"You must be very proud of your sister. She is very skillful in handling the household funds and she is still able to save money for special occasions," stepped in John.

"Yes," said Philip, pleased to hear John thought favorably of his sister. "Yes, thank you, Adah. Because of you we will have the finest Passover we've ever had. Let us sit and plan."

Philip and John walked to the synagogue with a lamb trotting between them. They were sharing it with Zebedee and his family whom they would meet in front of the synagogue along with Jonah, his two sons, Simon and Andrew, and the rest of the community. It was a very warm for early spring.

By this time in Jerusalem the forecourt would be crammed with pilgrims from all over Israel. Families bought unblemished lambs in the Temple market to be slain on the stone altar where their blood would be poured out in remembrance of the passing over of the firstborn of the Chosen People by the Angel of Death and their liberation from Pharaoh's slavery.

As at the Temple, a stone altar was raised in front of the synagogue. John stood with the rest and watched as lamb after lamb was brought forward, slaughtered, its entrails cut out and thrown into the fire pit, then the carcass handed back to its owner to be roasted whole over the wood of the vine for the Passover feast.

The morning was becoming hot. Philip left their lamb, so docile and pure, with the others in the corral waiting their turn to be slaughtered. Blood oozed down the altar into gutters. The smell of burning offal filled the air. John had never been this close to the sacrifices. In Jerusalem the crowds were such you didn't see anything. He noticed a man robed in white standing among the yearling lambs. His chestnut colored hair and strong profile reminded him of someone.

John rubbed his eyes; he was tired. Simon had them working day and night for the last few days because Passover and the Sabbath fell alongside each other so there would be no work for the next three days and extra fish was needed to be shipped to the Holy City for the Feast. John looked again.

The man was closer to the gate. Then he stepped through the gate and stood behind the altar facing the people. It was Jesus! The priest helped Jesus onto the altar. Words repressed for many, many years came hurtling back into John's mind: '…for the salvation of all I will lay down my life for my sheep. I am the Lamb of God.' The revelation that Jesus would be sacrificed out of love for us for the liberation of our sins, once and for all, came crashing back into John's consciousness.

"Stop. No more," bellowed John rushing forward though the crowd to stay the hand of the priest holding the knife. He threw it down. "What care I for the count of your sacrifices, says the Lord. I have had enough of burnt offerings.

In the blood of lambs I take no delight. Who asks these things of you? Bring me no more meaningless offerings; these are loathsome in my sight when your hands are full of blood!"

With raised voice John turned to the assemblage and cried out, "You are an abomination in my sight. Put away your misdeeds; end your wickedness. Repent; learn to do good, hear the orphan's cry, protect the widow!"

Andrew and young John were immediately by his side trying to calm his sudden outburst. When he stopped, each took hold of an arm and led him through the crowd. Simon, James and Philip cleared the way. As they moved through the people, John caught the eye of this individual or that and exposed them, saying, "Slanderer." "Lecher." "Idolater." "Coveter." "Hypocrite." "Thief." "Honor your mother." "Merciless." He growled, "Sabbath breaker." "Blasphemer."

The community of men had pressed forward to see what all the commotion was around the altar, disrupting the ritual. The man doing all the shouting was the fellow who had a growing reputation in the village for mildness and being willing to help those in need. At first, he was only echoing the prophet Isaiah, but then, when he moved through the crowd with those burning eyes that saw right down into the very heart of a man and began calling out their sins, they ducked away.

Past the crowds John shook off the two at his side and ran ahead away from them all. He had to think of what had just transpired. When he saw Jesus was about to be sacrificed he rushed forward only to see the priest about to kill another lamb. This vision of the Lamb on the altar was given him to revive what he had buried long ago in his mind because of his unwillingness to accept the mission of the Messiah. Words exploded from his mouth, reiterating Isaiah with fury and might. Next, after he turned to those gathered for the ritual and saw only falseness, wickedness, the blackness of people's hearts, he was compelled beyond his volition to expose all their faults.

John feared he was losing his mind. All his life his path was aimed at helping others: caring, soothing, giving, and loving his neighbor. Was this love? Was this his path?

Trembling overcame him for he believed what was revealed to him: Jesus was the Lamb of God, a pure and willing sacrifice for the sins of us all! What a paradox: Jesus-man-God-Messiah-Lamb-of-God. And his own role as herald threw his mind into a turmoil. With his heart at the point of breaking, he cried out in prayer, "Jesus! My God! Jesus!"

The fishermen were stunned by the ferocity of their friend's words before the altar and followed in silence as John strode blindly ahead, heading for the row of houses that lined the shore. He was only out of their sight for a moment, when they turned the corner of Philip's house and were aghast to see that John had collapsed in the yard.

Adah came running from the house when she saw John from the doorway raise his arms up to the sky, then crumple to the ground. She had her brother and Andrew carry John in and lay him on a hastily unrolled sleeping mat. The others huddled inside the doorway, but Adah pushed them all out and closed the door.

She knelt by his side and felt his forehead. Beads of perspiration covered his face and soaked his tunic. Adah washed his face, neck and arms with cool water, then covered him with a blanket. While she did all this, she crooned softly the psalm he had spontaneously sung just the week before, "...remembered our distress. God's love is forever!..." He was restless. For a moment his eyes seemed to focus on her face, then they closed and he fell into a deep sleep.

Once John was asleep, Adah stepped outside to question the men. Their muffled and worried sounding voices caused her to believe something terrible had happened to John. James and John gave a vivid account of John's bold words and actions: stopping the priest from killing another lamb, quoting Isaiah, admonishing the people for their sins...

They all wondered what had come over John. It was so unlike him. He was generally reserved, good natured. Just Adah knew of his penchant for helping the poor. Given the unusual heat of the spring morning and their working night and day, the friends put down John's behavior to exhaustion and were satisfied that if he rested he would soon be himself again. So the men dispersed and Philip went back to the synagogue to get his lamb. And Adah went back to doing her chores as quietly as she could in preparation for Passover.

John opened his eyes. It was dark. Only when the glow of a lamp caught his eye did he realize that he was not in the lean-to he had constructed for his sleeping in the side garden. Rather, he was inside Philip's house. His heart took a sudden leap when he recalled what had happened at the synagogue. Distress welled up again and he covered his eyes with clenched fists.

"Do you feel any better?"

John lowered his hands and saw young John sitting beside him. He rolled over to face the wall. What could he say? What explanation could he give for his actions and words: his condemnation of the people? What gave him the right to judge?

Young John was speaking and, though John was hardly listening, the tenor of the youth's voice seemed to indicate approval and respect. "… to call to mind their sinfulness. If they will not admit their sinfulness how can they amend their ways, turn to God, and be ready for when the Messiah comes? Your passionate words were as though you were their conscience…"

"Conscience," murmured John, "not judge." He reasoned: if his example of love alone was not enough, and if by the power of the Spirit he was given insight to see clearly into the hearts of people, and was then, by the same Spirit, compelled to expose their faults, then, maybe, this was part of his path also. Or…John rolled over again to face his wise young friend and asked, "Do you think me sane?"

"How can you ask such a thing?" exclaimed young John with unbridled admiration shining in his eyes. "You are everything I want to be!" And in saying that the youth saw signs of relief on his friend's face. He helped John sit up and said, "My parents and brother are already here. I came in to see if you would care to join us. They have already started eating. The feast has begun."

"Yes, I will join you." John rose, feeling somewhat relieved in mind as well as grateful for the youth's confidence in him. He resolved that if this was truly a part of his path, he would put aside all anxieties and anything else that could deter him from following it.

"Here. Put this on. Adah made it for you. Philip has one just like it."

John looked at the white coat the youth held up. His clothes, even his Sabbath tunic, were old and worn. Adah was thoughtful. He would be glad to wear it over his tunic. Feeling the warmth of the coat, the image of Adah leaning over him surfaced, covering him with a blanket and lulling him to sleep with the psalm. She was a very caring person.

Everyone stopped talking when the two Johns appeared. John smiled awkwardly at his friends and said, "I am sorry if I caused you any alarm today. I am much better now." He refrained, however, from giving them any explanation of his earlier behavior. And because they were his friends, they were relieved that he was himself again and respected his silence on the matter, for no one could fault him on what he had said to the crowds in front of the synagogue since it was the truth and everyone knew it. Adah got up and ushered him to a place on the right side of Philip.

It was a pleasant evening to celebrate the Passover feast under the full moon. Everyone resumed their eating and the Haggadah, the telling of the Exodus, which is interspersed with conversation, blessings, and food. Adah took her place opposite John. While the others ate, she had selected the choicest pieces of meat, herbs and unleavened bread. As soon as John was comfortable she offered him the food, not by simply passing him the bowl or plate, but rather by dipping her own hand into the dish and handing him each morsel. He accepted.

Philip stared at his sister and then at John. He was not surprised to see John's coat; Adah had made him one just like it. To seat John next to himself, the host was not unusual since John was his dear guest. But to hand him the food in such a manner was too great a show of esteem, and Adah's unguarded face glowed with affection. And all throughout this evening John remained unaware of the honor and love Adah was bestowing on him.

John put aside his earlier tension and was oblivious to Adah's attentions as he listened to the narrative and chatted with Zebedee and his wife, Rivka, who sat next to Adah. The elderly couple had been married for many years and it was plain to see that they were very much in love. They reminded him of his own parents who were comfortable with each other and filled with mutual respect and devotion. Rivka's eyes shone with adoration when she looked at her husband.

"John?"

He diverted his look from the elderly woman to Adah. She handed him haroseth, the brownish mixture of almonds, fruit, honey and cinnamon that represents the clay the Israelites used in the making of bricks in Egypt. He took it from her and glanced into her eyes and saw… adoration. He gazed at her in disbelief, yet she held his gaze in return with such hope and longing that he could not deny what he saw: Adah was in love with him.

A shy smile spread over her face, her cheeks colored; she lowered her eyes. He thought back on all that she was: her simple goodness and the way she always had something for him when he was about to leave to help the poor, and her interest and honest desire to learn more about the Sabbath and Passover. Her comforting him earlier, the coat she made him, where he sat at table, how she handed him his food…all done to show her love. He put the mixture to his lips and tasted the sweetness.

His heart was moved; how sweet it would be to accept her tender love. At that moment John remembered his resolve of just a while ago and put down the haroseth.

John kept to himself the next few days of Passover, contemplating his experience at the synagogue and his path as he understood it now. On the second night of Passover, and on the Sabbath, at the meal he remained reserved, for Adah sat at table and each time he saw the young woman John felt the attraction of her sweet love, though she did nothing more to charm him. Adah's simple presence had become alluring enough.

On the first day of the week he was glad to be out on the boat working again. The mindless physical activity of rowing, hauling nets and sorting the catch gave him relief from thinking of the one thing or the other.

On the seventh day of Passover the men came ashore from fishing in the afternoon as Simon's wife, Gali, and the children, accompanied by Adah, came along, having just bathed and washed their hair a short way down the beach. They stopped to chat with the men. Simon, a big man, whirled his little girl up onto his shoulder and poked and tousled his sons until all three were laughing. It was clear for all to see that he adored his children and wife and took great pleasure in having them about.

John smiled at the happy family, appreciating their amusement. Unintentionally, his gaze shifted to Adah amongst the group and rested on her smiling face. Before he realized it she was staring back at him, reflecting such promise in her eyes if only he would.... He turned and walked away.

In the garden he thought and prayed and tried to stop his beating heart. He had devoted his whole life to the service of the Promised One. John recalled at thirteen how he had pledged himself to Jesus before he even knew the why or wherefore. He never expected to experience the love of a woman, the desire for children. He could not break one promise to make another promise. His heart ached.

John decided to begin his mission. The final day of Passover was tomorrow. Jesus and Mary would be back in Nazareth in five days, at least. He would leave Bethsaida soon after this coming Sabbath to tell Jesus his plans. "God Almighty," John prayed, for he still felt unsure, "give me knowledge and strength to do what I am to do."

"John."

He turned to see Adah standing there. She was lovely to behold with her hair freshly washed, loose, long and dark. Her skin was the color of wheat; a faint blush touched her cheeks. Her deep blue eyes gleamed like lapis jewels, her lips…

"I brought you your basket. The poor will be pleased that you remembered them on the final days of Passover."

She had taken a few steps closer. He saw in the basket unleavened bread, wine, Passover figs and other such things. Being so wrapped up by his own predicament, he had completely forgotten the poor. How did Adah know he ministered to his friends in the village? She was so precious.

Adah handed him the basket and their hands touched. His hand cradled hers. Neither moved; John did not turn away and Adah would not. Rather, feeling the heat radiating from his body, Adah, carried closer by love, rested her head on his chest.

John drew in breath suddenly as Adah's tender body leaned lightly against his. Strong sensations surged through his being. Still, he did not step away. Delicately he fingered her damp hair, stroked her smooth cheek. Then he felt the young woman slip her hand from beneath his and slide both hands around to the small of his back. Her sure, light touch filled him with such fire that he immediately let go of the basket and lost his hands in her long, dim hair, pulling Adah closer. Closer. His senses reeled with ardor, intoxicated by her clean fresh scent. All his desire was for Adah. John never wanted to let her go.

Yet, when he opened his eyes to look on the one he loved, he caught sight of the basket with its contents spilled out on the ground. His heart stopped. The woman in his arms was only a dream, a dream that would not come true.

Adah could hear the pounding of John's heart. Her being tingled as he caressed her face, then held her tight in his ardent embrace. She was in ecstasy when he dropped his defenses and responded to her touch. John loved her! Then, as passionately as he had pulled her close, he now deliberately moved his hands to her shoulders and held her at a distance. Her joyous expression faded when she looked into his handsome, noble face and beheld utter sadness. A tear trickled down his cheek. If he loved her, why? Love was a precious gift given to them by God. Her heart went out to him as she reached up to wipe away the tears. But instead of yielding to her touch, he turned his face and released her. She watched as he stepped around her, stooped to pick up the basket and methodically picked up each item, one by one, that had fallen to the ground. His hands shook.

Bewildered, Adah knelt down beside him and laid her hands on his back. "John," she said gently. He continued. "John?" He stood up and left. Adah felt crushed. A moment ago he held her in his arms; she was sure of his love. How could he walk away without a single word? She cried out, "John!"

Philip came home to the house, hungry as usual. He expected to see everything ready, but found the bread burning on the hearth stone, the vegetable stew boiled down to nothing, the place disorganized, and no Adah.

It was then he heard a strange noise; muffled cries. He followed the sounds and found his sister curled up on the ground, weeping behind the small house. Her hair covered her face. Philip reached out and at his touch she rose and cried, "Joh…" but as soon as she saw it was only her brother, she collapsed again weeping.

183

Philip took in the situation with her one anguished cry: Adah had given John her heart and he broke it. Night was falling.

Inside the house Philip did the best he could to comfort his sister. His heart broke to witness her pitiable state and raged that John would wound her so. As soon as he could Philip left to defend his sister's honor. This could not go on. Down along the beach he did not find what he was looking for. He headed toward the village.

A figure was coming in the opposite direction. Philip called out in the gloom, "John?" The man stopped before him. Philip tried to control his anger at the man he loved as a brother, the man who had saved his life. But this man had also just deeply wounded his little sister. He confronted John with the words, "She is crying."

John's eyelids became unbearably heavy and closed for his own pain cut like a knife in his heart.

The brother said bluntly, "Will you take my sister as your wife?" When his friend did not answer Philip said, "Adah loves you."

John set himself like flint as to reveal nothing of how his whole being burned with love for Adah and spoke without betraying his own emotion, "I cannot marry."

"Then give her no false hope. Do not return to the house," shouted Philip. "You are no longer welcome in our home. Or village." He would not have his sister exposed to his friend's, this man's, this outsider's presence anymore.

John submitted to his friend's demand. He handed Philip the empty basket and with a heavy heart said in a tight low voice, "May the blessings of peace be with you. And Adah."

Philip heard John's voice break as he whispered his sister's name and was astounded. John did love Adah! Only then did he notice how his friend trembled beneath the rigid exterior. "Why, John? Why?"

184

"Shalom," said John, meaning peace in its fullest sense. He shook his head at the irony of that single word 'shalom' that meant to walk with integrity in the sight of God in safety, wholeness, harmony, health, prosperity, and happiness; peace. How could his friend, Adah, or he live in shalom when his answer to Philip had to be, "I cannot marry. Farewell. Shalom."

Philip clasped the man who had saved his life in a tight embrace. He felt horrible that their friendship had come to an end this way, but for Adah's sake... "Shalom."

XIV

"John! John…" The sudden cacophony of cawing ravens startled John awake. He had pressed on through the night as long as he could to put distance between himself, Bethsaida and Adah. When he could go on no further, he curled up beneath a stand of trees.

Philip was right to send him away. Torn between his path and a woman John, on his own accord, was already planning to leave right after the Sabbath to see Jesus. But now this had happened.

When did he fall in love?

When he first met Adah she was a wailing child whom he comforted in his arms. Afterwards, she was so quiet he barely noticed her. When he returned to Bethsaida she was still quiet. And yet, she was eager to please, anxious to learn and earnest in her desire to enrich her spiritual life and to know their God. He recalled the fleeting notion of what a lovely and appealing woman Adah was becoming the night she and Philip renewed their love for the Day of the Lord during that beautiful Sabbath celebration.

So, it began in innocence. He had pushed aside his feelings, but from then on, without his even being aware of it, he was being drawn to Adah. And then, without warning, looking into her eyes on the first night of the Feast of Passover, he realized Adah was deeply in love with him and, to his utter amazement, he felt the same way towards her. All during Passover week he shied away avoiding her, unwilling to face the truth.

Hence, when John woke, his heart was pounding, hearing Adah's cry in the cawing of the birds. He had dreamt of holding her in his arms. He wept. It was only a dream. Adah was only a dream. Through blurry eyes John saw the sun burst forth above the horizon. Wearily he stood and with constricted throat prayed, "Hear, O Israel: the Lord is our God, The LORD ALONE. You shall love the Lord your God with ALL YOUR HEART and with ALL YOUR SOUL, and with ALL YOUR STRENGTH…"

"Oh hi, I'm glad you're back," said a bright faced boy to Mary and Jesus.

"We are glad to be home, too, Ansh," said Mary. She asked playfully, "You look as if you know a secret. Can you tell us what it is?"

"It's no secret!" laughed the boy. "There is a man in your yard. He's been there since early morning. Amma told him you and the carpenter were gone to Jerusalem for Passover and might not be back for many days and invited him in but he said he'd wait. So the guy's been standing there in the yard staring at your house all day."

Mary casually continued to talk to the youngster while Jesus went ahead. Her son had wanted to return to their home almost immediately after they arrived in Jerusalem, but they stayed in the Holy City until the feast was half over. The only person to incite such deep concern in her son was John. She wondered if it was he.

Jesus walked around the man who stood in his yard with legs braced, hands fisted at his side and saw John's set jaw and knitted brow. His whole bearing bespoke something was troubling his cousin.

"I am ready to begin," said John in an even voice with his face set like stone so as not to betray his inner turmoil.

"Why tell me?" said Jesus as he turned and went into the carpenter shop.

John was stupefied. How could Jesus be so indifferent after he had just told him he was ready to begin?

"Come in out of the sun."

John stomped into the workshop. "You are the Lamb of God!"

187

"Yes, I am," said Jesus mildly. "What is troubling you?"

John's declaration came out more harshly than he had intended and Jesus repaid him with concern. He turned from his cousin and picked up a mallet that was lying on the table and began to tap on the workbench. "I saw you...amongst the lambs. A willing sacrifice. The revelation...for forgiveness...of sins...." With each stroke of the mallet every phrase was accented, getting louder and louder. "And I...reviled the people. Is that love? I will not...be judge!" John looked over to see Jesus' patient countenance and steadied his shaking voice. "I saw evil in their hearts. I will be conscience, not judge."

Jesus gave a slight nod and took the mallet from John's hand. "What happened next?"

John did not answer for his mind was in a whirl between recalling how fiercely he had admonished the people on the preparation day of Passover and the discovery of love that night. He would not speak of Adah as she was something that was never meant to be. He concentrated on the events of the morning and finally said in disgust, "I sounded like the worst kind of zealot! I thought I was losing my reason!"

"That was because there was more to be said. The Spirit moved you to speak to the people, yet you allowed your fears to dam up the flow." Jesus spoke reassuringly, "The Spirit is with you always. You must learn to give yourself over completely to the Power that is within you. Do not struggle. Deny yourself."

John turned away bitterly, hugging the knowledge of what he had denied himself. He longed to erase from his mind the sweet torment of the last few days. That is why he had come to Nazareth to tell Jesus he was ready to begin his path. When John saw Jesus calmly working the plane on a plank of wood he blurted out in frustration, "Put down your tools. Be about your Father's business."

Jesus raised his eyebrows and said evenly, "Soon."

188

Again John had spoken out of turn and his cousin's ensuing silence bore into his heart.

"Go before me, John. Prepare the way."

Jesus challenged him to go. At once John realized he was still unfit to go forth. But what else could he do? He could not continue as before, especially now that his heart was divided and he loved...them both.

"John, what is upsetting you? It is plain there is something more." John did not answer. Jesus said, "I think it would be wise then if you gave yourself a little more time before you began."

John felt crushed under Jesus' gentle advice, for he felt he was failing the one person to whom he had devoted his whole life.

Mary appeared at the door calling them in to wash for it was dusk and the Sabbath was about to shine. After they washed Mary handed John a white coat saying it was Joseph's and it would please her for him to have it. John stared at the coat remembering he had left one just like it that Adah had made for him back in Bethsaida and felt a sharp pain in his heart. Mary saw how he gripped the coat and asked if everything was all right. He smiled weakly putting on the coat, yet the pained expression remained on his face throughout the Sabbath blessing.

Few words were spoken as they ate. John owned the fact he could not marry Adah so, determined to concentrate on his calling, he finally said, "Jesus, I will do as you say."

Jesus stared at his cousin for a moment, then asked, "Do you feel you have no will?"

"My will is not my own," blurted out John, involuntarily letting some bitterness show.

"What is your will?" asked Jesus.

John would not speak his desire. "I was born for one purpose. As are you."

"You have a choice."

"Do I?"

"We all have free will," stated Jesus. "I come to do my Father's will, Abba's love. And still, to be true to myself, I must listen to what I experience all around me and weigh it against what I feel the Father asks of me and choose to do the thing that is the most loving and good and holy. With our God there is no past or future, only the now. And at this moment all things are possible. The choice is mine. Yours."

Jesus' simply-said, awe-inducing words tore at John's heart all the more. Was he free to choose? How could he be when he grasped that he had been elected from birth to be Jesus' herald? A heart fettered by another love was not free. And yet John still and truly desired to do the will of the Mighty and Gracious One.

"I, too, have listened to the Most High and have found pleasure in living out God's love," added Mary.

John pondered his cousin. She was a woman like him, someone selected to do a great thing. He always knew her to be at peace, in control. "Was it always so easy for you?"

"We all have choices to make in our lives," said Mary carefully. "If we truly love with all our heart, soul and mind and trust in our God, it is simple, though not always easy. Whatever good we choose to do in our lives is the Most High's will for us."

John's eyes widened and then watered. Jesus was all good, the greater good, while Adah was a goodness of another kind. The anticipation with which John looked forward to heralding the Messiah had disappeared because of Adah. In truth, preparing the way for Jesus, the Messiah, filled him with much anxiety for though he had been walking, sometimes stumbling, along his path, John now felt as if he had lost his way. There was nothing he could say. He had made his choice freely a long time ago. John rubbed his palms into his eyes, thinking how he must go blindly forward.

Mary, sensing more needed to be said, spoke, "We are all tired. All of us have traveled far. Let us say good night and rise refreshed in the morning."

190

In the morning they went to the synagogue. Despite John's effort to pray and listen to the scriptures, his mind was often far away struggling with his desire for Adah and his love for the man next to him, Jesus. As they came out, Jesus met some friends and stopped to talk while Mary beckoned him to come away with her.

At home they placed stools in the yard and broke their fast. Mary studied her cousin's face while he ate and wondered about the gloominess that hung over him. Wanting to share in his concerns she asked, "Why are you sad, John? Can you speak about it to me?"

Somehow he was afraid to tell Jesus about his predicament lest it impede, or bring to ruin, the design of his proclamation of the Messiah. For all that, he knew he needed to voice his feelings, and Mary's empathy gave him courage. Still, he did not know where to begin, so he asked, "Did you love your husband?"

"Ah," sighed Mary at once understanding the question and John's sadness. "Yes." And she told him the story of her betrothal to Joseph and the conception of her son, of her stay in Ain Karim, of John's birth and her wedding in John's parents' home. She explained that the Most High's Son needed parents and that she and her husband were in awe and wonder that they, the lowly ones of the world, were chosen. She spoke of the love she shared with Joseph over the years; though never consummated, it was deep, rich and true, and of all the many ways they shared their love throughout their married life. The Most High had truly blessed them in their love for each other and in their son, Jesus.

Mary peered at John's furrowed brow and realized he was not comforted. She had been married to the man she loved and had a full share of an affectionate family life, save for that one intimate thing. She knew it was essential to a man to feel the love of a woman and to have children. She understood his sadness and, as she tried to smooth his forehead, could only say, "Love is a beautiful thing."

"Then why are my heart and soul being torn apart?" agonized John, grabbing her hand away and holding it in his grip. "Because I desire something I cannot have: a wife and family. I have looked forward to being the messenger of your son. I have dedicated my whole life to his life, to my path. I am confused. A woman has shown me another path and I do not know which way to go. On the first night of Passover, I looked across the table and saw her holding out her hand, offering me love. I tried to deny what I felt inside, but my Adah…"

Mary smiled as he whispered her name. "Adah? Tell me about her?"

He gazed at his cousin for a moment, for he suddenly saw how much Adah reminded him of Mary: they were good, gentle, holy. He looked down at his hands and realized in his impassioned speech he was squeezing Mary's hands in his grip. "I'm sorry," he said releasing them and petting them gently. She only smiled at him, encouraging him to answer her question. He had no words to describe all his love's attributes - thus he merely said, "She is goodness itself."

"Is she pretty?"

"She is lovely!" he sighed and went on earnestly. "I saw her every day and never noticed what a beautiful young woman she was until the last day when I saw her in the garden with her black hair flowing and her deep blue eyes…" He closed his own envisioning her and a tear escaped from the corner, "…I held her in my arms. It was lovely. I am ruined."

"No John, you are not ruined," reassured Mary. "Love is a beautiful thing; a gift from God. Together you will find a way to share your love."

"How can I when I am your son's herald? I know I cannot marry."

"What did Adah say when you told her?"

John stiffened for it was Jesus who spoke from behind. He had no idea Jesus was privy to their conversation. In a way, he was relieved it was out in the open and, by his cousin's question, surmised Jesus understood that his heart was still heavy because of the way he had left Adah. Not turning around he continued to address Mary, "I did not explain why I could not marry her. I left without a word."

"John, John," said Jesus resting his hands on his cousin's shoulders, "when did you learn to be cruel?"

There was no hint of rebuke in Jesus' voice, only a tone of sorrow, yet those words wounded him more deeply than anything he had ever felt before. It was true. It was a cruel and cowardly deed to leave someone you love without a word.

"You leave much unsaid," chided Jesus ever so gently. "Do not be afraid to express what you feel and say what is in your heart."

"How can I tell Adah that I love her and not fulfill her expectations?" cried John, finally turning to Jesus. "I know I cannot marry and raise a family like an ordinary man and also be your herald. I cannot divide myself, my.heart, my soul and do justice to you and a woman."

Jesus remained silent, so his mother spoke, "Do not be afraid to tell her the truth. If Adah truly loves you as you love her, then you will both find a path you can walk on. It may well be very hard. And after you do speak with her, give yourself time to rekindle your heart for you may have to endure a great deal for the Messiah."

John's mind leaped to what the Messiah would endure: the Lamb, sacrificed for our redemption. But that was not to be John's message. He was to be the Messiah's herald preparing the way of the Lord, to make straight his path. Somehow he was beginning to believe again that his own path was still open because of the compassionate words of Mary and Jesus. Both of them encouraged him to be honest with Adah and to withdraw for a time to renew his dedication. A peace descended on John and, rising from his seat, he was able to respond positively, "I am your servant. Tell me what I am to do and I shall do it."

"Return to Adah and tell her the good news."

"Very well," said John, resuming his seat and thinking how ironic the good news, and all it implied, would sound to Adah and mean to them. Yet, he would trust in Jesus' word, and in Adah's love, that all would be well.

While he mused on these thoughts Jesus said, "Why do you hesitate?"

"Do I hesitate?" asked John, confused by the other's question. Did Jesus mean for him to leave immediately? It was the Sabbath. To walk further than from one's house to the synagogue was considered excessive, work. Walking to Bethsaida was out of the question, it would be wrong. He had never broken the Sabbath.

"Go," said Jesus firmly. And when John hesitated again his voice rose, "Which is more pleasing to Yahweh: Not to walk on the Sabbath or setting a wrong right and comforting one you love? Do not be paralyzed by ritualism. It obscures the beauty of the Day. Go! NOW!"

The color drained from John's face as he took a step backward frightened by Jesus' flash of temper. Mary, at her son's side, gave John an encouraging nod when he looked at her and mouthed, "Pray for me." John then bowed formally to Jesus and departed.

John stopped in the road and half turned when he heard his name being called. Jesus was coming after him. What more could be said? He fully accepted Jesus' will and was doing his bidding.

"I am the Messiah. Do you believe in me?"

"Yes," answered John.

"I am the Lamb of God. Do you believe in me?"

"Yes," answered John in a hushed voice, clasping his hands to his chest for pain pierced his heart as he contemplated the idea of Jesus' sacrifice. He was determined, however, to put aside his own feelings and ideas and to trust explicitly in the Almighty's plans; he turned squarely to Jesus and assented, "Yes, Lord."

"I am the resurrection and the life."

Like a high wave on the sea Jesus' words washed over him. The statement bathed him with awe and wonderment.

"The Lamb shall be handed over, made to suffer and die. However, on the third day I shall rise again."

At that Jesus seemed, to John's eyes, to become radiant; his face shone like the noonday sun and his garments turned brilliant white. As Jesus' words soaked into his mind John sank to his knees, overwhelmed by the mystery and the glory he saw before him. He had never imagined anything beyond the sacrifice. Peace and joyful hope buoyed his being at that moment with the assurance that death was not the end.

"Do you believe in me?"

"Yes, Lord," cried John, prostrating himself and kissing Jesus' feet, so humbled and grateful was he to learn this good news. He remembered now all that Jesus had told him: the sacrifice of the Lamb was for the salvation of all who believed and the promise of eternal life. He could not bear to hear it all those years ago, but now he embraced the message with his whole being. "I believe, Lord."

"The hearts of my people have become hardened. They stop up their ears and say they do not hear, they turn away and say they do not see. Who will open their ears and turn their eyes so they may see and be converted; their sins forgiven? Who will go before me? Who will prepare the way of the Lord? Whom shall I send?"

"Here I am, Lord. Send me," cried John sitting back on his heels with arms outstretched, beseeching. "Send me!"

"Go then, John. The season is here and the day fast approaches. Prepare the way." With that Jesus blessed John, laying his hands on the other's head. When John looked up, the radiance, the glory, was gone. It was just his cousin again. But as they were about to go their separate ways Jesus smiled and said, "The next time we meet - it is I who will come to you."

"Dry your eyes, little sister," said Philip, finding Adah in the garden. The Sabbath had ended and darkness was all around. Philip had left his sister to herself that day, knowing she needed to be alone and grieve the loss of John. He went on cautiously, "John has returned and asks for you. He says he brings good news."

"Where is he?"

"Down the beach with the men."

Adah rushed to the corner of the house and saw a fire burning high down the beach with the circle of men seated around it. All save one, John. She began to run but Philip restrained her. When John appeared in their midst and asked to speak with them all, especially Adah, Philip wondered if his friend had come back for her. However, he reasoned: If John had come back for his sister, would not that be a private matter between himself, John and Adah, and not something to be discussed in front of friends? Philip held his sister in check gripping her arm. Her heart was broken once and the fishermen, their friends, were not unaware of Adah's feelings and of John's sudden disappearance the day before. He had cause to be wary and would protect his sister.

Adah was filled with hope. John's arms around her the other day proved his desire, yet the tears he shed told her the man she loved could not give himself to her. Adah felt crushed. And when he did not return, or rather the basket returned without him, she mourned John's going and the refusal of her love. She cried and prayed, pouring her heart out to God. If only John could confide in her his doubts and fears - she was sure nothing would be impossible for two people who loved each other. Adah was willing to do anything for him. And now her prayers were answered for John had returned with good news.

The fishermen were overjoyed when John appeared out of the darkness. They peppered him with questions, but he remained silent until all were present. Over the last two days they had asked Philip what had happened, but Philip would not speak a word, not wanting to defame his friend or expose Adah to pity. As brother and sister approached, the men became quiet and noticed the intensity with which John and Adah gazed at each other.

"Thank you for coming. Please be seated," said John barely above a whisper. He looked around at the men, his friends, sitting at his feet and flushed seeing their curious, expectant upturned faces. He cleared his throat and began, "My friends. I have been strange of late and went away without explanation. I have come back to tell you good news." His voice sounded weak. He averted his eyes to the fire to gain control, to find the right words... no, to lose control, to stop struggling, to surrender.

"The world is in darkness. The people have closed their minds, ears, eyes. Hearts have become stubborn following their own designs. The lowly and the just are taken for sinners. Where is justice? Where is mercy? The day draws near when the Promised One of all the ages will come to this waiting world. Heed my voice: I am called by One greater than I. Consecrated from my mother's womb, I have been given a tongue to speak to my people Israel: open your ears and eyes and hearts. Repent your ways for I, the herald of the good news of salvation, give a joyful shout: THE MESSIAH IS COME!"

John breathed deeply as his eyes focused once again on his friends. Never had he been filled with such burning passion. By the astonished look on the men's faces, he knew he had to speak on. Humbly he said, "I have not lost my reason. When the Spirit is upon me, like the day of preparation for the Passover, the words of the Almighty and Merciful One stream forth from my lips."

The men now understood John's uncharacteristic outburst at the slaughter of the lambs and all began talking at once with excitement.

John, embarrassed by their exuberance, raised his hands to quiet them. Speaking earnestly he continued, "Unlike the other day, when I was unwilling to give you an explanation of my words and actions because of my fears, I will say all that needs to be said: I have seen the evil in the hearts of the children of Israel. And yet, I have seen the glory of the Lord. An abyss, dark and wide, separates them. Yet, the Carpenter is building a bridge! And I, I call from the side of those in darkness, 'Come Lord. Lead us to your Light. Let your Light shine on us and we shall be saved.'"

The fishermen rejoiced at his words and began calling John a prophet. Filled with excitement and questions, they badgered him to say more. All John would say was that the season was fast approaching and he needed to retreat into the wilderness so that he might prepare for his mission.

One by one they came forward and asked for his blessing. Simon wholeheartedly hugged John and pledged his support. Andrew, who was speechless, could only stare in wonderment at the man. James predicted John would make a better prophet than make a profit in the fish trade. And young John was bursting with pride remembering how John had hinted not long ago that the Messiah would come during their lifetime.

Philip was next and John turned to him and said, "Do you understand why?"

"Shalom, John," his friend replied enfolding him in his arms. "May the peace and fullness of our God be with you always."

"And you."

Because Philip understood what was in John's heart he ushered the other men away so his dear friend and sister could speak privately.

They were alone. John beheld the beautiful woman, golden against the firelight, who had remained seated throughout his discourse and blessing. Her eyes were cast down; tears glistened on her cheeks. Tears welled up in his own as he pulled her to her feet and held her in his arms. "I love you, Adah."

She broke into sobs. She had prayed for his return and for him to confide in her, yet now that she heard why he could not be hers, she wept. She understood his words, respected him for his honesty and was proud of him. But her heart still wanted him and, as impossible as it may seem, loved him even more.

After a while she became quiet in his arms and he gently released her and gave her his blessing. When she was able to look up at him he said, "I am sorry."

Adah grabbed his hands, "Don't say you love me and that you are sorry. I love you and am not sorry. I will mourn, yes. But I am not sorry."

John looked down at their hands and remembered how earlier that day he had gripped Mary's hands in much the same way. He spoke tenderly to her, "It is true, I too am not sorry I love you. I am sorry that I am not another man who could take you into his home, love you, give you children, and grow old with you."

"Oh, John," her voice was sad but sure, "I would not have it any other way. You have changed my life in so many ways and I am grateful. I understand now that you are the Lord's chosen one and our God must always be first in your heart."

"Adah," as John spoke he brought their clasped hands to his breast, "but I want you to know that you will always be in my heart."

"You are the Lord's, not mine."

"Yes. And we must part." He sighed deeply and said, "Give me your blessing before I go." John felt her squeeze his hands tighter. Her mind knew what was right but her heart held on. "Adah, do you know the hand gesture the Rabbi signs over the people at the final Sabbath blessing at the synagogue?"

"No. We women all bow our heads for the blessing."

"Let go of my hands and I will teach it to you so you can give me your blessing."

Adah gazed up at him, "Is my blessing so important?"

"Yes!" he said with all his heart. "I cannot leave without it."

Tears started to flow down her cheeks again as she leaned close and kissed his hands before she released them.

"Put your palms like mine," he instructed holding his hand up, palms facing out. She did it. He said, "Now divide your four fingers; two and two, with your thumb spread out to the side. That is the first letter of the Holy Name of the Almighty, Yah."

Adah found it awkward to do, so she pressed her hands against John's to maintain the position but found her fingers interlacing with his.

"Adah, we must not hold on to each other so. Or thus," said John releasing his fingers and rearranging their hands into a firm clasp. "Rather, may we always hold each other without grasping; supporting, and being supported by one another through our love." As he spoke he rested one palm lightly on hers, receiving support while the other hand gently gave support to her other hand from beneath. Then slowly he guided her hands to an upright position.

"They look like hands praying," perceived Adah.

"Yes," agreed John. "Let us be this way: together yet separate; loving and free. Praying." He smiled when he saw she understood and said, "Do you feel the power as we touch? The power that is between us as we stand this close together?"

"Yes," whispered Adah. How could she not help but feel the energy between them?

John moved his hands ever so slightly from her palms, "Do you feel the power?"

Adah nodded. John took a step back. With his hands still out towards her asked, "Do you feel the power?"

"Yes," said Adah with a strange feeling of excitement in her heart as she held her palms out to John.

200

John backed away a few more steps. "I feel it. Do you?"

"Yes!"

Now outside the ring of light cast by the fire, his voice called from the blackness, "Do you still feel the Power?"

"Yes!" exclaimed Adah. Her heart was filled with joy, for now she understood how two lovers could be apart yet still remain one.

"That Power is love. Love is a blessing from our Gracious God. That Power is Love Itself! We are held in the loving hands of our Creator. How can we ever be separated?"

Adah raised her hands aloft in the Sign of Yah and prayed, "Dear God, bless this man whom I love. Give him the strength and the words to tell all people the good news of the Messiah's coming. Guide John and keep him safe and hold my John always in your loving hands."

"Amen, My Love."

XV

For six months John wandered alone. He left Bethsaida in the spring when the steppes were crowned with glory after the rains with scarlet and purple anemones, bright yellow iris, crocus and saffron, white narcissus and hyacinth. As the beauty of nature blossomed, John's heart was revived by the splendor of spring.

John was grateful that Jesus and Mary had encouraged him to speak from his heart to the woman he loved, and was pleased to have begun his path by proclaiming his mission as herald of the Messiah to his friends first, before retreating into the wilderness to contemplate and prepare for his role as the bearer of the good news. And with Adah's blessing he was freed to fully ponder the mystery and glory revealed to him, and ready himself for the unleashing of the Power of the Spirit that would gather all peoples to the Messiah.

As days turned into weeks the desert bloom withered and dried, leaving the ground brown in the summer's heat. The land was stripped of its glory. So too was he. The solitude of the wilderness stripped John of all pretenses, leaving his heart bare before the Almighty. Removed from daily labor, family, friends and love John cried out to his God to be his stay, his guide, his love. Only the Omnipotent could fulfill all his needs now. In that realization his faith grew hard as iron, hope anchored and strengthened his soul and, though his life still seemed black as night, he was consumed from within by a burning love that blazed as hot as the noon- day sun.

John became a student of nature. In the likeness of creation to its Creator, all that is true and always will be presented itself before his eyes. The promise of dawn during an endless night taught him to trust in the ever Faithful One. The constancy of God was displayed in the cycle of the moon in her waxing and waning. The cleansing power of a storm's fury that left in its wake a rainbow was parallel to the infinite mercy of the Eternal Judge.

One morning he awoke to find himself encircled by a flock of gazelle, quietly nibbling on the dew moistened grass. Not wanting to disturb their peace he remained perfectly still, surrounded by their gentle beauty. Yet, all at once, they stiffened, ears twitched, tails flashed and they bounded away hither and yon. A lioness raced across the plain and pulled down an old buck and within moments the whole pride joined in the kill. John's heart pounded at the ferocious beauty he witnessed. He stayed low and watched them take their fill, then move off to rest under a group of trees. Carrion birds that circled above now swooped down and picked at the remaining flesh. At dusk jackals howled and gnawed the bones. In the morning John inspected the scant remains which were being carried off by ants. John meditated on all he had seen and understood that though one perished so many were given the gift of life.

John walked the length and breadth of the land and finally came to the shore of the Salt Sea. The stark landscape and undrinkable water were in sharp contrast to the lushness and abundance of life that surrounded the Sea of Galilee. In their difference he found a metaphor between his worthless self and the Excellency of the Almighty God.

A young camel had died by the shore. John found it and thought it perhaps out of desperation, had tried to quench its thirst in the briny water. As he stood meditating on death, the wind whipped up sand. It stung his body. He realized how threadbare his clothes had become and how evenings were becoming cool. He decided to fashion himself a cloak out of the skin of the animal. It had been dead a couple of days; therefore the skin was already loose, so it was not hard to find a sharp flat stone to cut and peel off the hide. John brought the large piece down to the waterside and washed it in the salt water, recalling that tanners do some such treatment to preserve pelts. Then he spread and stretched it out to dry.

It was strenuous work so John rested by an outcrop of rocks that harbored a hive of bees and was fascinated by their busy coming and going. He prayed he would be that diligent in his mission. As the sun drew close to the horizon, he became aware of a humming sound. He looked up and saw a black cloud coming toward him. Thinking it was the swarm of bees returning to their hive, he crawled under the camel hide for protection. In an instant the buzzing was all round him although it was not so much a buzzing now but rather a clicking kind of noise. He peeked from beneath the skin and discovered it was locusts, not bees that had landed. To a farmer, locusts were a disaster that could devour a crop in less than a day, but to many people, they were a delicacy when prepared well. Suddenly, John felt hungry and started catching the insects. When he had collected a goodly number, he broke off their legs and cracked their bodies like a nut and ate the sharp tasting morsel. Then remembering the beehive, John carefully reached in and extracted some comb dripping with honey and feasted.

While he ate he tried to remember the last time he had eaten; whether it was days or weeks ago, he could not recall. He ate carob back in the mountains in the north but… it was true he had fasted in the past, yet now he just never thought of gathering food and was not hungry until this present moment. He marveled at the mystery of it all and thanked El Shaddai…Almighty God who nourishes and satisfies…for the abundant blessings of food and clothing.

Weeks had turned into months and it was autumn now. He always kept track of the days and would gravitate toward some small village when the Sabbath was approaching that he might worship in the synagogue. And it was thus, when he came to Bethlehem on the day of preparation, he heard not only the Sabbath trumpet but the long blast of the Shofar, the ram's horn, signaling the first day of the year, Rosh Hashanah, the day one's name was written in the Book of Life.

On the Day of Remembrance, Rosh Hashanah, the Rabbi of the synagogue bade the worshipers to emulate the holiness of Abraham and Isaac and Jacob as the way to salvation. This was the beginning of the High Holy Days during which the people would repent their transgressions against the Law with fasting and pray for divine forgiveness. In ten days, on the solemn feast of Yom Kippur, when their fate was sealed in the Book of Life, they would be pardoned and found acceptable in the sight of the Great Judge.

During the High Holy Days John quietly attended the services. Many priests, scholars and affluent men rose up in public and professed their need to reform their lives. On the last day the people processed out to a nearby stream and threw bread crumbs onto the water as a sign of their casting away their sins. John was aware that at the Temple, the High Priest would likewise be driving a goat with the sins of the people on its head over a precipice as the same sign.

John saw into the hearts of those around him and was not convinced of the depth of their repentance. He left after the ritual and made his way to the Jordan River. He realized deep within himself that now was the time: the fruit had ripened; the season was upon them all. It was time to gather all the people and prepare them in holiness for the coming Messiah.

At the river he threw off the camel cloak he had fashioned and shed his tunic and stood naked before his Creator. John raised his voice in supplication, "Almighty God and Judge, show your mercy to your wandering people. Let me be your Shofar calling out to your Chosen Ones a time of true repentance. I am your instrument. Play me, O Spirit of Divine Justice, that they may hear my call, repent their sinfulness and be a holy people ready for the One who comes. I tarry no longer. Have mercy on me, your servant. Wash away my iniquities and cleanse me from my sins!"

And with that, John cast himself into the river and submerged himself beneath the watery darkness. He held his breath until every fiber in his being felt as if it were about to burst, then rose up as if from a tomb, gasping for air and feeling reborn.

Mosallam rushed into the courtyard calling for his wife. Little Zechariah stopped playing and toddled over to his father who picked up his son and twirled the chubby fellow overhead. Zara came down from the terrace hearing the commotion and asked her husband the meaning of his early return home from the marketplace

"I have great news! A prophet has come to town!"

"Is it John?" Zara asked excitedly.

"We had just got our stalls in order and people were beginning to shop when a voice rose above the everyday hubbub," continued Mosallam without answering. "We quieted down to listen, then followed the sound. A man was calling to the people to repent their sins. He kept outside the market beyond the tax collector's booth. I don't think he had any money or else he would have come into the marketplace. When a crowd had gathered he began to revile the people for their sinfulness. He even directed his words to certain individuals. I know this for a fact because I could hear the gasps from this one or that when his words struck home."

"Was it John?"

"I don't know if it was John. His voice was loud and harsh. My friends told me the man looked like a wild-man with blazing eyes. His final words before he left were, 'Come with me.'"

"Did anyone go?"

"No. We were all too shocked by his words. But if he is the prophet I think he is, he won't give up and will come again tomorrow to call the people to repentance and this time we shall be ready to follow him."

The next morning Mosallam and Zara were not the only people waiting on the side of the road. Many from Ain Karim anticipated the prophet's return. Some were curious, some were just interested in the commotion the stranger stirred up, while others, like the blind man and his wife, earnestly wanted to hear the words of the prophet and follow him.

It was not long before a voice was heard. But no one was on the road; rather the voice came from below the terraced slopes. He was climbing up to Ain Karim, "Repent. Repent, oh Children of Israel. The reign of heaven is at hand. Your wicked hearts are an abomination before the Lord. Let not your fate be sealed in the Book of Death. It is not too late. Let those who have ears heed my words. Be cleansed of your sins…"

The townsfolk were awestruck as the man continued to rebuke them. When he finished, only a few people made motion to follow the prophet when he ordered, "Come with me."

When only a few moved, the prophet shouted, "Woe to you who hear my words but harden your hearts; you will not escape the day of the Lord. Come and be cleansed," and began to walk up the road toward Jerusalem.

Zara had steered her husband to follow after the first reproach. She whispered to Mosallam that it was indeed John. He looked different since they last saw him for he was long bearded and his sun-streaked hair was braided back from his intense face. He wore a camel skin over his lean bronzed body. His voice was no longer gentle.

Another group complied with the strange man's call after the second reproach. But the prophet stopped and hung his head for a moment. He turned around and faced the small group following him and said, "Take comfort my children." He passed through them and went back down towards the townsfolk for a third time. The people braced themselves expecting another reproach when they saw him returning. He stretched out his arms to them and raised his voice, yet this time it was full of compassion, "Comfort my children. The reign of heaven is at hand. The One promised us through our ancestors has come. His love is everlasting, his mercy infinite. The day of the Lord is at hand. Let us wash ourselves clean that we may welcome him without fear. Come with me."

The sound of tenderness in his voice and his words of encouragement touched the hearts of many more and they obeyed the prophet's command.

They walked up the road toward Jerusalem and were surprised when the prophet veered off, going around the Holy City. They had thought when he spoke of being cleansed that he was leading them to the Pool of Bethesda by the Sheep Gate where miracles were known to happen. Before that they thought he would lead them to their own spring with its pure abundant water or some other stream along the way. Now they did not know where the man was taking them so they prayed and sang psalms as they journeyed. The townsfolk were disconcerted when they began down the Red Ascent. Zara had to help Mosallam pick his way down the rough and narrow trail. Perhaps they were going to Jericho which had some fine springs and even a Roman bath. But they were not. The prophet led them through the wilderness and stopped at the Jordan River across from Bethany where the water was plentiful.

Evening was closing in on them and the people were tired and hungry from their day-long march. They drank their fill by the side of the river and picked wild ripe dates and nuts that grew along the banks. It was now dark and the prophet motioned for them to take their rest here at the oasis. Away from the comfort of their home-fires the townsfolk whispered among themselves about the now silent prophet and wondered why they had come and what the morrow would bring.

"Awake! Awake!" cried the powerful voice.

The people of Ain Karim scrambled to their feet in a state of confusion, wakening in unfamiliar surroundings.

"Make ready the way of the Lord. Make straight his paths. Every valley shall be filled and every mountain made low and all the ways made smooth; then shall all the children of earth be gathered to see the salvation of our God."

Alert now to what was happening everyone recognized the words of the prophet Isaiah and the promise of salvation.

But they remembered the harsh words this prophet had had for them the day before and tried to defend themselves, "We follow the commandments. What more does our God want from us?"

"Hypocrites!" roared the prophet, flinging off his camel skin and wading out into the river. "You robe yourselves with insincerity. Be earnest in your desire to love the Almighty and your neighbor." Bracing himself against the current he urged them, "Repent! Confess your sinfulness. Come to the water. Be cleansed of all your impurities. I will baptize you with water that you may be prepared for the One who is more powerful than I. He will baptize you with fire!"

Despite his urging the people stood hesitant on the banks of the Jordan. Mosallam could feel the tension of the people in the mix of the uneasy silence with the buzzing of the bees, the cawing of the birds and the rush of the water. He measured his own heart, weighing it against the words of the prophet and regretted all the things he had done, or left undone, regarding his family, his friends, his business affairs, his Creator. John had told him, when he announced the good news to the lepers just a few years ago, that Messiah was coming. If John, as herald of the good news, now offered baptism as a means to come closer to their God, he would not draw back. The blind man saw clearly what he must do. He removed his cloak and sandals and edged himself down the river bank into the water. The morning air was cool and the water brisk, yet he did not flinch from his resolution. Feeling the rush of the water he called out, "Take my hand. Baptize me, a sorrowful man who longs for salvation."

Instantly two hands grabbed his arms; Mosallam held on to the prophet's forearms which were sinewy and reassuring.

"Kneel down, my friend."

That was the voice of the John he knew. Full of trust the blind man knelt down and the waters lapped around his shoulders.

"Do you confess your sins and resolve to amend your life?"

"With all my heart."

"Lean forward and immerse your head."

Mosallam felt the Baptizer pull him forward a little and the water flow over his head. When he emerged from the water he felt enveloped by a sensation of profound peace and joy which he had never experienced before.

Standing in the water Mosallam's wife took hold of her husband as the Baptizer passed him to dry land. Zara had followed her husband into the river to help and as they began to leave the Baptist took hold of her wrist. She resisted the intention his clasp held; she was nothing like the woman she had been before in the Red Inn days. She had put that life behind her and was now a respectable wife and mother. Zara strained against his pull defiantly as he dragged her deeper into the river. She growled, "Let go."

"Pride is a sin, too!" the Baptist growled back.

Zara recoiled from his blazing eyes. John had never reviled her even when she abused him so cruelly that first time long ago when he held her wrist and said he was her friend. She became frightened and tears sprang to her eyes because she knew her faults.

"Lack of compassion is also a sin," he said softly to himself as he loosed her hand. "We are all sinners. The Messiah will soon be among us. Do you not want to be pure when you meet him again? Be baptized."

Zara emerged from the water rejoicing in the goodness of God, as did the others who came forward to be baptized that morning.

Whilst the people were organizing to leave for Ain Karim, the Baptist said, "Now that you have washed yourselves clean, put away your misdeeds, cease doing evil, robe yourselves in humility, kindness and mercy. Love one another. 'Be comforted my people,' says the Lord. 'Your iniquities are pardoned.' "

Mosallam and Zara lingered behind the rest - they hoped to speak with John. The Baptist stood by the Jordan. Timidly they approached, but they all ran to each other when John turned and smiled. They embraced with joyful cries. To Zara he said, "I am your friend." Together they laughed, remembering. To them both John said, "I wanted you to be the first to hear the good news and be baptized. Let us give glory to our wonderful God!"

The couple was overjoyed to discover that John was still the same warm man he had been before. John explained that when the Spirit was upon him, he was God's alone. When they were about to leave John saw how Zara was biting her tongue trying hard not to ask something. He laughed at her in a loving way and said, "What do you want to know?"

"What did you mean by, 'When you meet again?' Have I already met the Messiah?"

"Yes," answered John joyfully and volunteered the next answer knowing she would be beside herself until she found out who it was, "in truth, you have both met the Messiah. He is Jesus of Nazareth."

"Your cousin!" exclaimed Mosallam.

"My Savior," nodded John humbly. .

"That Passover, when we were all together, we discussed the Messiah with him and you said nothing!" cried Zara. Then she remembered how Jesus had touched her belly and the baby inside moved... came back to life! Her eyes widened as John nodded silently, reading her thoughts. She whispered, "Tell him I am truly grateful."

"He knows," said John, embracing her and then Mosallam. "Go now my friends. May the peace of our loving God be with you always!"

Adah ran to the seashore to interrupt her brother and the other fishermen with news from the market. "A traveling merchant up from Judea just told me that there has been a zealous holy man preaching by the Jordan River. He demands repentance and baptism for the forgiveness of sins," she exclaimed jubilantly, "And they call him John the Baptist!"

The men let out a whoop of joy. It was almost winter and John had retreated into the wilderness in early spring. He had begun his mission at last.

"I want to go to him," Adah told Philip.

"Oh, Adah," he sighed, noting her seriousness. "He is called to be a servant of the Lord and can offer you nothing."

"I accept that. I want to go and be in the service of the Lord, also. I want only to help him in his work."

"Adah," groaned Philip, questioning in his mind whether her motives were pure. Seven months ago she willingly let John go to prepare himself for his mission and seemed at peace with her decision. He was surprised by her request. Philip knew her not to be a foolish child in love with a dream, but in good conscience he could not let his sister go. He said, "It would be unbecoming of an unmarried woman to be following a man, let alone a prophet..."

"I'll go!" jumped in John. "I wish to be in the service of the Lord, too!"

"No," said James flatly. "You are too young. No."

Philip nodded in agreement: both of them were too young to go to Judea alone.

"I wish to go."

"What is this? A mutiny?" shouted Simon. Andrew, his brother, had made the request and he, at twenty, was no child easily led. If he wanted to do something, it was not to copy the two others; it was Andrew's own desire.

Simon, James and Philip put their heads together; it seemed, if truth be told, even they wanted to go but realizing their responsibilities could not. So, as a compromise, it was decided that the three younger siblings would go and represent them all with the stipulation that Andrew would be responsible for their welfare and, it was made clear, if one had to return for any reason, the other two would escort the other home. To this all the siblings were amenable.

Philip questioned his sister privately when they reached their house. "What will you do if John sends you home?"

"If John sends me home I will be disappointed. But I will be at peace," Adah spoke with conviction. "It will mean I am to do the work of God some other way, as I do now."

Philip had heard of his little sister's reputation for caring for the poor and ill. She seemed secure in whatever life held for her. And if she still loved John, it was not grasping or demanding. He believed she could be trusted to let John carry out his mission without hindrance. He was satisfied and gave Adah his blessing.

The very next morning Philip, Adah, John and Andrew climbed into Simon's boat and he ferried them across the Sea of Galilee to the southern shore. As the three disembarked they bade their brothers and friends a poignant farewell. It was the first time any of them would be separated from family and village to travel in Judea. Philip hugged his sister and whispered for her to come home soon. John had said his good-byes to James and his father and mother in Bethsaida before they left. Simon gave Andrew a pouch with enough money in it for three weeks provisions. He cautioned them to stick together, especially in Samaria, to protect Adah and, if need be, guard her safe return. And most of all to tell John they had kept him in their prayer all this while and would continue to keep them all in their hearts. Simon and Philip gave them a final blessing and the three were on their way.

Adah awoke and stretched. Three days had passed and they were sleeping in Judea. They had stayed close to the Jordan River because they were told that was where they would find the Baptist. The campfire was warm and burning high. She had just dreamt that someone was stroking her hair. She sighed and looked up to see the stars above and was surprised to see the dove grey sky of dawn. Adah recalled that as she drifted off to sleep the fire was merely glowing embers. She sat up. John and Andrew were sound asleep. Who built up the fire? Out of the corner of her eye she saw someone moving off. She whispered, "Who is there?"

"It is I, Adah. I did not mean to wake you."

Adah rose and hurried over to where John stood by the river. "We came looking for you and you found us!"

John smiled down at her and stroked her hair and asked, "Why have you come?"

"We want to be your disciples: Andrew, John and I."

"Why have you come?"

"I want to serve the Lord."

John stared at her solemnly for a while, then asked, "Do you love me?"

"Yes, John." And she spoke on as honestly as she could, "I confess I want to share your life. Thinking back on it now, in truth, I was your disciple from the first day you came back to us in Bethsaida after you left us that time to go to Jerusalem for Passover, though neither of us knew it. You opened my eyes to the beauty of our faith and taught me about respect and consideration for others, particularly the poor. You were an example to me of gentleness in action and word," as Adah spoke she held out her hands, then divided her four fingers in two in the Sign of Yah and joined them together so that her palms were lightly touching. "You showed yourself to be a man of integrity and holiness, prayer and love. Someone who could lead me closer to my God, someone I could give my life to."

John was silent, touched by her eloquence, and cast his eyes to the ground examining his own heart. He was illumined to the fact that Adah's love had grown pure and chaste as had his own. Time and grace had mellowed their passion and that was why, just a moment ago, he could so easily smile down on her beauty as she lay sleeping.

When he did not say anything and only stared at the ground, Adah presumed John thought it best if she did not stay. She, too, bent her head over her palms pressed together in prayer and humbly asked, "May I ask a favor before I go?"

John gazed at her in amazement; he did not say she had to go but because of his slowness to respond she was willing to leave without complaint if she thought her presence would compromise his path. He said, "What do you want?

"What I really came here for - to be baptized."

"Kneel down by the water side," he said, moved by her steadfast desire to be closer to the Almighty. "Do you confess your sinfulness and resolve to love our God with all your heart, with all your mind, with all your soul and with all your strength?"

"I do," Adah responded clearly. She shivered as the cold water drizzled over her head from the cupped hands of the Baptist.

"Rejoice! Put on a new life! Salvation is at hand!"

Young John woke with a start at the loud cry. Seeing Adah kneeling by the water and hearing the Baptist praying, he woke Andrew with a shove and they hurried over to join them.

Adah stood to the side as her companions, each in turn, knelt, were baptized, and pledged their hearts, minds and souls to God. Then all three men hugged joyfully and talked.

Afterward John called Adah over and said, "Andrew and John are going to stay as my disciples."

She was proud her two friends were going to remain with the Baptist. But she remembered and was embarrassed to say, "I have another favor to ask."

"What is it?"

"We promised our brothers that if one of us, me, had to return to Bethsaida the other two would escort that one home."

"I did not say you had to leave. You are not mine to command to come or go. Adah, follow your heart. Do as the Almighty directs you," said John honestly. "But I want to make myself clear: you said you would give your life to me; I am not the One. I am only his messenger, his herald." When John saw she understood, he continued, "For my part, I would not be averse to having a woman disciple." John laughed shyly, "Adah, you have not heard my outbursts. I often frighten people. Sometimes I even frighten myself. Thus a woman's presence may be helpful in easing the people's fears as they come to the Jordan to be baptized.

Adah was prepared to withdraw but was even more joyous at being accepted and exclaimed, "Then I shall stay, too, and be your - the Baptist's disciple!"

XVI

"Brood of venomous vipers..."

The Baptist had, a moment before, just finished telling his new disciples about his preaching in the towns and villages which had been so effective that people early on began to come to the Jordan of their own accord to seek him out, listen to his words, repent their sinfulness and be baptized. The Baptist had stationed himself where the three from Bethsaida found him, by the shallow waters near Bethabara, a section of the Jordan River where travelers and caravans could cross over easily to follow the trade routes.

A crowd of people had approached from the west. As soon as he saw them the Baptist was on his feet to scan the on-comers. Adah and her companions noticed the visible change that overcame John. Without hesitation the Baptist charged forward shouting at the top of his lungs, "...You cannot escape the wrath to come."

At the head of the group of pilgrims were the leaders of the area, the Pharisees. It was to them, mainly, that the Baptist aimed his words. It was they who protested, "Who appointed you judge? Abraham is our ancestor..."

"I am not judge," the Baptist declared, "but I see to the heart of things. I warn you, you whitened sepulchers, the Almighty is able to raise from these stones children of Abraham and Sarah worthy of the One to come."

The elders were about to refute his words but the Messenger continued, "You think you are solid as a tree? Show me your fruit. Every tree that does not bear good fruit is cut down and cast into the fire. Even now the ax is lying at the base. Bear fruit worthy of repentance. Dig into your souls! Root out all sin! Repent!"

The Pharisees glared at the man who challenged them while a few meek souls in the crowd called out, "What ought we to do?"

"Love your neighbor. Have you two coats? Give one to someone who has none. Have you food on the table? Share with those among you who are hungry."

A tax collector came to hear the word and asked, "Teacher, what should I do?"

"Do not deal shrewdly with your own people. Collect the just amount prescribed for you."

Even soldiers, when they saw the townspeople going out to the wilderness, followed them to the river, and absorbed in the moment asked, "What about us?"

"Be men of honor. You were sent here to keep the peace. Do not harass the people or extort money from the weak; bribe no one by threatening false accusations. Be satisfied with your pay."

The Baptist waded into the river and bade the people come. "Attend to the sound of my voice: anyone who abides by my words will bear much fruit," he said and continued, "the covenant with the Lord has been dragged through the mud by you ungrateful, decaying children of earth. Come and wash yourselves clean of the filth you wallow in. Be cleansed of every sin; rise from the mire for only those with a clean heart, pure eyes and open ears will be acceptable on the day of salvation."

The Pharisees seethed with anger when they saw all the people flocking around the Baptist to be cleansed. They feared they would lose their influence over the people and wondered by whose authority this man had the right to condemn, preach and baptize. They demanded to know, "Who are you?"

"I am not the Messiah."

"Are you Elijah?"

"No."

"Who are you, then?"

"I am the voice of one crying in the wilderness: prepare the way of the Lord."

"Why do you baptize if you are not the Messiah or Elijah?" they retorted, not satisfied with his merely quoting Isaiah.

"I will baptize you with water that you may be prepared for the One who is more powerful than I. He will baptize you with fire!"

At those words the Pharisees turned their backs on the Baptist, closing their minds to his words for they feared this one, mad ascetic, with his prophecy of an even more fanatic prophet to come, would upset the delicate balance of power they held in the shadow of their Roman occupiers.

"He comes to gather all the children of earth to Himself," cried the Baptist, chasing after them. "His winnowing fork is in his hand to clear the threshing floor and gather the wheat into his granary, but the chaff he will burn with unquenchable fire!" He followed them up the banks and down the road shouting, "He will baptize you with fire that you may be on fire with zeal for the Lord!"

When the Baptist returned, he took up his place in the Jordan and continued to exhort and baptize and proclaim the good news of the coming of the Messiah. There was much rejoicing among the people who accepted his words and they returned to their homes with the Baptist's blessing.

Adah, Andrew and young John sat spellbound throughout the day listening to the Baptist. Adah was more surprised than her friends because she had heard of his manner of reprimand from her brother only the day before Passover when John had rebuked the people in front of the synagogue. She was astounded for she knew John to be the gentlest of souls. She always respected the authority with which he spoke, yet now his words held so much more force - and how the words poured out of his mouth!

When everyone was gone John came out of the river muttering to himself, "They refused to turn and be saved."

Maybe one hundred people were baptized that day and merely a handful of Pharisees turned their backs on his preaching. Adah thought he should be pleased and wondered whether those who were not baptized deserved pity or compassion.

"They did not come to the Jordan out of faith. They closed their ears to my message of the coming of salvation. Tender words and compassion they do not understand or respect. I hurl my words against their hard hearts hoping to break their resistance. I fear they will not be ready when the Messiah comes."

"Do you condemn them, then?" asked young John, remembering the first night of Passover when John recoiled from the thought of being judge of the people.

"I am not judge. I do not condemn," said John evenly, knowing what his friend referred to. "But I see how stiff-necked they are. If they do not turn from their ways how will they be saved? I will not abide hypocrisy, or their questions, while others seek the truth." His voice was full of anguish knowing he did not reach all who came to the river that day. "Pray with me, my friends, that they will have a change of heart. Pray that our Lord will have mercy on them, and me, for I will not show them mercy; either they repent and are baptized or they doom themselves."

They prayed. The Baptist, practiced at meditation, blotted out all distractions and surrounded himself with silence. Inside he wept over his failings and begged mercy, pleaded for wisdom, courage and perseverance, and thanked, praised and worshiped the Almighty.

The three new disciples prayed for a while; however, they soon fell into whispering about the events of the day. Mostly they watched the Baptist's facial expressions as he prayed. They noted how he struggled within himself, but after a while his features softened and when he opened his eyes he was no longer the fierce prophet but the peaceful, good-natured John again.

John the Baptist and his disciples stayed by the Jordan River and ministered to all who came to hear the words of the prophet and receive his baptism of water. Young John's fervent enthusiasm inspired many people while Andrew's calm logic persuaded others. And still others, the women among the groups, were encouraged to approach the Baptist by Adah's gentle words.

Adah was also responsible for tending to their mundane needs. It was their custom to leave the river on the day of preparation to attend the services on the Sabbath at some town or village and preach to the people. On their way back to the river on the first day of the week, Adah would scavenge among the bushes and hedges for berries and nuts. But they never went hungry because, more often than not, the hundreds of people who came to the Jordan left offerings of food and the disciples were able to share with the poor as well as feed themselves; besides, Andrew and John always had a line in the water. Nevertheless, Adah became concerned for John since he never partook of their meals.

Usually, after a day of baptizing, while the men built a fire and Adah organized the food, John would cross the river to pray by himself on the other side. He encouraged fasting for all the disciples who joined him but never to the point of bodily harm. Consequently, it made Adah wonder when she began to notice that while she never saw John eat he was strong and vital, not wasting away.

Sometimes she followed him across the river after she had eaten and watched him immobile in prayer. She prayed also, but then left him to his solitude. After about a month of this she decided to ask him about it, and as she approached him she was stopped by a humming. Locusts fell out of the sky all around the Baptist. Immediately, John jumped up and dashed about like a child scooping up the insects. When he had caught a goodly number, he reached between the rocks and brought out a bit of honey comb and dabbed the morsels with each bite.

Relieved and awed by the mystery, Adah thanked El Shaddai for providing a feast for the Baptist and went back to report to her friends what she had just witnessed, as they also had wondered about John the Baptist.

Time went by and the crowds were growing in number. Thousands of people from all walks of life confessed their sins and were baptized. Disciples came and went. The Baptist kept young John, Andrew and Adah as a nucleus and let others go after he instructed them in prayer and fasting, and proclaiming the message of the good news, even to the point of giving a chosen few, like Apollos, the Jew from Alexandria, the authority to return to their homeland to instruct the Jews there and offer them the baptism of repentance.

One day, after the people had all gone home and the sun was sliding toward the horizon, Adah climbed the banks to the level ground to collect fuel for the fire. She gathered the dry brush into bundles and tucked them under her arms, all the while keeping a lookout for sticks. Her arms were full when she stooped down for just one more clump of dried grass before heading back to camp when, as she rose, she bumped into a man and dropped them all. She apologized profusely for her clumsiness and went to pick them up.

"I have come seeking the Baptist. Is he near?" asked the stranger, stooping to help her pick up the bundles.

"Yes," answered Adah. "I am on my way back there now. Please, follow me." She was embarrassed to have the stranger, a man, helping her and said, "Here, let me take them."

"No. I shall take them all," he said simply, taking the dirty sticks and bundles of grass from her. "Lead the way."

"Have you come to be baptized? Do you wish to be his disciple?" questioned Adah, sensing in this man a kindness, a generosity that she had experienced only once before in John back in Bethsaida. She continued, "It is late. John, The Baptist, has been baptizing in the river all day. Many people came to hear him speak today and have already started back for town. His preaching is often fierce, but really he is kind. So, if he is abrupt or harsh with you it is only because he desires all people to be ready for the day when the Messiah comes..." Adah blushed, wondering what had loosed her tongue to talk to a strange man that way. She glanced up and saw he was paying close attention to everything she said. He smiled so she went on, "It will soon be dark. You must share our meal and stay the night instead of trying to make it back to town in the dark."

John, informed by Adah that another had come, looked in the direction from whence she came and saw a man silhouetted in the flaming sunset. Feeling no urge to rebuke or exhort, but rather a pulling or a drawing of his heart, John merely beckoned the man to come.

The Baptist undid his belt, took off his camel skin wrap and entered the water. He turned to face the shore and almost became undone. John could plainly see the man removing his cloak was Jesus. When their eyes met John was unable to speak or move. His heart cried out, "It is I who ought to be baptized by you! How is it you come to me?"

"Let it be done so, for now. It is all in Abba's hand," came the silent reply which carried with it an assurance that John's own baptism was still to come. Then Jesus waded into the water obedient to the Father's design and humbly knelt before John.

John could not bear to see the Promised One kneel before him in this pool of shame so he lifted his eyes to heaven beseeching the Almighty for guidance, with unutterable groans from deep within his being because the Innocent Prince of all humanity had come to him to be cleansed from sin.

"Baptize!" he heard the command reverberate in his being.

John closed his eyes and soundlessly asked, "You would be totally one with us, Lord?"

"Baptize!"

Obediently, John cupped his hands and lifted the silty water above Jesus' head. As the liquid began to trickle down, John's eyes widened as he saw that which slipped through his fingers had become the purest of oil: clear, golden, fragrant. The oil flowed slowly, endlessly over Jesus' head, running down over his beard and shoulders, causing him to glisten as if the noonday sun was shedding its rays all over him. John murmured, "Truly you are the Anointed One, the Messiah of Yahweh."

The moment the Baptist separated his hands and raised them to praise the Father a dove flew down from the heavens and hovered over Jesus. "YOU ARE MY SON, THE BELOVED; WITH YOU I AM WELL PLEASED."

Thunder rolled in the clear sky startling the people journeying to town. Wind raced through the trees that lined the riverbanks, rousing Andrew and young John to their feet. Adah stepped back in awe for it seemed to her she heard astounding words. She had kept her eyes on the two men in the river and wondered why John was so still, like a statue, with his arms raised aloft.

Eventually, the two men, the Baptist and the baptized, came out of the water. It was difficult to say who assisted whom for they leaned on each other and continued to do so as they stood by the fire. By this time, the fishermen had come upon the scene and heard the stranger say, "I will retreat into the desert for forty days and forty nights. I shall return this way again."

John nodded and the other walked off into the direction of the last rays of the setting sun.

With the man out of sight Andrew helped the Baptist on with his camel skin, for John stood immobile, wet, and visibly shaking. Young John began to ask questions and persisted even though John stayed silent. Adah shushed him and led John closer to the fire. She could feel him trembling.

"Did you see? Did you hear?"

The three looked questioningly from John to one another.

"Did you?"

"The wind?" ventured Andrew.

"I saw a dove!" remarked young John at the same time.

John shook his head and spoke more plainly, "Did you hear the words from heaven?"

Andrew and young John shook their heads; they did not hear any words.

"They thundered from the sky!" cried John in disbelief that they did not hear it. "You are my Son, the Beloved; with you I am well pleased."

"I heard those words," said Adah, laying her hand on the Baptist's arm and added, "You spoke them."

John sank to his knees, curled over and covered his head with his arms, so overwhelmed was he by the thought that it was he who had spoken: his voice the voice of Yahweh. His disciples, his friends, bewildered by his words and actions, knelt down around him and also prayed.

By and by, John lifted his head and spoke to them earnestly, "After me comes a man who ranks ahead of me because he was before me. The One who comes after me is mightier than I. I am not worthy to unfasten the thong of his sandals. He, the man who was in our midst today, is the One of whom I preach, why I baptize. He is the salvation of the world. He is the Messiah!"

The disciples were amazed. As usual, the enthusiasm of the youth had to be expressed, but young John quickly silenced himself when he saw the Baptist's intense look. The Baptist said, "You will become his followers when he returns this way."

The Baptist's preaching increased in intensity and urgency. He cried, "Repent! I baptize with water, but in your midst stands the One who comes after me. He will baptize you with the Holy Spirit..." And the people flocked to the Jordan River.

Time held no meaning for the Baptist and he was stunned to see Jesus standing on the banks above the Jordan just as the sun rose one morning. How could forty days and forty nights have passed so rapidly, thought John, when there was so much more to be done; so many more people to be reached! All he could do was shout at the top of his lungs, "Awake! Prepare the way of the Lord!"

The Baptist had preached on the first day of the week in a nearby town and had led a large number of people out to the wilderness where they camped for the night beside the river. They were sleeping and Jesus, the Messiah, stood among them. "Awake! Awake! Behold the rising Son. See the glory of the Lord. With divine mercy he comes to save you! Repent! Here is your God!"

The townsfolk, startled from sleep, stumbled to their feet and rushed to the river past Jesus to John. Excitedly, the Baptist preached the presence of the Messiah while the Messiah looked on. All day he baptized and exhorted the people that he was not the One, only his messenger, and that they must look to the One who is now among them to be their savior, for that was something he himself was never meant to be.

When all were baptized and leaving to go back to their town, the Baptist saw Jesus moving off also. Quickly he grabbed Andrew and John by the arms and said, "Behold the Lamb of God who takes away the sins of the world!"

The two disciples did not understand the meaning of their Master's words, but heard the urgency with which he spoke and looked in the direction the Baptist pointed and spotted the man whom John had baptized forty days earlier walking off with the crowd.

"He is the Messiah!" uttered John, propelling the two from him. "Follow him."

Adah heard the Baptist's words and saw him pushing Andrew and John from him. She saw the man they followed; it

226

was he whom she had bumped into on the flat while gathering fuel, the man who John said was the Messiah. Her heart beat as she started up the embankment to follow, but at the top she paused to look over her shoulder. John stood alone. His eyes followed the man and when he was out of sight the Baptist turned and crossed the river Jordan.

She followed John across the river and at an unobtrusive distance prayed while he prayed. Suddenly, a cloud of locusts descended. She remembered the last time the locusts came was many months ago. To her knowledge John had not feasted since a time well before he baptized the man whom he called the Messiah. John remained immobile, so Adah gathered the locusts that had fallen from the sky and prepared them to be eaten. Then, as she had seen John do, she knelt before the rocks where the bees were flying in and out but was hesitant about reaching in for the honey.

"Here, Adah," said John reaching over her shoulder and retrieving a hunk of honey comb. He sat down with her and while he began to eat the locusts said, "Why did you not follow him?"

"Because you did not follow him," she answered simply. "I still want to serve the Lord by being your disciple. You told John and Andrew to go, not I."

"You ought to have followed him," sighed John. He saw Adah cast her eyes down and bite her lip. He was slightly disturbed by her remaining, while at the same time he was appreciative of her loyalty and dedication. He warned her gently, "I am just a man. He must increase while I must decrease. Do not put me above my Lord and Master." When she continued to bite her lip pensively he added, "Bless you for your faithfulness."

Adah looked up into the Baptist's eyes, and though they were steady, they were not stern. She smiled for she understood his warning and in her heart renewed her commitment to continue as the Baptist's disciple.

The next day only a small number of people came to the Jordan. After the last few weeks of intense preaching and baptizing it was not surprising. The following morning Adah awoke to find herself alone. John was neither by the river nor across it where he meditated. She waited and prayed, confident that the Baptist would return, and he did: alone. John had gone to the crossroads to preach, but no one followed him back to the Jordan that day.

"It is quiet," said John.

"Yes," agreed Adah. "I miss John's chatter."

John laughed. "Yes." It was only then that he realized that he had not spoken to her since the two other disciples had left almost two days ago. "I find the silence beautiful," he said, half explaining, half apologizing, "listening to the hundreds of little sounds that create silence."

John closed his eyes. To him silence was indeed beautiful; an ambience where one could retire into the stillness of the heart and be purified, rekindled and refreshed by the palpable love of the Almighty. The silence had made him whole when he retreated into the wilderness. In the silence he heard the voice of Yahweh speaking to the Son. A shiver ran down John's spine remembering that awesome experience when he had baptized Jesus and heard the Voice.

When he opened his eyes he saw Adah quietly sitting across from him. She was meditating but her expression changed from content to thoughtful to pensive. He asked, "What are you thinking?"

"About my brother, Philip."

"You miss him?"

She smiled and nodded timidly. How many months ago had she left her small fishing village and was now the Baptist's disciple?

"And?"

"And the rest of my friends. James should be getting married quite soon. Remember, he was betrothed about a year ago?   The harvest season is nearly over and the time for weddings to be held is almost here."

John was pleased that she was thinking about the future. He, himself, wondered in what direction the Spirit was going to lead him now that the Messiah was walking abroad.   Inspired by this opening she had inadvertently given him, John took the opportunity to say, "The Messiah has begun his way. I do not know if I am to continue baptizing or withdraw entirely. I need time to ponder these things. Would you oblige me a request and allow me to escort you back to Bethsaida? You would be home with your brother and friends again and be free to do as you are inclined."

For a moment, Adah was thrilled at the prospect of returning home and seeing Philip. However, she soon realized she would not be with John; she gathered he would not be staying on in Bethsaida.   She was willing to follow him wherever he went, to do whatever he did.   Nevertheless, she reasoned, if John asked this of her then this must be God's will. Adah would go home and favor his request but, whether she was with him or apart, she would still be his disciple. Adah pressed her hands together in prayer fashion and bowed in acquiescence saying, "I am your servant, Master."

"Goodness! Don't call me Master," John corrected her with a smile on his face, gratified that Adah was supple to the movement of the Spirit. "How many times do I have to say, I am not the One?"

Adah called John 'Master' out of the deep regard she held for him and was continually impressed by how humble John was in being able to brush aside any undue homage in such a light manner. Thereupon, she continued in a lighthearted tone, smiling herself, "Yes, Master."

"That's enough!" John laughed. "There are a few hours of light left. Let us be on our way."

When it got dark they stopped for the night. Though they had walked in silence most of the time, there was an easy feeling between them. They understood each other. It was only when they sat down around the fire that Adah wondered aloud, "How did you know that that man was the One?"

"In him all the prophecies are fulfilled."

She did not know which prophecies John referred to or how he knew they were fulfilled. What she really wanted to know was how John had recognized him, because she sensed when Jesus came to the river to be baptized that day John surely knew him. "Did you know him from before you became the Baptist?"

"My mother is his mother's aunt. I am cousin to his mother. So, I am his cousin, also. His name is Jesus."

"You've known him all you life..." marveled Adah, "...and knew him to be the Messiah!?"

"He is a Galilean from Nazareth. I am from Ain Karim in Judea. Our families met every year in Jerusalem for the Passover and sometimes his family would stay with us for a while. I did not know him to be the One until my twentieth year and even then I did not fully come to terms with his Messiahship until my thirtieth year when I truly began to follow my path."

Adah was impressed with John's candor, yet noticed how quiet John's voice became the longer he talked. He was not tired but full of awe, awed by something she did not comprehend - something which she could only guess at - the magnitude of his path and the reason he baptized.

Early on the third day of their journey to Bethsaida, outside the town of Tiberius on the east coast of the Sea of Galilee, they came upon a group of people also traveling north. Among them was a friend of Philip's, a man named Nathanael. At first the man looked at the young sister of his friend in a dubious manner, seeing her traveling alone with a strangely dressed man, but then inspiration dawned on him and he intuited her traveling companion to be none other than the Baptist all of Israel had been talking about. Immediately,

Nathanael fell to his knees and begged to be baptized for he so longed for the coming of salvation; the Son of the Most High.

"How is it that you know that salvation comes through the Son of the Most High?" asked John, astounded by the other man's words.

Bewildered by his own words Nathanael stammered that he only meant to say to be baptized.

John knew all too well the feeling of surprise and wonder at a mystery suddenly revealed without warning and put Nathanael's mind to rest, "Shalom, my friend. You have received a gift of knowledge from the Almighty and shared it with us. I will baptize you for the forgiveness of your sins, but know you are already near the kingdom."

After Nathanael's baptism, and of all those in the party with whom he traveled, John and Adah joined their company as they continued north. At the crossroads they paused. To the west was Nathanael's home, Cana, which was just to the north of Nazareth. John had a sudden urge to go and visit his cousin Mary and bring her news of her Son. But first he needed to escort Adah home to the northern rim of the Sea of Galilee. John expected to say farewell to his new friend when he learned that Nathanael was a relative of James' betrothed and was actually on his way to Bethsaida himself to finalize arrangements for the wedding which would take place in a few days. At this John asked Nathanael if Adah could join his traveling party and see her safely home to her brother.

John saw the look of disappointment on the young woman's face. He knew she wished they could all be together in Bethsaida again, but he reminded her of his need to be by himself and have the time to contemplate his path. "Until we meet again," said John, taking her hand in his as he gazed deeply into her eyes. He continued after a while, "Give my regards to your brother Philip and my blessings to James and his new bride."

As they stood together in that moment of silence, Adah felt herself to be his beloved disciple and was satisfied. She returned John's blessing and wished him well, bowed to her teacher and joined the other women who were traveling north.

Hence it was with peaceful hearts the Baptist and disciple went their separate ways.

The Sabbath was about to shine as John knocked on the door in Nazareth. He was dumbfounded when the door opened and there stood Andrew. Mary was behind him while Jesus and young John sat at the table.

"Welcome, my Baptist. Come in, come in, John!" cried Jesus waving him in.

But John felt awkward blundering in and stepped back out of the door frame. Mary, always perceptive, asked if he wished to wash and said she would bring out a basin and towel. John nodded.

Outside he could hear the youth remarking that he thought the Baptist was part fish on account of all the time he spent in the water and the laughter that followed. By then Mary had arrived with warm water and he was washing his face, the back of his neck, his arms up past his elbows... Washing was more than scruples or ritual to John; to him it symbolized a far greater meaning: to be cleansed of all impurity so as to be worthy to come before the Messiah, the beloved Son, on the day of the Lord.

Mary watched him knowingly. Wanting her cousin to be comfortable in her home, she also brought out a tunic, coat and sandals for him to wear and saw him hesitate, wondering whether these were Jesus' clothes or Joseph's. He sighed and put them on. When he was dressed Mary said, "Let me wash your feet after your long dusty walk."

Solemnly, and without protest, John sat on the bench and received this humble gesture of welcome performed by his cousin. She had a simple and giving way about her. He had always been inspired by Mary. The experiences of his life had taught him how to be a humble, giving, docile man, but she was always so.

Mary sensed John's apprehension and the awkwardness of the whole situation of his being present while Jesus, beginning his own path, was also present. Therefore, to ease the tension, she said with a sigh, "No webs. The way your friends talk I thought for sure I was going to find webbed feet."

John looked at his cousin incredulously, then began to laugh, hard, and threw his arms around the woman. "It's so good to be home."

As soon as John finished dressing in normal clothes he went straight into the house and into Jesus' arms. While they embraced they both said at the same time, "I'm so glad you are here!" They laughed, for the tension was completely broken and they could be completely themselves.

While his mother lit the candles making the Sabbath shine, Jesus took bread and prayed, "Blessed are you, God, Creator of the world, who has brought forth bread from the earth. Let us eat." He broke the bread and passed it to his friends around the table and they ate.

"He eats!" cried young John. "John never eats!"

"Never eats?" asked Jesus with wide-eyed astonishment.

"Adah says he eats locusts and honey," filled in Andrew.

"But that was many months ago," countered the youth.

"The locusts came the day you both became his followers," replied John quietly.

"Don't you hunger?" questioned Jesus, remembering how sorely he hungered in the desert for forty days.

"Yes," John's gaze penetrated deep into Jesus. "But not for food."

It was Jesus' turn to be awed; he understood his Baptist and was grateful.

"But as for tonight, while I am with you," John smiled, breaking the hushed atmosphere that had descended, "I eat whatever El Shaddai provides." And with a nod to Mary, he popped an olive in his mouth and said, "And tonight she has outdone herself."

"Master, how long have you known John?" asked Andrew, realizing the two had somehow made each other's acquaintance before meeting at the Jordan.

"I've known John all my life," Jesus exclaimed. "We are family. John, remember the time..." And the rest of the evening was spent reminiscing about their past, much to the delight of the two young disciples.

As the evening wore on John asked, "How is it that you came to be here?"

Young John piped up before Jesus could answer, "You sent us to follow the Master. And we did. We were walking in back of him when he turned around and said, 'What do you seek?' Well, Andrew and I were so surprised he had an accent like ours, Galilean. I said, 'Master, Where do you live?' And he said, 'Come and see.' And so, here we are!"

The Baptist smiled and put his arm around his young friend and asked Jesus, "Why are you here?"

"This is my home," Jesus laughed. "But really, Mother and I are invited to a wedding in Cana a few days from now and, it turns out, John's brother is the groom, so I am going to Bethsaida to meet him. And was it not you who told me I could find some good men there: the brothers of these two and their friend?"

"Where's Adah?" exclaimed Andrew, realizing she was not among them and remembering his responsibility toward her and Philip.

"Peace," said John. "As it turned out she wanted to return to Bethsaida again to see her brother and be present at James' wedding. On our way north we met Philip's friend, Nathanael, who happens to be a relative of the bride, and he and his group escorted Adah home since he had some arrangements to finalize before the wedding." The Baptist looked at Jesus and said, "Nathanael is another good man."

In the morning they all went to the synagogue. John, not dressed in camel skins, entered like all the other men and took a seat. Usually, he sat in the back not wanting to be conspicuous, but without fail he would be filled with the Spirit and would begin to exhort the assembly to repent their ways, to be baptized...

This morning Jesus was asked to read from the Holy Scrolls and give comment since he had been absent from their midst for such a time. He read from the prophet Isaiah, "The Spirit of God is upon me, because God has anointed me to bring good news to the humble of heart; God sent me to announce to the captives freedom, recovery of sight to the blind, the removal of oppression and to proclaim a year of favor." Rolling up the scroll and handing it to the hazzon, Jesus declared, "Today, in your hearing, this scripture is fulfilled."

All eyes in the synagogue were on Jesus for he read with such dignity; they were touched to the heart. Yet, his remark at the end made them wonder and they whispered among themselves, "Is this not Mary's son, the wife of Joseph?"

Jesus, knowing their minds, spoke out, "Solemnly I tell you, no prophet is believed in in his own home town."

The men became uneasy with the authority with which Jesus spoke and began to grumble, "Isn't he our carpenter?" "What right does he have to speak to us so?" "When did he become a prophet?" As Jesus tried to continue to teach them, the worshipers became more and more agitated, saying, "By what right do you lecture us so?"

"I say again," Jesus responded, "prophets are honored everywhere except in their home town and even among their own kin."

That offended the men in the synagogue even more and they moved as one to put Jesus out. With fists shaking and much yelling, they ran Jesus out of town and further up to the brow of the hill. Their village was built on the edge of a bluff. They would have thrown Jesus down over the steep hillside were it not for the eerie calm that descended on the crowd, making it possible for Jesus to pass through the mob without incident.

John's heart thrilled when he heard Jesus read from the scrolls and address the worshipers. But his blood rose when the community rejected Jesus and forced him from the synagogue. Because Jesus had begun his mission, John held back though his whole being screamed out to revile their blindness, their faithlessness, their pride. People were pushing and shoving. Outside the synagogue, John protectively caught Mary who was trembling with fright as she came down from the women's gallery. At the top of the hill the Baptist had had enough and stationed Mary between Andrew and young John and thrust himself into the crowd. It was at that moment all became silent and John saw why - Jesus had turned to face his people, the ones he had known all his life, and gazed at them with such love and mercy that the mob was sapped of their wrath; they were disarmed and allowed him to go his own way.

Back at the house John found Jesus in his carpenter shop, lightly touching the tools of his trade. Jesus said, "I will miss my wood working. And my home." John saw tears in his cousin's eyes. "I have begun, but my own do not know me."

The Baptist rushed in and knelt at Jesus' feet, and with his face to the ground he begged, "Forgive me, Lord. I have failed you. Bid me to leave your presence immediately and I will prepare your way."

"No, John," said Jesus lifting up the humbled man. "Stay with me today. Break bread with me. Pray with me. Tomorrow will be soon enough."

Just then Mary entered the shop and ran to her son; she had not feared so for his safety since the time he was lost in Jerusalem. She was heartbroken that their friends, neighbors and relatives had spurned her son. After they had comforted each other, Mary intertwined her arms with Jesus and John and said, "Come children, let us bless the Most High who has kept us safe this day. Oh, the mysterious ways of our God! We are together, so let us rejoice and be glad. Come into the house. Let us break our fast and give thanks."

When all three came into the house arm-in-arm and smiling, the two young disciples were relieved, for they feared their new Master was finished before he had even begun by the reaction of his townspeople.

While they ate, young John's mind turned to brighter thoughts as he anticipated his brother James' wedding. At one point he said, "John, come to Cana for the wedding. Mary and Jesus are friends of the bride and they will be there. So will all of us from Bethsaida."

"No," said John. His face hardened.

"Why? James loves you." cried the youth.

"And I him," replied John, softening a little, but went on, "Mary, where is my camel skin? Give it to me." John disrobed and put the skin on, fastening it with a belt. "This is why. You three will go off tomorrow, but I will stay and raise my voice against these dull, faithless people of Nazareth. And my voice will be heard in Cana, too, and in all of Galilee. I see my work is not yet done. Until then, I cannot rest."

On the morning of the first day of the week Jesus took leave of his mother along with his two disciples. It was just light and Nazareth was still sleeping. Outside the door the Baptist lingered behind; he wanted to prepare Mary for the onslaught of words that would reverberate throughout Nazareth and said, "These people have slept too long. They need to be awakened; therefore, my words will strike hard and to the heart of all those who rejected your Son."

"Will you call all the people of Nazareth to be baptized?"

"Yes. Once awake they will be open to the cleansing power of baptism and they, too, will desire to be made worthy of the reign to come."

"I wish to be baptized."

John stared at this ordinary woman; she was like any other widow in Galilee. Then, with his inner eye, he saw in this ordinary woman a heart so loving and open and free from any darkness or shadow that it instantly dazzled him. Her outward appearance showed nothing of the interior richness and beauty and wisdom that burned within her or the favor of the Lord that shone around her like glory.

"Oh, the secret way of the Most High!" said John and raised his arms in praise of the Almighty. He laughed joyously and said to her, "You are like a fish swimming who asks, 'Where is the sea?'" John exuberantly waved his arms around indicating everywhere.

"I could not deny your Son baptism." John spoke softly now as he let his hands drop to his side. "And I know now that that baptism was Jesus' complete surrender to be one with us, as well as being the anointing of the Messiah.

"Dear Mary," said John lowering himself to his knees, "What you desire you already possess and share with your Son. Do you not know that you have been pure love from your mother's womb? Rather," he said bending to kiss the hem of her garment, "I ask you to bless me."

John felt Mary's hand gently touch the top of his head and heard her say, "Let us bless each other."

John rose to his feet and tenderly encompassed her head with his hands and bending near, they touched foreheads. They stood in the street like that in silence for a long time, heedless of the villagers around them beginning their day.

When the Baptist did move away, he smiled broadly and, taking giant steps backwards, lifted his arms and raised his voice shouting, "Awake! The dawn from on high is upon you. The promise of mercy has come. Come out from the shadow of death. Repent!..."

XVII

The Baptist smiled. Inspired by this ordinary woman, the Mother of Jesus, and full of confidence in his mission as herald of the Messiah, John, brimming over with love toward the people of Nazareth, made plain to them their lack of insight in not recognizing the One in their midst. The Baptist urged them to be baptized with water that they might see with new eyes and hear with new ears and so come to recognize the man whom they ejected from the synagogue on the Sabbath as the true Messiah.

John's shout echoed throughout all of Galilee and many heeded his call. And as the time for Passover drew near, the Baptist began to make his way south passing through Samaria on the west side of the Jordan River.

Inasmuch as the Jews had nothing to do with Samaritans, the Baptist did not intend to preach in that region. Yet word of his righteousness went before him and they came out to meet him and begged the holy man to stay and worship on their holy mountain, Gerizen, where they, the true Hebrews, would offer the Passover sacrifice.

John argued for the truth. He did not deny that Mount Gerizen was a sacred place due to the altars of Abraham, Jacob and Joshua. But he testified that the Holy One's mount was, now and forever, Zion where David brought up the ark and made a covenant with the Almighty. The Baptist proposed that if they truly wished to give right honor and glory to God, they were to convert their lives and come on pilgrimage to David's holy city, Jerusalem, and there offer sacrifice in the consecrated dwelling Solomon had built for the Omnipresent. A few Samaritans accepted the Baptist's message of conversion, while the majority, because of centuries of division, refused to cross the line into Judea and accept that salvation came from the Jews.

By that time the streams of pilgrims making their way to Jerusalem flooded the road. On seeing the multitude, the Baptist exhorted the worshippers to offer honorable sacrifice by becoming as pure as the unblemished lambs they would soon be sacrificing. Rather than detour the faithful to the Jordan River from their pilgrimage to the Holy City, the Baptist imposed hands on all who confessed their guilt and blessed them on their way.

Entering the City by the Sheep Gate, John felt a wave of foreboding as he recalled how just the year before he had chastened the people of Bethsaida at Passover. He felt the same urge to revile the people of Jerusalem for their ungodliness as he slowly approached the Temple. First, he had to make his way through the marketplace filled with cattle and sheep and money changers. There were so many of them vying for business that they had, and for a long time now, occupied the forecourt of the Temple and threatened to spill into the portico and men's court of prayer. In the midst of it all, John paused to enter into that still place within his being from which surged the Power from on high.

Dressed as he was in his camel skin, the merchants recognized him immediately. The longer the Baptist stood motionless amongst them the greater their tension grew, waiting for his predictable outburst. Without warning a flock of pigeons and doves erupted from within the Temple. Animals began to skitter and jostle out of the archway. Men's angry voices were heard.

The Baptist, the one lone still point in the confusion, gradually opened his eyes and became cognizant of the furor and stormed into the portico to challenge all who dared disturb the holy precincts.

Jesus was the focal point of it all! Struck dumb by the uproar, John watched in amazement as his cousin swiped clean a table of money and weights and balances. Jesus then ran to another stall and released more doves. Simon, with Andrew's help, held back angry merchants while James and John engaged others in verbal debate. Philip and Nathanael, and other men as well, shouldered anyone else who tried to stop Jesus as he overturned more tables. Suddenly, one voice rose above all the rest, "Take these things out of here! Stop making my Father's house a marketplace! My house shall be called a house of prayer. But you, you have turned it into a den of thieves!"

John was close enough to see the glint in Jesus' eyes - tears. "Amen!" cried John and backed away, silencing himself from further speech. He recalled the time when he and Jesus were boys and his cousin had said he wanted to be about his Father's business. Now, behold, the Son was defending the integrity, the holiness of his Father's House.

From the shadows under the portico the Baptist took refuge from the commotion, yet stayed close enough to see and hear everything Jesus said and did. He saw the Pharisees and Temple guard approach to question the disturbers of the Holy Place. Not wishing to add to the clamor that disrupted the Passover celebration, and seeing the zeal the man had for the House of God, the officials asked Jesus for a sign to support his actions.

"Destroy this Temple and in three days I will raise it up," was his reply.

The Pharisees mocked him and dismissed him as a fool retorting that the Temple was forty-six years in the building. Jesus said nothing more. The elders thought it best to show clemency because of the holy season and allowed the foolish troublemaker and his followers to go their way with only a warning.

The Baptist bowed low in reverent awe hearing the Messiah's words, for he alone was mindful of the implication of this sign foretelling Jesus' death and resurrection. Hope, mingled with sadness, filled John's heart, for the Messiah had finally come to his own, to his Home, but the leaders of the people thought him a fool.

During the Passover John isolated himself from the crowds by praying in lonely places outside the city at night but then slipped into the Temple precincts at the first light of day. He kept to the shadowed corners so as not to attract attention to himself because he, as Baptist, had many, many followers among the worshipers. In no way did he wish to detract from the Messiah's mission. Along with everyone else he was entranced with Jesus' words and astounded by his power to heal.

When the holy festival came to an end and the pilgrims began their trek home, the Baptist took up his cry for repentance with new zeal inflamed by being in the Messiah's presence.

New followers gathered around the Baptist and consumed his every word. John was uneasy with this new lot for they were Zealots, a fanatical sect, who were drawn to his fiery preaching. Although they observed the strictest code of the law, they often took the law into their own hands and meted out punishment with concealed daggers on transgressors of the law, and they readily spoke of waging a holy war against Israel's oppressors, the Romans.

The Zealots looked to the Baptist as their spiritual leader. The more John reviled them for their duplicity, the more they were drawn to his zealous righteousness. The Baptist, abhorring all violence, denounced their tactics wanting nothing to do with it or them. Still the Zealots continued to cluster around him.

"Master, teach us to pray," asked a Zealot one day after observing the Baptist withdrawn into himself, morning and night, day after day, in prayer before and after baptizing in the Jordan.

"I am not your master. And you know how to pray," growled John, irritated by their outward subservience. "Our ancestors handed down the observances, prayers and benedictions which you learned at your mother's knee."

"Then tell us the source of your power."

"I have no power."

"Sir, your righteousness is beyond compare. Where do you get your strength, your fervor for the truth? If only you knew the power you have, thousands would follow you…"

"The truth?" said John, seizing the opportunity for their conversion. "You want to learn how to pray?"

"Yes," said the spokesman known by the name of Judas. All the others nodded likewise.

"Very well, I will teach you how to pray as I do, and where my so-called power comes from. Listen: there are times when one word spoken in the silent heart is the only word the Holy One will listen to."

"What do you mean?"

"Watch. I will show you my heart. And this, I pray, is how your hearts also will be."

The Baptist closed his eyes and inhaled deeply a few times. His shoulders relaxed and his head bent forward. In a while his eyelids raised a little. Fixing his gaze on the dead coals from the previous night's fire he went and sat down in the center of them. Scooping up a handful of ashes, he sifted them over his head, and with more handfuls dusted his shoulders, chest and legs. Tears streamed down his face. His lips quivered.

The Zealots were revolted by this show of abasement. When they saw his lips moving they concluded that he was finally, really praying and bade him to speak the words aloud.

"…mercy," he murmured a few times softly, then his voice gradually grew louder and more urgent. "…mercy… Mercy…MERcy…MERCY!"

Outraged, the men began to yell to break the Baptist's trance, for they were so scandalized that their leader would pray in such a fashion and bid them to follow his example. They had hoped he was the Messiah.

"I AM NOT THE MESSIAH!" blared the Baptist, jolted out of his trance. "Time and again I have said, 'I am not the One, but he who prepares the way.' That is my truth."

"Do you know there is another man preaching baptism where the Aenon River meets the Jordan not far from here?" said Judas. "He is drawing large crowds already. If we do not act now, his talk of peace, not to mention the wonders he is purported to be doing, will draw the people away from you and ruin our cause. You may be our last chance to restore the kingdom of David once and forever!"

"Now your truth is out," bellowed the Baptist. The Zealots were jealous for his sake and looking to make him their warrior king. "I am not who you suppose me to be. The One who truly is the king you desire – his kingdom is not of this world! I know he heals! Oh, that he would cure your blindness, your deafness!" Exasperated, the Baptist began shoving the Zealots away from him shouting, "Away from me you evil men. Go to him at the Aenon. Listen to him. He is the Truth! And woe to you if you believe him not, for surely the wrath of the Almighty will fall upon you!"

Finally they were gone. John was alone. And yet their presence, their odor of evil, still lingered. He paced the river bank trying to catch a breeze of fresh air but the air was dead. Killing thoughts entered his mind, and foremost was the sense that he had just let loose a falcon upon a dove.

Despite all his preaching and baptizing perverse men abounded. Were the children of Israel any more prepared for the coming of the Messiah than they had been before? Had his presence as Baptist failed? Fewer people were coming to be baptized. John wondered what he was to do now that Jesus was about his Father's business. He wished to become his follower, but he knew that was not his path.

Catching sight of Mount Nebo across the Jordan in the far east, John thought on Moses lying in his unmarked grave, forbidden to cross into the Promised Land because he had not trusted explicitly in the power of the Almighty and had struck the rock, twice, to bring forth the spring of water to quench the thirst of the Israelites in the desert. He questioned if he had

244

done all he could... Suddenly a feeling of aloneness, a total absence of any living presence, began to crowd in on him. Fear that the same fate would be his pushed into his mind.

He was alone in the blackness. It was as if the sun with its light and warmth had vanished from the sky. In this blackness John reached down into himself and pulled up his pride to combat these unseen forces that surrounded him. Along with it came temptations of anger and bitterness that he, the Baptist, should suddenly be left to himself. Had he not followed his path? Had he not baptized tens of thousands? Had he not prepared the way? And baptized Jesus? Had he not done all that he humanly could?

Humanly? Human. A mortal. A man of earth. Nothing but a man of earth. These last thoughts choked John with remorse for his conceit, as if he, and not the Almighty, was the one who had done all these things. John confessed that the Holy One was the Player, he merely the instrument. Sorrow for his lack of trust, his anger and bitterness, his forgetfulness, his pride... John wept and prayed, "MERCY!"

In his anguish John had fallen face down on the earth and begged God for mercy. And true to the lovingkindness of the Almighty, John's humble heartfelt plea was heard and he was again filled with light and warmth. Rolling over onto his back, John felt totally at peace and the energy of grace began to flow freely through his being. Words of praise and gratitude sprang from his heart and within moments he was up on his feet twirling and leaping about, glorifying God.

The sound of laughter made John freeze in mid-turn. At first he was embarrassed at being caught in such a fervent, and comical, display of devotion. However, when he looked over his shoulder and saw it was his friends from Bethsaida, he rushed to embrace them all.

Amidst the arms and beards and shining eyes and bright smiles and warm greetings, John felt a pair of arms encircle his waist and a wet cheek press against his side. Adah clung to him longer then she ought. John brushed his lips against her forehead and whispered, "Thank you, Adah." He felt her pull away, but he said, "Shalom," and kept his arm around her shoulder and close to his side while he continued to welcome the rest, then, naturally released her when they all sat down to talk.

"How did you know where to find me?" he asked.

"A Zealot," Philip answered, "came this day to Jesus and said, 'Master, there is a man baptizing and preaching down the river…' "

"TELL ME NO MORE!" exploded John. "Beware that…" John folded his arms across his chest and took a few deep breaths. "Forgive me, Philip. Friends. I did not mean to yell. Pray for that man Judas." His friends from Bethsaida looked at each other for no one had mentioned the Zealot's name. John saw their perplexed looks and waved his hand saying, "Let us speak of a more pleasant thing." And directing his gaze to the young woman hiding behind James said, "Are you not going to introduce your bride?"

"This," said James, pulling the woman to his side, "is Naomi. She has done me a great honor in becoming my wife. Already she is an anchor to my loose tongue when words storm out of my mouth."

The young bride blushed and smiled at her husband's words. John had understood that they were practically strangers to each other on the morning of their wedding, thus he was glad to observe an agreeable rapport between them. Spontaneously, in priestly fashion, John raised his hands over the newlyweds and prayed, "Blessed are you, Lord, Creator of joy and pleasure, love, peace and friendship. May this couple be very happy as once Adam and Eve were happy in the Garden of Eden. Blessed are you, Lord, who make groom and bride rejoice in each other when they become one soul in two bodies. And may this couple rejoice in the children you will bless them with."

"Amen!"

"Tell me about the wedding."

"Jesus performed a miracle at the wedding feast!" exclaimed young John before his brother James could answer. "His mother saw they were running out of wine, so she spoke to Jesus and then told the servants to do whatever he told them to do, and before we knew it, there were six more large stone jars filled to the brim with the best wine any of us had ever tasted."

John smiled, delighting in the miracle and at his loquacious young friend.

"And that is not the only miracle we've seen," attested James.

"Right," said Simon, speaking quickly so as not to be interrupted by the others. "Like the day Philip, James and I were called: we were fishing most of the day and had caught absolutely nothing when this stranger has the nerve to climb into my boat and ask us to put out a little and let down our nets. Well, I can tell you, I was in no mood, but something in his eyes convinced me to do it, and well, damn it, if we didn't catch the biggest haul ever. My boat was about to sink. James had to come and rescue us. The stranger sat calmly while all this was going on and when our eyes met he said, 'Follow me and I will make you a fisher of men and women.' The three of us, Philip, James and I, looked at each other, (Andrew and John were already following him) and we dropped our nets and here we are today."

"And how are Gali and the new baby? Where are they?"

"How did you..." stuttered Simon. He slapped his knees saying, "When will I cease to be amazed by what you, or Jesus, say and know and do?"

"Me?" laughed John. "I am nothing, just his worthless servant. But Jesus - may you all continually be amazed and moved to follow him always," replied the Baptist.

"Yes, I think we always shall," said Simon thoughtfully. After a moment he continued, "Well, anyway, my wife and new son and the children are with her mother in Capernaum. Did you know Jesus cured my mother-in-law, also?"

John shook his head as James interjected, "She wasn't sick; she just saw you and the lot of us heading her way and hid under the covers!"

Everyone laughed then grew quiet, lost in their own thoughts and marveling at all the wonders they had seen.

"Rejoice, my friends, and believe. Many signs and wonders shall you see." said the Baptist rising to his feet. "The prophecies of old have been fulfilled: 'Oh Capernaum: land of Zebulun, land of Naphtali, by the Sea of Galilee – on those who have sat in the shadow of death a great light has dawned!' The glory of God is upon us!"

It was time to be getting back. They all stood up and while they said their good-byes begged John to come with them to follow Jesus.

To this the Baptist replied, "I do not follow. I go before the Lord as herald, as decreed from my birth until my death, to prepare his way."

"Must you go alone? Do you not need followers to support you on your path? May I not serve the Lord with you? Do you no longer need me?"

John could clearly hear Adah speaking at the same time he spoke, yet, when he glanced in her direction, her lips were not moving. And she was staring across the Jordan at the wilderness that stretched out before Mount Nebo.

When John had bid farewell to all his friends he overheard Philip say to his sister, "Who knows what is in the heart of a prophet?"

"Are you blind? Could you not see he is covered with ashes and dirt?"

"He was dancing for joy when I saw him."

"I arrived well before you and the rest. I saw him a man of sorrow."

"And?" interrupted John. "Tell your brother everything."

With downcast eyes and her hands balled under her chin to keep her lips from trembling, Adah told her brother, "When I arrived John's proud head was raised high as he paced along the riverbank. But then the next moment he was on his knees, beating his heart with his fist. Then he sobbed and cried out for mercy and fell on his face and wept in the dust: such was the inner torture that bound him."

"And what did you do?" asked John softly.

"I prayed. From the moment I saw your agony, I prayed. Seeing you like that was breaking my heart...," Adah was speaking now to John but could not look him in the eye. "...And, indeed, if it had gone on much longer I would have gone to your side and eased your pain with my body."

"Adah!" exclaimed Philip horrified that she would compromise herself and the Baptist.

"Let her go on," said John calmly.

"But I am your servant, John," tears welled in her eyes as she sank to her knees. "So I only prayed and at last you became tranquil and let out such a sigh of relief and joy. It was then you did your dance." Adah buried her face in her hands and cried, "You don't need me."

Philip was frightened for his sister, that she, an unmarried woman, still had it in her mind to follow John, and tried to pull her to her feet saying, "Come away. You belong with us, following the Master."

The Baptist laid his hand on his friend's shoulder and assured him that all would be well and the right thing done.

"I will go ahead, Adah," said Philip. "Come when you are ready."

When they were alone, the Baptist spoke, "You indeed saw me when I was beset with evil. Thank you. It was your prayers that helped lift the unwholesome atmosphere that oppressed me." As he spoke to her he took her elbow and lifted her up, for she was still on her knees weeping. He continued, "When I felt your arms around me I was keenly aware of the battle your own spirit had just gone through and was instantly mindful of how your love is an embodiment of the Almighty's love and compassion towards me. By the support of your prayer, the purity of your love, and the Power of the Most High, we both were able to hold up our weaknesses and longings to our God and allow them to be transformed into strengths." He concluded with this assurance, "I will always need your love and your prayers."

Adah warmed to hear his words and thought on how she did love him and still wanted to be his disciple. Yet, how could she? Still not daring to raise her eyes to meet his gaze, she lifted them but a little and caught sight of the scar that ran across John's chest. She always wondered what could have caused such a wound; however, such questions were never asked of a man. In any case, Adah never wanted her love to hinder, imperil, or wound the Baptist on his path.

"Love and virtuous paths are both from our God," said John as he cupped her chin. "Your love and prayers invigorated me when fears and vainglory weighed me down. You watched over me and shared my pain." He smiled, and so did she when their eyes met for the first time. The Baptist said, "I am going to the river to wash. Come, let us purify ourselves and start anew."

After the ritual washing John the Baptist said, "As for being my follower – Are we two not one whether we are together or apart?"

"Yes, John, we are," answered Adah.

"Then you are to go your own way. Go where the Spirit leads you," said John the Baptist and began walking away. But he turned back to say, "Just know this: He, Jesus, must increase and I must decrease."

Adah began to mull over these things in her heart. She held up her two hands as John had taught her back in Bethsaida and felt the power between them: her love for John and her desire to sit at his feet as a disciple and to serve the Lord by being his follower, and the love she bore for her brother, her friends and the holy and gentle Master, Jesus. It was all there. She felt divided by two goods. She could hear her brother's words, 'Come when you are ready.' And John's, 'Go where the Spirit leads you.'

Lifting her hands aloft in supplication, Adah asked for a sign from God to show her which way she should go. She murmured over and over the Baptist's last words to her, 'He must increase. I must decrease.' Then, softly on the breeze, came a whisper, "Until he is no more."

A peace flooded over her. The words were foreboding, ominous, yet she now knew which way to go. For now, come what may, her life was with John the Baptist. With that knowledge such tranquility filled her soul that she praised the Holy One's goodness and mercy. Then, gesturing with her four fingers divided into two into the Sign of Yah as John had taught her, Adah blessed the direction of the ones she loved and followed the one she loved.

Adah had to run to catch up with John the Baptist. She remembered it was the day of preparation and he was making his way toward a town where he could worship on the Sabbath. When she caught up to him, she remained three paces behind out of respect, but to let him know she was there she said, "Shalom. Our God has directed that out of a thousand men, I am to be instructed in the ways of the Lord by you."

"Then know this," said the Baptist not stopping or turning, "Thus says our God: Faithful friends are a life-giving medicine and those who revere God will direct their friendships aright, for as they are, so also are their friends. And whoever finds a loyal friend has indeed found a treasure beyond price."

Adah's heart warmed anew by the Baptist's words, for he used her name, which literally means treasure, and knew for certain he was not displeased at having a woman as a follower, nor to call her a friend.

They had gone very far indeed that afternoon and were in view of Bethlehem as the sun began to set. A large flock of sheep blocked their direct route. When the Baptist and Adah began to wade among them a sheep dog, annoyed by their presence and for confusing the flock, came charging over. By its gait they could tell it was an old dog. They halted. The brown dog abruptly stopped barking, and with head down lumbered the rest of the way up to John with its ears back in submission, its eyes full of longing, wagging its tail. The dog sat down on the Baptist's foot and leaned its full wait on him. John rubbed her throat.

"Friendly old dog," laughed Adah.

"A dog will always know its true master," said the shepherd who followed the dog.

"Jacob," cried John as he gathered the man into his arms like a father who had been long separated from his son.

"You do remember me!" said the fellow, fighting back tears. "I came to be baptized months ago and you gave no sign of recognizing me though I knew you from the moment I heard you preach: the fire, the mercy and compassion."

"Shalom, my friend, I saw you coming to the river Jordan and my being rejoiced for your heart was as blameless as on the day I gave you into the hands of your father," said John. "How is Core?"

"He rests with his ancestors," replied Jacob. "He was true to his word and made me his heir. He even entrusted the welfare of his daughters into my hands. I have truly been blessed. But it is because of you that I am who I am today. Because of your generosity of spirit I am able to do right by my family and neighbors."

In the distance the Sabbath was being trumpeted in. "Please," said Jacob the shepherd, "share my Sabbath meal. I must stay with the sheep tonight. Come, join me."

As they spoke Jacob had been herding the sheep toward a corral. When all the animals were in he sat down at the gate's opening. "I am the gate," he remarked at the curious look of the young woman who sat slightly behind the Baptist. "There is no need for chains or locks out here; I alone am their protection. No wild animal can get in. Nor can the sheep get out without my knowing it. They trust me to care for all their needs." Jacob looked from the woman to John inquiringly.

"This is Adah, my follower."

"Welcome, Adah," said Jacob. Men normally do not speak to women other than their own family members and that only in private. However, if the Baptist saw fit to travel with a woman as a follower, who was he to question it? Meanwhile, he dug up from his pack two candles and flint and asked her to begin the blessing by letting the Sabbath shine.

The shepherd set out a simple meal. He invited the Baptist to lead the prayers and then the men talked about their lives. "When did you first meet?" ventured Adah and the shepherd told her how John had rescued him from a life on the streets and thievery. The tale ended with Jacob saying, "And John gave me his own dog, Spicy."

All throughout the meal and story Spicy sat in John's lap eating from his hand while John stroked her and rested his head close to hers.

Adah could see the undying gratitude in Jacob's eyes and marveled at the extent of John's selflessness. Her gaze moved from the man and his dog to the fields of grass and contemplated their beauty beneath the evening sky. She remarked, "In the moonlight the grass swaying in the breeze reminds me of the undulation of the sea." And Adah described her life by the Sea of Galilee.

Jacob took an interest in everything the young woman said and commented on how similar their lives were even though they lived in different regions of the country and the men she knew plied different trades. They agreed it was because they were both simple folk who lived off the land and trusted in their Creator and gave thanks for all the wonders God has done for them.

When the shepherd began talking about the yearling sheep he had sold last Passover and offered to show Adah the new spring lambs in the morning, the Baptist sprang to his feet, flung wide his arms and cried out in full voice, "The Father

Almighty will sacrifice his own Lamb and there will be no more need for further sacrifices."

In the silence that followed Adah noticed how the Baptist's eyes filled and glistened in the firelight.

John the Baptist groaned. He saw the concern in Adah's face and the alarm in Jacob's. "Peace, my children. Do not be afraid." Lightly he placed his hands on their heads and continued softly, "The Father will offer the Lamb he loves. The Good Shepherd will lay down his life for his flock." John blushed for his words were so inadequate. He tried to elaborate, "The Holy One's plan of mercy designed it to be so that you may have new life." Unable to make clear the profound mystery which exulted and grieved his heart, the Baptist strode away into the night.

The shepherd rose to go after him but Adah stopped him saying, "He goes to pray."

"He weeps."

In the distance they could hear the sound of weeping. "And for him, that too, is prayer," said his disciple, knowing the Baptist was responding to some inner mystery that only he fathomed. She had been with the Baptist long enough to know that all was prayer. She tried to explain, "You have heard him preach. His words are often a burst of fire. Most of the time, their flare exposes the hearts of others and burns with such intensity that they induce those who hear his words to come to the water to be purified and quench the fire. At other times, the Baptist's own words strike to the very core of his own being and he overflows with emotion." Adah paused. All was quiet. "He has gone within himself to pray now. Jacob, beneath all the fiery words there is the tenderest of hearts."

"I know," said Jacob. Then he asked, "Did you understand what he was saying, about the lamb and sacrifice and new life?"

Adah shook her head, "Sometimes, like now, his words glow with mystery. I know he speaks the truth, but I cannot grasp their meaning; they are like sparks of fire in the air. The

Baptist is a prophet and he alone possesses the full knowledge of their wisdom. He is God's trumpet blaring out a message that none of us will fully comprehend until the appointed time. Yet he goes on trumpeting the call of repentance and the coming of One greater than he, hoping that someday all will hear his message.

The next morning Jacob was relieved from tending the flock by his brother-in-law and went to synagogue with John and Adah. The night of prayer had renewed John's spirit and they all sang hymns of praise as they walked to Bethlehem.

After the scriptures had been read and the elders of the synagogue had spoken, the Baptist could not refrain from speaking of the Promised One and proclaiming his arrival. He spoke boldly of the Messiah and urged the worshipers to come back to the Jordan River with him tomorrow to receive the baptism of repentance.

When the service was over the elders followed the Baptist out and sought information from him. "We understand that you are not the Messiah and that you are only his herald."

John stared at them solemnly, for he knew their hearts.

"Since you are not the One, what we really want to know is: What do you know of this other man who is also preaching and stirring up the people?"

"Many things."

"Do you know his origin?"

"I go before him, yet he comes before me."

"How's that?" one asked.

"He comes from above and now his glory fills the earth," answered the prophet.

The elders whispered among themselves. They knew the Baptist to be a rigorously austere man, but this latest so-called prophet was preaching new things unlike anyone had ever heard before. Another said proudly, "We know the scriptures: the Messiah is to come from Bethlehem. Does this man come from Bethlehem?"

"He comes from Nazareth."

"That is in Galilee, isn't it? Nothing of any worth can come from there." They waved their hands saying, "He cannot be the Messiah."

"Nevertheless, it is for him that I baptize."

"Why? He is a no one," said one. Another said, "What name does he go by?"

"Wonderful!"

"That is not a name," a man muttered. An elder said, "It is claimed he does work wonders."

"Counselor!"

"They say he is wise." Many spoke at once. "I have seen this man and he is no older than this one." "He has not studied under any prominent Rabbi." "He has no authority to teach."

"Prince of Peace!"

"Is he the kind of man who could lead the people against our foes and free us from tyranny and oppression?"

"Everlasting Father!"

"He is quoting Isaiah," said a scholar. Another retorted, "Abraham and Moses are our fathers. Not this one." "Tell us, whose son is he?"

"Almighty Yahweh!"

There was an audible gasp when the Ineffable Name of the Holy One was spoken. The men fell back, covering their ears and eyes, for at that very moment a blinding light flashed all about. The elders tore their robes in protest of such a profanation. As one they grumbled and picked up stones to throw at the lawbreaker.

Adah had been on the sideline, standing with the women and townsfolk, taking in all that was being said. Toward the end she intuited that the Baptist was going into a trance. And when he uttered the Most Holy Name, he was completely enraptured; his whole being shone as he strained upwards to heaven, oblivious of all that was around him. It was then she noticed the elders picking up stones. She broke from the crowd and stood shielding the Baptist.

"Fool girl, get out of the way." "Whose daughter is she? Take her away," they yelled. "Don't protect a blasphemer." "Somebody get her away from that madman."

Adah turned to the Baptist and called his name, trying to rouse him, but he stood with arms, chest and face lifted high. Turning back again, she held out her hands and silently beseeched the elders and the others who were following their example by picking up stones. Wordlessly she begged them to show mercy and to be at peace.

The people were losing their patience and mocked her, "Are you his follower? Perhaps we should stone you, too!"

Adah cried out, "Don't! He is an angel!"

Now it was Jacob's turn to rush forward and stand between the elders, the Baptist, and his follower. He said, "Brothers. Peace. This man is a prophet known throughout the land. He is the Lord's messenger. Do not spill the blood of this holy man. It is the Sabbath; let us not mar the Lord's Day."

"He is a sinner," they shouted.

"Sinners shall all be destroyed," shouted back the Baptist. He had woken from his rapture. Laying his hands on the shoulders of his followers, he parted them and strode forward and said, "No future lies in store for those who heed not my words, nor believe in him of whom I preach." He stood face to face with those who intended him and his friends harm. The Baptist growled, "Who of us is without sin that any of us is free to cast a stone at another? Repent the evil within your hearts. Be baptized before it is too late."

With that he turned his back on the crowd and ushered Adah and Jacob quickly away. The three were quiet all the way back to the meadow where the sheep were grazing contemplating everything that had happened that morning.

When they had seated themselves at the campsite to break their morning fast the Baptist said, "Thank you, my friends. May our God protect us always."

"John?" asked Jacob curiously. "I am a humble man. I believe in your word and the message you preach, yet I did not understand the way you answered our elders' questions. Can you explain it to me?"

"For those who are humble of heart the answers are simple. To the self-righteous there is nothing to be learned." John laughed, "I confess, I was having a bit of fun with them. They asked me where he was from and I answered truthfully: the man of whom I preach is from Nazareth. Yet, he was born in Bethlehem and is of the House of David! Therefore, he is the fulfillment of that scripture, and others." And the Baptist went on to teach Jacob and Adah about Jesus, the Messiah.

XVIII

"Repent, oh House of David." That was the first thing the people of Bethlehem heard that morning when they woke on the first day of the week. "Oh Bethlehem, House of Bread! From you has come One who will satisfy your every hunger; the Promised One whose name is Peace. Behold, the Messiah has come! And he will reign over all of Israel. Prepare his way!"

Jacob took Adah aside while the Baptist preached, "He is returning to the Jordan and I must stay with the flock. But if there is anything I can ever do for John - I owe him so much - send word and I will be at his service."

By mid-day the Baptist was at the Jordan River baptizing all who had followed him into the wilderness. Many, away from the elders, clustered around him and hung on his words and begged to be made ready for the coming of the Messiah.

While the Baptist was still baptizing in the late afternoon a procession approached the Jordan to cross over at the shallows of Bethabara. It appeared to be a whole village on the move. In front were four horsemen riding black Arabian stallions followed by a unit of soldiers under a standard that bore a golden eagle on a field of blue. It was Herod's private army leading the royal household. A splendid palanquin, carried by eight slaves, veiled in green silk and embroidered with gold threads, shielded the reclining royal occupants from the sun and the gaping eyes of the rabble. It was followed by a smaller, but just as handsome chair litter carried by two men. More carts and chariots and horses bore other finely bedecked personages. They were Herodians, the Jewish nobility who, with Herod, collaborated with the Empire in hope that one day they would be rewarded by Rome with full governing power over their own land. Leading men of Galilee and Judea, as well as wealthy merchants, dignitaries and courtiers, rode in Herod's wake, eager to inflate Herod's ego and gain social recognition. Next were the court astrologers and magicians, musicians, acrobats and a retinue slaves. More soldiers brought up the rear.

Herod was moving his household after Passover and vacating his Jericho palace for his southern palace in Machaerus. His father, Herod the Great, had renovated the existing fortress on a mesa above the Salt Sea and transformed it into a resplendent place. Despite its grandeur, it was rumored to have a large arsenal of weapons and a huge cistern so that the citadel would be capable of withstanding a long siege if necessary. Also in its favor was the fact that it was far enough away from the prying eyes of Roman authority. It was said that this Herod, like his father before him, preferred this residence.

The people who had followed the Baptist lined the riverbank to watch the procession pass. Many began to whisper about mighty Herod's recent marriage. The Baptist was not unaware of the reason for the murmurs. His ability to read the hearts of sinners betrayed the royal couple's illicit union to which they had bound themselves, for Herodias was the wife of one of Herod's brothers, as well as being the daughter of yet another brother.

The Baptist turned to the whisperers from Bethlehem first. "Do not feel free to condemn others when your own sins keep you bound. Repent your sins and, if you will, pray for those who are far from the kingdom."

The people from Bethlehem, admonished, bowed their heads and began to pray while the Baptist boldly spoke out against the passing procession, "Thus says the Lord: A man shall cling to his wife and the two shall become one flesh. Woe to you who do what is evil in the sight of the Almighty. Woe to you who takes another's wife…"

The people trembled with fear because the Baptist dared rebuke Herod whose personal guard needed only a signal to put an end to the righteous man's denouncement and punish them all. A few of the guard did menace the Baptist and commanded him to cease, but he persisted fearlessly. When he saw that two servants had lagged behind and were listening to his words, John followed across the Jordan. Only after the guard had spurred on the two to keep up and the procession was out of sight did he stop.

Adah saw the Baptist standing on the other side of the river. There were still more people to be baptized, but she knew John the Baptist needed time to compose himself if he thought his words went unheeded. When he did cross back, she was relieved to see the look of contentment on his face. He said, "They heard my words."

That night, long after the villagers had departed for Bethlehem, John the Baptist and Adah sat in prayer after her meal. Suddenly, the Baptist's voice boomed out, "Draw near."

Voices called out in return and he went to the river and began to teach. Even though it was very dark, Adah gathered from what she heard that it was the couple who had lingered behind Herod's procession. They had harkened to the Baptist's entreaty for repentance and returned under the cover of night to be baptized. Adah built up the fire and invited them to warm themselves by the blaze. She offered them food before they headed back to Herod's camp. The Baptist remained by the riverside to give thanks and praise the Almighty God.

The man and woman, Cusa and his wife, Joanna, were servants in Herod's household. The two women talked as the husband sampled the food Adah offered them. He pretended not to be listening but often interjected here and there, this or that into their conversation.

"Adah!" cried the Baptist in a terrible voice.

She flushed with shame. She needed no more reproof than to hear the way he called her name. She and Joanna had been gossiping about the woman Herod had taken as a wife and Adah was repeating what she had heard from the whispering people of Bethlehem.

Though they were all a party to the situation, the prophet knew of Adah's instant remorse and addressed the other two, "Would you so quickly undo all you have just repented? Do not slander or spread rumor…"

"It is not a rumor," said Joanna, defending herself. "I am Herodias' personal maid and…"

"Do not say any more." The Baptist already knew. He saw it all in his mind when the procession approached and was filled with zeal to reprimand the Roman client-king and his blood relation, now wife, who considered themselves immune from the Laws of the Almighty. His hard silence silenced her.

But Cusa would not be silent. He knew the truth as well as his wife and stated, "Herod has married Aristobulus' daughter, who was married to yet another brother, Philip. Herod dared to shame his own wife by sending her back to her father Aretas, the Nabataean King of Petra.

"It is all because Herodias has bewitched him. With her father long dead, she is hungry to share in the power Herod now holds; she was not ashamed to be wooed away from her first husband and uncle. Those adulterers unabashedly married during the Passover celebration, of all times, disgusting the pious Jews in the Holy City."

"Her daughter is just like her in…" added Joanna.

"Enough!" shouted the Baptist. As prophet he issued a challenge, "Can you denounce Herod's sins to his face?"

Cusa blanched. Joanna covered her mouth. The husband sputtered, "It would mean death to anyone who tried."

"Then do not tear down what you are unwilling to rebuild." The Baptist continued in a voice free from all harshness, "Rather, pray for those ill-starred lovers that they may see and walk in the Light."

"Hear, oh Israel, the Lord is our God…" Under the starry night John the Baptist had followed the two servants of Herod and Herodias back to their encampment. Cusa and his wife safely crept back into camp as stealthily as they had exited.

The Baptist meditated as he waited for the morning light and when the sun burst from the horizon he prayed, "...the Lord alone."

Basking in the sun's brilliance, he ingathered the Spirit's power. Filled with the Truth and consumed with zeal for righteousness, the prophet's heart pumped, blood coursed through his veins, his breath deepened, and he was already in the camp before his bedazzled eyes could distinguish his location and was shouting, "Awake and hear me, oh wayward children of Israel. Awake!"

The drowsing guards stumbled to their feet at the roaring. A wildman had entered their camp; tall, lean and dressed in animal skins, the man strode toward Herod's tent. A strip of leather tied across his forehead framed his burning eyes while his long, sun-streaked hair was plaited down his bronzed back. It was the much talked about prophet from the river.

The guards, now alert, effectively blocked the Baptist's way so that he could no longer advance. Even so, he continued to raise his voice for all to hear, "Woe to those who bless evil and do in the daylight what is forbidden in the dark..."

And on and on spoke the Baptist, addressing his words not only to the royal couple in the tent, but to all those traveling with them, challenging the unrighteous and the self-righteous to true righteousness in the sight of the Almighty, that they might no longer be children of earth but rather children of Israel destined for the heavenly kingdom.

While the soldiers held back the servants and slaves who were inspired by the prophet's fiery words, the nobility came out from their tents and tried to justify themselves. No movement was seen from Herod's tent. Even still the Baptist knew they were listening. Herod was gripped by his words and restrained Herodias who was for putting an end to their denouncer right there and then. And it was by some perverse twist of fate that by the prophet's fiery words, and the royal couple's grappling, that their lust was fanned into flame and moved them to copulate.

The Baptist howled in outrage as his mind was seared by the scene his heart saw and he began to start away. He stopped and turned back after only a few paces demanding repentance. He said, "Turn back from your evil way; turn away from this path you follow. Come to the river and the Almighty will turn to you in great mercy."

No one made a move to follow him: not the merchants, the slaves, the guards, the unholy couple. He had pity on those among the travelers who longed for repentance but, because of rank or lack of freedom, could not outwardly follow him to the Jordan. John the Baptist faced them all and said, "The kingdom of God has come. Blessed are they who fear the Lord and walk in his way. Abandon this royal road you walk that leads to death, and come and walk on the holy highway that leads to new life!"

Adah had agonized over how John the Baptist called her name, for she immediately owned her culpability and was filled with remorse, fearing she had lost the regard of her teacher. She remained humbled until the Baptist and the two servants were about to leave and John crouched down beside her saying, "Peace, Adah." His face was illuminated by the firelight and she saw in it no reproach, only forgiveness and acceptance. She felt relieved. "Wait for me here," he said. "Pray for me. I shall return by midday."

The fire died down again and the moon was setting as she began her vigil. She prayed the rest of the night under the twinkling heaven and watched as the morning star faded into the dusty pinks of dawn. Adah said the morning prayers as soon as the sun broke over the horizon and implored God to be with the Baptist, knowing that at this moment he would be admonishing Herod and his followers.

At midmorning she moved closer to the river to escape the sun beneath the few trees that lined the riverbank and began to anticipate the Baptist's return. By mid-afternoon Adah became concerned when he had not come back. It was only when the sun reached the horizon that she guessed where he was and crossed the river and found him meditating in his solitary spot beside the bees' home in the cleft of the rock.

Adah advanced slowly so as not to disturb him. There were no locusts; his mission had been unsuccessful. His posture was rigid as he sat in the fading light of day. His lips were parched. Feeling his discouragement she went and fetched some water for him. "Drink," she whispered. He was not roused until she laid her hand on his shoulder and said again, "Drink."

John the Baptist inhaled sharply, flashed open his eyes and let out a long sigh. Seeing Adah and the gourd filled with water being held to his lips, he said, "I am sorry you were concerned." He took a sip from her hand. "I am well. Though, as you can see, no one had the inclination, or the courage, to submit to my baptism of repentance. Thank you for your prayers."

"They are all I can offer you as we serve our God together," Adah said simply and wished she could do more to further the cause.

"There is something more you can do for me."

"Tell me what it is. I am ready to do anything."

"Can you remain here, by yourself, for three days?" he spoke quickly. "I will not be daunted by their closed hearts. I mean to speak again to Herod and Herodias. I need to pursue them to Machaerus. I will have to charge them there with all the power of persuasion the Spirit grants me if I am to reach their hearts and lead them both to the true kingdom."

"I will stay here and pray and await your return," she said, obedient to her duty as disciple for she heard in his voice the urgency of the task ahead. "Go and do what you must," but she counseled, "It is a long journey and you have done so much already. Rest tonight, eat something, sleep and leave refreshed in the morning."

He agreed to rest and merely closed his eyes. Adah knew he would not eat even though she set out food. She wondered what kind of rest he got from sitting erect but soon saw his facial muscles soften, his shoulders relax and his hands unfold. As he rested she prayed for the success of his mission, then lay down to sleep.

"I will return in three days time," said John softly, waking her when there was only the faintest promise of dawn in the sky.

"I will be here," she answered. "May our God bless you and fill you with the Spirit."

A tall man, with torch in hand, ducked through the narrow door in the massive gate. The sun had set and the first watch of the night was beginning as he lit the other torches in their sockets along the wall and then leaned himself against the gate. As his eyes became accustomed to the night he caught sight of a form standing in the darkness just beyond the torch glow.

"Who goes there?"

No answer. The figure did not run as would one of the villagers who lived in the shacks outside the fortress if he had been spied lurking around.

"Who are you?" demanded the watchman. When the man did not answer the second time, the guard drew his sword with his right hand and lifted a torch from its socket with his left without turning his back. He advanced toward the stranger.

The light fell on the figure. It was the wildman the other officers had told him about on their return to Machaerus. They recounted how, twice, this skin-clad madman had attacked Herod and their group. The watchman eyed the stranger who stared past him. The man's eyes flickered in the torchlight yet, looking deeper, the guard discovered they burned with a fire all their own.

"Baptizer," the watchman addressed the man by the name by which he was known by – everyone throughout Judea knew of the man's renown. When the man shifted his gaze from the gates to him, the guard felt the Baptist's penetrating

266

stare. It bore down into his very soul. He was a mercenary, a soldier of fortune, paid well to protect the royal family as no Jews were permitted to join the army by Roman law. Coming up through the ranks by the use of his wits, brawn and ruthlessness he was now a leading officer, yet he felt suddenly uneasy facing this man. Mastering himself he ordered, "Leave before I raise the alarm."

The Baptist did not move.

Despite the thumping of his heart and as an act of intimidation, the tall soldier moved in closer and said, "The men will take as much pleasure in killing you as they would a rat." It was not a threat - it was a simple statement of fact. He himself had no quarrel with the Baptist as yet, and preferred to avoid any in the future. Though he was not a believer in the Jewish god, he appreciated that this man before him was a prophet and someone to be reckoned with. Besides, the watchman felt as if the prophet was somehow wrestling with his soul. "Be gone from here," he commanded and advised, "Your presence will have no effect on me - just as your words had no effect on Herod."

The Baptist did not move.

"I will have no part of you," said the soldier as he smartly sheathed his sword and strode back to his station at the gate. "Let your fate be on your head."

The Baptist was gone.

Through his morning prayers John could hear the village awakening. It was market day and people were taking extra care in setting up their stalls in the plaza before the fortress, for Herod had arrived at his southern palace with many guests.

John had withdrawn while the guard's back was turned and spent the rest of the night on a narrow path that skirted the fortress on the southern side. The fortress was built atop a mesa and its immense walls and parapets towered over the valley below. His journey the day before had led him through the desolate hills banking the Salt Sea. The spring rains did little for this region; nevertheless, from his vantage point above the valley, he saw a green oasis in the valley below. In the midst of the ochre, brown and rust-colored hills flowed a small river, the Arnon, which sparkled like a bejeweled necklace placed on a carpet of green velvet. John mused that a palace built like a fortress, with cisterns filled with fresh water and with easy access to the trade routes, yet some distance from the Roman center in Jerusalem which also housed a hidden arsenal at the ready, was indeed a small paradise for a man with ambition.

The Baptist appeared before the gates before anyone noticed. When the sentinels became cognizant of the man's presence, they grew tense fearing what could happen again. They had heard of what this madman had done just days before in assaulting Herod's traveling party. Word spread quickly among the village people in the market place on seeing the camel skin clad man - the mark of a prophet. They gathered around expectantly. Women who were fetching water from the well left their jars to summon those still at home. Even the elders joined in the semi-circle that had formed around the holy man to hear his words.

A hush fell as anticipation mounted. The unusual quiet drew the attention of the guards above on the parapet and they looked down. Some guests of Herod, who were enjoying the cool of the morning on the roof, followed suit and went to see what was happening below.

The Baptist turned his back to the gates and faced the villagers but spoke with full voice for all to hear, "Hear me, oh House of Israel, you who live in a false Garden of Eden far from the kingdom of God. Consider your ways. The King of Heaven is overcome with sorrow when you spurn his love by breaking the Law. Woe to you who claim to love the Almighty yet have done evil in God's sight against your neighbor, and yourselves…"

On and on he spoke, reducing some to tears by his emotional pleading for their repentance. Many came before him on bent knee admitting their sinfulness and begging for baptism. The Prophet was inspired to perform this ceremony not in the usual manner of leading the people out to flowing water, but by pouring over them water from the village well as a witness for all the stubborn on-lookers to see the great humility these simple hearts possessed.

The guards became uneasy at the villagers' increasingly loud demonstration of devotion and called for reinforcements. One of the first out of the narrow door in the gate was the tall guard from the night before. He took charge of the situation and instead of dispersing the mob, he ordered the villagers to line up and stop their wailing. His fellow guardsman questioned his actions but followed suit when they saw order was being restored. The tall guard, for some unknown reason, even to himself, felt impelled to facilitate whatever was happening and studied the Baptist. He found himself drawing closer and closer to the well to get a better look at the ritual and hear what the Baptist was saying. When the last person finished praying with the Baptist, the guard - a member of the Teutonic race: tall and fair with hair the color of flax and colorless eyes; not a common sight among the shorter, dark skinned Semites - found himself face to face with the Prophet.

"Clovis," the Prophet called him by name. "Our loving God comes to you, also. All who hear God's call are healed."

"Who? How?" whispered Clovis as a shiver of fear raced down his spine when he realized that this man knew not only his name but seemed, by his intense look, to know what ailed his heart and grabbed at his very soul. According to Jewish law, he was a pagan, yet could it be that their god loved him and knew the hollowness of his heart? The Teutonic was a man who prided himself on always being in control, but it shocked him to learn that he was personally included in the Baptist's call to new life and it stirred within him a queer longing to assess his life. It did not take much time to realize that his life had been one of violence and overindulgence in pleasures.

"Awesome is our God; a great King over all the earth," said the Prophet. "The Almighty sits enthroned over all the nations and judges with mercy and love."

Despite the drawing in his heart to accept this god's mercy and love, and his desire for a new life, Clovis could not bring himself to be humbled in front of the Baptist, the villagers and the other guards. He slightly bowed his head for a moment and said in a muted tone so none could hear save the Baptist, "Not now." Then he resumed his former posture of rigid control and said clearly, "Do you not fear King Herod here at his own fortress?"

"Whom shall I fear?" cried the Baptist, and in a sudden burst of energy, rushed toward the guards at the fortress. Surprised, they dodged and made way as the madman continued to rant and began to pound on the massive stone wall, "God is my Rock, my Fortress! This is nothing! I shall not fear. What can mortals do to me?"

Clovis was keenly aware of the danger on all sides; the guards would have taken hold of the Baptist were it not for his forcing them back. "Are you insane?" hissed Clovis in the man's ear, "They will kill you." He added louder so as not to be seen in sympathy with the madman, "Be gone or I will loose the men on you."

"No!" cried the Baptist and pulled away and yelled even louder to the people above on the parapet, "Repent. God loves you still! Return to God and you will live!"

The guards began to shout the Baptist down as the villagers, who were still assembled, called out for the Prophet to speak. Clovis, once again, took control and demanded order, saying with a sardonic laugh to ease the tension of his fellow guards, "Let him speak his piece. What could he say that you, or I, or Herod, for that matter, have not heard before?"

The Baptist smiled within at the cleverness of his friend Clovis who yearned to hear more and was open to the promptings of the Spirit; yet, to protect himself and the Baptist, in a crude way, gave him permission to address Herod and

Herodias who were, though unseen, above and listening to every word.

"Herod. Herodias. Children of the God of heaven and earth," cried the Baptist with outstretched hands raised aloft as one who beseeches. "Does not marriage reflect by its vow of love between spouses the covenantal relationship between the Holy One and the people? Why then have you broken your marriage bonds and entered into this twisted union?

"You are drunk on a heady wine. It has dazed you. The vagaries of the human heart have caused you to weave from your course in life. Come down from those dizzying heights. Make straight your ways. Come to the water, be refreshed, be purified. I know well it is a bitter thing I beg you to drink but think back, Herod, on that first wine you drank - your first love, your true marriage - and how sweet that was and how it was meant to ripen with maturity and mellow with age."

The Prophet paused to taste the atmosphere. It was dry and sour. The royal pair listened but was filled with revulsion toward the cup he offered them to drink. Zeal boiled within the Baptist and he vented his frustration against the couple whose hearts were sodden with lust and power. The Prophet said, "Thus says the Lord, our God, your Creator: Herodias, for this sin of yours you shall be barren from this day forth. Herod, for this sin of yours no sons and daughters will gladden your home because you have shamelessly taken your own flesh, your brother Aristobulus' daughter who was your brother Philip's wife, and have lived together in depravity."

The Baptist waited by the well the rest of the day for Herod and Herodias. A few who had not come forward before came and he listened to their sad whispered histories, counseled them, and poured water over their remorseful heads and prayed with them. The guards kept a tense watch, obeying Clovis' command to observe but not interfere. And when the shadows darkened the market place, the Baptist raised his voice once more, "Repent! The kingdom of God is at hand!"

XIX

The locusts came! Midmorning of the third day they came. While Adah was at prayer they simply dropped all about her and she gathered them up. She saw it as a good omen that the Baptist was making his return after being filled with the Spirit and that his mission was a success!

The day was hot and windy as she prepared for his return. She smashed the locusts with a rock and pulled off their heads, wings and legs and, with honey drawn from the cleft of the rock, made it into a paste. She beat the nearby bushes and trees along the river and came up with a handful of old berries, dates and almonds. She mashed these all together and made little cakes as best she could as a treat for John the Baptist's arrival.

Adah then collected wood and straw to have a nice, welcoming fire ready. The shadows were covering the ground by the time she finished and the wind of the day had calmed down. A layer of dust covered Adah. She decided to shake out her clothes, and went to bathe in the river and wash her hair.

Now she waited. The sun sank below the horizon and the crescent moon soon followed, leaving the dark sky twinkling with starlight. She would not eat, keeping her fast, until the Baptist was safely back and she prayed as the stars slowly glided across the sky.

All of a sudden she sensed a presence approaching in the dark. Hurriedly she built up the fire. She called out a few times but no answer came. Perhaps she was mistaken, Adah thought, only to feel all the more in her heart he was coming closer. Peering into the blackness she called out again.

"Here I am."

272

Adah ran out into the dark to meet him. With relief and in expectation of good news she exclaimed, "The locusts came!" When he did not respond, she sensed more darkness about him than night. Adah continued hopefully, "El Shaddai has prepared a feast in your honor."

"I saw your beacon from far off," he said with gratitude in his voice. "Come, we will eat."

As he walked he laid a hand on her shoulder. To Adah it felt weighty with unspoken cares. It was most unusual for him to readily accept an invitation to eat and out of character for the Baptist to touch her. She became anxious and longed to know what had happened. As soon as they were seated she said, "Please, tell me everything."

The Baptist related exactly all that had transpired since the time he left her and his zeal flared once more as he recounted every word he had said to Herod and Herodias.

His disciple sat motionless, listening intently, and when he had finished Adah bowed her head. After a moment, with head still lowered, she said, "Teacher? May I dare to ask you a question?"

"I am listening."

Raising her head, she stared directly into his eyes. Adah challenged him, "Was it you who cursed Herod and Herodias or the Creator of us all?" In her woman's heart she held the belief, as did every Israelite, that a person's life continued on through their children. "I pity them. Why curse? What does the Almighty feel toward them?"

John the Baptist inhaled sharply the Spirit. His eyes grew wide, then shut quickly so as to stop the tears from falling. He clutched his heart and his head dropped on to his chest as if he was pierced with an arrow. In a while he spoke, "The God of all mercies is heartbroken by their rebellion. I am overwhelmed by the feeling that the farther they run from God the closer, the more powerful is the Almighty's love for them!

"I did not curse them," the Prophet raised himself up again. "I foretold what would happen in the future if the present did not change. Our God is waiting for them with outstretched arms ready to embrace them.

"My words are like this:" the Baptist went on to explain, "Remember the first day we met, the day Philip had his accident? Did the fisherman tell you all that happened?"

Adah shook her head, "No, I really could not bear to hear of it."

"Well, when Philip was tangled in the nets beneath the water, Andrew dived in with his knife and slashed the nets to free him. When the fishermen got your brother to shore he was not breathing. The Spirit inspired me to push on your brother's back, to strike his chest with my fist, to breathe into his mouth to bring life into him."

It was Adah's turn to stare wide eyed.

"Peace. I did it so Philip would have new life." said the Baptist, seeing her wonder. He continued, "Such were my words to Herod and Herodias. My intent was to slash away the tangled nets they live in that they might be free of it. They are in a stupor from that heady wine they drank; they are drowning and close to death, though they do not know it. My words are meant to push and pound away all their desire for power and lust. My words are to purify and cleanse their souls. My words, also, are to breathe new life into them that they may be newborn, the children of God they were meant to be.

There was stillness between them as Adah took in all her teacher said. She understood his intent better now. At the same time, she was awed that he would humbly accept critique from a disciple.

"Thank you, oh daughter of Wisdom," said the prophet, breaking the silence between them. "You are truly a daughter of Wisdom. In your search you have found Her. By grace you have been given a share in the divine life and reaped the secrets of knowledge, temperance and prudence, justice and merciful compassion, and fortitude. Blest are you!"

Adah blushed at the Baptist's words of praise and spoke modestly, "If I am, then what of you? It is not I who am renowned and glorious as you are." She smiled and continued, "Blessed be our God who never fails either one of us at any given time or place." The Baptist was about to say something in return when she said, "As for temperance, El Shaddai has laid out this feast. Say no more and eat."

By the time they had finished their meal it was very late, so Adah lay down to rest. She had been cheered to watch the Baptist eat and savor every morsel. He once told her, when she asked, that he never took a vow to fast but was fed on solitude and the Word. Still, it was hard for her to understand. Yet the soundness of his body did not diminish by the withholding of nourishment; she sighed, believing he truly must be held in the Palm of God and nourished by El Shaddai, and went to sleep.

Something woke her. A sound. A grunt. Adah looked across the fire and saw the Baptist on his knees with arms outstretched. She wondered if he was praying even though Jews do not normally pray kneeling. She lifted herself onto her elbows to get a better view of his face and saw it was contorted. His breathing was erratic. She got up and stood before him and observed the rapid movement beneath his eyelids. What he was experiencing, whether dream or vision, she did not know, nor for how long this had been going on. His whole body trembled and he moaned softly calling on the mercy of God.

So empathetic was she to his distress that she stretched out her arms likewise and closed her eyes. Adah kything his pain, grief, fear, pain, aloneness, pain...prayed. By chance her left hand touched his right and his fingers instantly curled around hers. Adah called out his name, not out of pain, but in an attempt to break whatever tormented his being to bring him back to reality.

He did not respond. Rather the Baptist's prayer became more intense and he began to cry out, "Father, Father." She tried once more to rouse him by reaching out her free hand and laying it against his neck. "Fa…!"

John the Baptist collapsed to the ground. Bewildered and afraid, Adah gathered him close in her arms and rocked back and forth and took up his prayer, "Father. Your children are crying out to you. Have mercy on him. Father…"

With eyelids still closed John gradually awakened perfectly at peace. He thanked God that the terror of the night was vanquished when he felt himself enfolded in the wings of the Almighty. On opening his eyes, he was slightly perplexed to see darkness and then smiled when he saw the glint of sunlight; he was looking through Adah's hair. He was still nestled in her arms and her hair had fallen across them like a veil shielding him from the sun. Once more he thanked God for being manifested in this woman. It was her compassion and strength that had sustained him through the fear of the night.

John stretched a little and Adah woke with a start. She touched his brow, his cheek and knew him to be well but asked anyway, "Are you all right? What happened?"

"It is not of much consequence. It is rather what I experienced after that which makes me confident and unafraid to fulfill my path," he said serenely, and in a moment of tenderness, reached up and touched her cheek. "Thank you, Adah, for being one with me and holding me to your heart. To me you will always be the visible sign of the Invisible One's boundless love for me."

"You were in such agony," she whispered.

"Shhhh," he pressed his thumb on her lips. "Do not be concerned. All will be well. Trust in our God."

His tranquility calmed her mind as she flipped back her hair, splashing sunlight across his face. The Baptist did not need the sun, she thought; his countenance glowed with a light of its own. She loved him.

John smiled at her innocent thoughts. He loved her, too. "Come," he said. "We have a long journey today. Let us make ready."

After they had said their morning prayers, the Baptist went to the Jordan to perform his morning ablutions. When he came back Adah was still struggling with her long hair. She had neglected to tie it back the night before, letting it dry loose after its washing, and now it was all over the place.

"Get up," he said and she did obediently. "Turn around." Immediately John began to finger comb her hair and talked at the same time. "I want to go to Ain Karim for the Sabbath." Already he was deftly braiding her hair. "The morning is cool. If we cross the desert we can half our journey by detouring Jerusalem. Done," he said as he knotted off the ends. "Get your things together and let's be off." And with that he gave her a little push..

They crossed the Jordan River and were on their way westward, up through the wilderness of Judea. Adah fell behind more than her usual few paces for she was thinking. She asked, "Is not Ain Karim your home town?" The wind blew away his answer so she did not hear his reply. She asked again.

John stopped and turned around. "I said, 'Yes, I lived there until I was twenty-five.'" He waited for her to catch up.

"Tell me about yourself," she said, realizing how little she knew about his life before he became the Baptist. She continued speaking as she climbed, watching his composed face, "You know all about me. Tell me about your childhood, your family, how you became the Baptist..." As she spoke she saw his eyes flash and he reached out to grab her. She was not watching her step and was about to trip over a rock.

"Walk with me," John said taking her elbow. "I am an only child born to my parents in their old age. My mother was long barren; however, by the gracious will of the Creator I was conceived."

John became animated as he told Adah of the incidents surrounding his birth, of his relatives, Mary and Joseph, and the event of Jesus' birth. He told her of his boyhood, his schooling, his training with the Essenes as a youth, his sudden awareness of his destiny at the age of twenty with the death of his parents and the condolence visit of Jesus and his parents. John spoke of the people he loved, his friends, his struggle to comprehend and follow his path. John withheld nothing of his life from her and even explained how his cousin Jesus fulfilled all the prophecies written in the scripture regarding the Messiah.

It was a long hike across the hills and up the Red Ascent and then to skirt Jerusalem and come down to Ain Karim. Throughout the journey Adah was in perpetual amazement while John spoke. When he first began his story she wondered that if his father was a priest of the class of Abijah, would it not follow that John himself is a priest, also? But he was so eager to tell her everything about himself, she did not dare to stop and question him.

The shadows were lengthening by the time they reached Ain Karim and he was speaking of his friends Mosallam and Zara. "You mean they live in your house? You own a home?" Adah gasped excitedly. "Will we go there tonight?"

"No," John answered, his voice becoming more subdued. "I want to be quiet tonight and pray. But you will meet them."

"Tell me about them."

"Mosallam has more insight than anyone I know. And his wife, Zara, is a woman of texture."

278

Adah looked up at John and saw he was half smiling. "What do you mean?" He said nothing. "Is that a riddle?"

"Yes."

"Tsk, you prophet!" she laughed and he joined in her laughter.

"Seriously," said John, composing himself again. "It is the day of preparation of the Sabbath. Do you have any money left from the little traveling purse Philip gave you? Good. Go into town and buy what you need to eat."

"Won't you come with me?"

"No. I do not want my presence to be known at this time. As I said before, I wish to pray quietly for my path beckons me on." John added, "And Adah - trust in our God."

On the way to the synagogue Adah serenely sang the Sabbath psalms. She barely noticed John's silence, so full was she of her own joy remembering the journey they had shared the day before. As was the Baptist's custom, they arrived just as the service began so as not to draw attention away from the solemnity of the Lord's Day. Half way up the stair to the women's gallery John softly called her name. She turned and saw John had raised his right hand in the Sign of Yah as he said, "God bless you, Adah."

Adah smiled tenderly, her heart full of joy, raised her hand in the Sign of Yah and said, "And you, John."

As she sat among the women upstairs she wondered which one was Zara, perhaps the plainly dressed one in the corner, possibly that older woman over there, not that woman dressed in that richly embroidered coat with swathes of material draped around her head. Around her neck was a fabulous string of pearls and bracelets jingled on her wrists and a gold band circled her finger. Just as Adah was staring at her, the woman she turned her head in Adah's direction, though her eyes danced with exuberance. Adah shuddered and quickly looked away after seeing the ghastly scar that disfigured the woman's face.

When the service was over Adah hurried down to meet John. He was not there. She looked around and did not see him anywhere in the square before the synagogue. Maybe he was still inside with is friend Mosallam. She waited.

Almost everyone had gone. Adah's heart began to race. The woman with the scar was waiting for someone, also. Momentarily she was joined by a blind man being led by a little boy. Together they went off down the street. Adah was alone.

She went to the crossroads thinking John might be preaching there. He was not. She hurried back to where they had made camp last night hoping that John had preceded her there. She knew he needed his solitude. But after yesterday? She was confused and tried to pray for understanding; had John said something she did not comprehend? She pondered the last two days.

Adah contemplated the sign of the locusts, the Baptist's return from Machaerus, his night of agony, and his serenity the next morning. Only yesterday. Yesterday - how different the Baptist was and how different from the quiet John she had known in Bethsaida. He was glowing. He was...

Suddenly, with great clarity, she understood his terror on the first night; it was a vision, a premonition of what was to come - the Baptist was going back to Machaerus to charge Herod and Herodias today. Knowing that the Baptist's return from such a mission was doubtful, and for her to wait for him in the wilderness was unwise and unsafe, Adah began to weep, "My God, mercy!"

She knew in her heart of hearts that someday this day would come. Though saddened that John was gone, she was also so grateful that he had given her yesterday as a gift. They had shared one beautiful day together, but his path beckoned (she remembered his saying that just last night) and today the Baptist had gone to meet his destiny. Adah raised her hands in the Sign of Yah and prayed with all her heart, "God bless you, John the Baptist."

In her tears Adah remembered the Baptist's words to her, 'Trust in our God.' Gulping in air, she tried to pull herself together to think and pray. Adah realized John had brought her to Ain Karim for a reason. This was his home and he wanted her to be safe with the people he loved. The Sabbath was almost over and it would soon be dark and a new day beginning, so she collected her meager belongings and went back into town.

On her way Adah tried to picture Mosallam and Zara. She remembered her teacher's riddle: 'A man of insight, and a woman of texture.' She tried to recall all the people she had seen at the synagogue that day and could not sort out which ones they might be.

Adah composed herself outside the door of Mosallam the weaver. She had asked directions to the house and was uncertain to find herself standing in front of an impressive door. When an old woman opened the door she could think of nothing to say, except, "John?"

The old woman shook her head and was about to shut the door when another voice from behind said, "Who is it, Susannah?" The door opened wider and revealed the woman with the facial scar coming toward her. Sick at heart and not knowing what to say, Adah just stood mute in the doorway.

The woman, recognizing a person in need, took the initiative and drew the stranger inside. "May I help you? Who are you looking for?"

Adah allowed herself to be led inside and gaped about the courtyard. The light of many lamps cast a soft glow everywhere. An almond tree blossomed in the corner, baskets of flowers hung from the terrace, a carpet lay in the yard; a fine table with rich food was laid out. John the Baptist often asked people to renounce not only their sins but their possessions, too. Adah saw plainly all that John the Baptist had freely, even joyfully, renounced for the Messiah: home, wealth, priesthood, friends, a wife, children... and now his very life. Tears flowed down her cheeks; Adah had never loved John or revered the Baptist more than she did at this very moment.

"Who is it?" called a man's voice.

The woman gathered the girl into her arms saying, "Do not cry. You are safe here. Whatever is the matter, we will help you."

Zara, who is it?" It was the blind man from the synagogue getting up from the table. The little boy jumped up and steered him over to the door.

"I am Adah, Mosallam," she said finding her voice.

"You know me child?" he said touching her face, trying to recognize her, and wiped away her tears. "There, there. All will be well. Trust in our God. "

"A man of insight...," Adah sighed as she heard Mosallam speak the very words John the Baptist had spoken just the previous day. As she leaned on the scarred woman's chest and fingered her coat with its various threads and materials, it was not made for others to see, but rather to please her blind husband, "...and Zara, a woman of texture."

"You know John!" they said in unison.

"I am one of his disciples."

John had called to Adah as she climbed the stairs. He wanted to see her face one last time. When she turned, her deep blue eyes sparkled with pleasure. He blessed her and she joyously returned a blessing. He lingered for a moment, thanking the Almighty for giving them yesterday and for the gift Adah was to him. She had become a strong, confident, happy, spirit-filled woman. He trusted she would understand he had to go alone, and that the beautiful day they had shared together would sustain her, his disciple, his love, through the trial ahead.

282

He was away from the synagogue long before the service was over. John walked through the empty streets of his home town: there was the synagogue school, the marketplace, Mosallam's old rented rooms, his own front door. A flood of memories: family, Abigail, friends...John blessed them all. Reverently he kissed his father's mezuzah and went his way. He passed the spring outside Ain Karim and paused at the cemetery and prayed for his beloved ancestors who awaited the day of resurrection.

John the Baptist was a lone figure as he journeyed back down the Red Ascent and across the wilderness of Judea on the Day of the Lord. At dusk he stopped at a rushing stream that emptied into the Salt Sea at the base of the mesa that was Machaerus. There he rested and prayed. It was a moonless night and John the Baptist watched in awe as the stars circled a point of light in the north in their endless march around the heavens. He thought on how the Eternal One had made an everlasting covenant with Abraham and promised that his descendants would be as numerous as the stars in the sky. Abraham trusted and had faith in God even when he was asked to sacrifice his beloved son, Isaac. Abraham's son was spared from death, but now another son of Abraham, the Promised One, the Beloved Son, Jesus, would complete the sacrifice for the salvation of all. The promise of merciful love would be fulfilled by the Messiah's freely given gift of his life and death, which would lead all the children of earth to new, everlasting life.

As the morning star rose in the east John the Baptist prayed, "Merciful Love, I, who am nothing, beg you to make me worthy to be the true herald of your Son. Put into my mouth persuasive words that your wayward children may turn from their sinful ways and follow the Messiah who will lead them from death into life and into your loving arms, for with you is mercy and plenteous redemption. I humbly offer you all that I am to help you achieve the full redemption of all the children of earth. To you be praise and glory forever and ever. God of mercy and love, take my life, my all. Here I am."

Clovis could not believe his eyes. He had been summoned to the gate. The guard on the last watch of the night spotted that wildman, that Baptist, coming up the mesa. Clovis came out the door just in time to see the Baptist walking in a slow, steady pace making straight for the gate. Swearing beneath his breath, Clovis went out to intercept the prophet but was surprised when all of a sudden the Baptist veered off to the south and disappeared around the wall. The guards were puzzled and went to follow him, but Clovis called them back because the path that circled the fortress was narrow and fell steeply away on all sides, and Clovis did not want any casualties if there was an altercation.

As the morning sun rose, Clovis and the other guards waited, not knowing what to expect. When the new watch came out to take their place, the Baptist appeared from the north side and walked past all the guards and disappeared again around the south wall. Clovis, for a second time, tried to speak to him but got no answer. A third time the Baptist appeared. This time they all watched and let him pass freely. By now the villagers had gathered to watch the prophet pass and they, too, waited for his return, wondering what this circumambulating meant. High above on the parapet and roof of the fortress the Baptist's solitary procession was noted by more guards and dignitaries alike. The endless circling left them bored and they soon lost interest.

Clovis was all attention, though. He noticed the man's eyes were cast to the ground, half closed, as if the Baptist was in his own world. Another change of the watch; the sun was straight up - the fourth go-around. This time Clovis, alone, followed, begging the prophet to stop this madness, warning him of the danger if he continued to pursue whatever it was he was doing. The Baptist did not respond; he walked purposefully, slowly, acknowledging no one and no thing.

When they emerged from the north side, Clovis stopped and the Baptist continued. Five. Another change of the watch. Each time the Baptist appeared the villagers scrambled to their feet expectantly. In silence they watched him pass and then resumed their seats on the ground and waited. Six times around. Seven. The sun was setting. The watch changed and the Baptist did not reappear. It was dark.

Seven times John the Baptist walked the perimeter of the fortress, praying all the while that the walls that held captive the hearts of Herod and Herodias would crumble and fall and that they would be freed to turn from evil and do what is holy and just in the eyes of God.

The grey morning light revealed a lone figure standing in the market area in front of the fortress. Again, Clovis was summoned. He conferred with the watch, then went out to speak with the Baptist. Clovis whispered, "Do you not care for your life?"

"I am the messenger of the One, True, Loving God, Clovis," said the prophet to the pagan. "I seek an audience with Herod."

"You seek disaster," retorted the guard. "Up until now Herod has done his best to ignore you, knowing full well you are a holy and righteous man. If you dare meet him face to face, there is no way of saving yourself. Herod will be forced to silence you." Clovis tried his best to dissuade the prophet and protect him from a hellish fate. "I warn you - be gone before the changing of the guard."

Clovis returned to the wall just as the two new sentinels emerged from the narrow door. Immediately they tensed at the sight of the madman among them again. They were for arresting him before the villagers were about, but they consulted Clovis, he being the senior officer. He advised them, "Ignore the man. That is the best way to deal with the likes of him; he feeds on the attention given him by others. Anyhow, it is too late; the people are already gathering and staring at the Baptist." And he added with a hint of sadness in his voice, "Let fate take its course."

As the sentinels kept their silent vigilance, Clovis leaned against the wall, eyeing the prophet whose piercing stare wordlessly called him to conversion. No voice was heard but, as sure as if the prophet were speaking, the words from the day before echoed in his head, "The loving God comes to you, also. Be healed."

Clovis examined his life. As a child he was brought up to fear the many gods who controlled every aspect of life and rained down wrath on everyone without discrimination. When he was grown, he sold himself as a mercenary, took advantage of lesser men's wits to move up in rank, and used his brawn to intimidate the weak. He had stolen and plundered, used countless women and had sired who knows how many bastards.

What was his gain? He had nothing to show for his life except being the cause of much unhappiness, resentfulness, discarded women, and fatherless children. What a sick, wasted life! But the holy man's eyes told him differently. In those eyes he saw the reflection of a good man capable of so much more than what was in the past. In them he saw mercy, forgiveness, healing, love.

Though much of the righteous man's words were full of denouncement and woe, he also said there was one, true god who was a loving god. Clovis wanted to believe. His concept of many, angry, tyrannical gods was folly if one god is merciful and generous to forgive. He chose to believe in this God.

Clovis had let his body sag against the wall as he pondered his life. He was not a man to shed tears over the past but a man of action. Squaring his shoulders he went forward, oblivious of the other guards and the villagers in the market. He addressed the Baptist with the controlled voice of a soldier, "Is the door of salvation truly open to me?"

"Yes, Clovis," John the Baptist answered, mindful of the guards' outward pride but humble heart.

"What would you have me say to Herod?"

"God loves you." That shook the guard. John the Baptist went on, "The Savior of the world loves you, Clovis." When he saw Clovis' veneer crack and the corner of the fellow's eye water, John the Baptist said promptly, "Tell Herod: Greeting King Herod Antipas, Tetrarch of Galilee, and Governor of Perea. I, John the Baptist, son of Zechariah of the class of Abijah, request an audience. I am the messenger of the Promised One sent to prepare his way. I pray you will grant me a hearing."

Clovis was not surprised that this man could speak in courtly fashion, intuiting the Baptist to be no mean, ignorant, self-proclaimed prophet that often dotted the landscape; this was an educated man versed in etiquette.

As a well trained soldier receiving orders, Clovis struck his chest. John the Baptist pressed his hand over the soldier's fist and said, "Your sins are forgiven. Go in the peace of our God."

Clovis bowed his head and let out a long sigh as if a weight had just been lifted off his shoulders. He left the prophet, head held high, ignoring the water on his cheeks that flowed from release and joy, and passed through the narrow door.

XX

The gates of the fortress swung open and out came a party of wealthy women. They wandered out from behind the opulent walls to browse among the stalls set up in the common market to see if any of the goods caught their fancy. They were escorted by various servants, slaves and, as routine, a guard.

John the Baptist moved a little to the side when the gates spread and espied Herodias among the women, though he had never laid eyes on her before. She moved with regal grace: aloof, yet absorbing everything around her. She was stunning to behold arrayed in the finest linen, with jewels draped around her neck and forehead, arms and hands. Kohl elongated her eyes and color accentuated her lips and cheeks. As she passed, John the Baptist spoke, not overly loud but plainly, "God does not wish the death of an adulteress. Rather, brokenhearted by her shameful ways, yearns for her to return to her former innocence."

Herodias halted disbelieving her ears; it was that voice. A slight turn of the head showed her a thing wrapped in animal skins. Her companions began to whisper behind their hands and a hush fell upon the people in the market as they watched the royal personage and the prophet.

"Go back to your first husband, though uncle he may be," said John the Baptist gently without any kind of reproach or admonishment.

A suffocating stillness closed in on Herodias; her chest rose and fell with indignation at this public humiliation. How dare that maggot degrade her before the peasants, or anyone!

She had chosen Herod Antipas over his brother Philip, called, and with good reason, 'Philip Without Land,' because he was such an ineffectual ruler that the Emperor, on the death of their father, Herod the Great, gave Philip no realms of his own, but gave Galilee and Perea to Antipas. She had known both men in Rome where they were all raised. But it was her lot to have her marriage prearranged by her elders. However, after years of marriage to a soft, bland excuse of a husband whose only interest was in being a patron of the arts, she craved far more. Then Herod Antipas paid them a visit. Here was a man of power, prestige, wealth, virility. Antipas always prided himself on thinking that he had seduced her away from her husband, but in reality, it was she, with her feminine wiles, who enticed Herod.

Herodias burned with contempt for this thing that continually harassed and rebuked her life, and the husband she chose, the man she loved. With a flick of her wrist her two guards leapt on the man, beating him to the ground. Herodias took pleasure in seeing the thing made to suffer and walked away.

The pain was stunning. On his hands and knees John the Baptist struggled for breath; his ribs, back and head ached from the pounding. As his eyes cleared he saw two sandaled feet bejeweled with rings on the toes. He leaned back on his heels and beheld a girl of extraordinary beauty, a young Herodias, Herodias' daughter. "Child," said John the Baptist, finding the strength to speak. "Honor your father and return to his home. Do not be caught in their web of sin."

The girl had gazed impassively at the man, but when he advised her a smile spread across her face and she ambled away, following her mother and the others back into the palace.

A shiver ran down John the Baptist's spine as if the coldest wind of winter had just blown by; she was already tangled in their web. He bowed his head in prayer.

A hand touched his head for but a moment. He looked up to see Joanna, the maidservant, filled with concern but following the entourage back into the fortress. Until now the people standing about were in shock witnessing how the prophet was mistreated. Now he could hear other women weeping and men muttering. John the Baptist nodded to reassure Joanna that all would be well. Others then came to his side with water and sympathy and he blessed them for their kindness.

"Herod will see you," snapped a voice.

Clovis and three guards stood above the praying prophet. Because of the beating, and the depth of his prayer, John the Baptist was slow to stir from quiescence. A guard hauled him to his feet. Now cornered by the four men, John the Baptist was led toward the fortress.

The people in the marketplace raised an outcry when they saw the prophet being led away and would have rushed to his defense had not John the Baptist turned to them with outstretched arms in blessing and said, "Do not fear, my friends. I am ordained by the Messiah to be his herald and prepare his way. I willingly go to Herod to bid him make straight his paths. Shalom."

When John the Baptist passed through the gates, he was impressed by the beauty that hid behind the thick fortress walls. A glorious fountain sprayed a cool mist as they wended their way through the magnificent garden in the courtyard. Giant vessels painted with dancing figures held small trees that lined the colonnades on either side. They climbed three steps to enter into the palace and walked down a long corridor before the prophet and his escort reached the great hall. The floors were highly polished marble inlaid with red and green geometric designs. The lower halves of the walls were painted red with a pastoral fresco of lush fields and hills above. Cedar beams arched across the ceiling.

Herod's court was filled with the companions who had traveled down to Machaerus with him and they formed an open oval around the carpeted dais where the royal couple sat enthroned, framed by a tapestry hanging on the wall behind them. Herod was a man of lofty appearance with his hair and beard oiled and curled; a jeweled turban crowned his head and golden rings pierced his ears. His robes were ornate and rich in color. He reclined languidly on his throne with eyes half closed. John the Baptist knew, however, that he was being carefully scrutinized. On the other hand, Herodias hid nothing of her hatred.

The guard halted at an appropriate distance from the dais while John the Baptist continued further and raising his hands said, "Long have I yearned for the opportunity to spea…"

Before he could finish Clovis grabbed his arm, pulling the prophet back, and cuffed him across the face. "Do not speak until you are told."

Although Clovis' voice had been full of menace, the Baptist understood the pleading in the guard's eyes to mean to do as he said and he would protect him. Clovis was still a sworn officer of Herod's but, because he was converted, realized the only way to help the holy man was to become his guard.

"Bow to Herod," commanded Clovis.

John the Baptist paused for a moment lifting his eyes to heaven, then bowed his head and bent his knee, and said, "I bow to my King. I am his servant."

Herod smirked. He was not unaware that the holy man dressed in hides had just outwardly performed the ordered task but in essence proclaimed his servitude to God above. "Rise," he said in Latin. "I, too, have been interested in having an opportunity to speak with you." Herod prided himself on being a reasonable man. "You are my guest. What would you like to discuss?"

"Your life," replied John the Baptist in Latin. "I come to you, not to judge, but to enlighten your conscience and bring to you the good news of salvation."

"This will be illuminating," remarked Herod switching to Greek.

"Let us not play games," said John the Baptist in Greek. Herod's attempt to establish an advantage failed: the prophet had grown up in a town occupied by Romans who, in turn, were greatly influenced by Greek culture; John was well educated by his father thus he knew all the languages spoken in their land.

"Life is a game to be played, and won," retorted the man on the throne in Greek. He was excited that this man before him was no country bumpkin and said in Hebrew, "Your move."

The man of righteousness bore with patience the plays of the ruler's strategies. He began, "Under my feet I feel the seeds of weaponry where there should be grain. Why do you seek war? Seek peace."

"I am a man of peace," replied Herod. He raised his eyebrows, somewhat intrigued that the prophet knew about the arsenal he was accumulating and was amazed the Baptist had not begun where he had left off on those previous occasions. "However," said Herod Antipas, "one who governs needs to protect himself, and his interests, as well as those he rules."

"A man of peace keeps his treaties," said John the Baptist and he prophesied, "Because you have broken your treaty with King Aretas, he will overrun your borders and make war on you. Many will die."

"Is this something that will happen or may happen?" inquired Antipas, unconcerned of the possibility of a few skirmishes and ignoring the reference to the treaty he had entered into with Aretas when he married the daughter of the Nabataean King.

"You will be defeated by the Arabian King as long as you continue this path."

"She was not a Jew, you realize."

"Phasaelis was a convert. She put aside her gods and became a believer in the Almighty." John the Baptist went on, "Your own mother, Malthrace, was a Samaritan. Through her blood you are half Samaritan yourself and yet you worship in the Temple in Jerusalem with the rest of the pious. How do you glorify the Almighty?"

"I have always been a Jew like my father, Herod the Great," avowed Antipas. "Have you not seen how I have continued to glorify the Temple my father built for the Lord? How I have adorned it with gold and jewels?"

292

"You have," conceded John the Baptist. "And each time you have done so it has been at the expense of the poor whom you tax mercilessly. And who gets the glory for such a Temple gift? Not the Holy One." The prophet pressed on, "Now, what have you done to adorn the beggars who decorate the Temple gates?"

"They are all sinners. They are being chastised either for their sins or for the sins of their ancestors," Herod answered flatly.

"The Merciful One is ever ready to forgive. Are you? The Almighty is all lovingkindness!" exclaimed John the Baptist with voice full of warmth. "The Holy One hears the cry of the poor. Do you?"

"Why should I reward them for being charlatans, layabouts, or cripplers of their own children?" parried the wealthy man.

"Do you not understand they are children of the Creator, the King of the Universe, the same as you?"

"We each have our own lot in life," sighed Herod, simply closing the subject.

"Know this then, King Herod:" John the Baptist prophesied again. "Because you have been rewarded in this life with wealth and were not generous with your riches with those who stretched out their hands to you, you will soon learn what it is to be in need. The trade routes through Petra to Damascus will be blocked."

Antipas stared hard at the holy man; his fingers twitched.

John the Baptist merely stated, "You are a friend of the Romans."

Herod shifted on his throne. "I was educated in the imperial court." His whole family had ingratiated themselves with the emperor's family so as to enjoy their favor. Now as tetrarch, governor of the people, he wielded his power to suppress any disturbance that would endanger his good standings with the Romans and cause his removal. Balance was everything; by retaining his rule he could control the Jews, and the Romans, and preserve the luxury to which he and Herodias were accustomed. He informed his enlightener, "I often serve as mediator on our people's behalf with the Romans."

"Because of what she will mediate, Rome will cast you into exile and you will die far from the Promised Land."

Herod turned to the woman beside him with skepticism and murmured, "What does he mean?"

Herodias' cheeks colored; everything she had ever done was for the good of the man she loved. "How dared that maggot insinuate I would do anything to jeopardize our lives!" she blurted out, loathing the man who accused her of falseness. She hissed, "How long are you going to listen to this? Get him out of my – your sight."

"Beloved," soothed Antipas, "I do not believe half of what he says. But don't you find him intriguing, amusing?"

She looked at him coldly; sometimes he was such a fool. That is why she was so good for him; she had the power to foresee things her husband was blind to and had enough sense and enterprise to advise Herod, and because he loved her, Antipas heeded her counsel. She did not like how this game, as her husband called it, was going. Herodias entered into the fray, whispering in his ear with the most naïve voice, "Darling, what is he saying? I don't understand. I am frightened of this madman. Our spies inform us he has a large following. What will happen if all this talk leads this man and his people to usurp your power?"

Herodias was right. Antipas was well aware of the following the Baptist had but had weighed the risk and thought it leaned in his favor, because the Baptist would not abide any disciple to remain with him after they listened to him preach, were baptized, and taught how to fast and pray before being sent back to wherever they came from. They were just a lot of religious fanatics. Or were they? Suppose the Baptist turned the people against their ruler? His supporters would need only a word and there would be rebellion throughout the land. Herodias was right; Herod began to fear the Baptist.

"You are a holy and righteous man, John," Antipas said carefully. It was Herod's serve, yet curiosity got the better of him, "Do you work wonders?"

"I do not work wonders."

"Are you the Prophet?"

"I am not The Prophet," replied the prophet. "He of whom I preach is a wonder Himself. I am His herald. It is for the Promised One that I am the one calling in the wilderness, 'Prepare the way of the Lord. Make straight His paths.' "

The tetrarch felt perplexed; the Baptist was preparing the way for someone else, yet the crowds revered him. This man seemed to want nothing for himself. What did he gain from all this shouting in the wilderness and austere lifestyle? Despite all this, Antipas respected this herald and felt drawn to John. Herod was in a quandary between his wife who, regardless of her feigned composure, craved for his blood, and Herod's own strange desire to protect the Baptist.

"You don't appear to be a man of authority. We all know the Almighty blesses those who walk in God's ways. Look at me. I am a blessed man. I am a person of authority. Am I not?" said the ruler, trying to justify himself by indicating everything around him, including his beautiful wife. "You don't mean to suggest that we all put on smelly animal pelts and hunger in the desert like you, do you?" When the Baptist did not answer he said, "I am blessed and happy with my life. I do not need you to tell me what I should or should not do. I know the way I am going."

"Your riches will not go down to the grave with you. Do not seek your refuge in wealth or beauty," John the Baptist warned, then pleaded, "rather seek the things that are above. The reign of heaven is near. Put away your misdeeds and return to the Lord with all your heart."

"Now to which misdeeds are you referring? My conscience is clear," stated Antipas. He was resolved to master the Baptist, knowing the confrontation must come to a climax sooner or later. So far, the man of righteousness had not really accused him of anything – just set forth questions, or statements, and then made some prophecies that may or may not happen. To silence the Baptizer Herod needed a reason. He was a man of principle and required an authentic cause before he could exercise his authority without a qualm to silence the man. "I have done nothing to feel guilty about."

John the Baptist felt great sympathy for the man. The tetrarch was pulled by his passion for power, his love for the woman beside him on the throne, and his openness to hearing the prophet's words and heeding them, because in some small section of the man's heart he did fear God. They both knew that Herod's avowal of innocence did not bring the matter to a close. Rather, it obliged John the Baptist to make his final move. He prayed aloud, "Blessed be God, King of the universe, open the hearts of Herod and this woman. My children hear my words: though they cut like a two-edged sword they are meant to free you from the bondage of sin…"

"What sin…"

John the Baptist would not let the tetrarch speak, "The ruler of heaven has come to judge the earth in truth and justice, mercy and love! Woe to you, Herod, if you continue to tread this path. Let me instruct you in the ways of God. Put on a new mind that you may be a good and wise ruler of our people. It is within your power to cease aggression, give bread to the hungry, clothe the poor, and unburden the oppressed. Be a king who masters by serving."

"Herod, my Lord, beloved husband," whispered Herodias in all sweetness. "I am in awe of your fortitude in enduring this man's ranting. There is no one in all the land who is as just and tolerant as you. But my dear, how long are you going to abide this fool who dares reproach his king? Put an end to this. Put an end to him."

"The lips of an adulteress drip with honey," said John the Baptist who noted how Herodias' golden tone had gradually corroded away, exposing the iron beneath. "Her mouth is a black pit; her tongue strikes like an adder."

Herodias shrieked. But when she saw that Herod seemed unmoved by the insult directed toward her, she sobbed, "For my sake, Herod, terminate him."

Herod Antipas was not as passive in all this as it would seem, for the tetrarch was merely letting the man bring ruin upon himself. Herod had no illusions about his wife; she was beautiful, ambitious, and cunning. From the very beginning they craved each other, wealth, and their kingdom, and nothing then, or now, would separate them and the power they possessed.

"Thus says the Lord," declared John the Baptist, pointing to Herod Antipas. "You shall not uncover the nakedness of your brother's wife…"

"Half brother," corrected Herod.

"…it is depravity." Now John the Baptist pointed to Herodias. "She is your niece, the daughter of Aristobulus…"

"Another half brother."

"…Thus says the Law of God given by Moses: You shall not uncover the nakedness of your brother's daughter for her nakedness is your own. Blood is blood. You shall not have sexual relations with your kinfolk."

"We live, and love, by my own laws in my kingdom," Herod defied his accuser.

"Woe to you who defile the altar of the marriage bed profaning what the Creator has made holy: the communion of husband and wife."

As the prophet spoke these last words, he became aware of smoke wafting through the air. And heat. There was a strange glow around the dais.

"Fire!" shouted John the Baptist as the tapestry simultaneously burst into flame. "Fire!" he shouted again as it spread all around the royal couple. He charged forward to rescue them.

"There is no fire!" yelled Clovis in the Baptist's ear as he tried to restrain the man.

John the Baptist stood in horror as he watched the flames curl everywhere. How could this be? And yet everyone else in the room seemed unconcerned by what was happening. They only murmured about his behavior. Only he could see this vision, save it was no vision: it was a reality for those souls who put their trust in the power of their own selves and turned from the Face of God.

Isaiah's appeal came to the prophet's lips, "Who among us can live with the devouring flames? Who among us can live with the everlasting fire?"

In a burst of energy he shook off his guards and slowly, feeling the intensity of the heat, ventured forward into the fire extending one hand, then the other, as he spoke reassuringly to the frightened couple, "Come, and take my hands. Let me lead you to the cool refreshing waters of salvation. Wash yourselves; though your sins are like scarlet, they shall become white as snow; though they are crimson, they shall become white as wool."

John the Baptist was almost within reach of the couple and thought he saw Herod initiate a move to grasp his outstretched hand, but Herodias' clutch tightened on her husband's arm and Antipas shrank back further into his throne, engulfed by the fire.

"Restrain that man!" ordered Herod Antipas.

The guards were on John the Baptist, dragging him from the dais before he could say another word. Though he struggled violently, he could not break free.

"This poor man has lost his reason," announced Herod. "Years of asceticism have deluded his mind and caused him to make outlandish claims against his sovereign. But, out of respect for this holy man, I, a man of compassion, do hereby place him under my protective care where he may live out the rest of his days in tranquility and peace."

"Merciful Father, have compassion on..."

298

Someone clamped his hand over the madman's mouth, muzzling him from further outbursts as he was bodily carried out of the hall.

The tetrarch's tactical proclamation deceived no one. In fact, all thought it a brilliant move on Herod's part, except his wife.

The guards knew their duty. Solemnly, Clovis led the way down the dark stairway and pushed open a door. The three others threw the wildman into the blackness and slammed the door before he could spring to his feet. The key was turned.

Like a trapped animal John the Baptist flung himself against the door pounding and tearing at the solid mass that stood between him and freedom. Finally exhausted, bloody and bruised, he sank to his knees in the blackness. He moaned.

But then he stopped and prayed, "Fear not, my soul. Do not fret. Do not groan." He rose to his feet, "I praise you, my God. My life is in your hands. Father in heaven, into your hands I entrust my spirit."

Breath came easily now as his mind cleared. He reminded himself that the Messiah must increase and he must decease. Where one would expect to be overcome with anguish, considering the promise of darkness that lay out before him, hope instead swelled in his spirit.

"Jesus! Messiah, my God!" he was exuberant knowing his time as herald had come to an end. He petitioned aloud, "It is you who will redeem me! I wait for you." He began to dance and sing, "Blessed are you alone who has done this wondrous thing! May your fame rise like the morning sun! May your glory fill the earth!"

XXI

Adah was afraid for the Baptist's life. With vigils and fasting she joined herself to her master's mission, praying he would have the power to touch the hearts of those in Machaerus and, in the end, return to the peace and solitude of the wilderness which he so loved.

Each day she went out to the crossroads in expectation of his return, but he never came. As time wore on she clung to hope because, despite the distance and uncertainty, Adah could still feel his presence when she prayed.

Mosallam and Zara were wonderful to her. They became a family. They told her she could live with them as long as she desired, for they too believed that this was where John had wanted her to be. At times, when she felt as if she would drown in her tears, their compassion and support buoyed her up. She found solace in following the couple's example: the care of the poor and sick, which they had continued after John had left Ain Karim. Adah, likewise, took up again the ministry that she had performed in Bethsaida.

Adah needed water. The family she was helping had a desperately sick child. The boy lay with fever for days on end with no sign of relief. His father, a day laborer, found work only occasionally and could not afford money for a physician. The mother was worn out from hovering over her child while trying to care for her other children as well. Adah aided them as best she could by bringing them food, watching over the other youngsters, and fetching water.

As she approached the spring, Adah noticed a large crowd of men and women. It was unusual to see all those people at the spring at this time of day. They were listening attentively to whoever was addressing them. On any other day she, too, would have stopped to listen, but the family needed water. Unexpectedly, she heard the name of Jesus and halted in mid-step. She realized the speakers were not Judeans but Galileans like herself. While easing her way through the crowd to get a look, Adah recognized the voice. Voices. Another spoke. Breaking through the last group she saw her town mates, Andrew and John. Just at that moment a clap of thunder sounded and down came the rain scattering the people each to their own homes.

The teeming rain camouflaged Adah's tears as she embraced her friends. It did her heart good to see familiar faces and hear familiar voices, and she was proud that they were preaching in the name of Jesus. Straightaway, though, she remembered the family and bade her friends to accompany her to their house and then she would take them to a place where they could sit by a fire to dry and eat their fill.

When they arrived at the residence, the two young men stood just inside the insubstantial door out of the rain as Adah moved about the room adding wood to the fire, pouring more liquid into the already thin broth, handing a cupful to the weary mother to try to coax her child to drink. Then she offered her a wet cloth to cool the head and chest of the feverish boy. The child's limp body and shallow breathing bespoke the coming end of the boy's short life.

Regretfully, Adah told the family she was unable to do anything more for them and was about to take her leave when the mother laid her son down on his straw mat and began to sob uncontrollably over his motionless body. The father and children joined in the lament.

Andrew, moved with pity, came into the room, lifted the boy and placed him again in his mother's arms. "Woman," he said, "hold on to your child and let us pray to our Merciful God."

The mother clasped her limp son to her bosom and wailed. By this time young John had come to kneel on the other side of the woman. The two men placed their hands on the rocking woman and her child, and prayed, "God of all mercy, let this child and his mother know your love and compassion. Living Lord, grant this family peace and hope in this life and eternal joy with you in the next." The men continued to pray silently, then in unison said, "We ask this, dear God, in the name of Jesus."

Everything was quiet. The mother and family had ceased weeping, calmed by the faith-filled prayer of the two strangers.

The two rose and withdrew to the doorway where Adah awaited them. Touched by her friends' actions and words, Adah continued her prayerful gaze on the family, then turned and opened the door. At that moment, such a fragrant breeze swept through the one-room abode that one could almost smell spring in the autumn air.

"Amma, I'm hungry."

All turned to the voice. In astonishment the mother cried out praising the Living Lord as her once deathly-ill child tried to wriggle out of her too tight grasp. The boy was completely well! The whole family took up the joyful shout at the miracle. The three young people from Bethsaida joined in their rejoicing and John prayed, "Let us all give thanks and praise and glory to our Almighty God who has done this marvelous thing!"

Adah led the way out of the poor section of town and across the market place. They were so filled with excitement that before they knew it they were standing in front of a magnificent house. Andrew asked, "Where have you brought us? Surely you've gone too far? This is the rich section of town. Some rich man lives here."

Adah gazed solemnly at the two and said, "I live here. This is John's home."

"John!" exclaimed young John and burst through the door calling out his name.

"Steady lad," said the startled man sitting under the terrace. "John is not home. May I help you?"

302

"Mosallam," said Adah, quickly following the young fellow, "This is John, and Andrew. They are the town mates I have spoken of who were the first disciples of the Baptist. They now follow Jesus of Nazareth and were in Ain Karim preaching..."

"Zara," cried the blind man rising to his feet and making his way over to Adah. "We have company. Get the rooms ready. Put more lentils in the pot, bake more bread, and bring wine."

"Everything is ready, husband," laughed Zara from the kitchen doorway with hands on her hips. "As John would have it his home is always at the ready for anyone who may come through the door." And then addressing the two young men, said "Come in, friends. Welcome."

After everyone was introduced and dried and settled around the table, Andrew asked, "But where is John?"

"I'm not sure," answered Adah. "We separated in the spring."

"In following Jesus up and around Galilee we've lost track of the Baptist," exclaimed John, speaking over Adah's composed response. "Jesus has drawn such large crowds, what with his miracles and preaching, we never hear of John the Baptist anymore."

"Where is John?" asked Andrew, again noting the young woman's gravity.

"John the Baptist went to Machaerus, Herod's fortress by the Salt Sea, to urge him to repent his ways and return to the Holy One. After that..."

"Machaerus!" cried young John jumping to his feet. "Do you know what that means? Men like Herod Antipas don't let those who speak against him go free! And to charge the tetrarch to his face – John could be dead for all we know."

"No, no, no," breathed Adah. "He is alive!"

"How do you know?" asked Andrew, keeping calm.

Adah raised her hands, facing each other, feeling the power between them, "When I pray I beseech our God to guard the Baptist and I feel the master's presence."

"But what has become of him?" cried the youth anxiously as he began to pace back and forth. "He must be in the fortress dungeon!..." and he continued to fret and express his dismay and anger at the injustice of throwing such a holy and righteous man into prison.

"Son, come here," said Mosallam, who all the while had sat quietly with his wife, listening to the young people. When John sat next to the blind man Mosallam put his arms around him and said, "Trust in our God. All will be well. John is in our God's safe-keeping. Hold on to that. We are all in the providential care of the Holy One. Pray that you may have the strength, like John the Baptist, to follow your path wherever the Almighty leads you."

Consoled in the elder man's strong arms, and by his wise words, young John recovered himself. Andrew then leaned over and stated, "We will go to Machaerus and see John when we have finished here."

Andrew and John preached in Ain Karim a few more days before setting out for Herod's southern fortress by the Salt Sea. Adah accompanied them. As a disciple she wished to visit the Baptist also and the two would not deny her the chance to see John again. Along the way they reminisced about their discipleship to the Baptist and how much his life had inspired and changed their lives forever.

They planned to arrive on market day in Machaerus and the men took the opportunity to preach the good news. Each in his turn, in his own style, proclaimed that the reign of the Promised One was at hand.

While John and Andrew preached, Adah wandered among the stalls wondering how they would find out about the Baptist: where he was, if they could see him. Glancing at the massive fortress, she quailed at the thought of going in there.

304

"Are you not she who follows the man?" said a man in a low tone who stood next to her while he sorted through linens on the table. He did not look at her.

Adah saw that it was the man Cusa, Herod's servant who came with is wife, Joanna, to be baptized late that one night. "Is he here?" she asked softly, regarding the pile of material in front of her.

"I was there when he was not moved by the man's words. When the man started screaming about fire he said the man had lost his mind, was deluded. The man you seek is in the dungeon. Do not petition to see the man. It is too dangerous. Go to the southern wall. There are windows at the base. His is the first. Farewell."

Adah could barely take in the swift, cryptic, appalling account Cusa gave her. He was gone before she could ask him anything. Without losing a moment she found Andrew and told him the whole story and said she was going to see John and that they should join her as soon as they were finished preaching.

Cautiously, she made her way to the place; the path was narrow and the side fell straight away down from the brow of the mesa. She found the slit in the wall along the ground and fell to her knees, bent forward and peered into the blackness. "John?" whispered Adah. She could hear murmuring within. She called louder, "John?"

"Here I am," answered the voice calmly from within the darkness.

"John!" her voice shook. His was so serene. She thought by coming here she could comfort him in his time of distress but now, staring into the black pit, it was she who needed reassurance.

"Ah, Adah!" said the voice, light and full of warmth. "I thought your voice was one of the angels!" He sensed her emotion. "Give me your hand."

Tears sprang to her eyes. The reality of knowing that the one she regarded most in the world was all alone in this hole broke her heart. Adah lay flat on the ground and passed her arm through the opening, anticipating a clammy clasp. Instead she felt warm, rough hands firmly encompassing her hand.

"Do not weep, Adah. I may be by myself but I am not alone." He spoke easily to dispel her dismay and continued, "At first the darkness was overwhelming, but above me I saw this window and the blueness of the sky, a sign of hope and a promise of things to come, of Him who has come." He began to teach her, "Even in here my path continues. From the moment of my conception it was ordained that I would surrender my life to the Almighty to give witness to the One. I was never the One. I am the bridegroom's man who does all the preparations, then steps aside when the groom appears. And even though my voice is no longer heard in the wilderness, and I am removed from the sight of the children of earth, the Spirit of God is with me, prays in me and through me for all those who knowingly, or unknowingly, long for Him who has come."

As often would happen Adah became spellbound listening to the Baptist's words. She now believed wholeheartedly, as Mosallam had said that her master had the strength to follow the path the Almighty had laid out to the end. Even so she needed to ask him, "Are you really well? Are your guards kind? Do you get enough to eat?"

"You know my appetite, Adah" he laughed. "But yes, I get enough. As for the guards, they follow their orders - some happily, some not." He could feel the unspoken tension and, stroking the side of her hand with his thumb said, "Let me tell you an interesting story:

"One night, while I was deep in prayer, the guards came thundering into my cell and beat me. Their blows were heavy and I lost consciousness. When I awoke I was cradled in a man's arms. He cleaned my wounds. He whispered, 'Do not escape your cell again. I do not know how you did it while I was on guard, but to invade Herod's sleeping chamber again would mean your certain death, and mine.' I assured him I did not leave my cell but told him of the vision I had just had before the guards beat me.

"I saw an exquisite room, large and richly ornamented. In the center was a magnificent canopied bed. The bedposts were gleaming ebony and the netting was purple with spun threads of gold shaped like the stars of heaven. Through the curtains I could see Antipas and Herodias entwined in each other's embrace. The sight of them saddened my heart knowing theirs was a passion, yes, a love, which was never meant to be fulfilled. In their presence I prayed over them that they might have the courage to part and embark on a more holy life.

"My guard tells me he has been able to convince Herod that I did not actually escape. But I am chained for good measure because Herod complains that I continually haunt his dreams."

Adah stared into the darkness amazed at the matter-of-fact tone of the Baptist's voice. She intuited though, words unspoken on his part, that he was still being beaten.

"Do not let your heart be troubled, Adah. I am well," he said. They were silent for a moment, and then he said, "Who is with you? I sense more of my beloved disciples about."

"Andrew and John from Bethsaida are here preaching in the name of Jesus." She brightened recalling their reunion and added, "Oh, master, they worked a miracle. They came to Ain Karim to preach and cured a dying boy."

"They did not," he corrected her gently, patting her hand. "Give thanks and praise and glory to our Almighty God who has done this marvelous thing."

Adah tingled all over with wonder, hearing the Baptist say word for word the prayer of young John. At that moment Andrew and John quietly knelt down beside her.

"Friends! Give me your hands!"

Adah changed positions with the two men. They stretched out on either side of the window and grabbed the waiting hands of the Baptist. He said, "How is my Lord, Jesus?"

"Oh, John, I wish you were with us to see the thousands of miracles he has done."

"Is that so, Son of Thunder?"

"How - how did you know that is what the master has nicknamed me?" stammered young John.

That unaccountable knowledge on the Baptist's part left the youth speechless for a moment, so Andrew confirmed what his friend had said and added, "It is true. And not only that, but he teaches in the synagogues and sometimes challenges the elders. He preaches to the common folk in parables by the waysides, in the fields, and by the sea shore and then explains the parables to us later."

"And do you understand His meaning?"

"Not always," confessed Andrew. "But we know his words are true and will lead us to a new and better life."

"Tell me some of the things He says."

"Blessed are the meek and humble of heart; heaven will be theirs. Blessed are those who sorrow; they will be comforted. Blessed are those who show mercy; they will be shown mercy. Blessed are the single-hearted; they shall see God. Blessed are those who work for peace; they shall be called children of God. Blessed are those who hunger and thirst for righteousness; they shall be satisfied." Andrew had recited the list.

A light dawned on young John with the last saying and he squeezed the Baptist's hand, thinking how it applied to John the Baptist, and said, "And blessed are those who are persecuted for justice and holiness sake because of me. Rejoice and be glad, for your reward will be great in heaven."

Young John felt the Baptist's grip tighten in acknowledgement of his insight and exclaimed about the whole teaching, "Why, these are the keys to heaven! The promised hope of salvation and the special, tender care of the Almighty toward all those who love and serve the Holy One with all their heart. Those who possess these keys are fortunate, joyful, God-like!"

The simple young men did not fully understand the Baptist anymore than they fully understood Jesus but, like

Adah, were caught up with John's enthusiasm and devoured his every word. All afternoon they went on like that; the disciples recounted something Jesus had said and John would interpret it for them.

All too quickly it was getting dark and time to go. They had been warned it was not safe to be in the vicinity of the fortress after nightfall and had an invitation to stay with a family in the village. As they were about to leave, young John asked, "Is there any message you wish to send Jesus?"

"Are you the Promised One who is to come or should we look for another?"

Young John and Andrew stared at each other in disbelief; after all John the Baptist had said and done: his fire and zeal, his wisdom, his imprisonment for righteousness sake... How could he ask that? Shaken, the young men got to their feet and left.

Adah, who had sat with her back against the fortress wall listening all afternoon, prostrated herself and passed her arm through the black opening. Her hand lay free against the cool wall. She heard John the Baptist just below her whispering, confiding, "I must lessen in their eyes. They are to be Jesus' witnesses to what they have seen, and will see and hear: the blind regain their sight, the lame walk, lepers are cured, the deaf hear, and the poor have the good news proclaimed to them. The dead are raised to life. Blessed is the one who believes in me."

Adah recognized that by the time her master had finished speaking he was entranced and was not speaking as his own person but, rather, was saying words that Jesus would say in response to his question.

"How long?" asked the voice in regained lucidity.

"Six months."

"When, my Lord?"

Adah's heart ached for John's long loss of liberty. Her own throat was so tight she could not speak. The only thing she could do was try to stretch her arm farther down the wall hoping for contact, and when there was none she trusted that her simple presence would be enough.

"When will my Savior come to free me?" was the prayer she heard.

"Soon, John, soon," she whispered, longing to soothe his soul.

"Yes. I know my Savior comes. He will not delay," he prayed with confidence, then said, "The Messiah is the Lamb of sacrifice offered by the Father. He is the only perfect sacrifice pleasing to the Almighty that will redeem me and the whole world!"

Adah allowed the Baptist's prophecy to wash over her without trying to comprehend its meaning; just to hear his words was enough to give her hope for the future.

"...Ah, I see a Light, indescribably bright, gentle, soft..." once more he had become transported into a mystical vision, "Almighty El Shaddai! Thank you for nursing me at your comforting breasts making me strong and joyful to do your love. Shekinah! Your divine presence is with me always. I praise your glory!..." he was praying the ancient holy names of God, "...Elohim - One, True God! I place all my trust in you. Ruah - Breath of God! Blow away the chaos that fills our minds with doubts and fears. Shine your light upon us all that we may fulfill our mission. Oh, Wisdom! Teach us to walk in your justice. Mercy! Lovingkindness! Grant us peace..." He was no longer praying in his own name, or just for her benefit, but for all the people of earth.

Adah had fallen into rapturous prayer joining in John the Baptist's hymn of praise. She felt herself floating on light as if being taken up to heaven. In that moment of infusion their souls became one.

Their fingertips kissed.

"You are always with me."

When his fingertips came to rest ever so lightly on hers and she heard those words of comfort in her heart, Adah yearned to stay in that existence forever. Yet, when John the

310

Baptist delicately released his touch, she knew it was time for her to leave. The rush of love she felt during that blissful prayer reverberated throughout her whole being. Adah simply prayed, "Thank you, dear God."

The morning air was crisp as they loaded the cart and hitched the asses. Little Zechariah was bundled on top of all the pillows and mats and baskets and embroidered materials next to his nurse Susannah. Zara took her seat at the reins while Mosallam and Adah walked at the head of the animals leading the way. They were off to the southern palace of Herod for the grand bazaar and to visit John.

Invitations had gone out to all the master artisans throughout the land to come to Machaerus to show off their finest wares at a bazaar on the occasion of Antipas' birthday. Mosallam and Zara were excited about the opportunity to be there with other artists from around the empire and had worked diligently ever since the invitation had arrived. And all of their spirits soared knowing they would have a chance to speak with, though most likely not see, John.

With hand on the bridle, Adah walked along remembering how three months earlier she and Andrew and John had returned along this same route but with differing moods. The young men were confused and downcast by the question of the Baptist. They discussed his mission: he being the voice of conscience among the people and his baptism of repentance; how he pointed out Jesus to them – but now to turn around and ask if Jesus is the one – they did not know what to think.

On the other hand, Adah was light-hearted. So great was the outpouring of loving grace at their parting that any time she recalled that rapturous prayer, it was as if she were being taken up to heaven all over again. In that experience of peace Adah felt no need to say good-bye, for she was certain that she and the Baptist would forever be united in prayer and heart.

The next morning found them bustling about, setting up their goods. They had arrived by nightfall at the gathering place at the base of the mesa by the Arnon River where they made camp and left the setting up of their wares for the morning light. After the morning prayers and breakfast they transformed their wagon into a stall by taking off its sides. On them, and the flat bed, Zara arranged their collective merchandize for display.

When everything was in place Adah went ahead of the rest to visit John. She took her time; they were going to be there for the whole week and the diversity, artistry and opulence of the products held her interest. At one stall they were selling all kinds of delicacies and sweets. Among them were little honey locust cakes. Locusts had always been a sign of blessing, so she bought one for John. With gift in hand she climbed the steep slope leading to the fortress.

"John," she called into the dark hole. Adah had no problem crossing the regular marketplace. People milled around – mostly they were headed down the mesa to go to the grand bazaar. No one paid any attention to her as she slipped around the corner of the fortress. Adah could hear sharp intakes of air, then release. "John?"

"Leave."

Adah was puzzled by the strange command. "Leave?" she laughed and gently chided him, "Here I am to visit you, and you say leave, when you know we are never really apart. And I hoped to tempt your appetite with this honey locust cake."

"If you will not leave – prepare."

That was not John the Baptist; it was a stranger's voice, a foreigner's voice. Prepare. Prepare? Suddenly Adah began to shake. It was not the winter's cold – it had happened and she had not sensed it. The end had come. She groaned with immediate grief and rent her gown, then drew her coat tightly around her. She rocked back and forth on her knees sobbing. When she got hold of herself she said, "Tell me."

"Are you 'My Love'?"

Adah broke down again at the unexpected tenderness of the words. John had called her 'My Love' long ago when he left her in Bethsaida to begin his life as a prophet.

"The holy man prayed all day long lifting this person and that person - friends, strangers, people who were against him, even enemies - up to his God. The first person he always prayed for was 'My Love.' Surely, you are she."

"Yes."

Amidst this spell of sorrow was the bittersweet consolation to have it borne out by someone unknown to her that she was indeed always in John's heart. Humbly she asked, "Who are you?"

"I volunteered to be his guard. I thought I could protect him, aid and comfort him, be a brother to him. He was a holy and just man wrongly imprisoned."

Adah thought this must be the guard John had told her about who was so good to him when he was beaten. "May God bless you for your lovingkindness and mercy."

"Don't."

Adah heard him choke. "Why?" she asked. "You were his brother throughout all his confinement..."

"I have slain him."

"Dear God."

"I swear to you I was quick," said the guard straining to control is voice. "Shall I tell you how it happened?" The figure silhouetted against the blue sky in the opening above his head nodded. He began:

"Herod's birthday celebration week began last night with a banquet in the great hall. The place was filled with guests and visitors from far and wide. I came and stood on the side after I was relieved from my turn at watch in the dungeon. There was much eating and drinking going on and the musicians and acrobats and magicians were keeping them all amused. After the orator had performed his verse in honor of the milestone of Antipas' birth, the tetrarch still hankered for something more to commemorate the day. He was drunk.

Across from him reclined Herodias' daughter, Salome, on her couch, picking at the savories and sweets in front of her and licking her fingers.

"'Dance, Salome,' he ordered, but she was not inclined. 'Dance,' he shouted and said, 'I will grant you whatever you wish.' The girl closed her eyes and pretended not to be listening. 'I will give you whatever you ask for: clothing, horses, jewels...anything. Half my kingdom!'

"The young beauty stirred and stared at the drunken ruler. The rise and fall of her bosom betrayed her thirst for power and the thrill it fomented.

" 'For my birthday,' pleaded Herod.

"Salome sought counsel from her mother, who was lying beside her husband, and was beckoned over. The girl put her ear to her mother's mouth and smiled at Herodias' suggestion. Salome nodded to the musicians to play and she danced: slowly and sensuously at first to the rhythm, then as the music's tempo increased, so did her gyrating, faster and faster until she fell at the feet of Herod on the last beat.

"She was breathing heavily when she placed her hands on his knees and lifted herself up to his eye level. The fool leaned forward to gaze into her alluring eyes and feel her breath. Salome said evenly, 'I want you to give me at once...on a platter,' she paused to glance at her mother, who nodded, 'the head of John the Baptist.'

"Herod had reached out to touch her young flesh, but he quickly sobered and thrust the girl away, repelled by the beauty's words. He was about to refuse when Herodias leapt to her daughter's side repeating the demand and reminding her husband of his oath. For months Herodias had been looking for an opportunity to finally rid herself of the Baptist – with Salome as bait the trap was easily laid and swiftly snapped. Herod could not break his word with all the guests, courtiers and military officers eyeing him, so he solemnly gave the order.

"I stepped forward. I did not want one of the guards who hated the holy man to torture him or be slow about it. I brought a torch into the cell and found the Baptist on his knees praying with arms outstretched. His face was so peaceful. I drew my sword from its sheath. He opened his eyes and greeted me warmly. The glint of my sword caught his eye. I saw the corner of his lips turn up ever so slightly as if he welcomed this moment. He prayed aloud, 'Heavenly Father, forgive me my sins. Wash me clean. Do not hold my friend accountable for this deed as I do not. Father, Abba, receive your son into your arms. Ab...'

"Believe me, he felt no pain."

By some incomprehensible grace, Adah was inspired to move beyond the disgust and horror she felt and reached out to the executioner. She spoke as if in a dream, "You have done John the Baptist a favor by granting him his one desire."

"Death was not his desire."

"True. Baptism was his desire and you have baptized him in his own blood."

"You do not think me his murderer, then?"

"Come to the window, my friend," was her answer. Inside she could hear steps, something scraping along the floor, a step up, and then waiting. Adah lay flat on the ground and passed her arms through the opening. Just below she felt an up-turned face wet with tears of remorse. She laid her hands atop his head and spoke, "John the Baptist did not hold this act against you. Nor do I." She added, "He would have said to you, 'Shalom, in the eyes of our Merciful God your sins are like the morning mist. Do not look for them - they are gone. Turn to our Loving God; turn toward the bright sun of the future. Put on a new life. Bless you, my friend, my brother, shalom.'"

"I will put on a new life!" exclaimed the man, feeling free of guilt now that he was pardoned by the One True God with the blessing of this holy woman. "As of this moment, I resign my commission. My one purpose here is finished. I would have left nine months ago were it not to remain and protect my brother, John."

Those words would have sounded ironic given it was he who was John's executioner were it not for the abundant mercy he felt envelop him. He went on to plan, "I will return to my homeland where the fields glitter with snow at this time of year. And come spring, the land becomes green and stays so until the snow flies again. I will go home to where the mountains pierce the sky and where trees blanket the hills." He dreamed, "I will go home and find a good woman who will have me." He dared to pray, "But foremost, when I return to my homeland, I will spread the message of John the Baptist to my own people. May the One, True, Loving God be forever praised!"

"Amen."

The man moved away from the window and groaned, "Who will claim John's body?" He asked, "Is Jesus with you?"

"Jesus?" said Adah softly, then, "How do you know him? What made you think of him?"

"As I said in the beginning, John always prayed for you first. But Jesus was the name that on his lips with every breath."

"He is the One I must go to now," murmured Adah to herself. "No. I am here with John's friends, Mosallam and Zara."

"Tell your friends to come to the fortress. When I resign my commission I will petition Herod for the Baptist's body. He will grant my request; he is a superstitious man and will not want this holy man's bones entombed under his feet. I will bring John the Baptist's body out to you."

XXII

Mosallam tore at his beard. Adah broke the news as gently as she could but there was no way such brutal, shocking news could be conveyed without inflicting pain on the hearer. The blind man fought for control of his emotions; he was a realistic man and knew, as they all did, that death for the Baptist was inescapable. But John, his beloved friend - never to hear his voice again, or feel his presence...

Zara would not believe any of it; she ignored Adah and busied herself rearranging the items at their stall. Still, as much as she abhorred the telling of it, Adah felt compelled to relate the details of John's execution and turned to the blind man to give the account of the death of their loved one. "You're wrong. You must be mistaken," yelled Zara, suddenly turning on Adah, "we've only just arrived. John can't be gone. We haven't spoken to him yet."

Adah embraced the woman. Zara did not know what she was saying. The older woman pulled away, "No. Let me go. I'll go see for myself."

"Please, Zara, it's true," said Adah opening her coat and showing where she had rent her gown on hearing the news. Adah, then, unfastened her hair, shook it loose and picked up a handful of dirt from the ground and poured it over her head. "John the Baptist is dead."

"She is right," said a stranger. People had gathered hearing the commotion. It was a well-dressed man who spoke and added with a tinge of disgust, "For the price of a dance he lost his head."

"Mosallam," said Adah. "We must go up to the gate to claim his body. The guard said he would bring John out to us. The Baptist must be laid to rest."

"Where will we get winding sheets? And the perfumes? The spices? And a..." whined Zara, trying to accept what had happened but could not finish.

"We can buy all these things here, and a tomb can be purchased as well," said Mosallam, gathering his wife in his arms as she broke down weeping.

When the news began to spread throughout the bazaar, the villagers, who revered the Baptist, gathered and lamented the loss of the holy man who dwelt among them imprisoned in the fortress. Mosallam intended to make the necessary purchases but there was no need to buy; the people were generous and offered everything that was required wanting to venerate the dead prophet.

The three from Ain Karim, as the chief mourners, at the head of the procession led the way up the mesa. All the people wailed and cried aloud. Local musicians accompanied them playing a dirge.

The mourners assembled at the gate and waited. There was no need to seek admittance for the man at post expected their arrival. Presently, half the great gate inched open and four soldiers bore out the body. A fifth soldier, an officer, followed. Without a word being spoken the soldiers laid the body down on the litter provided by the villagers for the burial procession. A loud cry went up again when the people saw, though wrapped in many layers of material, the decapitated form of the Baptist.

Above all the rest was Zara's lament. In her grief she began cursing and looking for revenge; a just man had died in reprisal for a woman's pride. In her grief-born rage Zara screamed for the blood of Herod and Herodias.

Mosallam and Adah tried to calm her, but she would not stop. When she began yelling the names of the tetrarch and his woman, the officer pulled his knife. The crowd cried out at the threat of violence.

Clovis strode forward and grabbed the hysterical woman by the wrist. Up until now, he had watched in silence from the gate, caught between guilt and forgiveness. His last act as

318

officer would be to silence that woman. His first act as a disciple would be to give the woman what she cried out for. He slapped the dagger's handle into her hand.

Immediately, the woman flipped the dagger in her hand and she brandished it. His chest constricted as he saw the livid scar on that raging face; he realized she was no stranger to violence. If in her rage she struck him, so be it. He was not afraid to die for he had come to believe in something greater than himself. He eyed the woman carefully when she found herself with knife in hand, and in that pause, challenged her, "What would John do?"

The weapon slipped from her hand. The mixture of emotions had overpowered her reason and it took a knife to cut through the denial and fear, the anger and hate, and released the unbearable grief that gripped her heart. Zara fell over the body of her dearest friend and sobbed.

At first, fear ran through Adah when she saw the officer charge Zara with his knife. His looks were so alien: pale of skin, eye and hair, and very tall. His cold, hard, chiseled features reminded her of the Roman statues that had been erected throughout their land. After Zara's collapse Adah peered deeper into his face and saw integrity, a man whose stern eyes were rimmed red with regret. Here was John's executioner.

"Shalom, my brother," said Adah raising her hand in blessing. "We will take our beloved and leave here in peace." Staring straight into his eye she said, "Will you help us bear his body to his resting place?"

Clovis was stunned by the young woman's invitation and then recognized her also: her gown torn, her hair askew and covered with dirt. Her face wan with woe yet, beautiful. He was filled with awe at her bearing, sorrowing yet calm. She did not flinch from his presence and was generous beyond imagining by inviting him to join their company.

Laying his hand over his heart, instead of the customary salute of striking the chest, Clovis bowed respectfully to Adah

319

and took his place alongside the other men who would be carrying the litter.

The dagger was left in the dust.

The procession made its way off the mesa and into the wilderness. Mosallam had received many offers of burial spots from the faithful and choose the furthest one from the fortress. In the remote area they came upon a cave and laid the body deep inside. There was no rock large enough to cover the opening, so the blind man began picking up stones and placing them in front of the entrance, praying all the while. Soon everyone took their turn saying a prayer and setting a stone at the mouth of the cave. And when the chamber was sealed they silently returned to the Arnon.

Mosallam, Zara and Adah packed up their belongings to quit the bazaar. Even though it would soon be dark they set out into the dwindling light for they could not bear to stay a moment longer in that foul region. The moon was well-risen when they stopped to rest their exhausted bodies though none of them slept.

They arrived home in Ain Karim in the afternoon and Adah announced that she would be going on immediately.

"Where?" cried Zara. The young woman was like a daughter to her now and to have her go off when they should be mourning their loved one together for a whole week was beyond her ken. "You can't leave, now. We are in mourning."

"I have to," Adah said firmly. "Jesus needs to know."

"John the Baptist adhered to the strictest observance of the law and ordered his followers to do likewise," said the blind man. "Would you so easily dispense of his example and our traditions, Adah?"

"John the Baptist's life was one of mercy! I revere our laws but this…" She closed her eyes and listened to the stillness of her heart. "My own lips have to impart this message." She reached out to both of them. "It would be cruel for Jesus to hear of his Herald's death as gossip in the marketplace. I shall be the messenger of this tragic news. It is the least I can do for our beloved, and the Messiah."

Because of her wise words, they understood her unusual proposition and the couple gave their consent. Mosallam gave her a money purse as a blessing for the journey with the understanding, as was customary, that if she had any left over at her safe arrival, the money would be passed on to someone else in need.

Zara dashed upstairs. She, too, wanted to give Adah something for the journey. The young woman had come to Ain Karim with only a small sack of her few possessions. Zara returned with a bag and handed it to Adah saying, "I wanted you to have something of John's. It is clothing. I want you to wear them." She continued her explanation seeing the young woman's questioning look. "When John was a lad he lived with the Essenes. I've learned that after their ritual bathing the Essenes wore clothing such as these. I discovered John's tucked far back on a shelf while I was cleaning."

"Why do you give them to me?"

"You will need something to wear when you come before the Messiah. They will fit you. They are small enough and simply cut. John was only a lad when he lived there."

Adah began to cry as she thanked Mosallam and Zara for their thoughtfulness and for all the many kindnesses shown her during her sojourn in their - John's - home. Finally, she said good-bye to them all: the man of insight and the woman of texture, and little Zechariah and Susannah. She blessed them all and then began her journey.

Adah had not gone far along the main road going up to Jerusalem when she found herself surrounded by sheep. She had been walking with her head down, not paying particular attention to what was around her - just putting one foot in front of the other. Tired from everything that had happened the last two days she simply stood still hemmed in by all the white docile animals. A dog came to move the sheep along, but stopped and lay down on Adah's feet and gazed up at her with sad eyes.

"Adah?" It was the shepherd, Jacob, from Bethlehem, John's first friend, and Spicy. Even though the sky was darkening it was evident from the appearance of the young woman - her torn gown and unfastened hair - that someone had died. "Is it John?"

Adah nodded.

"I sensed it before I saw you," Jacob explained. "Two nights ago Spicy began to whine and then howl. I could find nothing wrong with her, but she knew."

Slowly, Adah related the painful story. They both shed tears and, standing apart with arms folded about themselves, hugged their own separate grief.

"But where are you going? Why are you on the road, alone, this late in the day?"

She explained her mission and the urgency she felt to get to Galilee.

"I will go with you," said Jacob. When he came upon her she looked like a lost little ewe lamb not knowing which way to turn. "You must not travel alone, especially through Samaria. It is already late. You will stay at my sister's tonight. Her husband can tend the flock while I am away. We will leave at first light."

It was settled. Jacob would not hear of any objections, and Adah, in truth, was too weary to dispute his plan and was genuinely relieved to have an escort.

The journey's length was five days. They walked from sun up to sun down, stopping only to pray and eat. Jacob always found a welcome and shelter for the night among the shepherds as they passed by the various villages, except in Samaria where it was safer to keep to themselves. On the Sabbath they stayed for the worship service at the synagogue before continuing their journey on the Lord's Day.

The shepherds who received the travelers sympathized with the two and were in awe of the young woman. Despite her obvious state of mourning, they respected the pilgrimage she was making and her sense of freedom of spirit. Shepherds, though vital to society, were often seen as lawbreakers because of their own freedom of spirit in their roaming ways and because of a few unscrupulous herders.

As their pilgrimage went on, Jacob began to admire more and more Adah's quiet dignity, fortitude, and her ability to praise God regardless of the heavyheartedness she felt. Her nature revealed a steadfast trust in the Shepherd of Israel and an honorableness that he never thought possible in a woman. In the beginning, he viewed her as a lost lamb, but now he was aware she possessed the heart of a ram. In the face of her being an insignificant peasant woman from a small fishing village, the ascetical life had formed Adah into a strong, prayerful and deeply compassionate individual.

Once in Galilee they began to inquire about Jesus and were told he was near the Sea of Galilee preaching. Further on they were told the teacher was preaching close to a village called Bethsaida on the north shore of the sea. Adah exclaimed, "That is my home!"

As they passed through Magdala and Capernaum they noticed the towns seemed almost deserted. Before they were in sight of Bethsaida, Jacob spotted in the distance the largest herd he had ever seen. As they got nearer, they realized the herd was people – myriads of people. Adah and Jacob were awed by the thousands and thousands of men, women and children who had gone from their homes to the steppes around Bethsaida to listen to the words of Jesus.

It was late on the last day of mourning when the two reached the outskirts of the multitude. The people were already settling down for the night as fires were being lit and children fed. Adah did not wish to approach Jesus in the dark, and besides, she needed to prepare herself for the encounter.

Adah fasted and denied her body sleep as she spent the night in prayer. At dawn she withdrew to a remote section by the sea and ritually bathed as she had seen John do ever since she met him. Her hair in the last seven days had become wholly disheveled from lack of attention; she had never shook out the dirt of the first day, nor had she attempted to tie it back. Patiently she sat combing her tresses with her fingers in the morning sun.

For the first time Adah opened the bag Zara had given her and put on the tunic, sash and coat. They were startling white: the color of mourning, the color of victory. Adah shivered in the cold air as she put on John's clothes. Her quivering was as if she were shedding the last remnants of mourning. She felt an unnatural calm – or, she wondered, was she just numb in body, mind, and spirit for certainly she did not feel victorious.

Jacob's eyes were dazzled when he beheld Adah; her clothes shone brilliant in the sun and accentuated her warm complexion, her deep blue eyes and shining black hair. It was as if she had been purified inside and out by some inner light. He, too, had bathed and was prepared to shepherd Adah the rest of the way. He asked, "Are you ready?"

"What will I say?" Adah said in reply. "My mind is a blank. I feel as new as these white clothes are to me. I am only an ignorant woman coming before the man to whom John the Baptist dedicated his whole life. What will I say?"

"Just speak the truth," counseled Jacob. "You are John the Baptist's messenger. You are a witness of his life and death. You are the one who was faithful to him till the end."

Adah nodded. That was why she had come. Yet, naturally, she felt trepidation; her heart thumped at the prospect of the task. Once more Adah turned to her Creator in prayer and, ingathering the rays of the morning sun, regained her inner stillness and was ready.

Jesus was in the center of the vast sea of humanity teaching the people. They were too far away to hear his words, but he stood out above the rest on the crest of a hill and slowly turned in all directions so all might hear his words. All eyes were fixed on him.

Adah approached the throng. Jacob followed. He had wanted to go ahead to clear a path through the dense crowd, however, Adah forbade him from doing so – she did not want to distract the people from the Teacher. She stood silently behind groups of people and patiently waited until they moved aside. The people, when they felt her presence, stepped out of the way and stared at the unusual woman dressed in stark white whose gaze was fixed on the Preacher.

Adah made her ascent slowly as she halted behind each group of people and then proceeded a few steps forward when they let her by. When she was close enough to see Jesus clearly, he had turned and was facing the other direction addressing the listeners on the opposite slope. Adah saw her brother Philip and their friends from Bethsaida and other men as well, sitting in a circle around Jesus, providing him an area to move about freely. The closer she got the thicker was the crush of hearers eager to catch his every word.

Jesus was addressing the people in parables: new wine, seeds, birds of the air, foundations, the reign of God.... Finally, she was upon the group of sitting disciples when Jesus turned and saw her standing at the circle's edge. Adah cast her eyes to his feet not wanting to interrupt his parables, knowing they were more than stories but truths to be weighed in the heart and cherished.

At last Jesus finished speaking to the crowd and faced her. He stretched out his arm to her. Adah understood she was being invited to join him in the circle. She remembered, though, the purse Mosallam had given her as a journey blessing and, now that she was home, gave it to an old woman who sat on the ground beside her. Adah's heart skipped beats as she stepped over his followers until she came up to him and touched Jesus' extended hand.

"Master," Adah said as she finally raised her gaze to meet his. Her eyes had been dry for days now having passed all crying, yet when she beheld his and saw them glistening already, her eyes began to fill up again.

Philip jumped up, as did the others who knew her, to move closer. Jacob took hold of an arm and the man retorted, "That's my sister." Nevertheless, the shepherd held back the man, and the others who got too close.

"John is no more," Adah spoke in a low tone, her throat tight with emotion.

Jesus' jaws clenched. Tears flowed.

"What?" The disciples cried. "What did you say?" "What did she say?"

Jesus laid his hands heavily on her shoulders and bent his head in sorrow.

"Come," Adah boldly enfolded the man in her arms. With her head close to his she said, "Your Herald is dead."

"How?" "Where?" "The Baptist was in Machaerus." They were all questioning her at once. "When?" "How do you know this?"

"John was beheaded on Herod's orders," she spoke to him alone. "We buried him in the wilderness by the Salt Sea eight days ago." Adah felt the Teacher's knee buckle as he sank to the ground weeping. Holding him close she bore his lament.

"Oh Lord," she prayed, looking up to the Father in heaven with her own grief welling up again. "The Baptist called you his Savior. Could you not have saved him from this?" At her words Adah felt Jesus clutch her even tighter.

Still gazing upward, Adah caught sight of an eagle circling high in the heavens. Inspiration came, "Yet, John is free! He is no longer bound to this earthly prison." Cradling Jesus' head to her breast she stroked his hair until he was spent and limp. Then Adah whispered in his ear, "John freely died for love of you and now rests in peace in the bosom of the Almighty."

Jesus eased away from her enfolding arms and leaned back on his heels. Adah sat down before him and continued, "John the Baptist freely gave his life for you. You were the wine that inebriated him. It was for you that the Baptist planted and watered the seeds of repentance. Your Herald believed in you. You were his rock that upheld him. Every breath was for you. John the Baptist loved you with all his heart and with all his soul and with all his strength." She gave Jesus this testimony on behalf of the man she had followed as disciple and confessed in conclusion, "As I do, Master. I believe that you are the Promised One, the Messiah. Blessed are you who have come in the name of our God."

After saying that acclamation Adah splayed her hands in the Sign of Yah on the earth between them and bowed low before the Lord.

"My Love," said Jesus, "I thank you for all you have told me and for your dedication as a disciple of John the Baptist. Blessed are you for your heart was open to hear and see what many of the wise will never understand. The Spirit that filled John has alighted on you, as well." Then he said in a voice only she could hear, "Thank you for believing I Am."

Jesus called her 'My Love' and to hear Jesus say the Name of the Ineffable God in regard to himself left her breathless with awe. Despite all the lamenting going on around her Adah was graced with serenity. It was indeed the touch of the Spirit that had inspired her to say those words to the Messiah and bless him. And when the Master called her by the same name John had, the sensation was not one of bittersweet dissonance that so pierced her soul as when the executioner had done so, but rather, it was a feeling of being caressed and strummed like a precious harp.

Jesus remained in quiet reflection until he sensed the stirring of the multitude. The news of the death of the Baptist had spread like fire across dry grass. Among those who mourned the prophet were some who were indifferent and some who were even pleased that the fanatic of the wilderness had finally been taken care of.

Indignation welled up in Jesus and he poured out his anger, "My Herald is dead. You were pleased for a while to hear his words, but they found no home in your heart because he was an offense to your ways; his solitude, his camel skin garment, his burning zeal and flowing mercy, his prayer and fasting, his righteousness made him a madman in your eyes. He came not in finery, eating and drinking, but came simply speaking the truth for all to hear.

"You were disappointed and now you come to me." Bitterness toward the cold-hearted people stuck in Jesus' throat and he needed to spew it out before it festered. A spate of words rushed past his lips, "You were looking for a prophet. I assure you, John the Baptist was my prophet. And more: I tell you he was Elijah come again, and you did not recognize him. I tell you he was Isaiah shouting in the wilderness, 'Prepare the way of the Lord. Your God is here!' and you did not hear him. I tell you, John the Baptist always thought he should decrease in the eyes of you all, but I say he was the greatest among those born of woman. His was a burning, shining lamp and now his flame has gone out."

Jesus continued to warn the self-righteous in the crowd, "Remember his words. I tell you the prostitutes and tax collects remember his words and will enter the reign of heaven before you."

Then Jesus closed his eyes, blocking out all the faces before him.

Adah, still sitting at the Master's feet, recognized the tactic from being the Baptist's disciple as a means to withdraw into oneself to pray to the Almighty and re-focus on one's intention: how to reveal the love of the Most High to the listeners. Adah saw Jesus' facial muscles soften and shoulders drop, his fists unclench. She heard him whisper a prayer, "I praise you, Abba, for now all things have been handed over to me so that your children may know your everlasting mercy and love."

Jesus spread wide his arms as if to embrace the whole multitude and said, "Come to me, all you who are confused and weary, and I will give you hope. Learn from me the compassion of our tender God. Let my words and deeds light your way and you will be blessed. I am the Light. Come, follow me and I will give you the Light of Life."

The crowd cringed when the Teacher unleashed his anger at the non-believers and then pressed in closer when Jesus proffered his gentle command. That day many came to believe and were healed by the wondrous power of the Master.

It was not until after Jesus had begun to move among the people that Jacob, who proved quite strong for a small man, allowed the brother to go to his sister. When Adah was reunited with Philip, friends, and their womenfolk, she found that each new meeting was a blessing for in sharing their sorrow the collective pain in their hearts over the death of their friend was eased. As for Jacob, he was in continual admiration of the young woman and, when things settled down, planned to speak with Philip.

The day was full of wonders. It was mid-afternoon before anyone realized that there was hardly any food and they were hungry. The multitude had been on the steppes for days and had eaten almost all the provisions they had brought with them. The people's stomachs were rumbling but no one wanted to leave this place of miracles and hope. Jesus' disciples had only a little food of their own and wondered what to do. They were discussing the matter and trying to figure out a way to get rid of the people when Jesus turned to them and said, "There is no need for them to leave our company. Share with them our food."

His followers were perplexed as they had only five loaves and two fishes among the twelve or more of them – and that was hardly enough to touch their own hunger. At a loss as

329

to what to do, they just stood there until the Master went over to the basket of bread. He paused quietly for a moment, broke the loaves, divided them among other baskets that were lying around, and gave them to his disciples to distribute.

Cries of rejoicing went up among the various groups which lounged on the hillside. They praised the God above for the miraculous bounty. Only when the people were satisfied did Jesus give the disciples leave to encourage the multitude to return to their homes before it was too dark. And so those who had gathered on the steppes left the area singing the praises of the wonder-worker who cured their ills, filled their hearts with hope, and filled their bodies with the finest bread.

Evening was upon the disciples by the time they moved down the hill and up the shore. They were just outside Bethsaida when the women built a fire to chase away the night chill. It was the disciples' turn to eat and, sitting around the fire, they feasted on the left-over bounty. Adah was not hungry and wandered close to the waterline reliving the events of the day. So many feelings, so many wonders.

Someone else was by the waterside gazing out over the expanse. Jesus. She felt drawn to him but kept her distance, sensing his need for solitude to pray - the same as John.

Philip came to her side. "Jesus has told us to get in the boats and go over to the other side of the sea," he said. "Will you come with us?"

Adah was tired. She was so close to home and had been away for so long that the thought of living a wayfarer's life, as she had done as John the Baptist's disciple, at this time held no allure. Adah loved her brother dearly and wanted to be with him following Jesus, but she told him she needed to be settled for a while and rediscover who she was and what life held in store for her.

Philip accepted without question everything his sister told him about her feelings and desires. Adah was home and he would not deprive her of it. However, he had responsibilities toward his young sister and said, "You have been an independent woman ever since you left to follow the Baptist, but it is my duty to be concerned for your welfare…"

He was speaking very earnestly and Adah wondered what he was about. If he wanted her to come along with the Master's disciples she would. If he was afraid of her living alone in Bethsaida there was no problem because she could live with friends in the village.

"…he spoke to me," Philip was saying, "Jacob is a good man. I approve of him."

Adah failed to understand her brother's meaning and said, "Yes, Jacob has been very good to me. All week he never left my side, yet never once tried to take advantage of me. I am grateful for his help during this time of distress." Feeling numb from everything that had happened this past week she turned to Philip and said, "What do you want me to do?"

"Stay here," he said, seeing she was worn out. He kissed her forehead and said, "Listen to your heart and you will know what to do."

The young woman said good-bye to her town mates and the other disciples as they crowded into Simon's boat and pushed off from shore. Tears stung Adah's eyes as she watched them go, feeling suddenly alone. She turned and went back to sit by the fire.

Jacob stood as she approached and added more logs to the fire. He offered her bread and drink. When she had eaten he said, "I will be leaving in the morning to get back to my sheep."

"I don't know how to thank you for all you have done for me," replied Adah. "I am in your debt."

The young man's heart pounded at Adah's words; he did not want her thanks, nor did he want her to feel indebted to him. He wanted her. Jacob said, "I have spoken to your brother and he said it was your choice. Adah, I am in love with you."

Adah was astonished. She hid her cheeks with her fingers as she felt the flush rise and fixed her eyes on the man who spoke on.

"I want you to be my wife, the mother of my children." He was a simple man of few words. "You have my heart. May I have yours? I know this is not the time to be asking but I humbly ask: Will you marry me?"

Silence ensued as Adah thought. Her stare wandered to the fire as she looked deep within her self. The flickering flames rekindled in her the dream of long ago of being a wife and mother.

New tears came forth as she relived how she had given her heart to John and how he had walked away because of his destiny as messenger and prophet. Her love for John had evolved but remained a strong and dominating force in her life. Adah realized clearly her desire to serve God was clouded by her desire to somehow be a part of the Baptist's life. Shame filed her soul as she pondered this and she turned away from the warmth of the fire to look at the cold sea - for that was how she felt inside: cold.

At that moment Jesus, who had not gone off in the boat with his disciples, turned his gaze on Adah and she was instantly flooded with warmth and a feeling of being unconditionally loved. It was almost as if Jesus had enfolded her in his cloak to comfort her and whispered, "You were not meant for shame, but for love. Only walking again through our past can we see what our lives have meant. You loved truly. And love, when it is true, transforms us and those to whom we give it. John needed your love as much as you needed to give it. And both of you, in the sincerity of your hearts, were transformed and served me, my child."

Adah seemed to melt from the heat of the inner locution as it deepened. "You cannot see into the future as your back is to it. But now you have someone in front of you who is offering his hand so that you may walk together the path of life in peace and love. Love extends his hands."

A hand touched her shoulder. "You are crying. It was too much to ask. I am sorry." Jacob said to tenderly. "Perhaps in the spring..."

"Yes, Jacob, in the spring," responded Adah full of joy. She raised her shoulder and tilted her head sideways to caress his hand with her cheek. Her heart was brimming over with hope for the future: a tender husband who loved her and the promise of children at the breast. "Yes, come to me in the spring and I shall be ready."

Jacob could not believe his ears and dropped down by her side. Was she really saying yes?

Adah smiled at his dumbfounded expression and said, "Yes!" She extended her hand. "I will enter into a covenant of love with you, Jacob. I give you my hand. I give you my heart."

The couple sat hand-in-hand close to the brightly burning fire. Jacob told his betrothed all his dreams for the future and Adah was happy because they were her dreams also.

"May I warm myself by your fire?"

"Please, sir," said Jacob getting up and putting another log on the fire as Jesus took a seat opposite the couple.

The young people became suddenly shy when the wonder-worker joined them, for they had witnessed many miracles that day and were in awe of his presence. Besides, Adah was still elated with the feeling of having her spirit lifted by Jesus when he spoke those words in her heart.

Eventually, Jacob took up where he had left off and discussed his plans of returning to Bethsaida in the spring right after the sheep had been sold at market for the Passover. This year promised to be a good one since many ewes were heavy with young and there would be plenty of lambs for the sacrifice.

At this Adah gasped. Jacob, seeing her fearful reaction, asked what upset her.

Adah received a sudden illumination into one of the last things the Baptist had prophesied in her presence and darted a glance at the Master. His eyes were closed and he did not seem to be paying attention to their conversation. She whispered, "John the Baptist said that ..." she felt shy saying 'the Messiah,' "He will be the lamb of sacrifice offered by the Father. The only…"

"Do you understand what my Prophet meant?"

They both turned to Jesus. His eyes were still closed, his face composed. Jacob had no idea what the woman was saying. Adah bit her lip.

"Adah?" Jesus now looked intently at the Baptist's faithful disciple.

Such a day filled with valleys of tears and mountains of gladness! How could she endure another plunge of emotions? "Oh…," she moaned and began to rock forward and back. "…no, Lord. No." It wasn't that she did not understand, but rather she did, and could not bear the thought of this great and holy man's death and its implied manner.

Jacob threw his arms around his intended and held her tight, unable to comprehend the exchange going on or think of words to say that might give her solace.

"Peace, Adah. Do not be afraid."

She swallowed hard and tried to calm her beating heart. She remembered everything John the Baptist had told her. She prayed. She listened to her heart. Adah gazed at the Messiah and he gazed at her. He was waiting for her to speak. Holding his gaze she felt her heart expanding and found the courage to prophesy, "Your death." Adah corrected herself, "Your life and death will set us free so we might be holy and righteous all the days of our lives. With you, Lord, is love and mercy, the forgiveness of our sins," she joyfully declared. The words, which she herself uttered, filled her with trust and awe and a new sense of hope.

"You have spoken well," affirmed Jesus, "But there is more." He looked on her with such love then stated, "I am the resurrection and the life. All who believe in me - even if they have died - will have eternal life."

Astonishment filled her heart on hearing this revelation of love, mercy, and eternal life. Adah bowed low and said, "Praise be to you, Lord. You are the Holy One of heaven and earth."

Jacob still did not comprehend their conversation, but he followed Adah's example and bowed as well and gave praise to God.

Without warning the wind began to blow. Adah stood and looked out over the waters. There was a squall line right in the direction of where her brother and the others were headed. Living this close to the sea she knew the danger of being caught on the open water when a gale was blowing.

"Dear God," she prayed in faith. "Keep them safe." Then to Jacob, "They are in the hands of the Almighty. Let us make our way to my home where we will be safe from the weather. Master, you are welcome, too. Come."

"Thank you," said Jesus. "But I must go to my disciples. Shalom, my children."

Adah led Jacob up the shoreline the short distance toward her house. The Master had gone the other way. For some reason Adah glanced over her shoulder to look at Jesus and saw that He was not skirting the waterline – rather He was in the water. No, not in the water – Jesus was walking on the water.

Epilogue

"...ba!" John's consciousness awoke from his ecstasy to an even higher reality. And he continued to sigh, not in longing as before, but rather with a sensation of bliss that comes when one is whole, happy beyond all telling, full of perfect peace and joy, and overflowing with love and gratitude. "Abba, Yahweh!" He opened his eyes and there was, "...Jesus!"

In one step John clasped the embrace of a Love that had no beginning, a Love that would never end.

Jesus said, "Thank you. I celebrate you, my beloved Baptist."

John was humbled and amazed by these words spoken to him, a mere man, yet was pleased to rest in the arms of Yahweh Jesus. Then something sparked a prophecy of old as John felt the welts on Jesus' back and words came to his lips, "By his stripes we are healed..."

John let his hands slide down Jesus' side and felt heat on the left side of His body. John took a half step back to see – it was a gash, a wound. His eyes caught sight of Jesus' hand, then the other – pierced. "...Pierced for our offenses."

"Dear God," he exclaimed stepping further away, examining Jesus' whole body. In astonishment John said, "What we have done to you!"

Overcome, John fell down in homage. Not because of the method of death inflicted - crucifixion – but because Jesus' body was clothed in a glorious light and the wounds shone brilliantly as if they were living jewels afire with love.

"Rise, my dearest prophet," said Jesus joyfully. "Love has conquered! Victory is mine and redemption won! And you are One with me!"

John said in wonder, "You underwent this for me?"

Then John was not alone. Voices echoed, "…for me?" "…for me?" Countless voices of those long departed, "…for me?" Myriads of voices mingled with voices of generations yet to be, "…for me?" "…for me?"

"Yes!" Jesus declared to John, and to every soul, "Yes, I have redeemed you. I created you and gave you breath. You are precious to me. In love I lived among you that you might know that I Am One with you. Out of love I died that you might be One with me, so that where I Am you also may be. I love you! Come, share in my glory!"